The de...
eldritch...
as blac...
Quarhaun swung it at the...
darted in at the same moment, sinking his razor-sharp dagger into its flank. The demon roared and crouched low, its eyes darting around in search of an escape.

"Where do you think you're going?" Shara growled, cutting a gash across the demon's shoulder.

In answer, the demon sprang toward Uldane. Shara and Quarhaun both swung their blades as its attention turned away from them, and the two weapons clattered together instead of striking true. The demon sailed over Uldane's head, but the fearless halfling thrust his dagger up to cut another gash in its belly as it went over. It landed with a grunt of pain but didn't slow down, charging at full speed toward the ruined wall.

Shara cursed as she shook her sword free from Quarhaun's blade. "After it!" she yelled, already starting her run.

She heard Uldane fall in behind her, but Quarhaun wasn't moving. She shot a glance over her shoulder without breaking stride.

"It's a trap," the drow called after her. "There's bound to be more."

"So we kill them all," Shara snarled back. She heard the drow sigh, then his footsteps joined hers, quickly closing her lead.

Titles in the
DUNGEONS & DRAGONS® novel line

The Mark of Nerath
Bill Slavicsek

The Seal of Karga Kul
Alex Irvine

The Temple of Yellow Skulls
Don Bassingthwaite

The Last Garrison
Matthew Beard
December 2011

Novels by James Wyatt

In the Claws of the Tiger

THE DRACONIC PROPHECIES

Storm Dragon

Dragon Forge

Dragon War

THE ABYSSAL PLAGUE

The Gates of Madness (ebook)

Oath of Vigilance

DUNGEONS & DRAGONS

JAMES WYATT

OATH OF VIGILANCE

THE ABYSSAL PLAGUE BOOK 2

Oath of Vigilance

©2011 Wizards of the Coast LLC

All characters in this book are fictitious. Any resemblance to actual persons, living or dead, is purely coincidental.

This book is protected under the copyright laws of the United States of America. Any reproduction or unauthorized use of the material or artwork contained herein is prohibited without the express written permission of Wizards of the Coast LLC.

Published by Wizards of the Coast LLC

DUNGEONS & DRAGONS, D&D, WIZARDS OF THE COAST, and their respective logos are trademarks of Wizards of the Coast LLC in the U.S.A. and other countries.

Printed in the U.S.A.

Cover art by Wayne Reynolds
Map by Rob Lazzaretti

First Printing: August 2011

9 8 7 6 5 4 3 2 1

ISBN: 978-0-7869-5816-0
ISBN: 978-0-7869-5932-7 (ebook)
620-31728000-001-EN

The sale of this book without its cover has not been authorized by the publisher. If you purchased this book without a cover, you should be aware that neither the author nor the publisher has received payment for this "stripped book."

U.S., CANADA,	EUROPEAN HEADQUARTERS
ASIA, PACIFIC, & LATIN AMERICA	Hasbro UK Ltd
Wizards of the Coast LLC	Caswell Way
P.O. Box 707	Newport, Gwent NP9 0YH
Renton, WA 98057-0707	GREAT BRITAIN
+1-800-324-6496	Save this address for your records.

Visit our web site at www.wizards.com

For Carter.

This is a book about growing up, about learning from good teachers and bad, about the value of true friends, and about the power that comes from knowing yourself. I'm so proud of the young man you're becoming.

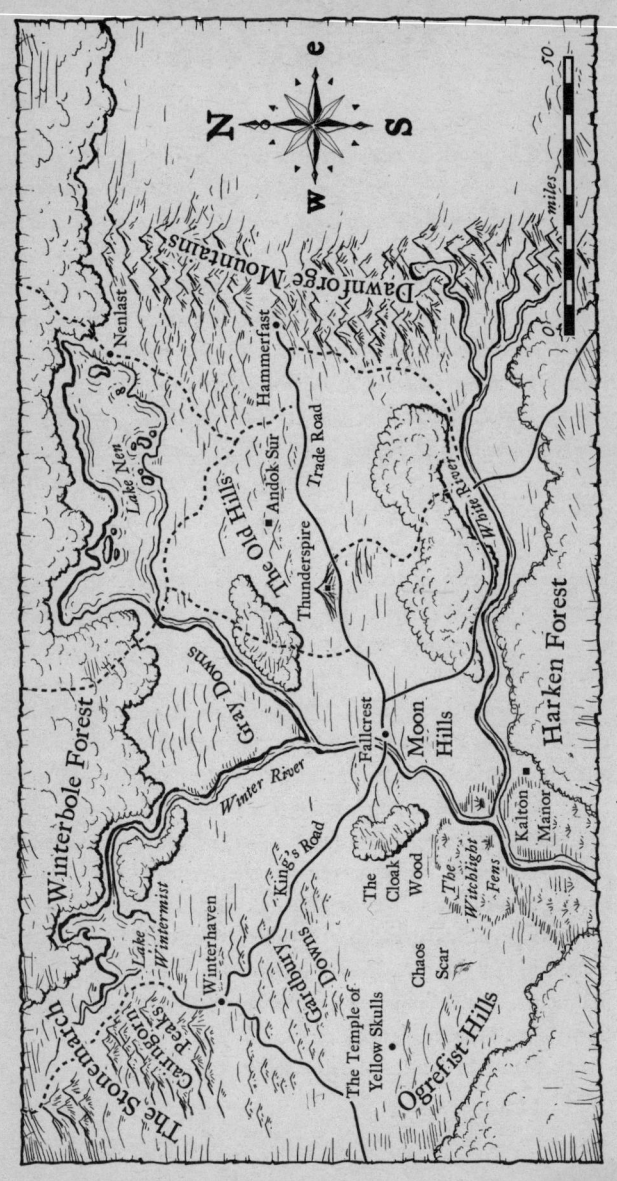

Dungeons & Dragons

In the shadow of empires, the past echoes in the legends of heroes. Civilizations rise and crumble, leaving few places that have not been touched by their grandeur. Ruin, time, and nature claim what the higher races leave behind, while chaos and darkness fill the void. Each new realm must make its mark anew on the world rather than build on the progress of its predecessors.

Numerous civilized races populate this wondrous and riotous world of Dungeons & Dragons. In the early days, the mightiest among them ruled. Empires based on the power of giants, dragons, and even devils rose, warred, and eventually fell, leaving ruin and a changed world in their wake. Later, kingdoms carved by mortals appeared like the glimmer of stars, only to be swallowed as if by clouds on a black night.

Where civilization failed, traces remain. Ruins dot the world, hidden by an ever-encroaching wilderness that shelters unnamed horrors. Lost knowledge lingers in these places. Ancient magic set in motion by forgotten hands still flows through them. Cities and towns still stand, where inhabitants live, work, and seek shelter from the dangers of the wider world. New communities spring up where the bold have seized territory from rough country, but few common folk ever wander far afield. Trade and travel are the purview of the ambitious, the brave, and the desperate. They are wizards and warriors who carry on traditions that date to ancient times. Still others innovate, or simply learn to fight as necessity dictates, forging a unique path.

An extraordinary few master their arts in ways beyond what is required for mere survival or protection. For good or ill, such people rise up to take on more than any mundane person dares. Some even become legends.

These are the stories of those select few . . .

THE ABYSSAL PLAGUE

ORIGIN

The Gates of Madness
James Wyatt

The Mark of Nerath
The Abyssal Plague Prologue
Bill Slavicsek

THE PLAGUE STRIKES

The Temple of Yellow Skulls
The Abyssal Plague Trilogy, book 1
Don Bassingthwaite

Oath of Vigilance
The Abyssal Plague Trilogy, book 2
James Wyatt

The Eye of the Chained God
The Abyssal Plague Trilogy, book 3
Don Bassingthwaite
April 2012

THE PLAGUE SPREADS

Sword of the Gods
Bruce R. Cordell

Under the Crimson Sun
Keith R. A. DeCandido

Shadowbane
Erik Scott de Bie
September 2011

OATH OF
VIGILANCE

PROLOGUE

Vestapalk perched on the lip of the crater and stared down into the tumult below. A red glow from the bottom cast sickly shadows from the boulders and other debris that littered the slopes of the old caldera, but occasional lightning in the heart of the central shaft turned the rubble into stark silhouettes. Deep within the shaft, the Voidharrow was doing its work, slowly breaking the earth down into its component elements and infusing them with some distant echo of its malignity, creating a sinkhole of evil, a new Abyss that would spawn plague demons enough to overrun whatever was left of the world when its work was complete.

It was beautiful to Vestapalk, his creation as well as his source. He had poured himself into its genesis, vomiting forth so much of the Voidharrow that he was left little more than an empty husk at the rim of the volcano's crater. He had lain there, spent, for weeks as the Voidharrow bored down toward the world's core, birthing this maelstrom. Slowly, his exarchs and his minions had found their way to him, joining Nu Alin in keeping watch over him as he rested. As the new Abyss had grown, they had moved down into it, making it their home. They were its demons.

Vestapalk spread his leathery wings and leaped into the air. He circled the caldera a few times, riding the warm updraft from the sinkhole, then folded his wings and dived into the shaft.

His Abyss swirled and churned around him, bathing him in its chaotic surges. First lightning crackled and danced along his wings, then a jet of flame washed over the scarlet, crystalline scales that covered his head and neck. Mighty as it had been, the mortal body that was the dragon Vestapalk would have been destroyed if it had flown through the midst of the storm like this. Something akin to laughter rumbled in his chest.

He spread his wings to arrest his fall and circled again, gazing down at the bubbling pool that was the Voidharrow, the origin of his own transformation as well as this new Abyss. Wisps of steam rose from it and shone in its red glow like an aurora of blood, and at the edges, where it slowly ate into the earth, it unleashed flashes of fire and lightning, rumbles of thunder and cracking ice. Vestapalk circled lower until his claws trailed across the surface of the liquid crystal. It lifted slender tendrils to meet him, brushing them against him as he passed over, sending electric tingles through his claws.

With a splash that sent waves of viscous liquid sloshing against the walls of the cavern, Vestapalk settled into the pool. The Voidharrow embraced him, rising around him in a thin film that slowly spread to cover every scale of his body, just as it had when it first infused his mortal body and began his transformation. It crept under his scales and flowed into his veins, coursing through him and reinvigorating him.

He looked down at his body, shining like a distant, crimson star. He was the Voidharrow now—the dragon's mortal body and the fragment of its mind that persisted within his own were nothing more than a framework for his power. He was the lord of this Abyss, master of the plague demons that walked and crawled and flew among the swirling elemental forces. He closed his eyes and extended his mind throughout the liquid pool, sent out a call to all those he had infused with its power, his exarchs. He summoned them, and he felt them respond, turning their steps toward the Voidharrow.

He closed his eyes and settled into the pool to wait for them as the Plaguedeep grew around him.

The demons came quickly, gathering around the edges of the pool amid the churning entropy of elemental forces liberated from the earth. They prostrated themselves before Vestapalk, and he extended his mind to touch each of theirs, to ensure that no doubt or resentment or ambition had taken root in his exarchs. Satisfied, he lifted his head, sending a slow cascade of liquid running from his chin to splash back into the Voidharrow, and then he addressed them.

"Our time has come," Vestapalk said, his voice filling the cavern and resounding from the walls. Beneath him, the Voidharrow whispered its echo of his words, and all around him his exarchs murmured their agreement. "The Plaguedeep has taken root in this place, and it grows with every passing hour. With it, our power grows, and the world's destruction grows ever nearer."

The murmurs around him grew louder with excitement, and he paused to let them quiet again.

"So now this one sends you forth to carry the seeds of annihilation beyond this place. You shall carry the Voidharrow to every corner of the world. The demons at your command shall spread terror and destruction everywhere. Our plague will spread until the world is gone and only the Plaguedeep remains."

Now the murmurs rose to eager shouts. Vestapalk cast his eyes around at his exarchs and the other demons capering grotesquely near the edge of the pool. He saw one of his exarchs, hulking Churr Ashin, lash out with a massive claw to take the head off a lesser demon that pranced too close. The demon's headless body twitched and danced for a moment more before it tumbled into the viscous pool and the Voidharrow dragged it down to fuel the plague.

"Wherever you go, this one goes," Vestapalk continued, roaring above the noise. "As you spread through the world, you spread my power. This one is the Voidharrow, the plague, and the Plaguedeep. Go forth and consume the world!"

More violence erupted around the edges of the pool, and Vestapalk felt a slow surge of power as demon blood spilled into the pool and flowed into his veins through the

Voidharrow. He let the excitement rise to a fever pitch, let the ecstasy of power build within him, until he felt that his exarchs were sated. Then he roared once more, "Go!" and the demons hurried to disperse.

Vestapalk settled back into the pool, the blood eddying around him. He closed his eyes and drank in the intoxicating flows of power within the Voidharrow for a moment before turning his gaze to Nu Alin.

The body thief stood calmly at the edge of the pool, a stark contrast to the bestial demons that had thronged the shore moments earlier. He looked almost perfectly human, though he made no effort to conceal the red liquid that welled in his eyes like bloodstained tears. He must have seized a new vessel only recently, shedding the battered corpse of the drow he had taken at the Temple of Yellow Skulls. Now he wore the body of a strong, fair-skinned man, perhaps one of the Tigerclaw barbarians from the northern forest.

"What is it, Nu Alin?" Vestapalk murmured. The Voidharrow's echoing whispers were indistinct, like a susurrus of wind.

"There was another purpose that drove us once," Nu Alin said. His voice was low and rumbling, and it echoed softly on the cavern walls and stirred gently in the Voidharrow. "Before you joined with the Voidharrow, you scoured the land for a sign of my presence, driven by visions of the Eye. And I . . ."

"You were a disciple of the Eye. What of it?"

"I was a disciple of the Chained God, and I sought to win him his freedom. Three hundred years have passed, and still he waits."

"Let him wait," Vestapalk spat. "We have no need of him. He and his disciples were a means to a greater end."

"Even you and I?"

"Even the flesh this one wears. The flesh of your first host is long discarded."

"Indeed." Nu Alin gazed into the pool by his feet. "And yet . . ."

"You carry his memories. That is all."

"Sometimes I think that is no small thing. Even you still speak as the dragon spoke."

"Perhaps you are right," Vestapalk said. He drew a deep breath, the glowing mist from the pool billowing around his nostrils. "The Elder Eye stirs," he said. "Dreamers hear his whispers in the night."

Nu Alin met his eyes. "I have heard them, too."

"It does not matter," Vestapalk said, making an effort to lend his words a finality he almost believed. "This one is the Voidharrow, the plague, and the Plaguedeep."

Nu Alin bowed deeply and turned away, leaving Vestapalk to his dreams.

CHAPTER ONE

Albanon glared up at the center of the vague circle of lighter gray in the overcast night sky. A gentle breeze, laced with a hint of winter's approach, did nothing to stir the clouds from the face of the moon.

"Looks like there'll be no passage this month," said a voice at his shoulder. The halfling innkeeper, Cham, set another glass of wine down in front of Albanon. "Will you gentlemen be extending your stay at the Cloudwatch Inn, then?" He tucked his thumbs under the straps of his filthy apron and smiled first at Albanon and then at his companion.

Kri let out a slow breath and opened his eyes. "Some say it's ill luck to disturb a priest from his prayers," the old cleric said. Cham blanched and the smile dropped from his face. "The night's not over yet," Kri added.

"Those clouds aren't moving, Kri," Albanon said. "Cham is right. There'll be no moonlight to open the Moon Door tonight. We're stuck." A bitter taste rose in his mouth. Another month's delay meant another month that Vestapalk's demons could spread the abyssal plague, another month that Shara and Uldane would be fighting the demons without his help. He glanced over his shoulder at the inn building that had already been their home for a month's time. A few other stranded travelers sat on the porch nearby, watching the sky with an equal mixture of hope and irritation.

"I've also heard it said it's not wise to pretend you know what the gods intend," Kri said, a smile crinkling the corners of his eyes.

"The priest is right." A tall man swathed in an emerald cloak settled into a seat at the next table and spoke loud enough for the other travelers on the porch to hear. "Blessed Sehanine will open the Moon Door if it pleases her to allow us into the Feywild."

Albanon noticed the moon-shaped pin that fastened the man's cloak, identifying him as a devotee of the moon god, one of the deities traditionally revered by the fey folk. Then the man pulled his hood back to reveal the long, pointed ears and opalescent eyes of an eladrin.

"They say Sehanine and Melora must agree to open the Moon Door," Cham said. " 'Sehanine swells the light of the moon and Melora parts the veil of cloud.' It seems to me it's Melora we're waiting on."

"When you should be waiting on me, innkeeper," the eladrin said. "Bring me a glass of whatever my kinsman there is drinking." He pointed at Albanon's untouched glass.

"Of course, good master. I apologize." Cham bobbed in a bow and disappeared back inside.

"My name is Immeral," the eladrin said, reaching a hand toward Albanon.

"Albanon." He clasped Immeral's hand in greeting, then turned back to his wine.

"Heading home?"

A flash of annoyance stung Albanon. He had left his family estate years ago to study magic with a human wizard, Moorin. Now Moorin was dead, but the old wizard's tower had become his home. The thought of returning to his family had never seriously occurred to him. "No," he said after a moment. "My friend and I have other business in the Feywild." On his shoulder, Splendid roused enough from her sleep to give an irritated chirp. Moorin's pseudodragon was not at all pleased with Albanon's plan to accompany Kri into the Feywild, and she had made her displeasure known frequently and loudly over the course of the last month.

Kri extended his hand to the eladrin as well. "I'm Kri Redshal," he said.

Immeral shook Kri's hand but never shifted his attention from Albanon. "In Celduilon?" he asked. Celduilon was the eladrin city closest to the other side of the Moon Door, and the most common destination for travelers from Moonstair. A longer journey through the Feywild was not something most mortals undertook lightly.

"No," Albanon said, glancing at Kri. The priest's frown was barely noticeable, but Albanon got the message. He didn't trust Immeral's curiosity. He fingered his wine glass, trying to decide how to deflect the eladrin's questions. "Our business . . ."

"Our business is nothing anyone else would find interesting in the least," Kri interjected, smiling broadly and shifting his chair closer to Immeral's line of sight. "But what of you, my friend? No doubt you're returning home to Celduilon."

Albanon saw a look of annoyance flit across Immeral's face, but the eladrin wrenched his mouth into a polite smile as he turned to Kri. "My home is not within the city, but yes. My lord's business has kept me in Moonstair for entirely too long, and I am eager to rest in my own chambers tonight, Sehanine permit it."

Albanon stared into the overcast sky again, grateful to Kri for distracting Immeral's attention. He'd rarely spoken to another eladrin since leaving years ago, and he found the subject of his Feywild home distinctly uncomfortable. Kri led Immeral through a conversational labyrinth, to a range of topics safely distant from their business in the Feywild, and Albanon lost himself in the play of moonlight filtering through the shifting blanket of thick clouds.

He was dimly aware of the two men discussing the history of Moonstair when he realized what he was seeing. "The clouds are parting!" he blurted, interrupting Kri's discourse on some ancient troll kingdom in the region. The moonlight was growing brighter, and as he glanced at the river he saw colored lights beginning to shift and swirl in the air over the rocky island that held the Moon Door. "The door is opening!"

His words sparked a bustle of excited activity on the porch and inside the inn as travelers gathered their belongings, settled their accounts, and said their farewells. Albanon lifted his pack to his shoulder, dislodging Splendid, who took to the air in a flurry of wings before settling back on top of his pack. He swallowed the last of his wine and hurried after Kri to reach the portal before it closed once more.

"You're determined to go through with this, then?" Splendid said in his ear.

"Nothing has changed, Splendid. Moorin would have wanted me to do this."

"Moorin was content to stay safe in his tower and teach you there. I still don't understand how you can let it lie vacant like this. That tower should be yours."

"If it's mine, I can choose what to do with it. I'll go back to it eventually. You're free to wait for me there."

"And eat what? The rats that are certainly crawling all over the place now?"

Albanon smiled. "Well, someone has to get rid of them."

"I am *not* a mouser!"

"Oh, well, I'm sure you're good for something."

Splendid hissed and fell silent on his pack, sulking.

A gravel pathway led from the inn's porch around the small keep that served as the mayor's home and out to the series of rocky islets that gave the town of Moonstair its name. As they reached the rushing water of the river, the face of the moon appeared full and bright in the sky, and the aurora over the river blossomed into a riotous explosion of color.

Albanon helped Kri jump from one islet to the next until they reached the rocky slope of the last island. A well-worn path took them to a tiny plateau encircled by a ring of moss and dotted with flowers that retained their spring bloom despite the autumn chill. Silver and blue light danced in sheets and ribbons through the air above the faerie ring like a cascade of moonlight spilling from the sky. Where the light touched the ground at the center of the ring, it formed the faint outline of a doorway, the Moon Door.

Immeral rejoined them, now mounted on a dusky gray horse with dry brambles woven into its mane. "Well, Albanon," he said, "perhaps I'll see you on the other side and we can continue the conversation we never quite began." He reached down to shake Albanon's hand, then turned with a smile to Kri. "And Kri Redshal, your skill at diversion and misdirection is worthy of the fey. I salute you." He clenched a fist over his heart, nodded to the old priest, and guided his horse to the Moon Door. The light danced and shimmered around him as he rode into the portal. He paused in the center, looked around with a broad smile on his face, then spurred his horse and disappeared.

Albanon and Kri fell into a vague line with the handful of other travelers and shuffled toward the portal, waiting their turn to cross into the Feywild. Albanon felt a gnawing dread and thought one last time about turning back, going to find Shara and Uldane. They could use him, he suspected. Vestapalk's demonic exarchs and their bestial minions were rampaging across the Nentir Vale, carrying havoc and destruction with them and spreading the abyssal plague. After leaving the Temple of Yellow Skulls, they had decided to split up—Shara and Uldane, with the drow they had rescued from the dragon, were looking for signs of the dragon's new lair while Albanon and Kri ventured into the Feywild in search of something—anything—that might help them defeat the dragon when they found it. One of the founding members of the Order of Vigilance, Kri had explained, had been an eladrin noblewoman, and they sought her tower and her library in the hopes that they might find some knowledge that hadn't been passed down through the order. Albanon worried what might happen to Shara and Uldane without his magic, though, and without Kri's power and guidance.

Well, Shara and Uldane could take care of themselves, and he'd see them again. He had made a commitment to Kri to stay with him and learn more of his Order of Vigilance. He wasn't going to fail in that commitment just because it meant traveling dangerously close to his family home.

Stepping into the portal was like settling into a warm bath, though the chill didn't fade from the air. At first everything muted—the roar of the river around the rocks below, the chirping of frogs and crickets on shore, the evening bustle of the town behind him, and even Splendid's yowl of alarm. A moment later, the world erupted into vibrant life. Frogs and night birds sang a chorus; the air was awash with autumn scents; the moonlight painted the flowers in iridescent blue, silver, and violet; and the rushing of the river became a complex symphony. The pseudodragon leaped from Albanon's pack and circled him in the air, surprised and excited by the new experience.

Albanon closed his eyes and took a deep breath, savoring the bouquet of pollen, leaves, moss, earth, and mushrooms. A sudden memory struck him. As a child, he'd been tumbling down a hill, laughing, with a giggling girl beside him. They landed tangled at the bottom of the hill, her hair tickling his nose and the pungent aroma of broken mushrooms surrounding them. He smiled as he cast about in his memory, trying to remember the girl's name. Instead, Tempest's face came to his mind.

"Come along, lad, you're blocking the doorway." Kri's rough hand gripped his shoulder and drew him out of the dancing lights. "Is it good to be home?"

Albanon drew in another deep breath as he walked. "I wouldn't call it home any more, but I never realized how much I missed it. Everything is so different, so much more *alive*."

"It suits you," Kri said. "You almost look like you're glowing."

Albanon laughed. "It's possible. I can feel the magic everywhere around me, fueling my own power." Drawing energy from the land and air around him, he casually tossed a burst of fire into the sky. "It's so *easy* here."

"Some say it's an advantage to study magic in the mortal world," Kri said, "because it's harder to work magic there."

Albanon nodded. "Magic comes so naturally to my people that they're lazy about it. That's why I wanted to study with Moorin."

"You weren't satisfied with the easy route."

"I suppose not."

Kri clapped him on the shoulder. "And that's why I want you with me, learning beside me. You're not going to settle for easy answers or look for shortcuts. That's what I need, and it's what the Order of Vigilance needs if it's going to survive to another generation."

Albanon swelled with pride. Since Moorin's death, he'd been adrift. His adventures with Shara and Uldane and the others had been important, but Kri was beginning to show him hints of a greater purpose, as well as a goal for his own growth and learning. Kri would be his mentor as Moorin had been, and would teach him the things Moorin hadn't been able to—starting with the ways of the order of which Moorin and Kri had been the last members.

The Feywild side of the Moon Door was like a distorted reflection of the world they'd left behind. Actually, Albanon supposed it was the mortal world that was distorted—the Feywild was the world as it ought to be, flowing with magic and unspoiled by the spread of cities and farms. The landscape around them was mostly familiar, but varied in a few details. A narrow strip of grassy earth replaced the rocky isles on the fey side of the door. An ancient grove stood in Moonstair's place at the confluence of the rivers, but faerie lights weaving among the tall trees pointed the way to the pavilion that passed for an inn on the Feywild side of the Moon Door.

"I've been here before," Albanon said, the memory dawning suddenly. "Midsummer's eve, years ago now." For a moment he could almost hear the music filtering through the trees, the laughter of the gathered fey. He laughed and shook his head clear. "This place is beguiling."

"We'll stay here for the night and set out at sunrise," Kri said. "We should be able to reach the tower by the end of the day tomorrow, if we keep up a good pace."

"Oh, it's closer than I thought. Where is it, exactly?"

"Southeast," Kri said. "Beyond the Plain of Thorns. You know the area?"

The smile faded from Albanon's face. "I do."

"We need to petition the local lord for access to the tower."

"Indeed." A chill dread gripped Albanon's chest. "We should have discussed this earlier."

"What's wrong? You know this lord?"

"Of course I do," Albanon said. "He's my father."

CHAPTER TWO

The thick air over the Witchlight Fens gave no hint of the coming winter. Sweat trickled down Shara's back, tickling under her armor like a lover's playful touch, but the black flies that swarmed her head kept any longing at bay. She waved her hand uselessly through the buzzing cloud. The bite of the insects was a sharp reminder of her more vexing concerns.

"There's something moving around by that old wall," Uldane said, pointing ahead and to the right. Shara swatted at the bugs again and peered through the haze. She spotted the wall on a low rise, part of some ancient ruin long ago claimed by the expanding swamp, but she couldn't make out whatever Uldane had seen.

"I don't know how you two can see anything in all this light," Quarhaun muttered. The drow had stayed with them since they left the Temple of Yellow Skulls, but the weeks he'd spent on the surface world had done little to ease the discomfort he felt being out of the dark and confined tunnels of the Underdark.

Shara sighed. "I can't see it, Uldane. Is it a demon?"

"Is it the dragon?" Quarhaun asked.

"It wasn't big enough to be Vestapalk," the halfling said. "And I lost track of it, but I think it might have been one of his minions."

"Then let's go kill it," Shara said. "Sooner or later, these things will lead us to Vestapalk."

Quarhaun spat. "Are you sure? The more we hunt the dragon's minions, the farther we range around this valley. We don't seem to be getting any closer to our prey—quite the contrary, in fact. We're southeast of the temple now, and the dragon flew to the west."

"But the demons were following the dragon," Shara said. "Anywhere we find them, we could find Vestapalk."

"And besides," Uldane said, "it's still worth doing. We've killed a lot of these demons, and they were causing harm to a lot of people. We're making a difference."

"But I've yet to repay the dragon for the injuries he dealt me," Quarhaun said.

Shara gripped her greatsword and clenched her jaw. The drow didn't seem to care much about the spread of the abyssal plague, but his hatred for the dragon was the one thing that the drow had in common with her, the reason that Quarhaun had helped her and Uldane hunt the demons that were spreading around the Nentir Vale. The dragon had killed her father and her lover, and Shara had already killed him once in exchange, or at least she thought she had. Perhaps it was appropriate that she'd have a chance to take the dragon's life again, payment for the second companion he'd taken from her.

Her eyes burned. Slowly, over the past months, she had begun to feel alive again, secure in the belief that Vestapalk was dead. She had started to feel something other than pain and grief over Jarren's death; she had been able, from time to time, to think of him and smile. Then the dragon reappeared, back from death and infused with the same crimson substance, like liquid crystal, that marked the demons they'd been fighting. All her pain and rage had returned, and all she knew was that she needed to kill the dragon again.

"We'll find him," she said. "He's the source of these demons. If they're coming from him, we'll find him where they are most abundant."

"Like a lava flow," Quarhaun said. "The source of the eruption is where the lava is thickest."

"Exactly."

The drow scowled and shifted his grip on his own sword. "I suppose I am willing to kill more minions if it will lead me to their master."

"Is that really all you care about?" Uldane said, looking up at the drow with wide-eyed curiosity rather than judgment.

Quarhaun crouched beside Uldane and put a hand on the halfling's shoulder. "Care?" He snorted. "Where I come from, to care about something is to watch it die, slowly and in great pain, for no other reason than because you cared about it."

Uldane scowled, knocked the drow's hand from his shoulder, and stepped back. "I'm not a child," he said. "And I saw this dragon kill three of my dearest friends in the world. I hate him, too, but I'm not going to let my hatred and pain turn me into a monster."

Quarhaun laughed and straightened up. "Give it time. Let it fester long enough, and before you know it you will be a grim, merciless killer like me." He clapped Shara's shoulder. "And like Shara."

Shara looked at him in surprise. His pale, pupilless eyes showed genuine approval. "I'm not sure whether to be flattered or disgusted," she said. But it had been a long time since any man looked at her that way, and when he lifted his hand from her shoulder she felt its absence.

Quarhaun's eyes met hers. "You know I mean it as a com—"

"Quiet!" Uldane whispered. "There's someth—"

A horrible shriek split the air and something slammed into Shara, knocking her to the ground. Claws scrabbled against her armor and a tooth-filled maw lunged at her throat before Quarhaun hacked at the creature and hurled it off her. Shara scrambled to her feet and saw a creature the size and rough shape of a panther snarling up at her, blood running from a gash across its face. Its body was long and sinuous, as much worm or snake as big cat, tapering only slightly at the wide, flat head. Familiar red crystals grew organically from its joints and crusted around its eyes and gaping mouth.

The demon shrieked again and leaped at Shara, but this time she was ready for it. Gripping her sword tightly in both hands, she slammed it into the beast's flank, knocking it out of the air and opening a gaping wound in its side, splintered ribs jutting out from the gash. Its shriek turned into a howl of pain, and it landed hard on the ground.

Shara shifted her grip and brought the blade around to take off the thing's head, but it rolled to its feet and her sword bit into the soft earth instead.

The demon's roll brought it within reach of Quarhaun's eldritch blade, a jagged greatsword of some infernal metal as black as night. The blade thrummed with power as Quarhaun swung it at the creature's neck, and Uldane darted in at the same moment, sinking his razor-sharp dagger into its flank. The demon roared and crouched low, its eyes darting around in search of an escape.

"Where do you think you're going?" Shara growled, cutting a gash across the demon's shoulder.

In answer, the demon sprang toward Uldane. Shara and Quarhaun both swung their blades as its attention turned away from them, and the two weapons clattered together instead of striking true. The demon sailed over Uldane's head, but the fearless halfling thrust his dagger up to cut another gash in its belly as it went over. It landed with a grunt of pain but didn't slow down, charging at full speed toward the ruined wall.

Shara cursed as she shook her sword free from Quarhaun's blade. "After it!" she yelled, already starting her run.

She heard Uldane fall in behind her, but Quarhaun wasn't moving. She shot a glance over her shoulder without breaking stride.

"It's a trap," the drow called after her. "There's bound to be more."

"So we kill them all," Shara snarled back. She heard the drow sigh, then his footsteps joined hers, quickly closing her lead.

Quarhaun laughed as he passed her, less burdened by his light mail armor than she was in her heavy scale. Shara grinned in acceptance of his challenge and pushed herself harder, her breath coming faster as her legs carried her up the low rise behind the drow. The exertion was exhilarating, particularly after the thrill and terror of the brief battle. For all her effort, though, Shara fell behind as Quarhaun was the first to reach the wall.

The wounded demon pounced at Quarhaun and knocked him down, as it had Shara, but instead of sprawling to the ground, the drow and demon both disappeared from Shara's sight. Shara reached the spot a moment later and saw a stone stairway descending below the rise. The daylight reached only a short way down the narrow stairs, and in the darkness beneath she heard the thud of metal on stone and Quarhaun's grunt of pain as he hit another stair.

"Damn it, Shara," she breathed. She fumbled in a pouch at her belt for a sunrod. "That was really stupid."

A blast of blue eldritch fire lit the darkness at the bottom of the stairs, farther down than she had expected. In the brief flash, she saw Quarhaun back on his feet, fire wreathed around the demon's body as it screeched in pain. She breathed a little easier as the sunrod sputtered to life. Uldane caught up with her and followed her down the steps without a word.

Uldane speechless—that was a bad sign. It probably meant that the halfling was as disappointed in her idiotic foot race with Quarhaun as she was with herself.

But she'd berate herself later. In the darkness below, a faint purplish glow lit Quarhaun's inky-black blade as it swung in a wide arc. Shara thought she saw the blade bite into several demons, and she quickened her pace down the steps.

The sunrod's light reached the bottom, revealing Quarhaun standing in a circle of six crouching beasts. One lay still on the ground at his feet, its shattered ribs identifying it as the one that had attacked them on the surface—the one that had led them into the trap as Quarhaun had predicted.

Shara dropped the sunrod, gripped her sword with both hands, and charged down the remaining stairs. Swinging the sword fiercely, she knocked the nearest demon aside and stepped into the ring of them beside Quarhaun. She slashed at a demon as it lunged toward the drow, cutting its face and driving it back. She put her back to Quarhaun's and they both held their long, deadly blades at the ready.

"I win," Quarhaun said over his shoulder.

"You take the prize, all right," Shara shot back. "I should have just left you here."

"But you didn't. That was foolish."

"We'll see about that." The demons were holding back, assessing them, looking for an opening in their defenses.

The demon nearest the stairs screeched as Uldane's dagger slid between its ribs, and it wheeled on the halfling in surprised rage. Shara lashed out at it and it turned back to her, batting uselessly with an enormous claw, weakened by Uldane's strike.

"They're still coming," Quarhaun said.

Shara glanced behind her and saw two more of the creatures fill in the circle around them, and she noticed dark shadows moving just beyond the sunrod's light. "That's a lot of demons," she muttered.

"So we kill them all."

"Right." Shara scanned the circle and found the one Uldane had stabbed. Blood from its side ran down its front leg, leaving sticky footprints glistening in the light as it stalked around the circle. She lunged at it, bringing her sword down in a mighty swing toward its neck.

Her target hopped back away as the two demons beside it leaped at her. The one on her left clamped its jaws around her arm, pulling her sword off target, though her armor kept its teeth from biting into her flesh. On her right, sharp claws cut through the leather and mail that protected her knee, but the wound was shallow. She slammed the pommel of her sword into the face of the demon that held her arm, but it held her fast.

Uldane appeared out of the shadows again and drew his dagger across the beast's throat. It yowled and released Shara's arm. Its voice died in its throat as Shara brought her sword down to split its skull.

"We need to get into a passage or something," Quarhaun said, "a narrower hall where they can't surround us."

Shara glanced at the stairs where the sunrod still sputtered, and she saw Uldane nod. "Right," she said. "Follow me."

With a roar, she slipped between two of the creatures and made for the stairs, swinging her sword in a wide arc to slash at the demons as she passed. Uldane shadowed her movement toward the stairs. Shara turned and paused to let Quarhaun get behind her, but the drow was nowhere in sight.

"Quarhaun!" she called.

"I'm here." His voice came from somewhere beyond the pool of light the sunrod shed, and he sounded annoyed. "In the hall I was pointing to."

Shara slashed at a demon that came too close and called back, "I can't see you!" Even as she spoke, though, she saw a flash of fire illuminate the drow, two demons snarling as the flame licked around them, and the mouth of a narrow tunnel a half dozen paces ahead and to the right.

The beasts were tough, and there were a lot of them crowded into the room. The smart thing to do would have been to get to the stairs and retreat. On the narrow stairs, the demons couldn't surround them, and they could fight just two or three demons at a time. Quarhaun's idea had been sound, but he'd apparently had a different narrow passage in mind—one that he could see but that her human eyes couldn't.

At this point, retreating up the stairs would leave Quarhaun stranded in his hallway with no way out. Shara doubted he could hold the passage by himself—the demons would get around him, attack from both sides, and bring him down in a minute or less. She changed her plan.

"Uldane, light another sunrod," she said.

Her heart pounded as she rushed at the demons again, hacking furiously on every side, her sword cracking through bone and drawing spurts of blood. She advanced in the general direction of where she'd seen Quarhaun's fire, keeping an eye out for any other sign of his presence. Another sunrod sputtered to life behind her, and Shara gasped as she realized just how many demons were crowded around them. But then Uldane rejoined the battle, slicing and cutting with his dagger, making up in precision what he lacked in strength. Together they carved a path through the demons until the mouth of Quarhaun's passage came into view in their circle of light. The drow wasn't there.

"Quarhaun!" Shara called. The only answer was the roar of another demon as it lunged at her, clawing the wounded spot on her knee. This time the claws went deeper and pain shot up her leg. Her knee buckled under her and she stumbled, giving another demon the chance to lunge in, slashing at her side, slamming against her ribs without piercing her armor. Then another pounced onto her back, and she fell under its weight.

"Get off her!" Uldane shouted, and the demon's weight lifted from her back. Uldane might have been small, but he wielded his dagger with such speed and skill that he could outmaneuver even much larger and stronger foes, positioning them just where he wanted and driving his dagger home.

"There's too many of them," the halfling said as Shara found her feet.

Shara roared and whirled in a complete turn, unleashing a hail of steel on the demons that had closed in for the kill, driving them back again. "We can't just leave him," she said.

"Of course not." Uldane didn't sound convinced, but Shara knew the halfling would never abandon a friend. Or even a casual adventuring companion, or whatever the drow was.

Shara scowled. She and Uldane were risking their lives for Quarhaun. Just a few moments earlier, Quarhaun had chided her as foolish because she hadn't abandoned him to the demon. He was a drow, after all—born and raised in a society that exalted scheming and treachery as the highest virtues. She had no reason to believe that Quarhaun would even inconvenience himself for her benefit, let alone put his life at risk. Why should she do any more for him than he would for her?

"Come on, Uldane," she said. "We're almost there." Back to back, they fought their way to the hall, a raging storm of steel and fury cutting their path through the demons. Uldane held the sunrod up to light the passage where they'd last seen Quarhaun, a hall running straight, as far as the sunrod's light could reach.

Quarhaun was gone.

"Now what?" Uldane asked.

"We have to find him."

Uldane nodded, and Shara smiled grimly. He didn't ask why. He knew, just as she did. They would risk their lives for Quarhaun, even if he wouldn't do the same for them. They'd do it because it was the right thing to do.

CHAPTER THREE

Tempest was silent as they walked, and Roghar recognized her expression—her brow creased, her eyes on the cobblestone beneath her feet, her lower lip caught between two sharp teeth, pinched almost tight enough to draw blood. He rested a big, gentle hand on her shoulder but left her to her silence. The past months had taught him that nothing he could say would be any greater help than that simple reminder of his presence and his concern.

He'd thought at first that time would heal the wounds that her brush with possession had left on her soul. In those first weeks, though, she'd been haunted by constant reminders of Nu Alin, terrified that any stranger they met might be harboring him, ready to assault her again. At times she even looked at Roghar as though she thought he might be possessed and waiting for the right time to attack her. Finally he'd decided that she needed to leave the Nentir Vale, and they'd traveled together to Nera, where they first met. Somehow he'd thought that removing her from the scenes of their last adventures and immersing her in places that evoked happier memories might help her forget the ordeal.

It stung his pride, fleeing the Vale like that. It felt like running from a battle, which Bahamut taught him was a sin to be shunned. But once Nu Alin had left Tempest's flesh, it had ceased to be a battle he knew how to fight.

So instead, he and Tempest had thrown themselves into fights they did understand, confronting extortionists, bandits, and a crazed necromancer in the streets of the fallen capital. In the hundred years since the emperor's palace sank into the earth and the empire crumbled, Nera had gone from a bustling city with tens of thousands of residents to little more than a frontier town, leaving the manors and estates of the city's vanished nobility to crumble into ruin around the crater that marked where the palace once stood. For its size, though, it had more than its share of crime and evil, from madmen working dark magic in ancient laboratories to bands of gnolls picking through the ruins and occasionally attacking families that lived too close to the decaying manors.

Their work of the day seemed like something in the latter category. They had arranged to meet Travic, a cleric of Erathis, in a tavern near the ruins, and agreed to help him investigate some disappearances. Roghar had every expectation that they'd be fighting gnolls before the day's end, and that suited him fine. Fighting gnolls was a bit like fighting demons by proxy, since the foul, hyena-headed humanoids revered demons and worshiped a demon lord as their god.

He squeezed Tempest's shoulder as they approached the tavern, and she seemed to shake herself out of a reverie. She glanced at Roghar's hand on her shoulder as if noticing it for the first time, and she smiled up at him.

"We're almost there," he said.

"I know." She drew a deep breath and let it out slowly. "What do you suppose Travic has for us today?"

"Gnolls, I expect."

"Filthy beasts."

"Indeed."

Roghar spotted the tavern by its sign, a crudely painted basilisk's head with glowing green eyes. At that hour of the morning, no boisterous crowd marked it as a tavern at all, let alone one of the busier gathering places in the city. "The Stony Gaze," he announced. "Are you ready?"

"Of course."

Roghar pulled the tavern door open and scanned the room inside, his senses alert for danger. Travic was there, a warm smile spreading across his weathered face as he recognized the dragonborn. A young woman with a mop glanced up at the doorway, looked back at Travic, and returned to her work. Otherwise, the place seemed deserted.

"Roghar, thank you so much for coming." Travic stood up and bobbed his head in greeting. A lock of salt-and-pepper hair fell into his eyes, and he brushed it aside.

"Good morning, Travic." Roghar stepped to the side and let Tempest enter before him, then followed her to Travic's table.

"Tempest, lovely to see you," the priest said. "Thank you, as well."

Tempest took his outstretched hand and started to sit.

"I have to apologize," Travic said. "I planned to meet you here, buy you breakfast, and discuss the situation while we ate. I did not plan on this establishment's excellent cook being abed at this hour."

Roghar laughed. "Fortunately, we have eaten already."

"I'm glad. And I believe it's to our advantage to get an early start. I've heard a report of another couple gone missing, so perhaps we can look into that while it's still fresh."

"Very well," Roghar said. "Shall we leave right away?"

"I'll tell you what's going on as we walk. Or at least as much of it as I understand." He patted the mopping woman on the shoulder as he walked to the door. "Thank you, Jesi." She returned his smile.

Outside, Travic started walking in the direction of the ruins. "The cases I've looked into so far have had much in common, things that set them apart from the troubles we normally see near the ruined part of the city."

"Gnoll attacks and such?" Roghar asked.

"Exactly. When gnolls raid the city, they leave an unholy mess behind them. Blood everywhere, bodies half eaten and mutilated, stores of food plundered, that sort of thing. It's obvious there's been an attack, and quite clear that gnolls were responsible—few other creatures are both so savage and so cunning."

"How common are gnoll raids like that?"

"Actually rare. The watch patrols those neighborhoods pretty heavily, and when gnolls do attack, the watch strikes back fast and hard. Otherwise, no one would live in those areas."

"But you said these cases are different?"

"Yes. No blood, no bodies, nothing missing or plundered. It's like these people just disappeared—just got up and left, taking nothing with them."

"Maybe the gnolls have new leadership," Roghar said. "Maybe they've started carrying victims back to their lair, making offerings or sacrifices or something."

"Anything's possible, I suppose. But I've never heard of gnolls behaving like that."

"What does your god tell you?"

Travic stopped walking and sighed. "Nothing clear. But the whole thing feels wrong to me. Dangerous and important."

Roghar closed his eyes for a moment, letting his thoughts settle and fall still. His spine prickled at once, and a sense of urgency rose in his chest. At the same time, a gnawing dread took root in his gut. He opened his eyes and nodded. "Lead on," he said to Travic. "Dangerous and important is about right."

Travic led them around a corner, and the ruins emerged into full view. The street, a broad thoroughfare that once must have carried carts and wagons to the city's finest homes and markets, sloped gently upward and then suddenly dropped off into the crater that marked the site of the fallen palace. Majestic stone buildings lined the sides of the street, but the ones nearest the crater were only crumbling façades over ruined husks, the gutted interiors visible through gaping windows and empty doorways.

"I dream about this street sometimes," Travic said. "I see it as it once was, flowers and banners in a riot of color, the wealthy and powerful of the empire walking along its smooth cobblestones, the palace rising in majesty at the crest of the hill. Except instead of the emperor in his palace, I see Erathis, bathed in glory, the sword of her justice in hand and flames of inspiration around her head. Her eyes pierce me, and she commands me to rebuild."

"That's not a calling you could easily ignore," Roghar said.

Travic sighed. "It makes me so tired. I'm just one man."

"Today we are three. And we'll shine the light of the Bright City into this desolate street." Erathis, the god of civilization and law, was said to live in a celestial realm called the Bright City of Hestavar.

"Thank you, my friend. Bahamut's work will be done as well."

Roghar noticed the cleric's gaze wander, a little uneasily, to Tempest. Travic understood why Roghar was helping him—as a paladin of Bahamut, Roghar had a divine calling, just as Travic did, and the goals of their gods were aligned in many cases. But Travic didn't know what to make of Tempest and had no idea why a warlock whose power ultimately came from the powers of the Nine Hells would participate in this work.

Tempest wasn't like them, it was true. Her power didn't come with a divine mandate—it wasn't granted on condition of service. In fact, as far as Roghar understood it, Tempest had stolen the power she wielded and used it without permission from the powers of Hell. And he had made it his mission to make sure she used it in ways that would infuriate the devils it came from, which brought him a perverse sort of pleasure.

"It's just up here," Travic said, starting toward one of the more intact buildings. "This street's not entirely desolate. Many of the poorer people of the city find homes here, living in buildings whose owners are long dead. It's dangerous—between the gnolls and other creatures that haunt the ruins and the risk of collapsing floors or ceilings, there's a lot that can kill you. But it's better than a lot of the other options the city offers to the poor."

"I lived here," Tempest said. Her voice startled them both—she hadn't spoken since she entered the tavern. "For a little while."

Roghar studied her face, but couldn't read any emotion in her expression. Her eyes were turned toward the crater at the top of the hill.

Travic nodded. "Then you know what I'm talking about."

"I know."

Tempest fell back into silence, and Travic, apparently lost in his own reverie, led them off the street through a doorway draped with a tattered curtain.

The space inside had once been a grand entrance hall for a stately home. The morning sun poured down through an open skylight, warming the ancient stone and illuminating every corner of the room. A graceful stairway swept halfway up the wall on one side before dissolving into rubble. A moldering tapestry that might once have been a carpet hung askew over another doorway opposite the stairs, the hinges of the original doors still visible at its sides. A pile of straw and rags in the far corner must have served as a bed, though it was too thin to offer much protection from the hard marble floor.

As Travic had said, no sign of violence marred the scene. If gnolls had attacked this place, Roghar thought, they would have torn the curtain they came through, for starters. They would have killed the residents of the home, and gnolls prefer to kill in ways that leave blood all over the floor, the walls, and sometimes the ceiling.

"Who lived here?" Tempest asked.

"Their names were Marcan and Gaele. An older couple, humans in their fifties. Marcan was a cooper, but he lost his arm at the same time as they lost their children, about fifteen years ago. Gaele earns a pittance washing clothes and linens."

Roghar growled, a low rumbling deep in his throat. "So the weak become prey for the ruthless," he said.

"Indeed."

"That's not what it looks like to me," Tempest said. "Maybe they found a better place to live. I don't see anything here that I'd take with me if I left."

"If they had simply moved, I'd have heard about it," Travic said.

"Are you sure?"

"I spend a lot of time with the people on this street. They know me and trust me. I was with Marcan and Gaele when they lost everything. They'd share the joy of a new home with me."

"Then I say we venture into the ruins and look around," Roghar said. "Maybe we'll find a threat other than gnolls lurking there."

"I'm confident we will," Travic said. "The gods will guide us."

Travic led the way back out to the street and up toward the crater where the jewel of Nerath, the emperor's glorious palace, had once stood. They passed more makeshift homes like the one Marcan and Gaele had claimed, marked by curtains hanging in empty doorways or clothes hung in broken windows to dry. Here and there, a potted plant lent a splash of color to the barren stone walls.

The closer they got to the crater, though, the more infrequent such signs of habitation became. Fewer buildings could boast four walls and a roof, and soon Roghar was helping Tempest clamber over rubble that choked the street. The few sounds of human activity faded, replaced with the scurrying noises of vermin and the occasional snarl of a larger scavenger picking through the ruins.

"Look over there," Travic said.

Roghar shielded his eyes from the morning sun and followed Travic's pointing finger. It took him just a moment to find what the cleric had seen—the mangy pelt of some beast, hung like a banner on a crumbling wall a few dozen yards away. "Gnolls," he said.

Travic nodded and slid his mace out of the loop at his belt. Roghar drew his sword and adjusted his grip on his shield, glancing over his shoulder at Tempest. She still seemed distracted, distant, but she held her rod resting on her shoulder, ready to blast any enemies that appeared out of the ruins.

Roghar led the way, picking his way carefully through the rubble. Gnolls were not known for laying traps and deadfalls near their lair, not least because they'd be likely to stumble into their own traps in the madness of their hunting fury. Even so, the ruins could hide any number of dangers, from lurking scavengers to unsafe floors. As he neared the wall with its grisly banner, he slowed his steps in a futile attempt to move more quietly, but for all his efforts every step was a grating symphony of crunching gravel and clanking armor.

Despite the noise, no gnoll appeared behind the wall, no spears or arrows shot out at him. With a glance over his shoulder to make sure that Travic and Tempest had kept up with him, he ran the last few yards and fell into a crouch at the base of the wall. He signaled the others and they froze in place, crouching low to take whatever cover the rubble afforded. Roghar cocked his head and listened.

Wind stirred through the ruins, making the pelt rustle against the ancient stone. Claws or teeth, still attached to the pelt, clattered against the wall. Somewhere far off, he thought he heard a flute playing high and sweet. But nothing stirred behind the wall.

Slowly, as quietly as his armor would allow, he rose from his crouch and peered over the crumbling edge of the wall. The building was a gnoll den, certainly. Filthy piles of furs and grisly trophies decorated the space defined by the broken ruins of four stone walls. Gore-stained bones, some gnawed and broken, littered the center of the space. Dried brown blood was smeared on what walls remained, in patterns he imagined the gnolls found artful or symbolic in some way. But he saw no gnolls, and none of the fierce hyenas they preferred as pets.

Gesturing the others forward, Roghar stepped around the crumbled wall. The stench of death assaulted his nostrils, and he silently thanked the wind that had carried it away from him earlier. He moved carefully about the den, peering around the other walls, straining his ears for any sign of life.

"It's abandoned," Travic said.

Roghar looked down at the gory mess in the middle of the room. Maggots writhed on the bones, fighting over what meat was left on them. He glanced around again, his eyes taking in details he'd missed the first time—shiny black beetles scurrying among the furs, a spider the size of his fist perched on an ornate web in one corner. He nodded. It was possible the gnolls were simply out hunting, but the place definitely gave him the sense that no one had been there for days, perhaps weeks.

"Just like the house," Tempest said. "Just like Gaele's house."

CHAPTER FOUR

"Your father?" Kri said, his eyes wide.

Albanon nodded slowly. "The Prince of Thorns, yes."

"You're not smiling."

"You don't know my father," Albanon said. "Or do you?"

"No, no. In all my years and for all my study, this is my first visit to the tower where the Order of Vigilance began. My first visit to the Feywild at all, actually. So what kind of reception should we expect?"

Albanon frowned. "A very cold one. He was not pleased with my decision to study in the mortal world."

Splendid alighted on his shoulder. "He should have been proud," the little dragon huffed. "Moorin was the greatest wizard in all the world."

"The world's greatest wizard is not good enough for the Prince of Thorns," Albanon said. "In his mind, even the lowliest eladrin mentor would have been preferable."

Kri stroked his beard. "Well, a cold welcome is better than an armed one, I suppose."

"Don't insult him, or the one could turn into the other."

"Understood," Kri said. "We'll make our audience as brief and as polite as possible."

"Brief is good," Albanon said. He stared at Splendid. "Polite is essential. Even if he says things about Moorin that are . . . less than complimentary."

"He would insult the great wizard Moorin?" The pseudodragon sounded incredulous.

"Speaking from ignorance. But this is not the time and place to educate him. It's probably best if you just stay quiet."

Splendid huffed and settled into a more comfortable position, stretched across Albanon's pack and shoulder. Her needle-sharp claws bit ever so slightly into his skin, making him wince and shift his shoulders so her claws had more cloak to pierce than flesh.

"Well, let's get to the inn," Albanon said. "Tomorrow's a big day."

Albanon woke before dawn from a sleep troubled by dreams of his father, and he lay awake listening to the riotous chorus of birds greeting the first light on the eastern horizon. He saw Splendid as a silhouette on the windowsill, head cocked at the unfamiliar songs. He got up and walked to the window, idly scratching the pseudodragon's cheek and chin as he watched the sun rise and thought about his father. Before the sun set again, he'd be standing in the audience hall of his father's manor, facing that imperious glare and a host of questions he didn't feel prepared to answer.

Kri woke before long, rescuing him from his thoughts by launching into the bustle of getting started on their journey. They left the inn with the sun still hidden behind the eastern trees.

East of Moonstair in the world, the desolate expanse of marshy woodland and low hills called the Trollhaunt stretched for miles, strewn with ancient ruins and troll-infested caves. In the Feywild, the land was not much different, though both trees and hills stood taller. Albanon led the way southeast, along a river that shimmered with faerie light. Around midday, they found a dry spot overlooking the river and sat down to eat. Kri made a few attempts to start conversation, keeping to light topics, but Albanon kept getting lost in his own thoughts, sometimes trailing off in midsentence, and Kri soon gave up.

After eating, they left the river and struck out due east. The trees grew taller, and an increasingly dense undergrowth of thorny bushes suggested that they were approaching their destination. Albanon found it easy enough to pass through the brambles without harm, and as long as Kri stayed close at his back he didn't have much trouble. A few times, Kri's cloak or robe got caught on a thorn and Albanon drew farther ahead; then Kri became lodged in the thorns until Albanon doubled back and helped him free.

"The brambles know their master," Kri observed as Albanon worked his cloak free for the third time.

"I just know how to navigate them. I walked this forest a great deal as a child."

"The thorns recoil at your touch."

Albanon laughed. "Nonsense. My father is the Prince of Thorns, not I."

"Are you not his heir?"

"It's not that simple. Nothing is here. Please try to keep that in mind when we see him."

A few hours after leaving the river, they came to the forest's edge. The trees gave way to a wide plain, dry and brown, choked with thorny bushes and tangled vines. To the north, the forest jutted a little farther into the plain, and Albanon could just make out the spires and halls of the Palace of Thorns among the trees. He waited to see how long it would take Kri to spot it, a game he had always enjoyed playing with visitors, even eladrin from other realms of the Feywild.

"What are we waiting for?" Kri said. "Isn't that your father's house?" He pointed right to it.

Albanon's mouth fell open. "Didn't you say you'd never been here before?"

"I haven't. But it sure looks like a Palace of Thorns, doesn't it?"

"It usually takes longer for visitors to spot it among the trees."

Kri laughed. "Ioun is the god of knowledge, prophecy, and insight," he said. "I make no claim to possess more than a fraction of her wisdom, but she does grant me eyes enough to see much of what is obscured to others."

Albanon's gape widened into a smile. He had much to learn from Kri, and moments like that made him all the more eager to start learning. Ioun was also the patron of sages, scholars, and students, so it seemed appropriate for him to study with one of her priests.

His smile lingered as he led Kri through the briers, but faded quickly as the shadow of his father's house fell over them. The dread that had haunted his sleep the night before returned in full force. His steps slowed without him fully realizing it, but they still brought him to the vine-wrapped outer gate all too quickly. Thorns jutted from the vines, nearly indistinguishable from the mithral bars of the metal gate that supported them. Albanon knew that on either side of the gate, a high fence of mithral and briers extended all around the Palace of Thorns, a warning as much as a physical ward.

"How do we pass through the gate?" Kri asked.

Albanon didn't answer, but stepped closer to the gate. Silently, the huge gate parted in the middle and opened before him, as if welcoming him home.

"I am not the Prince of Thorns," he said, "but I am still a member of this house."

Tall trees with prickly leaves stood like columns in two straight rows ahead, ending at another gate—the inner gate, the entrance to the Palace of Thorns. Holly branches and thorny vines twisted together in an arch over the gate, which was a door made of white wood. Again the doors swung open at Albanon's approach, but this time two guards stood behind it, eladrin women in fine mithral chainmail, holding slender spears and staring at him with more than a hint of surprise.

"My lord Albanon," one of the guards said in Elven. "You were not expected."

"You will announce me to my father, please," Albanon answered in the same language. It felt strange in his mouth, it had been so long. "As well as my companion, Kri Redshal, priest of Ioun."

"Yes, my lord." The guard turned briskly and walked into the palace. Not once did she look back to make sure Kri and Albanon were keeping pace, and she didn't slow or stop until she reached the ornate door of the audience hall, made of the same white wood but carved with intricate designs of flowers and vines. Then she turned and said, "Wait here, please," before passing through the door. It closed behind her with a definitive thud.

Albanon's heart was pounding, making his head throb. Splendid paced from one of his shoulders to the other until he hissed at her to be still. He couldn't form a coherent thought. Snippets of sentences chased each other through his mind, refusing to resolve into anything he might actually say to his father, the Prince of Thorns. Kri smiled reassuringly at him, and he was unable to return the gesture.

The door swung open again, and Albanon stopped breathing. The guard stood in the open doorway, spear held to the side. She didn't look directly at him, but focused her gaze up and out as she made her formal announcement.

"Lord Albanon and Kri Redshal, you are welcome in the Palace of Thorns. His Eldritch Majesty, the Prince of Thorns, requests that you appear before him, that he might offer his welcome personally."

With that, she stepped to the side, clearing the way for Albanon and Kri to enter, and Albanon's eyes met his father's.

Albanon had a fleeting impression of a predatory insect, tense and waiting, claws poised to lash out and seize its prey. His father's features were sharp, and he leaned forward on his throne, his hands clutching the arms. The Prince of Thorns was an old man, though the signs of it were more in his bearing, his perpetual scowl, than in his physical features.

"Albanon," said the Prince of Thorns. "Tell me, how are your studies progressing?" The old man's face was neutral, but his disdain was clear in his voice.

Albanon decided to ignore the question as he strode forward and knelt briefly before his father's throne. The throne was carved from the living wood of the tree that also formed part of the back wall of the chamber, adorned with images of thorn-bearing plants.

"Father," Albanon mumbled as he rose.

"And you have brought a mortal man into my hall. Therefore, I assume that this is not a social visit. You might as well come quickly to the point."

Albanon bristled, but struggled to keep his face and voice from showing his anger. "A tower stands on your lands, beyond the Plain of Thorns. We seek your permission to visit this tower."

The Prince of Thorns scoffed and waved one clawlike hand dismissively. "Ridiculous," he said. "The Whitethorn Spire has been abandoned for generations. None of our people venture there any more."

"With respect, father, we'd like to change that."

"It's sure to be infested with monsters."

"We believe we can take care of ourselves."

"Can you? Then your studies must be coming along very well indeed."

"Moorin taught me much before his death, and I have had several opportunities to practice my magic in dangerous circumstances."

"Your teacher is dead? I told you, Albanon, humans are so short-lived. If you had studied with Darellia—"

Albanon interrupted, steel in his voice. "Moorin was murdered."

"How unfortunate." The prince's voice was not the least bit sympathetic, and Albanon felt Splendid stir on his shoulder, growling softly.

"Father, just grant us your permission to visit the tower and we'll leave your hall and trouble you no more."

"What do you seek there?" the Prince of Thorns asked. "I told you, the tower is long abandoned."

"With all due respect, Your Eldritch Majesty," Kri said in perfect Elven, "Sherinna's tower is abandoned because her son refused to fulfill the duty his mother laid on him at her death."

The Prince of Thorns sat up taller on his throne, glaring at Kri for a long moment before turning his attention back to Albanon. "I never cease to marvel at the ways of humans," he said. "They can be taught to speak, but they cannot learn manners."

Kri drew himself up, and Albanon could feel the power gathering around him. The air shimmered with it, and even the Prince of Thorns seemed to diminish slightly in the face of it. Kri's voice rumbled like distant thunder in the hall. "Sherinna was the sole custodian of knowledge that might prove to be vital to the fate of the world. She intended for her heir to safeguard that knowledge after her death, but her son refused and humans took on that responsibility. Now three hundred years have come and gone, and I am the last member of the order founded to take on the burden that *you* refused."

Albanon stared at Kri. The founder of the Order of Vigilance had been Albanon's own grandmother?

The Prince of Thorns stood, and Albanon took an involuntary step back. Kri's wrath was like a nimbus of divine power around him, but it paled in comparison to the raw fury of the Prince of Thorns. The room darkened and seemed to constrict, the thorny decorations of the throne loomed behind him, and the prince himself seemed to tower above them and at the same time to lean hungrily forward like some feral predator.

"Do not presume to lecture me about my duty, human," he said. "I am the Prince of Thorns. My duty is to this land and the people who dwell in it. You have no claim on me."

Kri did not recoil from the Prince of Thorns's anger. In fact, he presumed to step forward as he tried to argue. "But the fate of the world—"

"The fate of *your* world is not my concern."

Albanon swallowed. He had to try to calm both men before the argument turned into something worse. He put a hand on the priest's shoulder. "Kri, there is no need to cast blame for what has already happened. The Order of Vigilance took up my grandmother's burden after her death, and that is all that matters. Perhaps it was meant to happen that way—after all, isn't it fitting that the knowledge needed to save the world should lie with the humans of the world, and not hidden away in the Feywild?"

Kri's gaze stayed fixed on the Prince of Thorns, but he took a slow breath, and the palpable aura of anger around him diminished slightly. "No doubt Ioun saw to the preservation of that knowledge," he said.

"And Father, whether you knew it or not, you acknowledged our family's role in preserving that knowledge when you allowed me to study with a wizard of the order."

The Prince of Thorns also seemed to diminish slightly, and he let his eyes stray to Albanon. "Of course I knew it, my fool of a son."

Albanon blinked. "You did?"

A hint of a smile crossed his father's face, and he settled back into his throne. "And so with you, the legacy of the Order of Vigilance passes once more into Sherinna's family."

"You intended that all along?" Albanon said. "Then what are we arguing about? Why not just grant us permission to visit the tower and be done with it?"

"You still have not told me what you seek in the Whitethorn Spire."

Kri smiled and leaned on his staff, suddenly seeming old and harmless once more. "I believe, Majesty, that the knowledge passed down through my order is incomplete. Moorin knew more than he was able to pass on to Albanon, and his knowledge might have complemented my own. We hope to find records in Sherinna's tower, writings or artifacts or . . . or anything that might help us face the threat my order was founded to combat."

The Prince of Thorns scowled and stroked his chin. "First you blame me for shirking my duty, then you admit that your order failed in its sacred trust to preserve and transmit what Sherinna learned."

For a moment, Albanon thought that Kri was going to erupt in wrath again, but instead the old man's shoulders slumped. "You are correct," he said. "I am sorry that I cast blame before admitting my own failing."

The prince regarded Kri for a long moment, then turned his gaze to Albanon. "I cannot deny you your birthright, my son. But heed my warning—my huntmaster has reported strange creatures in the vicinity of the Whitethorn Spire. I was not speaking idly of the place being infested with monsters." His face softened, to Albanon's amazement. "Be careful."

"I will, Father." He fell to one knee again, and Kri followed suit. "Thank you."

"I hope you find what you seek," the Prince of Thorns said. He waved a hand to dismiss them, and Albanon and Kri stood and left the palace.

CHAPTER FIVE

"Get behind me," Shara said, and she turned to face the demons. She and her greatsword could almost completely block the passage, so a demon that tried to get past her to Uldane would pay for it in blood.

"Do you have a plan?" the halfling asked.

"Step one," Shara grunted as her sword bit into a demon's shoulder. "Don't die."

"Sounds good so far."

Another beast pounced, sailing over the demons closest to Shara and hurtling at her face. She brought her sword up just in time for the creature to impale itself on the blade. Shara staggered back under the sudden weight and almost tripped over Uldane, and then the demon nearly wrenched the sword from her hands as it fell lifeless onto its companions. Another one took advantage of her lowered defenses to lunge in, raking her leg with its claws before she could twist her body out of its way. She yanked her sword free and smashed the pommel into the demon's face, driving it back.

"I don't know what step two is," she said. Her breath was coming harder and faster, and she finally had to acknowledge the doubt nagging at her mind, questioning whether she and Uldane could get through this alive.

"I figured as much," Uldane said. He threw a dagger past Shara's hip to sink into a demon's eye. The enchanted blade wrenched itself free and sailed back to Uldane's hand, trailing pale red blood. "How about this? We make our way down the hall until we find either Quarhaun or a strong door we can put between us and these demons."

"What if we find more demons?"

"That's not part of the plan."

"I like this plan. Stay close."

Shara lunged forward and swung her sword in a barrage of cuts that belied the weight of the blade, driving the demons back. Then she countered with several quick steps back—and stepped hard on Uldane's foot. The halfling yowled and Shara stumbled, nearly dropping her sword as she flung her arms out to keep her balance. One of the demons darted in and clenched its jaws around Shara's leg, piercing armor and skin right below her wounded knee. Shara gritted her teeth and brought her sword around to cut into the creature's shoulder, even as Uldane slipped around her and drove his dagger into its throat. It released Shara's leg, she found her footing, Uldane got behind her, and they were more or less in the position they'd started in. Except that blood was trickling down Shara's calf and jolts of pain shot up her leg with every step.

"Let's try this again," she said. "But this time, stay a little less close."

"Sorry," Uldane said.

Shara gave up on the idea of driving the demons back and concentrated on keeping their teeth and claws away from her body as she and Uldane shuffled backward down the hall. Uldane kept a safe distance from her feet but still managed to throw his little blade past her to harry their foes. She focused her attention on the demons, trusting that Uldane was keeping at least one eye on the hall behind them.

A long moment later, Shara could no longer see the mouth of the tunnel in their circle of light. Four more corpses littered the hallway in her wake, and they still had not found either Quarhaun or a door. Or more demons—which was good, since their plan didn't account for that possibility.

"How long is this hall?" Shara asked.

"I can't see the other end," Uldane said.

"And I can't see where we started. So apparently it's endless."

"Maybe we're already dead and this is our eternal fate," Uldane said. "Fighting demons in an endless hallway."

"In that case, we might need to switch places for a little while. My arms are getting tired."

Uldane laughed. The sound made her smile, and she imagined that it made the demons pause. Uldane amazed her—his ability to find joy and humor in the worst of situations was inexplicable, sometimes infuriating, but more often than she would admit it was a comfort.

They retreated a few more paces down the hall, then Uldane swore under his breath.

"That doesn't sound good," Shara said.

"Well, there's one good thing. I found a door."

"And how many bad things?"

"I only see two right now, but they're at the edge of the light. There's probably more behind them."

"More demons?"

"I'm afraid so."

"That wasn't part of the plan," Shara reminded him.

"I guess it's time for a new plan."

Shara risked a glance over her shoulder and spotted the door Uldane had mentioned. It was a heavy wooden door bound with iron, but that was no guarantee of its strength. After uncounted years buried beneath the Witchlight Fens, the wood might be all but rotted through. Shara decided it didn't matter.

"Run for the door," Shara said, driving back a beast that lunged at her injured leg. "We have to get there before those demons."

Uldane took off down the hall. As soon as he was clear, Shara took a few quick steps backward, then turned and followed him at top speed. Her injured leg sent jolts of pain through her with every step, and for a moment she was afraid it would give out beneath her. She heard the demons snarling and scrabbling on the stone floor behind her. Ahead, Uldane was racing toward the door as the other group of demons stalked forward. Fortunately, those demons saw no reason to rush forward when their prey was apparently running right into their waiting jaws.

Uldane reached the door, pushed it open, and looked inside, then planted himself in the doorway. His eyes widened as he looked back at Shara, and before he could shout a warning Shara dived into a roll. A demon sailed over her, jerking in midair as Uldane's dagger bit into it. Shara somersaulted to her feet and sliced the demon half open before it hit the ground. She vaulted over its corpse, then she was in the doorway with Uldane.

"Thanks," she said, panting.

"Uh..."

"Check out this door," Shara said. "I'll hold them back."

The halfling stepped back as the first wave of demons crashed upon her. She lost herself in the rhythm of slaughter, no longer feeling any pain, though her sword seemed to grow heavier with each swing. The demons that had been at the other end of the hall reached the doorway as well, and Shara was pleased to see some of them batting claws at demons from the other group, as if competing for this choice prey.

"It's strong," Uldane said. "There's a bar on this side, and a heavy table and some other things we can pile against it."

"Is there any other way out?"

Uldane paused, swallowed hard, and said, "No."

"Doesn't matter," Shara said. "It's all we have. Get ready to close it."

She hacked around at the arc of demons in front of her, causing just enough pain and confusion to buy the space she needed. Then she stepped back and leaped to the side, and Uldane pushed the door closed with a solid slam. She heard claws scrabble against the wood as she helped Uldane maneuver the bar into place, but the door held.

She rested the point of her sword on the floor and allowed herself a deep breath as she looked around the little room. It had evidently once been an office or study, with a large work table and a couple of low bookshelves, now empty. A tapestry hung on the wall, so discolored with mildew and stains that she couldn't tell what it depicted. Uldane was making a circuit of the room, checking the walls for any secret doors and gingerly lifting the tapestry to make sure it didn't hide another door.

A heavy body slammed against the door, and it buckled slightly. With a glance at Uldane, Shara went to the table and started shoving it toward the door. It was heavy, and she was more tired than she'd been willing to admit, but with Uldane's help she managed to tip it across the doorway, and the next time a demon slammed into the door the table kept it from buckling at all.

"I need to rest," Shara said. Without waiting for a response from Uldane, she slid her sword into the sheath on her back and slumped to the floor. She shrugged out of her backpack and rummaged inside until she found a roll of bandages, then she gingerly removed the armor that covered her injured leg.

"We need a new plan," Uldane said. He started shoving against one of the low bookcases, inching it toward the door.

"Saving Quarhaun seems to be off the table." She frowned. The thought stung more than she thought it should.

"It does seem a little less urgent than saving ourselves." Uldane scowled at the bookcase, which was about as tall as he was. "I think I'll wait until you can help me with this."

Shara cleaned the blood away from the wounds on her knee and lower leg and examined them carefully. There was an angry redness to her skin around each cut that caused her some concern. She remembered Vestapalk commanding his demonic minions to go forth and spread the abyssal plague, and she washed the wounds again, wincing in pain as she scrubbed at the torn flesh. But for all the wounds hurt, they weren't going to kill or cripple her.

So I'll be able to stand when the demons finally get through the door, she thought.

She looked around the little room again. "I don't want to die here," she said. "I'm not ready."

"Shara—"

"Not while that damned dragon is still alive. If I don't kill him, who's going to? How many more people is he going to kill?"

A look of terrible pain contorted Uldane's face, but it passed quickly, as it always did. The halfling seemed immune to grief, sadness, and anger—no negative emotion could hold him for long. "You know," he said, sitting down next to Shara, "I keep thinking about that day. The fight with the dragon was horrible. But the part I like to remember is the time just before the fight. When we knew we were getting close. I remember you teasing Jarren, making light of the danger. I remember the way he looked at you, the love in his eyes. Borojon chided you two for dawdling on the path, and scolded Cliffside for making so much noise."

Tears ran down Shara's face. She had thought of that day countless times, but all she could remember was the horror; the dragon's jaws clamped on her father's shoulder; the sickening sound as the dragon literally tore Cliffside apart; the sight of Jarren, her love, looking over the cliff as she and Uldane fell toward the river; the dragon looming over Jarren's shoulder. Vestapalk might as well have torn out her heart that day, and the only joy she'd felt since had been when she thought the dragon was dead.

But Vestapalk wasn't dead. And the thought that a swarm of demons might prevent her from killing him was more than she could bear.

"I guess what I'm saying," Uldane said, "is that maybe you'd feel better if you try to think about the good times that you and Jarren spent together, instead of dwelling so much on the pain of having lost him."

Shara wiped her eyes. "It's been so long, Uldane. Sometimes I can barely remember the good times—as though my pain is all I have left of him."

"Don't do that, Shara. He was a good man, a good friend. He deserves better memories."

Shara wrapped a bandage around her knee in silence, trying to dredge up happier thoughts of Jarren.

"I remember the first time I snuck his lucky coin from his pouch," Uldane said. "He got so mad he could hardly speak, and his face was so red I couldn't help but laugh!"

Shara smiled. "He got used to it soon enough."

"I made sure he did." Uldane's laughter bubbled out again, high and infectious.

A renewed scrabbling at the door wiped the smiles from their faces. "Let's get that bookcase to the door now," Shara said.

The scratching sounds continued this time, as if the demons were determined to dig through, or under, the door. With Uldane's help, Shara got one of the bookcases—made from hard, heavy wood—in place behind the table, strengthening their barricade. As they started toward the next bookcase, though, the sounds on the other side of the door changed. Yowls of fury or pain started up, then the scratching at the door stopped. The howling grew louder, and Shara heard the ring of steel and a blast of fire.

"Perhaps we're not going to die here after all," she said.

"Is it Quarhaun?" Uldane asked brightly.

"I don't know." She went to the door and pulled at the bookcase they'd just put in place. "But someone's fighting out there, and now that I've caught my breath I think I'd like to be a part of that."

"You never put the armor back on your leg."

"It's full of tooth holes anyway." She dragged the table a few feet back, walked around it, and pressed her ear to the door.

A fight was definitely going on. She heard weapons thudding into flesh, the snarls and howls of the demons, and what might have been speech in a language she didn't understand, full of sibilant sounds and low rumbling vowels. More sounds of erupting fire and a crack of lightning suggested that at least one spellcaster was present at well. "It might be Quarhaun," she said, half to herself, and she lifted the bar from the door and opened it just enough to peek out.

Quarhaun was there, his black eldritch blade crackling with lightning in his hand. His newfound allies were lizardfolk—tall and burly warriors with reptilian heads and long tails, wielding mostly clubs and maces of bone and stone. Angry orange crests adorned the tops of their heads, and their bodies were covered with fine green scales.

"Shara!" the drow warlock called.

Something like joy surged through her as she flung open the door and waded back into battle.

CHAPTER SIX

Roghar scratched his head. "So whatever we're dealing with is preying on gnolls as well as humans," he said.

"Well, it makes sense, in a way," Travic said.

"How so?"

"I mean, the idea that gnolls had dragged Gaele and Marcan away without leaving signs of a struggle was unlikely. I was trying to come up with a theory that fit, and it becomes easier if we abandon the idea that gnolls were the captors."

"Perhaps there's some kind of mind control at work," Roghar said. "Someone enchanting them, luring them away."

"That opens a whole world of unpleasant possibilities. The best is that it's some rogue enchanter, more or less a common criminal with magic at his disposal."

"While the worst is . . . a lot worse."

Travic nodded. "A vampire or succubus, maybe even a mind flayer."

Roghar glanced at Tempest, who had turned away to look out at the ruins again. "Or some kind of possessor," he whispered to Travic.

The priest's eyes widened and shot to Tempest as well. Roghar had told him about Tempest's experience with the possessor demon, and warned him that it was a painful memory for her. "Should we turn back?" Travic said, keeping his voice low. "I can find other help—"

Roghar shook his head. "It'll be all right."

"What will?" Tempest asked, turning back to face them. "What are you two whispering about?"

Roghar stammered, trying to find a plausible and gentle lie. While he struggled, Travic stepped forward and put a hand on Tempest's shoulder.

"I'm just concerned for you," the priest said. "I don't want to put you into a situation that's going to bring up too many difficult memories."

Roghar rolled his eyes. Honesty was always Travic's preferred approach, even if it was insensitive or vaguely insulting. But he was a kind man in general, which usually allowed him to speak the truth without hurting feelings.

"You think Nu Alin is involved in this? Here?"

"We have no idea," Roghar said. "We were just discussing the possibilities. The demon that possessed you, or something like it, is at the outer edge of those possibilities."

"It's far more likely an enchanter, maybe a vampire," Travic added.

"A comforting thought," Tempest said, the hint of a smile touching her lips. "You know you've found success as an adventurer when a vampire is one of your better possibilities."

Roghar guffawed as a sense of relief washed through him. Such glimpses of Tempest's wry humor were rare since her possession, and he missed them terribly.

Travic looked toward the morning sun. "Well, if a vampire is what we're after, we've chosen the right time of day," he said. "Shall we explore farther into the ruins?"

Tempest nodded, still almost smiling, and Roghar's heart felt light as he lifted his sword to rest on his shoulder and stepped onto the crumbling street that led deeper into the ruins of Nera.

The road that Roghar had chosen more or less at random led quickly to the lip of a crater, one of a few places in the ruined city where the earth had opened up and swallowed the streets and buildings. The largest such crater marked the site of the imperial palace, but several smaller ones were arrayed around it. He sighed and chose a different path that would take him around that obstacle, but Tempest put a hand on his arm to stop him.

"What is it?" he asked.

"Look." Tempest pointed into the crater.

The depression was a couple dozen yards across, the sides worn almost smooth by a century of rain. Larger chunks of rubble littered the bottom, including recognizable pieces from some of the buildings that lined the edges, as though the crater were slowly expanding and drawing more of the ruins down to its heart. Roghar followed Tempest's pointing finger and saw what looked like the mouth of a tunnel in the crater's wall, about halfway down the side opposite where he stood.

"The gods have led us true," Travic said.

Roghar nodded. The tunnel mouth was clearly in use. Even from his position, he could see a rough path leading up the side of the crater from the tunnel mouth, and the pattern of debris beneath the tunnel suggested that rubble had been cleared out from the interior to make a clear route—presumably leading to some secret lair.

"I never met a tunnel mouth I didn't like," Roghar said. "Adventure awaits!"

He started circling around the edge of the crater toward the path, and Tempest hurried after him.

"Roghar, wait!" Travic called.

"What's the matter?"

Travic frowned, staring down into the crater. "I'm not sure," he said. "I have a strange feeling about this place."

"You said it yourself. The gods led us here. You're not getting cold feet now, are you?"

"Of course not. I just think we should approach with caution."

"Live while you can, my friend!" Roghar said, starting toward the path again. "No telling how long you have left."

"I'd prefer to prolong those days by exercising the caution and discretion I've been given," Travic muttered, quickening his steps to catch up.

Roghar laughed, but he stopped abruptly when the bowl of the crater sent the sound echoing back to him, louder and harsher. He frowned at the echo and started down the path. His armored feet crunched in the gravel, sending a trickle of pebbles off the side of the path and down into the crater. The crater seemed to magnify every sound.

He made his way along the path, cringing at every sound the crater echoed back to him. As the path took him lower and the earth took him in, the echoes surrounded him—his own footfalls and those of his companions, every crunch of gravel and rustle of cascading debris. He started hearing whispers in the echoes, words he couldn't understand, although they felt threatening. He stopped and turned to look at Travic and Tempest, and found them glancing around as he was to find the source of the whispers.

"Now I see what you mean about that strange feeling, Travic," Roghar rumbled. The sound that came back to his ears was like rolling thunder.

Travic and Tempest both nodded, unwilling to speak. Roghar swallowed his fear and continued down the path, treading as lightly as he could manage.

Tempest's scream echoed into a shrieking assault on his ears. He tried to turn to see what was wrong but found the world spinning around him, and he lurched sideways, nearly hurling himself off the path. He crouched and put one knee down to steady himself, and managed to look over his shoulder without falling over.

Travic was sprawled on the ground, his back to the crater wall. He clutched one of Tempest's hands in both of his own, struggling to pull her back up over the rough edge of the path.

Roghar turned himself and dove for Tempest's other hand, which was scrabbling for purchase at the edge. Flat on his belly, he caught hold of her, then braced himself as she started pulling herself up. In the space of a few pounding heartbeats she was back on the path, leaning against the crater wall, terror showing in her wide eyes.

"What happened?" Roghar asked. The flurry of echoes made him wince, and Travic's face grew a shade paler.

"I slipped," Tempest whispered. Her eyes met his, and he saw the same fear he often saw when he rushed to her bedside in the middle of the night. He furrowed his brow in concern, but she gave the slightest shake of her head before turning to Travic. "Thank you for catching me."

"The echoes of your scream threw me off balance," Travic whispered back. "You almost had a nasty tumble."

"Sorry," she said. "It just came out."

Roghar got to his feet and helped Travic stand. He put an arm around Tempest's shoulders and looked into her eyes. "Are you all right?" he said.

She nodded, but her eyes couldn't hold his gaze.

"We can still go back," he said.

"No." She shrugged out of his half embrace and nodded toward the tunnel mouth, no more than ten yards away. "It was just a slip."

Roghar scowled. The storm of whispering echoes was growing unbearable, making it impossible to think. He resolved to discuss the "slip" with Tempest later, and he started back down the path. The echoes of their footsteps grew more intense as Roghar went on, but despite his growing sense of anticipation, he reached the tunnel mouth without further incident.

The tunnel had been dug out of the earth, and it was shored up with a mix of fresh lumber and ancient stone columns. It ran even more steeply downward than the path in the crater, and curved sharply around to the left, cutting off Roghar's view. He saw no sign of light coming up the tunnel, so Roghar reached into the pouch at his belt and found a sunrod. Before he could light it, Travic came and stood beside him.

"I'll take care of the light," the priest said. He rested a hand on the seal of Bahamut that adorned Roghar's shield and closed his eyes for a moment, then a mote of light like a tiny sun sprang to life on the shield.

"Now my enemies can have no doubt where I am," Roghar said, smiling.

"It's no different than if you were carrying that sunrod," Travic replied.

"I wasn't complaining. Let them try to get past this shield and my armor. Better that than have them attacking the two of you."

"Roghar," Travic whispered, with a glance at Tempest. The tiefling was staring into the crater.

Roghar raised an eyebrow.

"She screamed *before* she fell," Travic said. He stepped back and gestured toward the tunnel mouth. "Shall we?"

Roghar watched Tempest as she turned back toward them, her eyes still wide and her mouth set into a thin line. Had she experienced some kind of vision? Perhaps her nightmares had come to plague her by day as they did every night. Was she going mad?

Just a slip, he thought. But a slip of her foot? Or a slip of her self-control?

Tempest kept such tight rein on her thoughts and her emotions—it was part of what allowed her to keep control over the sinister power she wielded. If that control was slipping . . .

"What are we waiting for?" Tempest demanded. She met Roghar's gaze with a mischievous smile, and he couldn't help but smile back at her.

"Travic needed a moment to pluck up his courage," Roghar said. "The older he gets, the longer it takes."

Travic laughed. "That's true of a lot of things, but not this. Let's move."

Roghar turned to the tunnel mouth. He'd have to duck his head to enter, and if anything attacked in the tunnel he'd be at a disadvantage, fighting in very close quarters. On the other hand, the curve to the left was slightly to his advantage, giving him better reach with his sword hand than an opponent coming up the other way. Assuming his hypothetical opponent used weapons.

"Who's plucking up his courage now?" Travic said behind him.

Shooting a grin back to the priest, Roghar stooped and entered the tunnel. The bedeviling echoes ceased at once, and his footsteps seemed muted by comparison. The light Travic had put on his shield shone clear and bright, filling the tunnel until it curved out of sight. Alert for any sound around the curves, Roghar advanced as fast as the low ceiling would allow.

He saw nothing to indicate who might have excavated the tunnel or why. The shoring was crude but effective, employing scavenged materials that had evidently been well chosen for strength and size. The tunnel spiraled down until Roghar figured they were lower than the bottom of the crater and then, without warning, it opened up into a wider hallway with a gentler downward slope. The hall looked like it had been part of a manor house above ground before the cataclysm that dragged it into the earth. Smooth stone walls gave him ample room to move and swing his sword, and the ceiling accommodated even his nearly seven-foot height. The hall showed signs of its displacement, though—jagged cracks ran through the walls, crumbling masonry littered the floor, and the two doorways Roghar could see leading off to the sides were half collapsed. Roghar eyed the ceiling cautiously, wondering how many tons of rock were overhead now.

He paused as Tempest and then Travic emerged from the corkscrew tunnel and found their bearings in the new hallway. "I see light coming around that corner," he said, pointing down the hall.

"Smells like incense," Tempest added.

Roghar took a deep breath through his nostrils and noticed it as well—sandalwood or something similar.

"I'd wager we're about to walk into a secret temple," Travic said. "Tiamat?"

Roghar bristled. As a paladin of Bahamut, he had a special loathing for the cults of Tiamat, mirroring the enmity between the two dragon gods, the twin children of Io. But this didn't feel like a cult of Tiamat to him. The whole arrangement suggested devils—the temple nestled in the ancient ruins, the menacing whispers in the crater, and the spiraling descent, like a passage through the Nine Hells. "Five gold says it's Asmodeus," he said.

Travic sniffed the air and smiled. "You're on. There's no hint of brimstone."

Roghar scowled. "I stand by my bet. Come on." He shifted his grip on his shield and started down the hall.

"Stop!" Tempest said quietly, but with an urgency that stopped him dead. She moved up to stand beside him and pointed at the floor just in front of his feet.

Roghar crouched and squinted, and finally saw the slender tripwire stretched across the hall a few inches off the floor. "Thank you," he breathed. He cast his eyes around the hallway but didn't see any other sign of a trap—no block of stone rigged to fall from the ceiling, no slits in the walls where blades might spring out. It didn't matter. Even if it was only rigged to ring a bell in the secret temple, alerting the cultists to their approach, he'd almost walked right into it. He stood and put a hand on Tempest's shoulder. "Do you see anything else?"

"Not from here. But maybe I should go first."

Roghar didn't like the idea—it would make her more vulnerable in an attack, and possibly cost them precious time in a fight as she fell back behind him. On the other hand, she was probably more likely to notice signs of an ambush or hear approaching attackers than he was, as well as being more likely to spot traps and tripwires. He nodded and squeezed to the side of the hall so she could get past him.

Tempest stepped carefully over the tripwire and paused to make sure Roghar crossed it safely. Roghar mimicked her motions, provoking a snicker that Tempest quickly hid with a cough. He grinned at her, then pointed out the tripwire to Travic so the priest could step over it as well.

Roghar nodded to himself as he followed Tempest down the hall. This is how it's supposed to work, he thought.

Teamwork, each member of the team relying on the others' strengths and covering each other's weaknesses.

I'm starting to sound like a priest of Erathis, he thought with a laugh. The god of civilization promoted the ideals of people working together to build and invent and civilize, sometimes even to conquer. But those ideals were not far from Bahamut's—the Platinum Dragon exhorted his followers to protect the weak and defend just order, order that might be established in Erathis's name.

Tempest led them past several collapsing doorways, the rooms beyond mostly or completely caved in, showing no sign of having been touched or inhabited in the last century. An alcove on the left side of the hall held a decorative guardian, a stone sculpture in surprisingly good condition, depicting a proud human knight in plate armor. Roghar paused as the knight's stone eyes caught his gaze—they were so lifelike, so expertly carved, that he found himself wondering for a moment if the statue might be a living man turned to stone by a medusa or basilisk. But the pose was that of a watchful sentinel, not a man turned to stone in midstride, and he dismissed the thought.

Travic lingered at the statue as well, admiring the sculptor's art. Tempest held up a hand and hissed a warning, wrenching Roghar's full attention back to the end of the hallway.

"I hear voices," she mouthed, pointing to her ear.

Roghar tried to listen, but a sudden sound of rumbling stone from behind him drowned out all other sound. He whirled around in time to see the stone knight, emerged from its alcove, swing its sword down in a deadly arc toward Travic's head.

CHAPTER SEVEN

The way to Sherinna's tower lay across the Plain of Thorns, the aptly named expanse of brown bush and sharp briers that stretched from the edge of the forest for miles to the south and east. Albanon led the way through thorny vines that did, he had to admit, seem to yield at his approach. He moderated his pace to make sure Kri could keep up—the thorns started closing in behind Albanon as soon as he passed, forcing Kri to pick his way more carefully through the brambles.

The sun settled on the horizon, bathing the dry plain in blood-red light. Albanon frowned at the sky, looked back to the forest where his father's palace stood hidden among the trees, and searched the fields ahead for a sign of the tower.

"I don't relish the thought of having to find the tower in the dark," he said to Kri.

"It can't be much farther," Kri replied. "And the sky is clear—we'll have moonlight to guide us."

"Can you see the tower? Am I just blind?"

"If you are, it's because you rely too much on your eyes instead of letting yourself feel the magic around you."

Albanon sighed. "It's overwhelming here. So much magic."

"That's what makes it so useful. If you can open yourself to it, it will show you more than your eyes ever could. Imagine you're a fish that can feel everything the water in the ocean touches."

"I'd go mad."

"No!" The vehemence of Kri's reply surprised Albanon. "If you're unwilling to use the power given to you, you'll never learn anything."

"Moorin always taught me to use my power with caution."

"Moorin held you back."

Albanon glanced up to where Splendid circled in the sky, glad the little drake wasn't present to hear her late master insulted. He knew he should probably take offense as well, but he couldn't quite manage it. He had loved Moorin—"like a father" didn't seem to quite cover it, considering his relationship to his own father. But he'd also long felt exactly what Kri had just said, that Moorin was holding him back, unwilling or unable to see his true potential. Moorin had dismissed his grumbling as the discontent common to every young apprentice, but now Kri seemed to be validating it.

Splendid swooped down and landed on his shoulder, making him stumble a few steps forward under the sudden weight. With her return, Albanon felt a blush of shame for the thoughts he'd been harboring, the disrespect he'd allowed himself to feel for his departed master. The shame was followed by a surge of anger, though, at the mentor who was supposed to train him and heighten his skills and instead held back his growing power.

Why should I be ashamed of wanting to claim the power that is mine? he thought, casting a dark glance sidelong at the pseudodragon.

"I found your tower," Splendid said.

"You did?" Albanon's face brightened, but then he heard a sound that sent a thrill of fear down his spine. Hounds bayed in the distance behind them.

Kri cocked an eyebrow at him. "A hunt?"

No trace of fear showed on the old priest's face, and Albanon could understand why. In the world, the sound of a hunt meant a party giving chase to a stag or a boar. It was nothing for the people of the world to be afraid of, and might send a flutter of excitement in a listener who had participated in such a hunt before. But the stag or boar who was the quarry of the hunt would flee in fear, and rightly so.

"The nobles of the Feywild do not hunt beasts for sport," Albanon said. "If there is a hunt on our heels, it means we are the quarry."

"But your father granted us passage," Kri said. "Did he change his mind?"

"Perhaps he decided that the insult you gave him could not be allowed to stand. I've rarely seen him that angry."

Kri drew himself up. "He needed a slap in the face."

"Not where others could see, not from a stranger in his court, and certainly not from a human. Even if he had been willing to ignore your insult, he might have felt he had to punish you in order to save face with his courtiers."

"So what now?"

"Now we run. Splendid, lead the way to the tower!"

"If what?" the drake said.

"If what? I don't think I understand you."

Splendid's voice dripped with disdain. "If you please."

"You must be joking."

"Am I a pet? A servant? A slave? I think not."

"Fine, Splendid. Please!"

The drake sniffed. "That will have to do."

She pushed up from Albanon's shoulder, sending him off balance again, and flapped into the air. She circled a moment as Albanon watched, then flew away in more or less the direction they'd been heading, but a little more to the south.

"And now we follow, as fast as these damned thorns will allow."

Albanon hurried after Splendid, the thorns parting in front of him and closing in behind. He searched the rolling plain ahead for a sign of the tower, cursing himself for forgetting to ask Splendid how far away it was. Then he crested a rise and spotted it, nestled in a thicket at the top of another low hill. Too far away—they'd never make it, if the hunt was as close as it sounded.

"Albanon!"

He turned and saw Kri ten yards behind him. Grasping thorns pinned the priest in place, caught in his clothes and piercing his skin. Albanon growled in frustration. They'd never escape the hunt if Kri kept getting snagged in the brambles.

"Use your power, Albanon," Kri said. "The thorns respond to your mere presence. If you command them, they'll respond to that as well."

Albanon's eyes widened. Why didn't I think of that? he thought. I am a wizard and the scion of an eladrin prince. Did Moorin utterly crush my sense of my own abilities?

He stretched one hand toward Kri and the other, gripping his staff, in the direction of the tower. Drawing a deep breath, he focused his will and his magic, then with a grunt he extended both out through his hands. Kri staggered free of the thorns, and a path appeared through the brush and vines, a hundred yards long.

"That's more like it," Kri said. His broad smile filled Albanon with pride, and together the two men raced for the tower.

When they reached the end of the first path, Albanon thrust both hands in front of him and made a longer one. Over the sounds of the baying hounds in the distance and Kri's wheezing breath, he heard the high, clear notes of a horn urging the hunt onward. Too close. At least Kri was moving faster, but it still felt too slow.

When they reached the end of the second path, Albanon had an idea. First he summoned his will to clear a new path in front of them, the longest one so far. He could feel each individual thorn and vine when he stretched out his senses, feel the magic in them and shape his own magic to control them. It was so easy, now that he understood it.

Why did I never learn this before? he wondered.

With fierce joy surging in his heart, he turned around and lifted his arms over his head. He watched as the vines surged back over the path he'd left in his wake, then thickened still more, growing taller and tougher. In a moment they were a wall behind him, studded with terrible thorns.

"That should slow our pursuers," Kri said.

"Yes. Even if they carry my father's authority, it'll take them some time to clear a path through that, or to go around it."

Each time they reached the end of a path, Albanon set up a new barrier behind them. Soon the tower loomed close, and Albanon finally allowed himself to believe they might reach the tower before the hunt caught up to them.

Splendid swooped down and landed on a thick bush, nimbly twisting herself around the large thorns. "I have to admit, apprentice," she said, "your control of the thorns is admirable. The great wizard Moorin would approve."

Albanon turned away before Splendid could see him scowl, then found himself blinking back tears. What would Moorin have thought? he wondered. He still missed the old wizard, despite the resentment that seemed to be growing in his heart. And despite the excitement he felt at the thought of learning from Kri.

Splendid jumped onto his shoulder and they hurried along Albanon's path. The horns blared with a new urgency, as if the hunters had realized that their quarry was escaping them. But the thorny barriers didn't seem to be slowing them as much as Albanon had hoped, which only confirmed his fear that the huntmaster carried the full authority of the Prince of Thorns, allowing the hunt to clear a path as easily as Albanon did.

Albanon cleared one more path, and the thorns fell away from the base of Sherinna's tower. It was a slender spire of white marble draped in ivy, five or six stories high. It had weathered the centuries well—but most structures built in the Feywild by eladrin hands did. The tower's entrance was a door of stout oak reinforced with mithral bands, and Albanon felt a sudden worry that they'd reach the tower only to find themselves unable to open the door to escape their pursuers.

He turned to raise a thorny barrier behind them, and caught his first glimpse of the hunt. The hounds at the lead had glowing green eyes, and with each yowl and bark they belched a puff of emerald fire. Behind them, a half dozen eladrin nobles rode white and gray horses, the pennants of the Prince of Thorns trailing from their upraised lances.

So there was no denying it—the Prince of Thorns had sent them out to kill his own son.

Albanon raised the barrier just in front of the lead hounds and heard them crash into it with yelps of surprise and pain. Smiling with bitter satisfaction, he nodded to Kri. "Almost there," he said.

Only then did he see the toll their flight had taken on the old priest. Kri was bent over, hands on his knees as he tried desperately to catch his breath. His ashen face was twisted with pain and streaked with sweat.

"Oh, no," Albanon breathed, stepping to the old priest's side. "Come on, Kri." He put an arm around Kri's shoulder and tried to help the priest walk to the tower. "We're so close."

Kri accepted his help and they hobbled together along the path, the yelps and barks behind them growing more intense as the hounds forced their way through Albanon's thorny barrier. The hunt was so close that Albanon could hear the eladrin spewing colorful curses as their horses balked at the rising brambles. The tower seemed impossibly far away.

Every few paces, as Kri caught his breath, Albanon threw back one hand and summoned another surge of thorns to slow the hunt. Slowly—painfully slowly—they drew nearer and nearer to the tower, and their pursuers remained at bay. Each step stretched to an agonizing eternity.

Somehow that eternity drew to an end, and they stood before the mithral-bound doors to the Whitethorn Spire. Albanon glanced over his shoulder and saw two riders circling around the end of his thorny barrier, spurring their horses for a charge.

"Open the doors!" he urged Kri.

Exhausted as he was, the old priest tugged with all his remaining strength on the mithral ring that hung from one door. The door didn't budge.

"Is it locked?" Albanon asked. "Do you have a key?"

"No! There's not even a keyhole." Kri raised his staff and chanted a few arcane syllables Albanon recognized as a simple charm of opening, but again the doors showed no hint of movement.

"They're coming!" Splendid chirped in Albanon's ear.

Albanon put his back to the door and clenched his own staff. The lead rider was about twenty paces away, but riding hard and fast. Albanon called up another surge of thorns to slow them, simultaneously trying to prepare his mind to unleash a spell of fire or lightning on the riders. Panic and his pounding heart shattered his concentration, making both efforts ineffective.

The door suddenly slammed hard into Albanon's back, knocking him to his knees as Kri yelped and staggered back. Albanon twisted around to see what had opened the doors.

His guts wrenched in fear as he recognized the monster in the doorway—a hulking brute, almost like some kind of beetle, standing upright but hunched forward. Four arms tipped with heavy claws sprouted from its torso. Its red eyes glowed in the shadow inside the tower, set above a mouth full of sharp teeth. A massive carapace of reddish crystal covered its shoulders and back and rose in two sharp spikes above its head. It was one of Vestapalk's minions, but larger than any he'd seen before. A plague demon, born of the Voidharrow.

Smaller demons swarmed behind the one in the doorway. So Vestapalk's corruption had already spread as far as the Feywild, to the very tower that Kri believed held the secret to defeating them. Albanon scrambled to his feet, his eyes darting between the demons in the tower and the charging fey hunters.

On one side, the claws of the demons held the promise of torture and death, or worse. On the other, the hounds of the fey charged forward, ready to tear him to shreds, and the spears of his kin were aimed to pierce his heart. But the thought that came to mind was Tempest's face, smiling in her determination. She would have gone down fighting. He could do no less.

CHAPTER EIGHT

The demons shrieked as Shara's sword cut into them. The arrival of Quarhaun and his lizardfolk allies had thrown them into confusion, and Shara's whirling fury broke their resolve completely. Those that could turned and fled back the way Shara and Uldane had come. The rest were trapped between Shara and Quarhaun, and a hint of her old exultation coursed through her as she hacked and stabbed a path to where the drow stood.

He came back, she told herself, singing the words to the rhythm of her blade.

A quieter voice in the back of her mind kept reminding her, the way Jarren can't.

In a matter of moments the demons were all dead or dispersed, and Shara leaned on her blade beside Quarhaun. Her exhaustion couldn't keep the grin from her face, and Quarhaun returned the smile, a little sheepishly. Their eyes met for a moment, which did nothing to calm her pounding heart.

One of the lizardfolk nudged Quarhaun's arm and he looked away, reluctantly, to answer some question in their sibilant language, pointing to the demonic corpses that littered the hall.

"Ow," Uldane said.

Shara turned to find the halfling, pale and frowning, slumped against the wall behind her. He was picking at the torn scraps of leather armor that had covered his chest, pulling strips of it from a bloody wound.

"Nine Hells, what happened to you?" Shara said, dropping to her knees beside him.

"You missed it!" Uldane said, the beginnings of his smile turning into a wince of pain. "One of the demons had me in its mouth and it was shaking me back and forth, and I stabbed it in the eye!" He drew a ragged breath and forced a smile to his face. "Do you have any idea how hard it was to get it in the eye when it was shaking me like that?"

"I can imagine," Shara said. She tried to keep the concern from showing on her face as she helped him pull the armor away from his wound. His cut had the same angry red swelling along the edges that her wounds had. "I don't know how I could have missed it."

"You were busy protecting Quarhaun." His voice was matter-of-fact, but there was an edge of disapproval in his eyes.

Shara frowned. "We need to put both of you in heavier armor. I'm not sure I can keep every enemy away from the two of you."

"I don't like wearing heavy armor," Uldane said. "It slows me down."

"I know, Uldane." Shara brushed a long braid of dark hair out of his face. "I've got a potion in my pack that should take care of this wound. It's not as bad as it looks."

"It feels even worse than it looks."

"I'll be right back." She stood and picked her way through the demon corpses back to the room where she and the halfling had holed up. Quarhaun was waiting for her at the door.

"You came back," she said quietly.

"That was the plan, right? Kill them all?"

"You risked your life to save us." The words had a hard time escaping past the lump in her throat. "That was foolish. You said it yourself."

"You did it for me." Quarhaun touched her chin softly with his gloved hand, and a shiver went through her. "And if you did it, it must be worth doing."

Her thoughts a jumble, she squeezed past him into the room and grabbed her pack. "And you found friends," she said.

"A hunting party. They were following our tracks into the ruins, actually. I convinced them to help me kill the demons."

"How did you do that?"

Quarhaun shrugged. "By convincing them we could, I guess. They fear the demons and hate them for thinning the prey. I showed them an opportunity to give up one hunt in order to get better hunting in the future."

"Give up one . . . they were *hunting* us?"

"Prey is scarce in the fens."

Shara found the potion she needed and stepped back to the door. "Quarhaun . . . thank you."

The drow scowled, speechless.

Shara went back in the hall to find Quarhaun's lizardfolk friends crouching there, their glassy eyes fixed on her, and she wondered if they were assessing her ability to fight back if they decided to make a meal of her. She looked down the hall and saw one of them crouched beside Uldane, prodding at his wound with a feather-bedecked length of bone.

"Hey! What are you doing?"

The lizardfolk turned its head slowly and its eyes fluttered open to stare at her. It opened its mouth and hissed something low and rumbling.

"Quarhaun!" she called. "What's it saying?"

"Shara," Uldane said. "Don't worry. I think it's helping."

Shara stepped closer and saw that the color had returned to Uldane's face. She dropped to her knees and took his hand. "I'm sorry," she said to the lizardfolk. "Please go on."

Quarhaun spoke in the lizardfolk's hissing tongue and the healer or shaman or whatever it was turned its attention—and its bone totem—back to Uldane. The halfling winced and squeezed her hand, but the wound began to knit itself closed and the angry red color faded from his skin. Uldane's bright eyes opened again and a smile spread across his face.

"What an interesting feeling!" he announced, trying to sit up. "I felt like I was swimming."

Shara looked at her friend's chest. Water soaked his clothes and had washed the blood away from the wound, which was still a bit pink but otherwise completely healed.

"Looks like you were," Shara said, smiling at the halfling.

"Oh! I'm all wet." He looked up at the lizardfolk. "How did you do that?"

Quarhaun hissed a few words, and the shaman responded in kind.

"He says the water spirits healed you. He just brought them where they needed to be."

Uldane sprang to his feet, all the pain of his injury forgotten. "Ooh! Do you think I could learn to do that, Shara?"

Shara just smiled and wished that she could learn to recover so quickly and so completely from her wounded heart.

"We should leave this place," Quarhaun announced. "The demons might come back in greater numbers."

"You're right," Shara said. "We should hit them before they can regroup."

"Hit them?"

"Of course."

"Shara," Uldane said, "just a few minutes ago you were saying you didn't want to die here. You want to have your revenge on Vestapalk before you die, right?"

"I have no intention of dying," Shara said. "We're stronger than ever, and the demons are on the run. We need to root them out of here."

Quarhaun caught her gaze with his blank white eyes. "Why?"

Shara's face flushed and her words were heated and fast. "You've seen them. Whatever has changed Vestapalk, whatever he tried to do to you—that same substance is here. It made these demons. They're all part of the same

. . . the same disease. For all we know, Vestapalk could be here, somewhere in these ruins, spreading his plague from here."

Quarhaun held her gaze for a long moment until she looked away, uneasy.

"You are quite a warrior," he said at last.

"What does that mean?"

"It's not our way, you see? Among the drow, women hold sacred positions, ordained by the Spider Queen. They're the matron mothers and priests, generals at times, but not warriors. I've never known a woman like you."

"Does that mean we're going to explore these ruins some more?" Uldane asked.

"I suppose it does," Quarhaun said.

"Well, that's a bright side to it. I wonder how far down the tunnels go? It can't be too far, or they'd be full of water, wouldn't they?"

"It depends. Sometimes stone tunnels jut up all the way from the Underdark, solid and dry even when they touch the surface in swampy areas like this."

"Really?"

"It's rare, but it does happen."

"I'd like to see that."

Shara let Uldane pester Quarhaun with questions as she tried to sort through the feelings the drow's words had stirred up in her. *It's natural that he'd respect a skilled warrior like me,* she told herself. *And the fact that I'm a woman makes me . . . a curiosity. That's all.*

And the way he touched my chin . . . the memory of it brought echoes of the shivers it had sent through her.

Who knows what that means to a drow like him? Maybe it's a warrior's sign of respect.

She felt a grin creep into the corners of her mouth. *I wonder what else drow warriors do as a sign of respect* . . .

She shook her head to dispel the thought. "Are we ready to move on?" she asked.

Uldane stepped closer to her and looked up at her seriously. "Are you sure about this, Shara?"

"Of course I am. Vestapalk might be here. How could I live with myself if revenge was within my grasp and I let it slip away?"

"Do you think he's here?"

"We've seen more demons here than anywhere else in the Vale. Remember what Quarhaun said earlier? It's like a lava flow."

Uldane nodded. "We'll find the source where the lava is thickest."

Quarhaun turned from the lizardfolk shaman and put a hand on Shara's shoulder. "Kssansk says his people will continue to help us until we've rooted the demons out of here."

"And they won't eat us?" Shara asked, smiling.

"No promises, but I think we're safe at least until the demons are gone."

"No promises?" Uldane said, his eyes wide.

"If Kssansk had wanted to eat you, he had the perfect opportunity while you were passed out on the floor."

The shaman cocked his head, presumably recognizing the sound of his name, and Quarhaun said a few words to him.

Kssansk responded with a short exclamation and two chomps of his enormous jaws.

"Two bites, he says," Quarhaun translated.

Shara laughed as Uldane's eyes widened further.

"Where did you learn their language?" she asked the drow.

"They speak a dialect of Draconic, same as troglodytes."

"And dragons, I take it."

"Yes. But my house had troglodyte slaves, not dragons. Some of my people think it's beneath them to speak in the languages of their slaves, but it's hard to argue that it's very useful to be able to understand it."

Something in his grin suggested that the most useful thing about understanding the language of slaves was the ability to quell any uprising before it took root and spread. Such a vivid reminder of the very different world he came from made her uncomfortable. She turned away from him to shoulder her pack.

"Which way?" she asked.

"We follow the ones that fled," Quarhaun said. "They'll lead us to the heart of their lair."

"Maybe," Uldane said, "by the most roundabout path imaginable. More likely, they'll just lead us outside."

Quarhaun arched an eyebrow. "You know so much about the behavior of these demons?"

"It's common sense, and the way most animals would behave. They don't want us to find their lair."

"They do if that's where they're strongest. That's what I'd do—pull all the survivors back to a defensible location."

"They're a pack, not an army," Uldane insisted. "I don't think that's the way they think."

JAMES WYATT

"Shara, help me here," Quarhaun said.

"I think Uldane is right," Shara said. "I think they'd try to lure us away. They know they can outrun us and make their way back to their lair by a back route."

Quarhaun scowled, and for a moment Shara thought he might lose his temper. The air thrummed with his gathering power, and dark energy coalesced around his hands before he took a deep breath and made a visible effort to calm himself.

"Fine," he said at last. "We go the way they didn't go. Lead on, sir halfling." He gave an exaggerated bow.

Uldane frowned at him and started down the hall, in the direction he and Shara had been going before they ducked into the room. Shara took up a position just behind him and to the left, which allowed him a chance to notice any traps or other dangers before she blundered into them, while keeping her close enough to step in and protect him if anything leaped out to attack. It was their established procedure, and at that point Shara was happy to ignore Quarhaun and the lizardfolk.

Let them protect each other, she thought.

Uldane wasn't trained as a tracker, but he noticed details that most other people would miss—a bloody print on the floor here, there a scratch in the wall gouged by one of the crystalline growths that sprouted from the demons' backs. In each case, he chose the path the demons had not taken, and soon they were heading down a damp, moss-covered stairway.

"Looks like we're reaching the water level," Shara said.

"That's really interesting," Uldane said. "But this isn't an Underdark tunnel like Quarhaun described."

"I think this whole structure used to be above ground," Quarhaun said. "The swamp has slowly swallowed it up."

No hint of his earlier anger tainted the drow's voice, and Shara felt her own fading. So he doesn't like being contradicted, she thought. Or he just doesn't like being wrong—who does?

As she walked, Shara's foot slipped out from under her on the stair, and she hit the stone hard, with a clatter of armor. As she tried desperately to get hold of something solid, she slid down a dozen more stairs, each one raising a new racket as her sword and pack jangled against her armor and the stone beneath her. Her helmet slammed against the stairs several times as well, sending shocks through her skull. By the time she caught herself, her ears were ringing from the noise.

She looked up and saw Quarhaun bending over her, offering a hand to help her to her feet. She tried to grab his hand, but her hand didn't find it where her eyes told her it was. She held up a finger and tried to make her head stop swimming.

"Don't move!" Uldane whispered suddenly, a step or two above her.

Shara peered into the darkness below her, but her eyes still weren't cooperating. "What is it?" she whispered.

"There's something moving down there," Uldane said. "Something big."

CHAPTER NINE

Travic barely dodged the stone knight's sword. As the animated statue pulled its weapon back, Travic slipped behind Roghar and shot a ray of divine light from his hand to erupt in the statue's face.

"That's one of the things that takes longer as I get older," he said.

Roghar laughed as Tempest hurled a blast of eldritch fire over his shoulder. "Good thing you're not that old yet," he said. He raised his shield as the stone knight's sword sliced down at him, blocking the blow. He staggered under the force of it, and his shield arm tingled furiously. "Oh, that would have hurt."

His own sword clattered against the knight's stone armor, to little effect. The statue's perfectly sculpted eyes bored into him, unmoving and unblinking. It reminded him of the stone guardian he and Tempest had encountered in the Labyrinth beneath Thunderspire Mountain—except that Tempest hadn't been herself at the time. During that fight,

Erak had stabbed Tempest in the gut, letting the demonic possessor spill out with her blood. And their companion Falon, a cleric of noble ancestry, had discovered that he could command the stone guardian.

"Stop!" he ordered the knight, in his most authoritative voice.

In answer, the stone knight thrust its sword forward, right at his heart. Dodging to the left and parrying the blade to the right, he managed to avoid the stab, but it was too close.

"So, I take it you weren't created to obey the orders of Bahamut's paladins," he said. "How about clerics of Erathis? Tiefling warlocks? Either of you two want to try giving a command?"

"Kill!" shouted a growling voice somewhere behind him. "Smash the intruders!"

"Not what I had in mind," Roghar muttered. He landed a solid blow on the statue, hard enough to knock a few large chips of stone loose and drive it a few steps back. He used the opportunity to glance over his shoulder.

A group of bedraggled looking humans huddled in the hall, taking shelter behind what must have been their champion—a huge, mangy gnoll whose foul hide was marred by several burned, hairless patches. The gnoll held a heavy spear with a brutally serrated head, somewhere between a whaler's harpoon and a butcher's cleaver. The humans, though they were dressed like beggars, clutched an array of makeshift weapons and seemed determined to fight—at least for as long as they had the protection of the gnoll.

The gnoll charged Tempest.

And Tempest was still staring at the stone knight, probably overwhelmed by the same memories that it had stirred up in Roghar.

"Tempest, behind you!" he shouted. "Travic—"

The stone knight's sword slammed across his chest and pounded him against the wall, knocking the breath from his lungs. Roghar's armor kept the blade from cutting him in two, but the metal crumpled beneath the force of the blow and bit into his flesh.

A soft white light washed over him as Travic murmured a prayer. Air flowed back into his lungs and the pain in his chest lost its edge, and he looked up just in time to see the gnoll's spear turned aside an instant before it cut into Tempest's spine. Tempest whirled around and uttered a terrifying wail that battered the gnoll and the humans behind it back the way they'd come, giving her room to move.

"Now for you," Roghar said to the stone knight. "Bahamut, bless my blade!" Power coursed through him, ran down his arm, and poured into his sword as he struck the statue with all his strength. His blow connected with a crack of thunder that knocked the statue off its feet and sent it crashing to the ground.

"Marcan?" Travic called behind him. "What are you doing here?"

"Mind control it is, then," Roghar muttered to himself. He rushed forward as the animated statue tried to get to its feet, smiting it again with as much power as he could draw from his faith and his fear.

"You should leave this place, Travic," an unfamiliar voice said. "We have left that life behind us."

"Is Gaele here as well?" Travic asked.

"Heed me, priest. You should not be here."

A growl that could only be the gnoll punctuated Marcan's words, and Travic cried out in pain.

Roghar risked another glance over his shoulder. Travic was staggering back from the gnoll, and blood sprayed from the tip of the gnoll's spear as it pulled free of the priest's shoulder. That's not good, he thought. The humans, emboldened by the gnoll's successful attack, crowded forward to get in on the action. He didn't have time to worry about Travic. The stone knight was on its feet again, though it seemed a bit unsteady.

"Had enough?" Roghar asked the statue, making a few tentative jabs with his sword.

In answer, the knight slammed its sword into Roghar's shield again. A jolt of pain shot up his arm, then his arm went numb. He could barely hold his shield any more, let alone move it into position to block the knight's next blow. He tried to step back out of the knight's reach, but he bumped into Tempest and the tip of the stone sword bit through the armor plates at his shoulder.

"I need more space!" Tempest shouted, her voice high with fear and frustration.

Roghar nodded. Using his sword hand to help raise his shield in front of him, he ducked his head and rushed forward, inside the knight's reach. His shield slammed into the stone knight's chest, sending a fresh wave of pain through his arm but pushing the statue back a few steps, giving Tempest the room she needed.

As the animated statue fought to catch its balance, Roghar stretched his jaws wide and exhaled a blast of fire that covered the stone knight. The flames had little effect on the stone itself, but it concentrated and lingered on the places where Roghar's sword had already made gouges and chips in its surface. Fighting a magical construct like the statue involved more than wearing down its physical substance—it was a creature of magic and will bound to a material form. The divine power that flowed through his sword, the raw elemental energy of his draconic breath, and his own powerful will would cause as much damage to the statue as the steel of his blade, maybe more.

Indeed, the fire seemed to sap the statue's strength. It staggered back another couple of steps and sagged to one knee. Roghar pressed the attack, drawing his arm back for a mighty blow.

With his shield arm still numb, he left himself completely open to a counterattack, and the statue, even weakened and off-balance, was quick enough to take advantage of it. Springing up from its crouch, it rammed its shoulder into Roghar's chest, knocking the breath out of him again and sending him flying back to land at Tempest's feet.

The hall spun around him as he lay on his back. He heard the statue's footsteps as it advanced—he felt them reverberate through the floor—but he couldn't lift his head to see it coming.

Tempest screamed his name, panic filling her voice in a way he'd never heard before.

A murmured prayer helped bring the spinning world to a halt, and he felt strength surge through his body again. His shield arm tingled fiercely, but at least he could move it. He sat up just in time to knock the stone knight's blade aside with his shield and struck a solid blow on the statue's neck with his own sword. Had he been facing a human opponent, his blow would have decapitated his foe, and it was a solid enough hit to drive the statue back again.

Roghar stole a glance around as he got to his feet. Travic was struggling to hold his own against the gnoll and the ragged humans who occasionally lunged forward to take advantage of an opening. They were wearing him down and driving him back, crowding Tempest from that side too.

Tempest wasn't holding up well, he could see. Her eyes were wide, and power crackled in the air around her. Streams of fire circled around her head and tongues of flame leaped from her shoulders, signs that her tight control over her infernal magic was slipping. More than the actual threats they faced, the thought of Tempest losing control filled him with fear.

Roghar gritted his teeth. He didn't like having a whole separate battle raging behind him, out of sight, where he was powerless to help and protect his friends. He didn't like forcing Travic to hold off the gnoll and the others by himself, but he also knew that the priest would have crumpled under the stone knight's assault. And he didn't like forcing Tempest to split her attention, unable to catch the stone knight in the same fiery eruptions and thunderous blasts that she used to batter the other group of foes. Fundamentally, he hated everything about this fight, and wished he'd been smart enough to recognize the threat of the statue before it came to life and attacked from the rear.

"Your eyes should have tipped me off," he growled at the stone knight.

The statue's unblinking eyes gave him an idea, and he began gathering divine power for another strike, one he hoped would finish the statue. He lifted his shield to bat the knight's sword aside again, then Travic cried out and Tempest screamed his name.

He risked a glance behind him. Travic was down, and the gnoll stood over him with a leering grin twisting its blood-soaked muzzle. Taking advantage of Roghar's distraction, the knight's sword sliced past his upraised shield and bit deeply into his arm.

"Enough!" Roghar shouted. Ignoring the pain in his shield arm, he swung his sword with all his might. As it whistled through the air, it began to glow, and it struck the knight's head with a blinding flash of light. After the initial flare faded, the statue's eyes continued to glow, and an instant later, the statue's head erupted in a shower of stone fragments. Its body froze in the midst of staggering back, as if it had been sculpted in that position.

Roghar wheeled to face the gnoll and found Tempest raining all the fires of the Nine Hells upon it and its human allies. Her hands were a blur of motion, snatching fire from the air and hurling it at anything that moved. A cloak of smoke and fire surrounded her and flames danced in a ring around her feet—dangerously close to where Travic lay. The fury of her assault was keeping the gnoll back, for the moment, but it also made it impossible for Roghar to get past her and fight the gnoll or tend to Travic's injuries. Tempest might not have needed his help, but Travic's lifeblood was spilling out onto the floor as he watched.

"Tempest, back up!" he shouted over the roar of her eldritch flames.

She didn't respond. The firestorm around her grew larger and hotter, forcing her opponents and Roghar back several steps. Smoke started to curl up from Travic's robes.

Roghar let out a wordless shout and reached through the flames to grab Tempest's shoulder, yanking her backward. Flames lashed out at his arm, and Tempest whirled on him, ready to throw a handful of hellfire at what she perceived as a threat behind her.

"Tempest!" Roghar shouted again, lifting his shield to ward off the blast.

The blast never came, and the fury of the firestorm diminished a bit. He glanced over the top of his shield to see Tempest, eyes wide with shock, fear, and the dawning realization of what she'd almost done. Still using his shield to ward himself from her flames, he pushed past her to Travic's side.

The gnoll stood over Travic's body, its heavy spear clutched in both hands, its grin daring Roghar to come closer.

"I'll take that dare," Roghar muttered.

His first swing cut the brutal blade from the head of the spear, and his second cut a wide gash across the gnoll's throat. Before it could fall, Roghar planted a kick in the center of the gnoll's chest and sent it sprawling back into the clump of humans behind it.

As they staggered back from the corpse of their champion, Roghar dropped to one knee and rested his palm on Travic's chest. Fierce joy surged through him, Bahamut's delight in a battle well fought, and he felt Travic draw a ragged breath as healing power flowed through his body.

Roghar bared his teeth as he looked back up at the ragged humans. They stared at him in undisguised terror, then broke and ran back the way they'd come, making no effort to cover their retreat.

Roghar's roar of triumph pursued them, echoing down the hall.

CHAPTER TEN

The hounds of the fey hunt crashed into Albanon's thorn barrier as the smaller demons spilled out of the Whitethorn Spire. The first rider to reach the barrier stood in his stirrups, then disappeared, reappearing with a soft popping sound just outside of Albanon's reach. Albanon's mouth dropped open as he recognized Immeral, the eladrin they had met in Moonstair.

Albanon gripped his staff and braced himself for an attack, preparing an arcane shield he could throw up in case the eladrin's spear or a demon's claws came too close. In his surprise, readying that spell was all he could manage—all his thoughts of searing foes with fire or lightning had scattered like dry leaves in a storm wind.

Nodding a salute to Albanon, Immeral lowered his spear and charged the large demon. The other riders appeared behind him with a series of pops and engaged the smaller demons, slashing around them with long, slender swords.

They weren't after us? Albanon thought, suddenly feeling very foolish.

He gestured to dismiss the thorn barriers where the hounds were still thrashing their way through, and the hounds surged forward, leaping at the demons with teeth bared. Albanon stared dumbly as a fierce battle erupted on all sides around him.

"Are you going to stand there like a statue while the priest dies?" Splendid chirped in his ear. The pseudodragon pushed off his shoulder and took flight, circling his head as she continued to speak. "Not that I would be terribly surprised. Or disappointed, come to think of it."

The pseudodragon's words jolted Albanon out of his stupor. Kri, still sagging with exhaustion, was surrounded by the smaller demons, which stood almost as tall as he was. They were built much like dwarves, and some part of Albanon's mind wondered idly if these creatures had been dwarves that had been subjected to Vestapalk's transformation. Kri looked as though he could barely lift his heavy mace, let alone swing it effectively, and the demons surrounding him were making the most of his exhaustion. Like wolves encircling a tired stag, they darted in from behind to slash with their four clawed arms while the demons in front of him concentrated on dodging and blocking the weak blows of his mace.

It took only an instant's concentration for Albanon to work the same fey magic that had brought Immeral and the other hunters past his thorn barrier. He took a single step that carried him six long strides to Kri's side. Demons growled in surprise all around him, but he stilled his mounting panic with a slow breath and extended his senses to feel the magic flowing all around him. As Kri had said, the magic was everywhere, and he found it easy to pinpoint the location of each demon, like an interruption in the flow, a snarl in the weave. With a short string of arcane syllables, he unleashed the merest fraction of the latent power in the weave of magic, causing the air around him to explode with fire. Searing flames engulfed each of the demons within five yards, but left Kri and the eladrin hunters untouched.

The injured demons raised a terrible keening cry of pain and shuffled back from Albanon. In that moment of respite, he put a hand on Kri's shoulder.

"Gather your strength, my friend," he said. "The fight's not over yet."

"I have no strength left," Kri said.

"Call on Ioun's strength, then. I can't lose you now."

A few of the demons fell still on the ground, flames smoldering on their bodies, and the others pulled together on one side of the fray, pinning Albanon and Kri between them and those that were locked in battle with the eladrin hunters. They crept forward cautiously, as if waiting for the next burst of fire to erupt around them.

"That's right," Albanon said. "You should be scared."

He drew in his will as he lifted his staff above his head, then slammed the end of the staff down on the ground as hard as he could. The ground shook with the arcane power surging through it, and thunder pealed in front of him. The clump of demons was blasted back and scattered. When the rumbling ground settled, they all lay dead, leaving Kri and Albanon safely out of reach of any of the remaining demons.

Albanon turned to check on Kri. The old priest was clutching the stylized eye symbol of Ioun he wore around his neck, his eyes closed in fervent prayer. He looked a little stronger than he did before, but he was obviously not fully recovered. He drew a deep, shuddering breath and his eyes fluttered open.

"What's wrong?" Albanon asked.

"It's hard," Kri said, shaking his head.

"Drawing on your magic?"

"No, the magic is fine. It's harder to feel Ioun's presence, though."

"Can you fight?"

"I think so."

The eladrin hunters and their hounds had surrounded the large demon, though a few of the smaller ones remained on their feet, mostly locked in deadly grapples with the hounds. A few hounds lay dying or dead, and as Albanon turned to look, the large demon struck a solid blow on one of the hunters, knocking him to the ground.

Albanon pointed the end of his staff at the towering demon, and a line of lightning joined him to the demon with a loud crack. Smaller bolts of lightning extended from the demon to strike two of the smaller demons nearby. Beside him, Kri stretched out both hands and bathed the demon and the downed man in brilliant white light. The demon writhed in pain from the twin assaults as the smaller demons collapsed. Immeral shot a smile over his shoulder at Albanon.

"That's it!" Immeral cried. "It doesn't have much fight left in it!"

The demon's writhing stopped abruptly, and it fixed its small, gleaming eyes on Albanon. Its mouth opened and a voice came out—or two voices, rather. One was a bellowing roar befitting the body it issued from, and the other was powerful but strangely distant and alien . . . and familiar.

"So you appear again to disrupt this one's plans," the voice said.

Vestapalk! Albanon took an involuntary couple of steps back.

"Know this," the voice continued. "You strive in vain against this one. The Plaguedeep is planted, and its touch spreads to all the worlds. You are far too late to stop what has already begun."

Kri stepped forward, surrounded by a faint nimbus of holy light. "We will stop you, dragon," he declared, and his voice carried the ring of divine authority.

"Foolish priest. You do not know what you are doing, and you know nothing of this one. No mere dragon is this, though Vestapalk was mighty among dragons. This one is now mightier still."

"Keep it talking," Albanon muttered, hoping Kri could hear. The hunters had backed away from the large demon and were carving through the remaining smaller ones. Albanon closed his eyes and extended his other senses to feel the pattern of magic around him.

As before, he felt the power coursing through the air and the ground, and experienced the demons as dark tangles in that weave. The eladrin warriors and their hounds were bright threads, part of the same fabric as the Feywild itself, shining with life and their own magical power. Kri was a different sort of brightness, something foreign to the weave but congruent with it, shining with tremendous power of a different kind. The priest was speaking to the dragon-demon again, but Albanon paid no attention to the words. His attention was focused on the dark tangle of magic where the large demon stood.

A lot of power was packed into its four-armed frame, power that was both alien to the Feywild's weave of magic and antithetical to it—the magic of chaos and destruction. But there was more, something else occupying the same space. It was a faint presence, like an image in a mirror, similar to the demonic tangle. Albanon also noticed a churning undercurrent of elemental power, pointing to Vestapalk's draconic nature.

"Have you seen what you wanted to see, wizard?" Vestapalk's voice seemed to ring in his mind as much as in his ears, and Albanon's eyes popped open.

"You're projecting your consciousness through this demon, somehow," Albanon answered.

"And what have you seen of this one?"

Albanon frowned, trying to make sense of what he had seen. "You're not just a dragon any more," he said.

"This one is a dragon, the Voidharrow, and the Plaguedeep. This one is the plague that will consume you."

The demon's mouth opened wide, and a cloud of vapor billowed out. Tiny red crystals shimmered in the air and spread slowly out from the hulking creature.

As Kri jumped back from the spreading cloud, Albanon hurled a blast of fire at the demon. It roared its pain and lurched forward, sending the scarlet cloud eddying around it. Kri called down a column of light that sent the demon sprawling to the ground and also dissipated the portions of the cloud that it touched.

A lingering wisp of cloud touched one of the fey hounds, seeped in through its nostrils, and immediately started to alter the poor beast. Jagged crystal protrusions sprouted from its back as it howled its agony. Its forequarters flattened, its legs splayed to the sides, and its head curled in on itself.

Careful not to get too close to the remaining wisps of the toxic cloud, Immeral cut the hound-demon's head from its broad shoulders with a single swing of his sword. With a gesture, the huntmaster ordered the other eladrin and their hounds away from the tower, back to where their horses waited.

Albanon followed, forming a clearing among the thorns for the eladrin to sit comfortably. Kri threw himself down on the ground, still short of breath from the exertion of their long flight across the plain. Albanon settled with the others, enjoying a moment of quiet after all the chaos of the battle.

"Well," Immeral said after a moment, "had I known at Moonstair that I was speaking to the son of the Prince of Thorns, I would have offered to escort you to your father's palace."

"And had I known you were my father's huntmaster," Albanon said, then paused. "I don't know what I would have done, actually."

Immeral laughed, the clear, musical sound of the fey's wild delight. Just like the smells on this side of the Moon

Door, that laugh stirred up Albanon's memories of home, of feasts in secluded glades and races along woodland trails.

"Why did you come to the tower?" Albanon asked.

"As soon as you left the Palace of Thorns, your father turned his attention to the Whitethorn Spire. He had paid it little heed for decades, and it had almost faded from his consciousness entirely. When he cast his gaze this way again, he discovered that the tower was breached—something was here that shouldn't be. Well, we saw what that was."

"And he sent you here, to . . . ?"

"To protect you, yes."

"And we thought you were chasing us."

Immeral laughed again, but without mockery. "Oh, my friend," he said through his laughter, "if we had been chasing you, you would not have reached the tower."

"Although your command of the thorns was impressive," another one of the hunters added.

"Indeed," Immeral said. "You gave us a worthy chase—better than we've had in years." The smile faded from his face. "Of course, that left us all more tired once we arrived than we might have been. Probably cost us a couple of hounds."

"I know I'm lucky to be alive," another hunter—the one Kri had healed—said. He nodded to the priest. "Thank you."

"Without your help in that battle, Albanon and I would be dead for certain," Kri said. "We owe you our gratitude and our lives."

"You are the son of my lord and master," Immeral said to Albanon. "You need only to ask my help, and I will give it. Whatever the circumstances."

"Thank you."

Albanon sat back and looked up at Sherinna's tower. Splendid, the last legacy of his apprenticeship with Moorin, was perched atop the arch over the open door. Everything else around him was a part of his life that was new and at the same time old. Kri, his new mentor, was passing on to him a tradition that came from his own grandmother, whose tower this had been. His father's huntmaster had just promised Albanon his aid, and the very brambles of the Plain of Thorns acknowledged his noble birthright.

This is who I am, he thought. A prince of the Feywild, heir to the legacy of the Order of Vigilance. His eyes found Splendid again. Not some bumbling apprentice. Not anymore.

And not ever again.

CHAPTER ELEVEN

"Is it the dragon?" Shara whispered.

"I can't tell," Uldane replied. "It's dark down there, and . . . foggy?"

Shara's vision cleared enough to show her what the halfling was talking about. Eddies of mist billowed up the stairs from the chamber at the bottom. She took Quarhaun's hand and got to her feet, as slowly and quietly as she could manage.

"Should I take a look around down there?" Uldane asked.

"No. Whatever it is, it knows we're here. You're not going to sneak past it. The first one down is going to be the first one attacked. And that's going to be me."

"We should send some lizardfolk warriors down first," Quarhaun said. "Get a sense of what we're up against. Force the dragon to reveal itself, if it is him."

Shara looked for any hint of humor in the drow's face and saw none. "What?" she asked.

"They're expendable, Shara. You're not."

"I don't send anyone into danger I'm not willing to face myself."

"Officers with that attitude rarely live long enough to get promoted."

"I'm not an officer, Quarhaun. I'm an adventurer. I'm not here because some baron or general sent me here to achieve some military objective."

"Why are you here?"

"I'm here because that dragon killed almost everyone in the world that ever meant anything to me. And after I killed him once, he didn't have the decency to stay dead, which means I get the pleasure of killing him again. Maybe if I'm lucky I'll get to kill him a third time—once for Borojon, once for Cliffside, and once for Jarren."

"And so you're going to walk boldly into what's probably a death trap, not even knowing if whatever is down there is the dragon or not. You can't kill the dragon if you're dead."

"I have no intention of dying. Tell the warriors to come down with me, if you want. We'll face it together, whatever it is." With one hand on the wall to make sure she didn't slip again, she started down the stairs into the darkness and the mist.

Damned dragon probably heard every word of that, she thought. She smiled to herself. Good.

Quarhaun hissed instructions to the lizardfolk, and Uldane trailed behind her with a fresh sunrod. The sound of water dripping on stone and plinking into pools echoed up the stairway. Mist billowed around her feet as she reached the bottom of the stairs, and she peered ahead into a large, open chamber.

Water poured down slime-covered walls as the swamp worked slowly to absorb the ancient building. As it splashed to the ground it rose in fine droplets of mist that draped the floor of the room and rose in eddying clouds above it. Streamers of moss hung from jutting stones in the worn walls, waving in the water coursing over them. A gurgling sound came from somewhere near the center of the room, suggesting that the water was draining out before it could fill the room entirely.

Shara didn't see the dragon. It was hard to imagine the mist cloaking something that large, but not inconceivable—and there were corners of the room she couldn't see without stepping fully into the archway. She glanced over her shoulder and saw the lizardfolk warriors arrayed behind her, clubs and maces held at the ready, shields ready to block, and their eyes fixed on her.

Maybe Quarhaun was right, she thought. *Maybe I am an officer.*

One of the lizardfolk nodded its head at her in a gesture she interpreted as respect. She returned the gesture, then met each one's eyes in turn, excitement building in her chest.

No, she thought, *they follow me because I'm willing to lead them into battle. I've earned their respect.*

Eager for a fight, she turned back to the archway and took the last few steps that opened the entire chamber to her view. A large, sleek figure moved in the mist to her right, incredibly fast, snaking toward her to attack.

It wasn't the dragon. In its basic outline, it was identical to the demons they'd been fighting—vaguely pantherlike, with low forequarters but longer hind legs, a flattened head and torso that suggested the head of a cobra. This one was covered in red crystal protrusions that glittered in the light of Uldane's sunrod, jutting from its back, its hips, and the joints of its legs and forming horns and spikes around its eyes and mouth. And it was enormous, towering over her as it pounced, even its low-slung head far enough off the ground to let her pass underneath without ducking her head.

It slammed into her before she had time to do more than turn to face it, knocking her off her feet and sending her splashing into a puddle. Shara's ears rang as her helmet clanged against the stone floor again, and her shoulder burned where the demon's claws had raked her. Then the demon darted away, vanishing into the billowing mist.

The lizardfolk warriors gave a gurgling shout and charged into the chamber, fanning out as they passed through the archway, clattering their clubs and maces against their shields as if they were flushing game out from the reeds of the swamp. Uldane appeared in the archway next; he tossed the sunrod into the room and then slunk into the mist and shadows.

"This is no time for a nap, Shara," Quarhaun called as he stepped into the arch.

Shara stood up, scowling. "Listen, demon," she announced to the room. "I've spent enough time flat on my back in the last hour. No more."

Uldane's laugh betrayed his position, already almost a quarter of the way around the edge of the chamber. But the demon didn't reveal itself.

"Everyone get ready to hit it as soon as it shows itself," Shara said. "Hit it hard."

Keeping her center of gravity low, she stalked toward the middle of the room. The mist swirled around her feet and rose in clouds around her as she moved, and her feet splashed in shallow pools of water.

"It shouldn't be so easy to hide in here," she said. She stopped walking and listened. The lizardfolk were quieter than she was, but their feet made noise in the water as well, and the mist revealed the signs of their passage. But no such signs betrayed the movement of the demon, which meant it was either standing still or—

She looked up, and saw the demon slinking along the ceiling almost directly overhead.

"Up! Up!" she shouted. "It's on the ceiling!"

With a yowl that chilled her blood, the demon dropped down onto her, twisting as it fell so its ruby-tipped claws led the way down. Shara lifted her shield and crouched down, and as the demon hit she blocked its claws and drove her sword deep into its shoulder. Its yowl turned into a hideous, screeching scream as it crashed to the floor on its side, scrambling to get its feet beneath it again.

The two nearest lizardfolk were on it before it could stand, bludgeoning its head and its hips with blows from their maces. She heard the crunch of bone and saw some of the crystal growths on its hind parts shatter, then the lizardfolk who had struck the crystal shouted and drew back in pain. The shattered crystal had pierced the warrior's scaled hide, and he looked down at the wounds with wide, terror-filled eyes.

The demon found its feet and crouched to pounce. Shara's blade cut the creature's flank, then the demon leaped over the terrified lizardfolk and vanished in a rising cloud of mist.

"Quarhaun!" Shara called. "Bring Kssansk to look at this!"

The injured lizardfolk had dropped both mace and shield and started clawing at his own wounds as if trying to dig out the shards of crystal that had buried themselves in his flesh. Shara thought of the way Vestapalk's infusion had taken hold in Albanon and Quarhaun, starting to change them both into demons like these.

Again she was reminded of the dragon's commandment to his minions. "Spread the abyssal plague!" he had cried. She shuddered as the lizardfolk threw his head back and screamed.

Kssansk came and laid a hand on the frantic warrior, whose convulsive movements stopped at once, the scream squelched in his throat. Shara scanned the chamber for any sign of the demon's return, checking the ceiling as well as the billowing mist. This time, eddies in the mist signaled the demon's movement to her left, approaching the warriors on the far end of the lizardfolk line.

"This way!" she shouted, breaking into a run.

The demon was fast. It emerged from the mist and crashed into one of the lizardfolk, much as it had when Shara first entered the room. The lizardfolk, though, kept its feet and managed to get a solid blow on the creature's shoulder as it darted past.

The demon never stopped moving. After colliding with the warrior and his club, the creature leaped onto the wall and ran another ten yards before dropping back down into the mist. Shara stopped, frustrated.

"It's too fast," she said. "We could spend the next hour running back and forth across the room, and it'll just keep attacking one of us at a time."

"We need to group up," Quarhaun said. He shouted something in Draconic, and the lizardfolk responded immediately, pulling back to where Shara stood.

Kssansk led the injured warrior, the last to join the ragged circle. The wounds were still visible and the warrior's eyes had a glassy look, but he held his weapon and shield ready.

"How is he?" Shara asked.

"He's ready to fight," Quarhaun said.

"Will you ask Kssansk how he is?"

Quarhaun shrugged and relayed the question to the lizardfolk shaman, who answered with a long string of gurgles and hisses.

"He'll make it," Quarhaun translated.

"What else did he say?"

"I'm not an interpreter," the drow snarled. "I said he'll make it, he's ready to fight. What more do you need to know?"

"Shara!" Uldane's voice, full of terror, came from off to the right, not far from where Shara had last spotted the demon.

"Damn it, Uldane!" Shara shouted. "Join the circle!"

The halfling gave a short cry of pain, then Shara saw the demon leap up out of the mist again. It clung to the wall this time, craning its serpentine head around to watch the floor.

Shara saw the mist billow, then Uldane emerged from it, his face streaked with blood. He ran toward the circle as fast as his feet could carry him, then the demon hurled itself down from the wall to land right on the halfling.

A bolt of purplish lightning shot over Shara's shoulder to strike the demon, knocking it away from Uldane. Shara ran, calling for the lizardfolk to follow. Quarhaun echoed her instructions in Draconic and the warriors surrounded her, forming a tight clump around her as she moved to stand over Uldane. She reached a hand down to help the halfling to his feet. He managed to get up, but he was badly hurt.

The demon had vanished into the mist once more, though great clouds billowed around where Quarhaun's eldritch lightning had sent it sprawling. A reddish light filtered through the mist, as if the creature's crystal protrusions had started glowing. Then a voice whispered from the mist, and Shara's heart froze.

"This one is sorry not to be present. There would be pleasure in robbing the red-haired warrior of more of those she cares about."

"Vestapalk!" Shara cried. "Show your face and get ready to meet your doom!"

"This one is no longer called Vestapalk," the dragon's voice said. "And though there is pain in saying it, this one is not present to tear the halfling apart and bite the drow's head from his body."

"It's speaking through the demon," Quarhaun whispered in her ear. "Some kind of telepathic link."

"This one is the Voidharrow and the plague. Wherever the Voidharrow is, there are the eyes and the ears and the voice of this one also."

"I don't know what you're talking about," Shara said, striding forward. "But I'm about to poke out your eyes and cut off your ears to shut you up."

She took three steps into the billowing mist, then stopped as she realized, with a jolt of fear, that the mist right in front of her face was formed of tiny red crystals suspended in the air. The Voidharrow and the plague, she thought. That's not a plague I want to catch.

Behind her, Uldane cried out again, and she whirled around. The demon was right behind her, right in the midst of the lizardfolk warriors—and right on top of Quarhaun, its horrid face looking directly at her as it sank its claws into the drow's body.

CHAPTER TWELVE

"Roghar, wait," Travic said.

Roghar was poised to charge down the hall after the fleeing humans, but Travic's words brought him up short. He turned to look back at his companions, and the battle fury ebbed from his heart.

Travic still lay on the ground, barely strong enough to lift his head. Tempest sagged against the wall, breathing hard, her eyes looking around wildly as if following the movements of spirits only she could see.

"We're in no condition to keep fighting," Travic said.

"Of course," Roghar said. "I acted without thinking."

"Again," the priest said with a smile. "You need to learn to curb your youthful exuberance."

"Bahamut was with me," Roghar said. "Proud and fierce."

"For all his talk of nobility and justice, the Platinum Dragon is a warrior god at heart," Travic said.

Roghar stepped to Tempest's side. She recoiled, staring at him with wide eyes, then recognition seemed to sink in to her fevered mind. Her body relaxed, and she let her head drop onto Roghar's shoulder.

"Easy, Tempest," he murmured. "You're safe now."

Tempest threw her arms around Roghar's shoulders and pulled him closer. Hesitantly, gently, he enfolded her in his embrace.

As Roghar held Tempest, Travic managed to roll himself up to his knees. Roghar heard the comforting lilt of his prayers to Erathis and the warmth of divine presence around them all.

Erathis holds me, Roghar thought, and I hold you.

Finally, Tempest eased her hold on him and drew away, looking anywhere but into his eyes. Roghar felt strong and whole, and Tempest seemed stronger as well.

"What was it?" he asked.

"Nothing," Tempest said, still avoiding his gaze. "You know I hate being crowded like that, and Travic's no good at holding a line." Finally her eyes met his, and he saw a hint of the anguish she'd been feeling. "I felt trapped."

"Just like when Nu Alin was controlling your body."

Tempest looked away and pulled free of his hands. "Are we giving chase?" she asked.

"Are you up to it?" Travic said.

"Of course. Only, let's make sure we don't pass any enemies who can attack us from behind this time."

"Good plan," Roghar said. "But Travic?"

"Yes?"

"Are you up to this?" Roghar put a hand on Travic's shoulder.

"What do you mean?"

"Marcan was among them, wasn't he?"

Travic sighed, and some of the strength his prayers had lent him seemed to drain out of his body. "Yes, he was."

"Do you think something was controlling his mind?"

Travic turned and paced a few steps down the hall, stopping beside the decapitated statue. "I think something changed his mind. Obviously not for the better. But I don't think it's a spell that can be broken."

"Are you prepared to kill him?"

"If it comes to that, then . . ." Grief washed over Travic's face. "If there's no alternative, then yes."

"All right. We're dealing with humans, so if it's possible, we try to knock them out and bring them to the watch. Agreed?" Roghar watched Tempest carefully as he awaited her response.

"Of course," Travic said.

Tempest nodded, then frowned. "On what charge?"

"What?" Roghar said.

"We bring them to the watch on what charge? Do we know they're guilty of anything?"

"They attacked us."

"The gnoll and the statue did. What the humans were doing would be easy to paint as self-defense. We're barging into their home. Of course they're fighting back."

"We're barging into the temple where they're worshiping Asmodeus," Roghar said.

"Or Tiamat," Travic added.

"Or some other evil god or demon lord."

"We assume," Tempest said.

"Right. But I think it's highly unlikely we're going to round that corner and find that these ragged humans and their gnoll friend set up an animated statue to protect their little secret temple of Bahamut. Not to mention the whispers."

"Fine," Tempest said. "Assuming we round the corner and find a temple to some sinister power, I'll try not to kill them unless it's absolutely necessary. I'm just trying to make sure we're doing the right thing."

Roghar sighed and scratched his jaw. "Look, Tempest," he said. "I know it's not always easy to know what's right and what's wrong. And I know we're walking in a great gray area where the lines are even less clear than usual. But it means a lot to me that you're even trying to sort it out."

She smiled faintly. "So what's the plan?"

"Well, I don't expect they've gone far, unless they've fled out a back entrance. More likely, they're putting up their defense in their shrine or temple, or whatever is around that corner."

Tempest nodded. "So we charge around the corner—you first, naturally—and unleash everything we have. Trying not to kill them, of course."

"A little more caution is probably warranted," Travic said. "They've had several minutes to prepare their defenses. They might have activated traps. At the least, they've taken up the most advantageous positions they can find."

"Right," Roghar said. "But we don't have a lot of tactical flexibility. There's only three of us, and there's only one way we can approach, as far as we know."

He ran through other possibilities in his mind. Searching for another entrance could give their quarry a chance to escape, and it would mean navigating the whispering crater again. And he had no real reason to suspect that another entrance even existed, except that it would be tactically convenient.

Alas, he thought, reality rarely conforms to convenience.

"So I charge around the corner," he said, "cautiously. You two watch out for traps, and you help me flush out any cultists that are hidden behind cover."

"Is that what they are?" Tempest said. "Cultists?"

"That's my working assumption at this point," Roghar said, scowling at her.

"I suppose it helps to put a name on them. I mean, besides Marcan."

"Please stop it," Travic said. "This is hard enough for me already."

"Is it?" Tempest asked. "Can killing people ever be hard enough?"

Travic drew himself up, anger boiling in his eyes. "I will not listen to lectures on morality from a warlock who bargains with infernal powers!"

Tempest's eyes smoldered with fire as she glared at the priest. "Does the mouth that speaks it make the truth any less true?"

"I know the precarious path I walk," Travic said. "I grapple with these questions every night, when sleep eludes me. And now, because they seem to have entered your mind for the first time, I have to face them again? What I need now is resolve and certainty. Leave the doubts until darkness." What had started as an angry rant ended as a plea, and Roghar gaped at the priest, his heart aching for his friend.

"I see," Tempest said at last. "From now on I will keep my questions to myself, and see whether I am able to sleep after we've done what must be done."

Roghar reached a hand for Tempest's shoulder, but she pulled away.

"Let's do it, then," Roghar said. He closed his eyes, reaching for the sense of fierce victory that had filled him just a few moments before, grasping for any reassurance from Bahamut that his cause was just and his way true. A faint tingle brushed at the base of his skull and faded.

That will have to be assurance enough, he thought.

Without another word, he walked to the corner of the hall. Holding his shield up, he peered around the corner into what was indeed a small shrine. A simple wooden table stood as an altar, draped with a deep purple cloth embroidered with a jagged spiral in gold thread. A human skull adorned the altar, surrounded by five small cups. One of the cups held a greasy flame that licked up over the rim. Three long banners, similar to the altar cloth, hung on the walls of the chamber, each one sporting a golden spiral that reminded Roghar of a baleful eye staring out into the room. Behind the altar, a column of light filled a small alcove in the wall.

The cultists—it was a fair appellation, he decided—huddled behind the altar. Roghar almost laughed out loud. The cultists hadn't enjoyed many more tactical options than had he and his friends, trying to defend themselves in this small, bare chamber. They didn't have defensible positions to take, cover to hide behind, or, apparently, traps to set. So they had spent the last several minutes clumped behind their priest at the altar, clutching their weapons in trembling hands, waiting for the deadly assault they knew was coming. He almost felt sorry for them.

But not quite.

The priest was a middle-aged human woman with wild hair and wide eyes, draped in a formless black robe. A purple stole with the same golden spiral hung over her shoulders, and the symbol shaped from real gold hung on a slender chain around her neck. She held a gnarled quarterstaff carved and inlaid over and over with the same symbol, like a dizzying storm of eyes or whirlwinds.

"I admit," he said, "you are not what I expected. I trust you have had time to prepare yourselves to meet justice. Do you wish to surrender?"

One or two of the cultists behind the priest looked like they might be ready to throw down their weapons, but the priest just laughed.

"There need not be any bloodshed," Roghar said. "If you just put down your weapons . . ."

"There will be bloodshed," the priest said. "The Chained God will drink deeply of your lifeblood, paladin."

"The Chained God?" Roghar glanced over his shoulder at Travic. "I guess we both lose."

"No, just you," Travic said. "You bet it was Asmodeus, I said it wasn't." Travic rounded the corner, keeping Roghar between himself and the cultists in the shrine. "You owe me five . . . Gaele?"

Mouth hanging open, Travic stared at the priest of the Chained God.

"Hello, Travic," the priest said. "Marcan warned you to leave."

"What happened to you?"

Gaele scoffed. "You gave me comfort in my weakness. That's all Erathis could offer—the promise of a rebuilt empire where the rich still stand on the aching backs of the poor. The Chained God gives me *power*, Travic. Power to destroy you and the feeble comfort of your god."

Roghar shook his head. "Still up to this, Travic?"

Travic pulled himself together with a visible effort of will, then nodded.

"Good," Roghar growled. "Let's do this." Hefting his sword, he started forward.

"Stop!" Tempest shouted, and Roghar froze. "The floor," she said. "There's a glyph—a magic trap. You don't want to step on it."

Gaele laughed again. "I must congratulate you, tiefling, on your powers of observation. But let's see how they work through this."

She lifted her staff, and a cloud of darkness surrounded Roghar, enfolding him until he could no longer see the light on his shield. The cloud was cold, chilling his flesh and whispering madness at the edge of his mind. It pushed against him like water and sent twinges of pain through his entire body with even his smallest movement.

"Tempest?" Roghar said, gritting his teeth.

"I've got it," she said.

The darkness vanished and Roghar blinked in the sudden brightness of his glowing shield. Beside him, Tempest held a ball of inky blackness suspended in the air between her hands, and with a soft grunt of effort she hurled it at the priest. The ball dissipated into slivers when it hit Gaele's outstretched staff, but a few of the slivers tore small wounds in her face and shoulders.

"Travic," Roghar said. "Can you do anything about this . . . griffon? cliff? This trap, whatever Tempest called it."

"The glyph," Travic said. "I'll try." He dropped to his knees at Roghar's feet and started exploring the floor with his hands, not touching the stone, but reaching as if he were feeling the contours of the trap and its magic.

"Can I go around it?" Roghar scanned the floor, but still couldn't see any sign of what had alerted Tempest.

"No, it fills the entire hall."

"Why can everyone see this but me?"

"We know what to look for, that's all."

Tempest called up a storm of eldritch fire around the cultists, breaking up the clump of them as the fire ignited their clothes and hair. Only Gaele stood her ground as the rest of her little cult scattered.

"The Chained God take you, tiefling," Gaele said. She shook her staff, and rattling chains of red-hot iron appeared around Tempest, coiled around her body and cuffed to her ankles and wrists. Tempest howled in pain as the hot metal seared her flesh, and she thrashed against the restraints.

Travic looked back at Tempest, then up at Roghar.

"I'll help her," Roghar said. "You get rid of the glyph. I have to get up there and get your friend Gaele focused on me."

"I don't understand," Travic said, turning his attention back to the glyph. "What could have changed her so?"

"Later, Travic. Focus." Roghar stretched out a hand to cup Tempest's cheek in his hand. Her skin was hot, but as

Roghar breathed a prayer and channeled Bahamut's power into her body he felt her cool. Her thrashing stopped, and she drew a deep breath. Roghar's hand started glowing as bright as his shield, and Tempest let out her breath. The manacles sprang open and the chains clattered to the floor, where they writhed like snakes before vanishing in puffs of steam.

Tempest smiled at him, then conjured a shimmering orb of viscous green liquid in her palm. "Eat acidic slime, you lunatic," she said as she hurled the orb at Gaele.

"Travic?" Roghar said. "Progress?"

"I'm having some trouble concentrating."

"Fine. Forget it." Roghar backed up, crouched down, and ran at the glyph. At the last possible moment, he threw himself into the air, a strong jump that carried him almost all the way to the little altar. He braced himself, in case he hadn't completely cleared the glyph, but nothing erupted around him when he landed.

"Had any second thoughts about surrender?" he said, scanning the nervous faces of the cultists arrayed before him.

"Kill him!" Gaele screeched, clawing at the slime that was blackening her skin, and half a dozen cultists surged forward, closing their semicircle around him.

"I didn't think so." Roghar blocked the first half-hearted swing with his shield, then swept his sword low to knock two cultists off their feet. He caught three more in a blast of dragonfire from his mouth, but the sixth one managed to get past his whirlwind of attacks and land a solid blow with a shout of triumph.

The cultist's hammer hit his armor with a dull thud.

"You're going to have to do better than that," Roghar said, baring his teeth in the cultist's face. The cultist was a middle-aged man clutching a blacksmith's hammer in his one hand, the empty left sleeve of his tunic tucked into his belt to keep it out of the way. "Marcan, I presume."

Marcan paled and swung his hammer again, this time aiming for Roghar's unprotected face. Roghar knocked it aside with his shield and stepped to the side as another cultist stabbed at him from behind. The blade found a gap in the armor protecting Roghar's arm and sliced a painful cut.

Roghar kicked at the man who had cut him, knocking the cultist to the floor, and smashed his shield into Marcan's face. He brought his pommel down hard on the head of a cultist who was struggling to stand up, drove his knee into the groin of a man whose face carried fresh burns from his dragon breath, and cut the head clean off a man rushing in from his right.

It had been pure reflex, an attack without thought, and regret seized him before his sword even finished its swing. The dead man's face was still twisted in hate and anger as it fell to the floor, a moment before the body followed it down.

"You're all mad," Roghar said.

One dead, four on the ground in varying states of agony, that left one—

Something hit him hard on the head from behind, and his vision went double. He spun around and away from his attacker, willing his eyes to focus. The last cultist stood clutching a wooden cudgel in both hands, looking at once surprised that his blow had landed and terrified that Roghar hadn't fallen.

"That . . . hurt," Roghar said. "But it takes more than that to bring me down."

The cudgel clattered to the ground as the man turned and ran. Travic scrambled to his feet and drew his mace, placing himself between the fleeing man and the hallway.

"Let him go," Roghar said, turning his attention to Gaele.

Travic stepped aside, but an inferno erupted around the man as he stepped onto the glyph. His tormented scream turned Roghar's stomach.

"I guess Travic never managed to disable the glyph," Roghar said as he stalked toward Gaele. "Looks like your trap only managed to kill one of your own."

"You will never take me alive, paladin!" Gaele cried.

She didn't have much strength left, save what her defiance lent her. Tempest's fire and acid had left her scorched, scarred, and barely able to stand, but her eyes remained bright with madness and fury. She threw her head back, laughing maniacally, and just as Roghar reached her side the laugh turned into a howl.

Roghar's ears rang with the thunderous sound and his head started to spin. Malicious whispers coursed beneath the sound at the edge of hearing and sense, filling his mind with thoughts he couldn't follow, images of chaos and madness. The world disappeared from his view, and in its place was a starry void where chunks of ancient stone and pulsating globules of living flesh floated in graceful elegance. Wailing cries from no mortal throat echoed around him in the void as lightning and fire tore at his mind. He dropped his sword, which reverted to raw iron ore as it drifted away from his hand, and he clenched his ears, only to find that his body was no longer a body at all. Every atom of his substance floated apart, no coherence marking them as parts of a single being.

An anthem began somewhere in the void, whether near or far he could not tell. He heard it through a thousand tiny ears, and a thousand fractured minds heard the music of the Bright City, a hymn of praise to Pelor, Ioun, and Erathis.

Erathis. Travic. Somehow his shattered consciousness made the connection and recognized Travic's voice. Slowly his mind started piecing itself back together, woven with the texture of the music, which was more than Travic's single mortal voice. Just as the howling voices of the mad and the damned echoed Gaele's maddening scream, angelic voices and instruments undergirded Travic's hymn, growing in volume until they drowned out the scream and Roghar's mind was whole again.

Gaele was on her knees before him, the howl sucking the last ounce of breath from her lungs. He slammed his mailed fist into the base of her skull and she fell, gasping for breath as her eyes fluttered and closed. Travic stood at Roghar's side, shining with divine radiance, his face half hidden behind an angelic visage and his head thrown back in rapture.

"Enjoy your song," Roghar said, shrugging out of his pack. He pulled out a coil of rope and started cutting pieces to tie up the cultists who had survived.

CHAPTER THIRTEEN

Welcome to the Whitethorn Spire," Kri announced. "Your birthright."

The old priest stood outside the open doorway and bowed, making a sweeping gesture with his arm to invite Albanon inside. Albanon stepped over a demon corpse at the threshold and entered the tower.

The entrance hall was grandly elegant despite at least a century of disuse and the recent intrusion of the demons. Slender columns ringed the circular hall, supporting a staircase that wound around the wall. Living ivy spiraled up the marble columns as if sculpted there. A scattering of rubble and a few brown leaves cluttered the floor, which was tiled in an intricate mosaic depicting the stylized eye of Ioun set within the sunburst of Pelor. Far above, the domed ceiling was carefully painted with an array of figures Albanon couldn't identify at such a distance. One slender archway, directly opposite the entrance, led to a short hall with doorways on both sides. Similar arches led off from the stairway above it, granting access to the tower's five higher floors.

"Where do we start?" Albanon asked.

"Wherever you like," Kri said. "The tower is yours to explore now. Start at the bottom and work up. Start at the top and work down. Start in the middle and work randomly, following your instincts. It's up to you."

Albanon grinned, staring up at the stairway with its arches. Mine to explore, he thought. It's my birthright.

Part of him wanted to race through the tower, peering through every door, learning his way around as quickly as possible before deciding what to explore in more depth. But another part wanted to savor the discovery of it all, to choose one room and explore every bit of knowledge it had to offer up to him, whether it took hours or weeks, before moving on to another room. He let the two parts argue in his mind for a moment, savoring the anticipation and uncertainty.

"I want to see the mural," he announced at last. Without waiting for an answer, he walked to the stairs, stealing a glance down the ground-floor hallway as he went past. Three doors—two on the left, one on the right, all closed. He smiled, filing that knowledge away. Closed doors meant secrets awaiting discovery.

At each archway, he allowed himself no more than a furtive glance through, the merest hint of what lay beyond. More closed doors—three or even five on some floors, two on others. A large library full of dusty shelves, each shelf crowded with books and scrolls, was almost enough to make him stop and explore, but he stuck to his original plan, forcing his eyes back to the mural and his feet back to the stairs.

At last he reached the top of the stairs and found himself on a narrow gallery running almost all the way around the hall, except where the stairs emerged. A thin railing offered little reassurance when he looked down at the drop to the mosaic floor below. Wrenching his gaze upward again, he found that the gallery was perfect for examining the mural in the dome—but he still understood little of what he saw.

The dome was divided into eight segments. Each one featured a depiction of a short pillar topped with a crystal orb that glowed with purple light. Thirteen figures—not all of them humanoid, he realized—were arrayed around the dome, as if spread around a great vaulted chamber. In a focal position, right above the line of arches running up the side of the hall, stood an eladrin wizard, posed in action as if casting a spell.

"Sherinna," he guessed. He took a moment to study this depiction of his grandmother.

She was lovely, he decided, full of power and grace and wisdom. Or at least that's what the artist tried to convey, he reminded himself. And she was paying him to pull it off. He smiled, then let his eyes explore the rest of the paintings.

To Sherinna's left stood a human man in plate armor, locked in battle with a hulking brute of a demon, a monster with six claws and a massive carapace formed of red crystal.

Just like Vestapalk's minions at the Temple of Yellow Skulls. Albanon's heart quickened. Kri was right, he thought. Here we'll learn what's behind all this.

Next around the dome, an armored woman with the gently pointed ears of a half-elf swung an axe at a creature with the head and forequarters of the demons Albanon and Kri had fought at the tower, but its hind quarters were human legs encased in armor. In the background of that scene, a male dragonborn breathed fire over his own hand, but the fire coiled up and back on him.

In the next segment, an enormous mass of red spiders with crystalline shells swarmed around an elf female's face screaming in pain. There was no sign or depiction of the rest of the elf, leaving it unclear whether she had already been consumed by the swarm or was perhaps transforming into it.

Directly opposite Sherinna stood an archway formed of scarlet crystal, with a lush green landscape visible through the arch, forming a stark contrast to the dark chamber around it. A human man stood before the arch, but his legs were twin columns of red liquid shot through with flecks of gold and veins of silver.

"That's the Vast Gate," Kri said. Albanon started—he hadn't heard the priest approach, and thought he might have stopped off in the library or somewhere else in the tower.

"What's that?" he asked. "What is this scene?"

"Well, you're coming in at the end of the story," Kri said, stroking his beard. "But I have told you the story before. That's Sherinna, as you might have guessed." Kri pointed at the beautiful, powerful eladrin, and Albanon nodded. "Next to her there is Brendis, a paladin of Pelor. And that"—he pointed across the dome, where a male tiefling lurked in the shadows near a human whose hand glittered with red crystal—"is Nowhere."

"Nowhere? That was his name?"

"Yes. An expression of his alienation, I suppose. The three of them discovered a sinister cult operating in Nera."

"When was this?"

"Two hundred years before the fall of Nerath."

"So three centuries ago."

"Yes. The cult leader was that man there." Kri pointed at the legless human beside the arch. "Albric the Accursed."

"Nu Alin," Albanon said. "He's in the middle of transforming into the demon."

"Yes. He escaped the three heroes in Nera, but he left behind some writings that pointed to the ruins of Bael Turath as his next destination. Those writings also indicated that he was looking for something called the Living Gate."

"Not the Vast Gate?"

"No. As I understand it, the Living Gate was a mysterious portal located somewhere in the depths of the Astral Sea. I believe it actually shattered during the Dawn War, and what the cultists sought was just a fragment of its substance. Which, perhaps coincidentally, took the form of a reddish crystal."

"Perhaps not," Albanon said.

"Indeed. Anyway, in Bael Turath, Sherinna and her companions met another pair of adventurers. Miri"—he pointed to the woman with the battleaxe—"and the Sword of the Gods." This last hero was a fearsome man with pale skin and strange scarlet tattoos, holding a staff in one hand and an enormous sword in the other. A halo of divine light surrounded him, and the man he was facing recoiled in terror.

"The Sword of the Gods?"

"He was a cleric of Ioun, but he also seems to have been a figure of prophecy, something more than an ordinary divine servant. His origin is mysterious, and he did not survive this battle. But I am skipping ahead. Miri and the Sword of the Gods helped Sherinna and the others find the cultists, and they chased them through a portal leading to the abandoned dominion of Pandemonium, adrift in the Astral Sea. Which is here," Kri said, gesturing to the scene depicted on the dome as a whole.

"And you said before that they were trying to break open a prison? To free some great evil?"

"Yes. They used a shard of the Living Gate to open this portal." He pointed at the archway shown opposite Sherinna. "The Vast Gate, it was called—a doorway capable of reaching into many worlds and planes. They didn't free the entity they sought to release, but they did manage to bring the Voidharrow through their gateway. And by the time Sherinna arrived on the scene, several of the cultists were already in the process of changing into demons."

Albanon nodded, looking around at the variety of monstrous forms—all of which included some element of red crystal. "As the mural shows."

"Yes. And as you can see, they engaged the demons in battle. What the mural doesn't show is the outcome."

Albanon nodded. "The cultists defeated, the Vast Gate closed. And the Sword of the Gods dead."

"Although Nu Alin obviously survived the battle. At least one other cultist fled through the Vast Gate, and the Sword of the Gods was carried through it when he died. And Nowhere's fate is not clear to me. Perhaps most relevant to our investigation, though, Sherinna brought back with her a sample of the Voidharrow, sealed in a vial."

"Which the Order of Vigilance passed down until some of it ended up in Moorin's tower."

"Which the death knight stole," Kri said. "And then Nu Alin followed him across the Nentir Vale to find it."

Albanon rubbed his temples with his fingertips. "And Nu Alin, when he's not possessing someone, looks like a living blob of the Voidharrow. So what is the Voidharrow? Where did it come from? Did it come through the Vast Gate, or was it awaiting the cultists when they arrived in Pandemonium?"

"Those are the questions we're here to investigate. If answers exist, this is the place to find them."

"Here or Pandemonium, I suppose."

"Here at least we have the benefit of records, the fruits of Sherinna's own research and experience. Of all the founding members of the order, she was the most scholarly."

"Do you suppose that's why the demons were here? How much does Vestapalk know about the Order of Vigilance?"

Kri scowled. "Nu Alin was present at its founding, in a way. We must assume that his knowledge far exceeds our own."

Albanon stared up at the mural, his thoughts spinning. A few moments ago, he'd been so excited, eager to explore what the tower had to offer. Now he was confused and tired, confounded by the puzzle that lay before them and daunted by the prospect of trying to sort it out.

"I wonder," he said slowly, "do you think we might spend some time just getting familiar with the tower? Hold off on plunging into research until we . . . I don't know, until we know our way around a little better, maybe?"

Kri glowered. "While your friends fight the demons in our stead? While Vestapalk sends new minions to unearth whatever secrets this tower holds? While the abyssal plague spreads across the worlds? Of course! Take your time! Enjoy yourself."

Albanon felt his face flush crimson, and he turned away from the old priest. "I'm sorry," he mumbled. "I wasn't thinking."

"Clearly. Remember our mission, Albanon. We have to understand our adversary if we are to defeat him. Shara and Uldane are depending on us."

"I . . . I suppose I'll visit the library now."

Kri nodded, and Albanon slunk back down the stairs. He paused outside the doorway leading into the library and peered back up at the dome. Kri was still standing on the gallery, bony hands clenched around the thin railing, staring up at the depiction of the Vast Gate.

"Apprentice," Splendid chirped.

"Hm," Albanon answered, lost in a scroll in Sherinna's library. It was a fascinating study of the magical principles underlying the use of fire, outlining the problems and techniques of fire magic in a way he'd never even begun to consider. The author of the treatise, according to a line at the top, had been Sherinna herself, and Albanon enjoyed imagining that she was teaching him. He wanted to try the techniques she was discussing, but didn't want to stop reading long enough to leave the library and find someplace less . . . flammable.

"Apprentice!" the pseudodragon said again.

Annoyed, Albanon tore his attention from the scroll and scanned the library until he found the little drake perched on the top of a bookshelf, peering down at him.

"I'm not an apprentice any more, Splendid."

"Of course you are. The great Moorin never finished your training."

"The great wizard Moorin, in case you've forgotten, is dead and never will finish my training. I have no master, so I am not an apprentice. But the acquisition of knowledge is a lifelong pursuit."

"According to the ancient traditions of wizardry that the great wizard Moorin followed scrupulously, no apprentice can claim the title of wizard until a master has certified that his training is complete."

"Did you have something you wanted to say, Splendid, or can I go back to my reading now?"

"I wanted to say that you should be careful."

Albanon sighed. "About anything in particular?" he asked.

"About the priest. I don't trust him."

"*Now* you don't trust him? All it took was a few strips of honeybark and some kind words in Moorin's tower and you were his best friend. Practically everyone else we've met since we left Moorin's tower, though, smelled wrong to you, starting with Roghar and Tempest. 'The tiefling smells of pact magic,' you told me. 'And the dragonborn reeks of stale ale and—' What was it?"

"Stale ale and overpriced mead. He does!"

"And he's a paladin of Bahamut, and one of the most noble souls I know," Albanon said. "Even if he does call me an elf," he added under his breath.

"That doesn't mean I'm wrong about the priest."

"It means you're a terrible judge of character. What crime has Kri committed? Smelling like incense and scented candles?"

"Well, he does."

"That's because he's a priest, Splendid. He's a devotee of Ioun, the god of knowledge. And his knowledge is deep and wide! This library couldn't contain it."

"That doesn't mean he's working for good."

"He saved my life—twice—and kept me from turning into a demon. He fought by our side, helped us defeat Vestapalk's second in command, and helped fight off the demons we found here. What part of that doesn't seem like he's working for good?"

"He says he ran out of honeybark."

Albanon sighed. "Now you're just being ridiculous."

"But I don't believe him," the dragonet said, her voice growing shrill. "I can still smell it on him."

"Through the incense and scented candles?"

Splendid harrumphed, a sound somewhere between a meow and a squeak. "He's hiding something, apprentice."

"All right, Splendid. You don't trust him. What do you want me to do? I'll keep a close eye on him."

"Do you know where he is right now?"

Albanon looked around the library again, blinking. "I have no idea. He was here earlier."

"That was hours ago."

With a start, Albanon realized that the entry hall outside the library was dark—the sun had gone down as he read, and he hadn't noticed. Several magical lamps kept the library well lit, and he'd been engrossed in the abundant volumes the library had to offer.

"Perhaps he got hungry," Albanon said, "or tired. How long has it been dark?"

"I'm hungry," Splendid said.

"Fine. Leave me alone and get yourself some food."

"You should eat, too. The great wizard Moorin—"

"Splendid, enough about the great wizard Moorin! He's dead and gone!"

The dragonet seemed to get smaller, furling her wings and drawing her tail close around her legs. Her eyes grew wide, and she looked down at him with a mixture of grief and reproach that only fueled his anger.

"In fact, I've had about enough of you!" he shouted. "You've been following me around since Moorin died, hovering like a chaperone trying to keep me out of trouble. I don't need a chaperone—especially an impudent, self-important, overgrown familiar like you!"

With each word, Splendid shrank back from his growing anger, and with his final exclamation she turned tail and leaped off the shelf, flapping out through the archway in bitter silence.

"Good riddance," he muttered, trying to find his place in the scroll.

CHAPTER FOURTEEN

Shara roared her fury and charged the enormous demon. Quarhaun groaned weakly as its claws sank deeper into his chest.

"Get off him!" she shouted, then her sword bit into the thing's leering face.

"Remember, warrior," Vestapalk's voice said from the demon's mouth, "wanting a thing does not put it within your reach."

"Oh, I'll have my revenge," Shara said, aiming another slice at the demon's throat. It batted her blow aside, but at least that claw was no longer embedded in Quarhaun's chest. "Believe it, dragon."

"Not dragon. So much more."

The demon shuddered and Shara knew, in a way she couldn't explain, that Vestapalk was gone. The creature before her was full of destructive fury, intensified by the pain of its injuries, but it lacked the dragon's sheer malice—and, for that matter, its guile.

It doesn't stand a chance, Shara thought.

Her sword was a blur of motion as she jumped within the demon's reach, standing over Quaraun's inert form and slashing up at the demon's belly, the tendons under its forelegs, and, as it tried to back up and bite her, its throat. Every swing drew thick scarlet blood, gleaming like crystal in its wounds.

The lizardfolk had the demon surrounded, and they beat their clubs against it in a methodical rhythm, though they were attacking cautiously, avoiding the crystal growths on its back that had injured their fellow. Uldane danced in and out of the fray among the lizardfolk, always attacking exactly where the demon's attention was not, striking vulnerable spots that made it yowl in pain and growing fear. The demon crouched low, bringing its belly within Shara's reach.

"It's going to jump!" Uldane shouted.

Instead of striking its belly, Shara rolled toward its hind end and slashed at the tendons of its rear leg, just as it started to spring. Her blow sapped the strength from its leg and it barely cleared the ground with its jump, then staggered forward, dragging that injured leg. Shara chased it, but it spun around and swatted at her with one great claw.

Claws of red crystal slashed through her armor and bit into her chest, but fear drowned out the pain. *The red crystal's in my blood now,* she thought. *Am I infected with this plague? Am I going to change?*

And what about Quarhaun? She glanced back to where he lay and saw Kssansk crouching beside him, intoning his strange evocations to the water spirits.

"Let's finish this, demon," she growled, ignoring the fresh wave of pain in her chest. She whirled her sword in an intricate display above her head as she advanced on the demon, driving it back a few steps as it tried to anticipate her next attack.

Just when it thought it saw an opening and thrust another claw at her, she roared and leaped at it, driving her blade deep into its skull. It screamed in pain and thrashed around, knocking her away with one wild claw as it rolled onto its back, kicking at the air and the mist.

Then the lizardfolk were around it again, shouting in triumph as their clubs battered it into stillness. Shara turned, suddenly exhausted, and walked to Quarhaun's side. She crouched beside him and took his hand, and his eyes fluttered open.

"*Estessa tha meletiere iam,*" he said weakly, a faint smile on his lips.

Confused, she looked at Kssansk, but the lizardfolk didn't respond, and the words didn't sound like Draconic.

"What was that?" she said.

"I knew you cared for me," Quarhaun said.

Shara felt her face flush, and she laid his hand back down on his chest. "Of course I do. No one on my team is expendable."

His wounds were serious, but Kssansk's primal magic was already working to repair the deep wounds the demon's claws had made in his chest. Water flowed over his body in a thin sheet, carrying blood back into his body and—she realized with horror—liquid crystal out of the wounds, leaving it to pool on the floor beside him. Each glob of the stuff that was deposited onto the floor flowed into the last, staying separate from the water and congealing into a mass the size of Uldane's fist.

"And speaking of which, I need to check on that warrior who was hit by the shards. What is his name?"

"His name?" Quarhaun scoffed. "He's Third Lizardfolk from the Left."

"Those warriors saved our lives. Twice now. And their shaman is in the process of saving yours. I think they deserve more respect than that."

Quarhaun shrugged, then scowled in pain as Kssansk hissed a reproach. The words meant nothing to her, but the meaning was clear enough.

Shara smiled and stood, scanning the ranks of the lizardfolk warriors for the one who'd taken those injuries. She found him, a hulking specimen with a beaded band around his left bicep and a small silver ring pierced through his crest. Suddenly nervous, she approached him, carefully keeping her smile fixed in place.

The lizardfolk noticed her approach and her smile, and he raised his crest and bared his teeth, hissing in what looked like a very aggressive way. She stopped, taken aback.

"Don't smile at them," Quarhaun called from the floor. "All they see is teeth."

She let the smile drop as Quarhaun continued in Draconic.

"Now bob your head just a little—you've seen them do it."

She had, and she tried her best to imitate it, ducking her head like she was walking beneath a low beam, keeping her eyes fixed on the warrior. He returned the gesture, and she could see his body relax. She stepped closer, then put a hand on her chest. "Shara," she said, as clear as she could and a little too loud.

The lizardfolk cocked his head in a very birdlike way, then repeated her name. "Sssha'rra." He drew out the sibilant start, rolled the *R*, and inserted a heavy glottal stop in the middle, but she recognized her name and almost smiled again.

"They know your name, Shara," Quarhaun said, and she could almost hear his eyes roll with impatience. Kssansk shushed him, a look of amusement in his eyes as he observed the interaction.

"That's right," she said to the lizardfolk, realizing as she said it that she sounded like she was speaking to a child. "What's your name?" She put her hand on the lizardfolk's chest.

He lurched away from her touch and hissed again, his crest flaring like bright orange flame above his head.

"I'm sorry!" she said, bobbing her head again and stepping away from his bared teeth.

Quarhaun called to the lizardfolk and he turned slightly away from her, stretching his neck until she heard the muscles pop and crack. Then he bobbed his head slightly, only barely in her direction, as his lips twitched back over his teeth.

"Gsshin," he said, banging his club against his shield.

"Gushin?" She knew it wasn't quite right, but she hoped it wasn't so bad as to cause offense.

Gsshin bobbed his head and lowered his crest, and she knew she'd done well enough.

"I want to see your wounds," she said, pointing at the places she could still see where the demon's crystalline shards had burrowed into his flesh.

Gsshin flinched away from her finger, and looked over at Quarhaun as if waiting for a translation.

"No, look," Shara said, shifting into his line of sight. She pointed to her own eyes. "I look," she said slowly. "Look." Then she pointed at the largest gash, across his stomach. "At your wounds."

Gsshin rolled his eyes in a gesture so human it made her smile despite herself, and he called out something that could only mean, "What is this crazy human trying to say?"

With a rhythmic rumbling that might have been laughter, Kssansk stood up from Quarhaun's side and lumbered over to Shara. He bobbed his head at her, and she returned the gesture. Then he exchanged a few words with Gsshin, who reluctantly spread his arms wide so Shara could get a good look at his wounds. Kssansk pointed at the largest one and started speaking, addressing Quarhaun as if he expected the drow to translate.

And to Shara's relief, Quarhaun finally decided to cooperate. "He says that the crystal burrowed deep, and the water spirits had to work hard to flush it all out. He didn't have time to fully close up the wounds, but he's confident that the crystal substance is gone. And Gsshin fought bravely despite his injuries, and so on."

"Not 'and so on,' what did he say?"

"He says that a warrior could do no less, with your example to lead them."

Shara felt a flush of pride and satisfaction, but decided not to gloat over Quarhaun—at least not any more than was strictly necessary. She bobbed her head to Kssansk and Gsshin, then to all the warriors looking on, and turned back to the drow.

"And that's leadership, Quarhaun."

"Nearly got me killed," he grunted.

"Eh." She shrugged, holding back a smile. "Maybe you're expendable after all."

A search of the ruin revealed nothing to indicate that it was any more than an elaborate warren for the pack of demonic beasts, as Uldane had suggested. With the pack leader dead, the survivors from the battle upstairs scattered, apparently for good. And Vestapalk was nowhere to be found. Shara led the way back to the surface, and finally they emerged from the ruins into the dim sunlight filtering through a film of haze across the sky.

"Let's get out of this swamp," Uldane said brightly.

"I'm ready," Quarhaun said. Kssansk's ministrations had gotten him back on his feet, but he needed more rest before he could face any more combat.

Shara stopped and frowned back at the ruins.

"What is it?" Uldane asked.

"What are we doing, Uldane?"

"Going home, right?"

"No, I mean, what was that all about? I want revenge, so I led us into this swamp looking for the dragon. All we found was a nest of demons that nearly killed us all. And if it hadn't been for Quarhaun and the lizardfolk, we'd be dead down there. We're no closer to killing Vestapalk than we were when we started. Just worn out and broken down."

"It was worth it."

"Was it?"

"You bet! Watching you try to talk to Gsshin was almost worth it just by itself. The way he snarled at you when you touched his chest? Better than gold."

"Hm." Shara smiled. "I suppose I was hoping for something a bit more tangible."

"Gold and glory? The dragon's head on a pole? Shara, we made a big difference. That demon was spreading the plague, turning lizardfolk and the beasts of the swamp into its minions. And they were killing a lot of lizardfolk as well as the animals they eat. We saved them, Shara."

"Well, we helped them save themselves, I guess. And all this time I thought they were helping us."

"Isn't it funny how that works?"

Shara turned around and saw Quarhaun bobbing his head to Kssansk, evidently in the midst of a farewell. She watched, smiling, as he exchanged some more words with the shaman. He seemed at ease, in a way that made her feeble attempts to communicate with Gsshin all the more comical by comparison. And for all his talk about the lizardfolk warriors being expendable, his respect for Kssansk was plain to see, and somehow that increased her respect for Quarhaun.

Gsshin came and stood next to the shaman, speaking quickly to Quarhaun and gesturing in Shara's direction. Quarhaun laughed—covering his mouth as he did, she noticed—and nodded to both lizardfolk, then turned to her.

"Shara, Gsshin wishes me to convey his appreciation for your leadership and your martial skill."

Shara bowed, feeling overcome with emotion.

"He says that as soon as you learn to speak, you will be a human worthy of respect."

"How do you say 'thank you?'"

Quarhaun turned back to the lizardfolk, but Shara stopped him with a hand on his arm. "No, tell me. Teach me the words."

"Just one word. *Ashgah.*"

She stepped up to Gsshin, bobbed her head, and copied the strange sound as best she could. "*Ashgah,* Gsshin." She repeated the gesture to the shaman. "*Ashgah,* Kssansk."

Both lizardfolk rumbled with laughter and bowed to her. Then they turned and walked into the swamp, leading the other warriors back to their homes.

"Thank you, Quarhaun," Shara said.

He regarded her with a strange smile and said nothing, staring until she felt her face start to flush and she started looking for a path back to Fallcrest.

CHAPTER FIFTEEN

Roghar carried the four bound cultists, including Marcan, out to the hall and left Travic to keep an eye on them. He wanted Gaele to think she was alone, figuring that might make her simultaneously more afraid of him and less reluctant to show weakness in front of her followers. And Travic had been a friend of hers, which made him exactly the opposite of what Roghar wanted in the room. A hulking dragonborn and a sinister tiefling could scare information out of a helpless prisoner. A sympathetic, graying priest could not.

He leaned over Gaele, rolled her onto her back and gently slapped her cheek. "Wake up, Gaele. Time to answer a few questions."

Tempest stood behind him, arms crossed, a menacing cloak of shadows gathering behind her. He stood up and put his hands on his hips as Gaele's eyes fluttered open.

"Good, you're awake. I'd advise you against trying that scream again, unless you want to be knocked out."

Gaele opened her mouth and drew a deep breath, and Roghar tensed, ready to kick the air out of her if he had to.

"I will be free, the Chained God says." Gaele's words came fast and slurred, and her eyes weren't quite focused on him.

"The Chained God is going to free you, you think? I wouldn't hold my breath, if I were you."

"I will be free, and all will perish. The Chained God says, the Chained God says."

"Oh, dear." Roghar sighed. "This might be harder than I thought."

"So it shall be, so it shall be," Gaele said, her head rolling back and forth.

"Gaele, listen to me." He bent over her and tried to make her eyes focus on his face. "A few minutes ago you demonstrated that you were capable of coherent speech. Don't go all manic on me now."

"They will drown in blood. So it shall be."

"Gaele, I don't know what you're talking about. Do you know where you are?"

"You! You will go before me!" Gaele's eyes darted around the room, trying to see something past Roghar. He looked around.

"The altar?" he asked. He peered into the cups that surrounded the skull on the purple cloth. One held a thick jelly that burned with a guttering flame. Gravel and dirt filled the next. The third held some murky water, and a chunk of ice that had partly melted was in the fourth. The last cup was empty. Air, he thought.

"Before me to become the Living Gate, so it shall be."

Roghar lifted the skull and held it toward Gaele. "A friend of yours?"

She was looking past the skull, past the altar, to the alcove, he realized, looking at the strange shaft of light. He'd figured it was open to the surface somehow, maybe using mirrors to channel sunlight down from above. *Maybe there's more to it.*

"Tempest, will you take a look at that alcove for me, please? Maybe we can get a little more of Gaele's attention."

Tempest glared down at Gaele as she stepped around the altar, playing her part perfectly.

Gaele seemed oblivious, lost in her rambling. "To open my way to freedom, the Chained God says."

Roghar frowned down at her. "Your way or the Chained God's way? Whose freedom are we talking about?"

"We will soon be free, the Chained God says. Free to consume and destroy. Free to drown the world in blood. So it shall be, the Chained God says."

"No," Tempest whispered.

"What is it?" Roghar looked up to see Tempest staring aghast at something in the alcove, drawing back from it with an expression of utter horror on her face.

The prisoner on the floor forgotten, he rushed to Tempest's side and took her arm. "Tempest?"

"No no no no no!" Her voice started as a whisper but rose to a shriek of terror. She pulled away from him and fell to her knees, her back to the alcove and whatever horror it held.

"You will go before me to become the Living Gate!" Gaele shouted. "To open my way to freedom!"

"Silence!" Roghar bellowed, but neither Tempest nor Gaele heeded him.

Roghar stepped around Tempest and looked in the alcove himself. The light came, he saw now, from a clear crystal dome embedded in the stone at the top of the alcove, and it shone down in a perfect column to strike an engraved circle in the bottom, at about the height of his knee. The effect almost suggested a tube of glass, but Roghar could see motes of dust dancing in and out of the column.

He didn't immediately see what had disturbed Tempest so greatly. The alcove was bare of any decoration aside from the magical mechanism of the light, the dome in the top and the circle engraved in the bottom. He stuck his hand into the shaft of light. A brief tingle ran over his skin, and his hand felt strangely weightless.

Then he saw it. A glob of liquid hung suspended in the shaft of light, a little lower than his hand. It was no larger than the tip of his thumb, but it seemed to respond to the presence of his hand, stretching itself toward him. He yanked his hand out of the alcove and the liquid fell still. He bent down to examine it more closely.

It was red, and for a moment he thought it might be blood. But it shimmered in the light, almost like a gemstone with a million tiny facets. Gold and silver ran through it in streaks and flecks, just like—

Just like the thing that had taken Tempest.

"Oh, Tempest," he said, crouching behind her and putting his hands on her shoulders.

She pulled away from his touch and put her back to the wall, staring wild-eyed at the shaft of light. "I can't escape him," she whispered. "Not even here."

"How did that get here, I wonder?"

"Get it away," she said through gritted teeth.

"Tempest, calm—"

"Stop her!" Tempest shrieked.

Roghar spun around and saw Gaele on her feet, hopping around the altar. Before he could reach, she thrust her bound hands into the alcove.

"That's enough of that," Roghar growled, pulling Gaele away and throwing her to the floor.

"Now we spread!" Gaele cried. "The Voidharrow!" She lifted her hands to her face and covered it, as if cowering from him.

Roghar scowled down at her, then realized that the red liquid substance had clung to her hand and now stretched itself down to her face. He seized the rope that bound her hands and yanked them away from her face, but the liquid had pooled beside her nose. He reached for it, but hesitated just an instant before touching it, unsure he wanted it on his skin.

In that instant, it disappeared inside her nostril, and she screamed.

Like the howl she'd unleashed before, her scream was girded with supernatural force that sent him staggering away from her, clutching his ears and trying to keep his mind from splitting apart. But it lasted only a moment as her body writhed in agony and started to change, then the scream died with a gurgle in her throat.

"What in Bahamut's name?" Roghar said, stepping away.

"Roghar, what's happening?" Travic appeared in the entry, trying to keep an eye on his prisoners as he peered in to see what all the screaming was about.

"I don't know," Roghar said. "I think she might be possessed."

"Roghar, kill her," Tempest shouted. "Kill her now!"

"She's tied up—"

With a roaring howl, Gaele yanked her hands free of the rope Roghar had tied around her wrists. At the same time, shards of red crystal tore themselves free of her shoulders, forming a jagged cowl around her neck. The rope around her ankles, which had already proven useless in keeping her immobile, snapped as her legs thickened, the skin turning into a smooth, black armor.

"Kill her!"

Roghar fumbled for his sword, slid it from its sheath, and brought it down in a mighty arc toward her neck. A massive claw batted his sword away, and it took an instant before Roghar realized it was Gaele's arm.

"She's not possessed," he called. "She's changing!"

With a nervous glance down the hall, Travic ran into the room, pulling his mace free from its loop at his belt. "We've got to kill her before she finishes," he said. "She's only getting stronger."

Roghar drew in a breath and felt Bahamut's power welling in him. Even in that moment, he saw Gaele grow larger—her shoulders were now as broad as she was tall, and her head was turning into something alien and horrible. He swung his sword with all his might, biting deep into one of her tree-trunk arms. One of its arms, he thought—he couldn't possibly conceive of this monster as Gaele anymore. Divine radiance erupted around them both as his blow struck true, and the demon that had been Gaele howled in pain and rage.

Then Travic was beside him, and his mace crashed into the crystal growths on Gaele's shoulder, erupting in a similar flash of light. Travic recoiled as the crystals splintered and razor-sharp shards flew around him, but he seemed unharmed—until the demon's claw lashed out and fastened around his neck, lifting him off the ground.

"Gaele—" Travic gasped.

The demon hesitated just an instant, and Roghar used that instant to cleave its skull open with one more mighty blow. Its body writhed and changed a little more before finally lying still, and Roghar stood over it with his sword ready in case the red liquid oozed out, like the thing that possessed Tempest had done.

The room was still and silent. Though the demon bled, nothing flowing from its wounds seemed to have a life of its own.

"The danger appears to be over," he said at last, looking up at Travic. The priest nodded.

All at once, voices in the hallway started shouting. Roghar heard pieces of the same phrases Gaele had been repeating. "All will perish," "so it shall be," "open my way," and "the Chained God says" rang out over and over. Travic ran to the hall, but a moment before he reached the doorway the shouting stopped, as abruptly as it had begun. Travic stepped into the hall, peered intently at the prisoners, and cast a fearful glance back at Roghar.

"What is it?" Roghar said.

Travic didn't answer, but started down the hall. Roghar hurried to the door and watched him crouch beside one of the cultists—Marcan. He shook the man's shoulder, called his name, and felt in his neck for a pulse.

"He's dead." He repeated his efforts for each of the other three prisoners and stood, shaking his head. "They're all dead."

"That doesn't make any sense," Roghar said. A sudden fear struck him, and he spun around to check on Tempest. To his relief, she was still on her feet, slumped against the wall and curled in on herself. He hurried to her side and clasped her shoulder.

Her eyes shifted to look at him, but she didn't otherwise move.

"Let's get you out of here, my friend," he said softly. "Our work here is finished."

She closed her eyes. "They're all dead?" she whispered.

"Yes. I don't know what killed them."

Tempest sighed, and her long tail unfurled from around her legs. "Let's go, then."

Roghar helped her stand upright and guided her to the doorway. She didn't open her eyes until they were past the cultists' bodies in the hall, past the headless stone knight frozen in its death throes, and most of the way back to the start of the hall. After she did open her eyes, she never once looked back.

CHAPTER SIXTEEN

Eight slender windows at the top of Sherinna's tower, just below the gallery, let in moonlight that spilled down the grand entrance hall. Kri closed the door to his bedchamber as quietly as he could manage, not wanting to disturb Albanon's rest. The young wizard had spent precious little time in his trance since they'd arrived at the tower. Eladrin didn't sleep, but without at least a few hours spent in a peaceful reverie, they started to show the same signs of fatigue, irritable moods, and even hallucinations that plagued sleep-deprived humans.

Kri could understand the young man's excitement. He even shared it, to some extent. Here he was, after all, creeping to the library in the middle of the night to follow up a lead he'd encountered earlier in the evening. The thrill of discovery, of learning what had long been forgotten, was almost an experience of the divine for him. Sometimes he even imagined that he was waging war against Vecna, the god of secrets and Ioun's most hated foe, by unlocking the mysteries of things and expanding his own knowledge.

He made his way up the steps toward the library, but found himself diverted along the way. Between the library and the living quarters, the fourth-floor archway led to Sherinna's workshop. It was sparsely furnished and not half as interesting as the library for his purposes, but one item in there had caught his eye earlier, and he had resolved to investigate it further.

No better time than now, he said to himself.

He stepped through the slender arch and into the workshop. To his left, an identical arch, carved with the same gracefully curving lines, decorated a section of the wall. Had it been an actual archway, it would have opened into the empty air outside the tower, forty feet above the ground. But between the white marble columns was blank stone wall.

At the peak of the arch was the thing that had caught his eye before—a jagged piece of red crystal set into the stone.

"What is your story, crystal shard?" Kri whispered, peering up at the gleaming mineral. He closed his eyes and reached out with his other senses, the way he had taught Albanon. He saw it immediately—the stone was charged with magic, far more intense and wild than the focused energy that flowed through the columns of the arch. A glance at the overall flow of energies confirmed what he had suspected. The arch was a teleportation portal, serving basically the same function as the more common circle engraved on the floor and inlaid with silver. Properly attuned to a destination, it would allow instant transportation.

But how would one attune the portal? With an engraved circle, attuning the portal was a relatively simple matter of drawing a sequence of sigils into the circle's edge, sigils that matched those at the destination. With this portal, there was no obvious place to write those sigils, and he suspected the crystal was instead the key.

If the crystal is what I think it is, he thought, it's the key to a lot more than this portal.

He slid a dagger out of its sheath at his belt and stretched up to reach the blade to the stone. He pried it free from its setting with the merest effort, and fumbled to catch it before it clattered to the ground.

Peering into the crimson heart of the fragment, he left the workshop and climbed the next ring of stairs to the library.

"Ioun, guide me," Kri whispered, stretching out his hands as he stood before the shelves in the library. He drew a deep breath and closed his eyes as he held it, listening for Ioun's presence.

"Seek the Chained God," a voice said.

Kri opened his eyes, and his gaze fell on an unlabeled scroll on the shelf. He lifted the heavy scroll and carried it to a table, unrolling it enough to read the writing at the top.

"A research into the Living Gate," he read aloud. "By Sherinna, naturally." He closed his eyes and whispered, "Thank you," confident that Ioun had led him to the knowledge he sought.

"Three gods approached the Living Gate," he read aloud, "desiring to know what lay behind its gleaming scarlet surface. Pelor, whose light shines into all darkness, first discovered the Living Gate, though he later wished he had not. Ioun, whose mind ever hungers to learn all things, awoke the sleeping gate. And a third, nameless god, who feared no danger and doubted all authority, distracted the guardian of the Living Gate so all three gods could glimpse the madness beyond."

"The Chained God," a voice repeated. Kri looked around, but the library was deserted. A chill went down his spine. Did the voice belong to Ioun, rewarding his decades of faithful service by deigning to speak to him? Or one of her angels? Or perhaps Sherinna's shade, speaking from beyond the realm of death? He felt the weight of the moment as time seemed to stretch out, each passing second laden with significance.

"The gods were changed by what they had seen," Kri continued reading, "and they departed, swearing a solemn oath never to seek the gate again or speak of what they had seen beyond it. And for many long ages they kept their oath, even as the Dawn War raged throughout the cosmos, reshaping the world, the Astral Sea, and its dominions. But as the war raged on, one of the three gods returned to the gate, killed its guardian, and awakened the Living Gate from its eons of slumber. Madness burst forth through the gate and threatened to consume all that the gods were fighting for. Eventually, Ioun and Pelor cooperated to seal the gate once more, stemming the tide of madness."

"Something is not right here," a voice said. Kri jumped, startled, and looked around again.

"Something is not right," he echoed. He went back and reread the paragraph.

"Seek the Chained God," the voice repeated. Kri started reading again from the beginning, moving his lips with the words but no longer giving them voice.

"Everyone believes the Chained God was the one who returned and opened the Living Gate," Kri said at last. "But the Chained God was already in his prison, before the Dawn War even began."

"Who opened the Living Gate?" a new voice said. Kri didn't look up from the scroll.

"Either the legend is wrong in reporting that the Dawn War had already begun," Kri said, "or it was not the Chained God who opened the gate. Or else the Chained God was not imprisoned until later—I don't know. And I don't understand why it matters. What does the Living Gate have to do with Vestapalk and the demons?"

"Why don't you ask it?"

"Ask it?" He looked around helplessly, and his eyes fell on the crystal shard he'd brought up from the workshop. "Yes, of course. Ask it." He seized the fragment, bundled up the scroll, and carried both back downstairs.

"What did the three gods see behind the Living Gate?" a voice asked on the stairs.

"Was it the same thing that burst forth when the gate was opened?" another voice asked.

"What did Ioun see?" Still a different voice, and this one made him stop.

"Who are you?" Kri asked, his voice wavering. "I sought guidance from Ioun."

No voice came in answer. Suddenly filled with fear, Kri hurried down the stairs until he reached the workshop and looked around for something he could use to seal the archway. He tried to drag a tall bookcase in front of the arch, but loaded with books it was too heavy for him to move alone. He threw books and scrolls onto the floor until one landed open on the floor beside him and he looked down to see a jagged spiral symbol on the scroll like an eye staring up at him.

He dropped to his knees beside the book and started reading about the Chained God. Sherinna had penned this scroll as well, and recorded her search, along with Brendis and Nowhere, for the cultists whose trail they had discovered in Nera—cultists of Tharizdun, the Elder Elemental Eye . . . the Dark God.

"The cultists were trying to free the Chained God," he breathed. "I never knew."

"You have much to learn," a voice said over his shoulder.

Kri spun around and let his eyes range over the empty workshop.

"You must understand your enemies if you wish to defeat them," came another voice.

He nodded. "Ask it ask it ask it—I'll ask it." He placed the crystal fragment on a table and rooted through the materials stored in flasks and boxes around the workshop until he found a tiny vial filled with a glittering silvery powder. "Residuum," he said. "Excellent."

He carefully opened the vial, the powder left behind from a broken enchantment, like crystallized magic, and tapped out just enough of it to trace a circle around the shard on the table's smooth surface. As the circle took shape, he began chanting syllables of power, inserting occasional pleas to Ioun into the fabric of the ritual. The voices around him spoke a few times, but he blocked them out, forcing his mind to focus on the words of the ritual. So ignored, the voices left him in disgust, withdrawing to plan their next assault on his mind.

"Reveal your secrets to me!" he commanded, gripping the shard to complete the ritual.

The room around him disappeared, and he stood in a dusty ruin. A long wooden staff was held in two wooden braces in the wall beside him, and his hand clenched the head of the staff—the shard—suspended in the crook by a network of woven gut strands. Suddenly the wall opposite him burst open and a man stepped through, a man he recognized as the cult leader depicted in the mural at the top of the tower.

The man seized the staff, wrenching Kri's perception as the world turned around him so his perspective on the crystal remained unchanged. He cut the strings holding the crystal in place and cradled the shard in his own hands, oblivious to Kri's presence and his own hand on the shard.

And then Kri was the cult leader. "Albric," he said. "My name is Albric."

With his own hands, he killed one of his acolytes for impertinence, obeying the will of the Elder Elemental Eye. Then he used the crystal fragment to trace a circle on the wall where the staff had stood, opening a portal to a crowded city some part of his mind knew as Sigil, the City of Doors. He led his acolytes through the city until they were confronted by three robbers. One of the robbers was seized by the Eye, caught up in an ecstatic trance, revealing the presence and the name of Tharizdun, the Chained God.

Kri experienced Albric's thrill of excitement, his religious awe in the presence of his god. It was a perfect expression of what he longed to feel from Ioun but found increasingly difficult to claim.

And Kri experienced Albric's madness. He walked through a nightmare vista of liquid flesh and purple flame, and emerged in front of a ring of green flame. He howled in his madness, breaking the minds of those who heard him. And he stepped through a portal into Pandemonium.

Kri felt his pulse quicken as Albric began his ritual in the heart of the Chained God's abandoned dominion. He chanted invocations to Tharizdun, the Patient One and the Black Sun. He watched the shard of the Living Gate rise into the air and open the tiniest of portals, a narrow wormhole leading to the prison that held the Chained God bound. And he watched with a mixture of Albric's elation and his own dawning horror as a red crystalline liquid seeped out through the portal.

You must understand your enemies if you wish to defeat them, Kri reminded himself.

Then the vision became more confusing. Kri felt the tug of two different desires. The Chained God wanted him to fuse the red liquid—the Progenitor, he called it—with the shard of the Living Gate, and thereby create the Vast Gate. The red liquid itself, the Voidharrow, wanted him to fuse itself with him. He—or, rather, Albric—tried to follow the Chained God's will, and he guided the fusion of the Voidharrow and the Living Gate until it grew into the archway depicted in Sherinna's mural. His acolytes, though, obeyed the Voidharrow, and he saw them transform into demons.

The Chained God, he realized, had been betrayed. He felt the distant echo of the god's fury as he—as Albric—fought to carry out Tharizdun's will . . . and failed.

He felt what Albric did as the Voidharrow claimed his body, transforming him from the legs up into a creature of liquid crystal. He felt the tiefling's dagger slip into his side and end his body's life.

But Albric was no longer just his body. His will had fused with the Voidharrow as much as his body had, and he became something else. He became the creature that Albanon had described, a serpentine creature of red liquid.

"I am Nu Alin," Kri said aloud.

"Who are you talking to?" asked a voice in the room.

Kri's mind was jolted out of the vision, but he grasped at one last fragment of knowledge and experience. "I am in the Tower of Waiting," he said.

"Kri? What are you talking about?"

Kri saw the crystal fragment on the table in front of him. Sherinna's workshop came slowly into focus, and he turned toward the voice, fully expecting to see nothing there.

Albanon stood in the archway, a look of concern on his face.

"It's time for us to leave," Kri announced. Nu Alin was the key, he realized. Nu Alin was present at the beginning of it all. He had tried to fight the Voidharrow's will, to do instead what the Chained God wanted.

"What?" Albanon whined. "We've barely gotten started here!"

Kri turned his back to Albanon. "I've uncovered some new information," he said. As he spoke, he lifted the crystal from the table and slid it into a pocket, keeping it out of Albanon's view.

"So have I! I think I might be close to finding the dragon. I've been analyzing the flow of magical energy through the Feywild and the world alike. It's like there's a great vortex—"

Kri shook his head sharply. "We have another quarry now." *I have to find Nu Alin*, he thought. *If the demon can be turned against Vestapalk, together we might defeat the Voidharrow at last.*

"What other quarry?"

Kri grimaced. The urge to blast the annoying young eladrin with so much holy fire that his entire body would be consumed filled him so suddenly that he almost gave in to it.

"I'll explain later. Collect your belongings."

"Now? It's the middle of the night."

Kri thought he heard lightning crackle around his head, reflecting his frustration. He clutched his temples and drew a slow breath.

"Kri, are you unwell? You're acting very strangely."

"Not enough sleep, clearly. I'm sorry. Let me try to explain. Come into the stairway." He shooed Albanon out of the workshop and followed him onto the landing beyond, suppressing a sudden desire to push the young eladrin over the railing.

Instead, he put a fatherly hand on Albanon's shoulder and forced a smile onto his face as he pointed to the mural on the dome.

"I know where Albric is—where Nu Alin is," he said, pointing to the man in the mural above, standing before the Vast Gate with his legs already transformed into red liquid columns. "He is the key to all of this. He holds the knowledge we seek."

Albanon's eyes widened. "He left the Temple of Yellow Skulls on Vestapalk's back. Where he is, the dragon probably is as well. But there's no way he's going to help us against Vestapalk."

"Perhaps not," Kri said. "But we are not the only ones opposing the Voidharrow. It may be that enough remains of Albric the Accursed to turn even Nu Alin against his master."

"Well, where is he, then?"

"In Fallcrest."

Albanon stared at him for a moment, then swore softly in Elven. "Shara and Uldane," he said. "Let's go."

CHAPTER SEVENTEEN

Albanon hurried into the workshop while he adjusted the straps on his backpack. He had decided to bring only the bare minimum of books from Sherinna's library, things he really couldn't do without while he and Kri went in search of Nu Alin, but that bare minimum had filled his backpack almost to bursting. And that was after he'd removed luxuries like rope, sunrods, and food.

"I can't find Splendid," he told Kri. "Have you seen her?"

"Not in days, now that you mention it. I thought it was pleasantly quiet around here."

"I argued with her in the library last week and she slunk away. I think she must have left."

"Whatever will we do without her wisdom and perspective?"

"Please, Kri. She was Moorin's."

"So let her go!" Kri said. "Along with the last remnants of your apprenticeship and your childhood. You're not in training any more—if nothing else, the way you handled yourself at the Temple of Yellow Skulls proves that. Now you are a man—and more than a man, a wizard. Nothing remains to hold you back."

Albanon stood a little taller, but then his face fell. "Except you ordering me around," he muttered.

Kri turned away from the arch set in Sherinna's workshop wall and put a hand on Albanon's shoulder. "I don't mean to order you around, Albanon, but we're pressed for time. I will explain everything when I can, I promise you."

Albanon forced a smile for his new mentor. "Thank you. I'll hold you to that."

"You'd better, because I'm sure to forget. The old mind's not what it used to be, you understand?"

"Oh, I've noticed."

Albanon cast a longing look around the workshop. During the week since they reached the tower, he had spent nearly every waking hour in the library, and felt as though he'd only scratched the surface of all there was to learn there. He'd had no time for the workshop, let alone all the other rooms of the tower—the room where Sherinna had displayed trophies from her adventuring life as if they were exhibits in a museum, or the greenhouse at the top of the tower, full of exotic plants. He had even wanted to spend time in the music room, with its dusty harp and collection of wooden flutes, maybe even learn to play those instruments. He'd felt, somehow, that it would bring him closer to the mysterious woman who had been his grandmother.

"Are you ready?" Kri asked over his shoulder as he made some final adjustments to the arch.

"Just a moment." Albanon stepped out onto the landing and looked up and down the entry hall. "Splendid!" he called. "Splendid, I'm sorry for what I said. We're leaving now, and if you want to come with us you have to come now. Please!"

He waited until he heard Kri clear his throat in the workshop, signaling his impatience.

"Splendid!" he called, one last time.

With no response, he turned and shuffled back into the workshop, ready for Kri's journey.

"You're better off, believe me," Kri said. "Now, I've modified this arch so that it works more like a traditional teleportation circle. That means, among other things, that we'll be able to use it come back here, without passing through the Moon Door and crossing the Plain of Thorns. After all, you never know when your father will tire of letting us walk across his lands. I have keyed the portal to the teleportation circle in Moorin's tower."

"In Fallcrest?" Albanon said, suddenly excited to return to the town that had been his home for seven years.

"Did Moorin have another tower somewhere?"

A thought struck Albanon. "Why didn't you use that circle before?"

Kri blinked at him. "What?"

"When we first met. You said you came to Fallcrest by boat. Why didn't you just teleport there?"

"Moorin never shared the sigils of his circle with me. I studied them when we were last there."

Albanon frowned, but something about Kri's tone made him decide not to press the question further. Instead, he turned his attention to the arch. "Are you sure it's going to work?" He pointed to the top of the arch. "It looks like there used to be something set into the stone at the apex. Maybe it won't function without whatever it was."

"As I said," Kri said testily, "I have modified the arch so that it will function in its current state."

"Oh, right."

"Are you ready?" Kri asked.

"Do I have a choice?"

"Of course you do, Albanon. But I thought you wanted to help me root out the source of this abyssal plague."

"I do," Albanon said quickly. "Forgive me. I spoke without thinking."

A spasm of fury passed across Kri's face, and Albanon stepped away reflexively. Then it was gone, and Kri was smiling again. "We'll leave when you're sure you're ready," he said.

"I'm ready. I'm sorry."

"Very well. To Moorin's tower!"

Kri raised his hands before the arch and the columns began to glow, casting the interior into strange shadows. He stepped between the glowing columns and disappeared.

Albanon took one last look at the Whitethorn Spire, half hoping to see Splendid speeding through the archway on her tiny wings, and followed the priest through the arch.

For the briefest instant he felt like he was falling, and as if some dark presence nearby was grasping at him. Then his feet stood once more on solid ground. It took his eyes a moment to adjust to the candlelit chamber, but he knew it well, and it brought a stab of pain to his heart. It was the very chamber where he had found Moorin's corpse after

Nu Alin—using the unassuming body of a halfling—had torn him to pieces. Blood had been everywhere, and for one horrible moment the memory of the smell—the acrid blood and his own vomit—threatened to overwhelm him.

"What have we here?" Kri demanded, jolting Albanon's mind back to the present.

Magical power shimmered in the air around them, forming a dome over the teleportation circle that was inscribed on the ground. Albanon wasn't immediately sure, but he guessed the purpose of the dome was to keep him and Kri inside. He was more certain about the intent of the trembling soldiers that surrounded the pair, pointing spears and halberds in their general direction.

"Intruders!" one of the soldiers shouted. "Get the captain!"

Another soldier, a young man who looked barely old enough for the militia, broke from the circle and ran down the stairs, presumably to carry out his sergeant's orders.

"What's the meaning of this, sergeant?" Kri asked hotly. "We're not intruders—this tower belongs to Albanon, here."

"Sorry," the sergeant replied, "but we have our orders. You need to stay here until we can make sure you're clean."

"Fine," Albanon said, cutting off what he suspected was going to be an angry retort from Kri. "But we've been away from Fallcrest for some time. Can you tell us what's going on while we wait for the captain?"

"The town's under siege. The invaders are everywhere in Lowtown and the west bank. Plague is breaking out, mostly among soldiers who have fought the creatures, but it's starting to spread. Hightown's crowded with refugees."

"So what are you doing here?" Kri demanded. "Don't you soldiers have better things to do than occupy a wizard's tower?"

"The town's locked down," the sergeant said. "No one enters Hightown until we're sure they're not carrying the plague or working for the enemy."

The young soldier returned, breathless from his run. "The captain's here, sir," he said with a salute.

"Thank the gods," the sergeant breathed.

Albanon had the opposite reaction as the captain strode in. The captain was a tall human woman, with dark brown skin and eyes that gleamed like amber. Albanon recognized her—she had tried to arrest him after Moorin's death and had testified at his trial before the Lord Warden where he was finally acquitted. The few times he'd seen her since then, he'd had the distinct feeling that she took his freedom as a personal affront.

"Well, they don't look like demons," the captain announced. "And I don't see any sores."

"No, Captain Damar," the sergeant replied, "but our orders—"

"Moorin's apprentice," the captain said, stepping closer to inspect Albanon. "Your dragonborn friend blinded my soldiers and carried you away before we could arrest you."

"I've faced trial before the Lord Warden," Albanon said.

"Indeed. He decided you were innocent. But I still don't understand why an innocent man would attack my guards and run like a rabbit."

"Roghar and I were chasing the creature that did kill Moorin. It had taken our friend Tempest, and we were afraid it might kill her as well, so we were trying to travel fast. We didn't have time—"

"Back up," Captain Damar said. "Who else was present that day, the first time we tried to arrest you?"

Albanon furrowed his brow. "Who else? Well, the Lord Warden was the one who ordered me to surrender myself. The High Septarch and his apprentice, Tobolar. You and a half dozen soldiers. Me, Roghar, and Splendid, Moorin's pseudodragon."

The captain nodded. "They are who they say they are, sergeant. You may lower the wards."

Albanon gaped at her, stunned into silence.

"If you were an enemy posing as Albanon—well, first, you'd be a damned fool to choose that disguise. But more important, I don't think you'd know all the details of that day. And I see no sign of contagion."

"So you believe I'm innocent?"

The captain scoffed. "At the time, you were the only suspect that made sense, and your explanation of a 'foul creature from someplace else' seemed far-fetched." She frowned. "Now it's all too real."

As she spoke, her sergeant manipulated some kind of pattern on a nearby table, shifting gleaming stones around on an engraved circle. The shimmer of magic in the air around Albanon and Kri vanished suddenly.

"So what are these invaders?" Albanon asked, stepping out of the circle. He suspected he knew the answer, but he didn't want to believe it until he heard the captain say it.

"They're not like anything I've seen before," the captain said, and Albanon's heart sank. "Creatures of blood and fire, some of them, and others are made of shadow and nightmare."

Albanon cocked his head. These didn't sound like Vestapalk's demons. "Fire and blood, you say? What does that mean?"

"They're formed of living flame, like elementals. But they have faces in the midst of the flame, faces formed of blood streaked with silver."

"The Voidharrow," Kri said.

"So they are Vestapalk's demons," Albanon said. "But a new kind, one we haven't seen before. And they're all over Lowtown?"

"Oh, yes," the captain said. "And the west bank of the river. We have soldiers and conscripts all along the walls, the river, and the bluffs to keep them from spreading, but I fear it's futile."

"Why?"

"A couple of people struck by the plague ended up . . . changed. Most of them, we had to kill. A couple got away to join the enemy."

"They turned into demons," Albanon said.

"Demons seems like as good a word as any. So tell me, how do you defend a town against something like that?"

Albanon stared at the floor, trying to comprehend what had happened to the town he'd called home for seven years.

Kri stepped forward. "I'll tell you how we defend it," he said. "We find the source of the plague and wipe it from the face of the earth."

CHAPTER EIGHTEEN

Once they left the Witchlight Fens, Quarhaun's recovery slowed dramatically, as if distance from the swamp prevented Kssansk's water spirits from working their healing magic on him any longer. By the time they made camp, just a few hours outside the borders of the swamp, the drow had a high fever. He babbled nonsense as Shara wrapped him in his bedroll and forced him to lie still beside their campfire.

In the morning, his fever was worse, and she could barely rouse him into wakefulness. He'd open his eyes, say something unintelligible in Elven or Draconic or some other tongue—often with a dopey smile on his face—then close them again, falling limp in her arms.

"This is bad," she said to Uldane, looking down at the drow with her hands on her hips.

"We're only a few hours from Fallcrest," the halfling said. "Do you think you can carry him that far?"

"If I do, it'll take more than a few hours, but it's possible."

"We could build a raft and pole it up the river to town. That's the halfling way, after all."

"I wish we'd thought of that while we were still in the swamp. With the lizardfolk's help, we could have built a raft in no time."

"Maybe we should just let him sleep another day," Uldane said, staring at Quarhaun thoughtfully. "Maybe by tomorrow morning, he'll feel better and be ready to walk himself into town."

"Or maybe he'll be dead," Shara said. "I'd like to get him to a healer as soon as we can. If Albanon and Kri have returned, Kri could help him. And it'd be good to check in with them."

"Do you think it's that serious?" Uldane said, his eyes suddenly wide. He took a few nervous steps toward where Quarhaun lay.

"Yes." Shara ran her fingers through her hair. "I have an idea. We'll build a small raft, just big enough for him to lie on."

Uldane brightened, nearly jumping up from his seat. "Like the one that carried the Sleeping Prince!"

"I don't know that story, but tell me later. We'll tie some rope to the raft, and we can pull him upstream. We walk on the riverbank or wade in the shallows, and he gets a smooth ride."

"You really like him, don't you?" Uldane's expression was serious again, a little crease between his eyebrows expressing a hint of disapproval.

"Like him? Not really, no. He's cowardly, insensitive, snide, and sometimes mean."

Uldane's face broke into a wide grin. "Yeah, he can be a real bugbear."

"But he has been an enormous help to us," Shara continued. "So as much as I'd like to just leave him here for the ankhegs . . ."

"He sure likes you, though."

"Stop it."

"It's a bit creepy, actually. The way he watches you, sometimes it's like a dragon watching its prey."

"That doesn't make it sound like he *likes* me. More like he wants to eat me."

"You know what I mean, Shara."

Shara felt her face grow red, and she turned away. "What can we use to make a little raft?"

Uldane proved surprisingly skilled at weaving reeds around a basic frame of branches to make a simple raft. Shara knew that halflings were river-dwellers, but in all their years of adventuring together she'd never seen Uldane demonstrate the skills he must have been born into. Shara held her breath as she gently lowered a moaning Quarhaun into the raft, and she sighed with relief when it held him afloat.

"Maybe this will keep him closer to the water spirits," Uldane said as Shara worked her rope into a simple harness.

"That would be good. Although I don't know if the river has the same spirits as the swamp."

"Do you suppose they're friends or enemies?"

"Who?"

"The water spirits. Do the ones in the river like the ones in the swamp? Or do they think they're dirty, ugly, lazy spirits because they don't flow bright and clear the way the river spirits do?"

Shara blinked at Uldane, then turned to look at the river. She felt, in a way, like she'd never really seen the river before—the way the sunlight gleamed on the water as it rushed by, the dance of the plants that grew beneath the surface as the water swirled around them, the darting fish and skimming insects. And beneath or behind all that, in a way that words couldn't describe, the spirits of the river, laughing as they tripped along through the banks.

She stooped and dipped her hand in the water, feeling the water tug at her fingers, inviting her to join their tripping band. "Please," she whispered, "help him." She scooped a handful of water from the river and sprinkled it on Quarhaun, then shouldered her harness and started walking upriver, toward Fallcrest.

As they walked, Uldane prattled on about the water spirits, marveling at the sensation of the water flowing over him as Kssansk healed his wounds, speculating at more length about the relationship between the river spirits and the swamp spirits, not to mention the spirits in Lake Nen and Lake Wintermist, at the heads of the river. Oh, and the ocean spirits, or bay spirits, or whatever lay far to the south where the river, under some other name, at last joined with the sea.

Shara just let his words wash over her—like the water spirits, she decided, soothing away her cares.

After an hour or so of uninterrupted talking, Uldane suddenly fell silent. Shara thought he might have been in midsentence, but she racked her brain to remember what he'd said, in case he asked a question and was awaiting a response. Something about . . . oysters?

"I don't remember that," the halfling said at last.

Shara looked down at him, then followed his gaze off to the east across the river, where a fire-blackened farmhouse stood beside the scorched remnants of its fields.

"I do remember the house," Shara said. "It's the Wintermoot place, the farthest farm outside of Fallcrest. When you leave the town along the river, it's the last farm you see before you're in the wilds. When you're coming back, it's the first farm you see, so you know you're almost there. I wonder what happened."

Uldane looked concerned for a long moment, then his irrepressible smile reasserted itself. "I remember people talking about how you couldn't start a meeting until the Wintermoots arrived. Once they were there, well, it didn't matter who else was missing, because you know they'd had plenty of time to get there. If the Wintermoots could get there, then why couldn't you, right?"

"Look, there's still some smoke puffing out of the house. It must have been recent."

"We passed a ford not too long ago," Uldane said, though he looked like he dreaded what Shara might say in answer.

"No, I don't think there's anything left to be done. I think it happened recently, but not today. I'm sure we'll hear what happened when we get to Fallcrest."

"And sleep in real beds!" Uldane said, starting to walk again. "If Albanon's not at the tower, are we staying at the Nentir Inn?"

"That's what I figured. Is that all right with you?"

"Well, part of me feels like we should give our business to the Silver Unicorn—you know, help out the clan."

"Are you related to Wisara Osterman?" The stern matriarch who owned Fallcrest's more expensive inn seemed about as unlike Uldane as Shara could imagine.

"Not in any way I could trace. But I'm sure there are ties."

"We can stay at the Silver Unicorn if you want to, Uldane."

"Well, the rest of me thinks Wisara is a crotchety old coot who doesn't deserve our business."

"Oh, good."

"Besides, I don't think she'd be particularly welcoming to our new friend." Uldane nodded toward the raft where Quarhaun was sleeping soundly.

"I've been thinking about that," Shara said. "I really hope Albanon is back and we can stay in the tower, because I'm not sure we're going to do much better at the Nentir Inn. You don't see a lot of drow in Fallcrest."

"That's true. I heard a story once about some drow raiding Fallcrest, actually."

"Really?"

"Well, I guess they never got farther than the outlying farms, but—hey, there's another one!"

Shara followed Uldane's pointing finger with her eyes, lifting her hand to shield them against the early afternoon sun. Clearly outlined on a hilltop almost due north of them was the wreckage of another farmhouse—the manor house, really, of the Dembran family, a clan of minor nobles who had held an estate south of Fallcrest since the Nentir Vale was first settled. Shara couldn't see the fields, which were situated primarily on the north side of the hill, but the house was in much worse shape than the Wintermoot farmhouse had been. And not just burned. Walls were broken down as if a siege engine had been set against the place.

Shara felt a sick feeling take root in the pit of her stomach. "This story about drow raids—that wasn't a recent event, was it?"

"No, hundreds of years ago. Why?"

"These farms were attacked," Shara said.

"You think drow were involved?"

"No way to tell from here, but I doubt it. More likely it was the dragon or his minions. Damn it! We chased him all over the Nentir Vale, and he attacked Fallcrest while we were away! Maybe even while we were talking to him in the fens!"

"Well, as you said, there's no way to tell from here. But we should go check it out."

"Something tells me we should get to town as quickly as we can," Shara said. She looked up at the sky, measuring the position of the sun. "And before dark, if we can."

She waded into the water and bent over Quarhaun, feeling his forehead. "The fever has broken," she said. "It appears the water spirits heard my plea."

Quarhaun opened his eyes and said something that sounded long and florid, probably Elven.

"Go back to sleep," Shara told him. "You're still incoherent."

"I said, how could the water spirits not heed your words, when they come from such lovely lips?"

Blushing, Shara turned to Uldane, who raised his eyebrow knowingly. She rolled her eyes at him and turned back to the drow.

"So you're feeling better?" she asked

"I'm cold and wet," Quarhaun said. "My mouth tastes like a fungus slug died in it, and I think my shoulder might be on fire. But better, yes. Am I . . ." He lifted his head, trying to look around. "On a raft?"

"Yes. We built it to carry you to town."

"How industrious. And it explains the cold and wet."

"Well, the last time I checked you were burning with fever, so cool is an improvement. Can you walk?"

"Help me out of this thing and we'll find out. Where are we?"

"The outskirts of Fallcrest," Shara said as she took his hand and helped him sit up. The raft bobbed dangerously low in the water as he shifted, and Quarhaun scowled.

"Now some parts of me are wetter than others," he said.

Shara got him standing in the shallow water at the river's edge, then draped one of his arms around her shoulder to help him walk to shore. He slipped once, throwing his other arm around her and clutching her in a way that was rather more familiar than it needed to be. She shot him her best withering glare and he withdrew his hand, making excuses.

"That's better," Quarhaun said once his feet were on dry land again. "How far is it to Fallcrest?"

"Two, maybe three hours at a normal pace. It probably would have taken us five or six if we had to keep pulling you along the river, and I guess I would've been carrying you to the Nentir Inn. So even if you can't sustain a normal pace, we ought to make it before nightfall."

"Do you think an inn is wise?"

"Uldane and I were just discussing that," Shara said, nodding. "Our first choice is to sleep in Moorin's tower—well, it's Albanon's tower now. But if he and Kri haven't returned, I think we'll be all right at the Nentir Inn. It might present some troubles, but they know me there, and they'll accept you if I vouch for you. And you really need bed rest, and maybe the attention of a healer. Do you think you can make it?"

"I'm not dead. I'll make it."

"You very nearly were dead. Remember that before you try anything stupid."

Quarhaun nodded seriously to her, but shot Uldane an obvious wink. "I'll try," he said.

Uldane helped Shara out of the rope harness, untied the rope, and let the little raft drift back down the river. Shara watched with amusement as Uldane performed what seemed like a familiar rite, a prolonged farewell to a craft that had served its purpose well. He watched it drift downstream until Quarhaun cleared his throat impatiently, and even as they walked Uldane kept looking back until he couldn't see it any more.

As they continued, Shara and Uldane explained to Quarhaun what they'd seen of the Wintermoot farm and the Dembran estate, sharing their concerns that Fallcrest itself might be under attack.

"I once returned from a hunting expedition and found the cavern where my city had been completely caved in," the drow said. "It took us three weeks to find where the survivors had established a new city."

"What happened to the city?"

"The matron mothers of the ruling house had angered Lolth, and she punished them with the cave-in."

"How did anyone survive?"

"Lolth warned the priests of the other houses. They had to figure out a way to evacuate as many people as possible—key people, anyway—without letting the ruling house know what was happening." He shook his head. "I have no head for politics."

"If that's what you call politics, I'm not surprised," Shara said.

Soon the road left the riverbank and ran through a little wood that divided the Dembran fields from the more tightly packed farms that lay across the river from Fallcrest's Lowtown. Shara started to ask Quarhaun more about his home city, but Uldane interrupted her.

"Listen," the halfling said, coming to a stop on the side of the road.

Shara and Quarhaun stopped as well. Shara slid her sword from its sheath as she looked around for any sign of danger.

"No," Uldane said. "Listen."

"I don't hear anything."

"Exactly. Where are the birds? Where are the squirrels fleeing through the branches at all the noise we're making? It's too quiet."

"Maybe we're not hearing them because we've already scared them away."

Uldane looked dissatisfied with that answer, but evidently couldn't refute it. He scowled as he looked around at the trees, ears alert for any sound.

Quarhaun shifted uncomfortably a few times before breaking the silence. "It's quiet, certainly. And that's unusual?"

"Of course," Uldane said. "There should at least be birds singing down by the river."

"I see. In the Underdark, silence is normal. If you hear something moving, it's probably coming to kill you."

"Good grief," Shara said. "What a terrible place!"

"On the other hand," Quarhaun added, a thoughtful look on his face, "if you don't hear something moving, there's probably still something coming to kill you."

"That might be what we're looking at here," Shara said. "Weapons out, eyes and ears open. Aerin's Crossing is just a little farther. Maybe we'll get a better idea what's going on."

Aerin's Crossing was the beginning of the town of Fallcrest, more or less. If nothing else, it was distinguished from the more southerly farms by the fact that it usually appeared on maps of the town. A half dozen smaller farms clustered around the crossing where River Road met the Old Ford Road, which ran through all of Lowtown on the other side of the river, then wound up the bluffs, passed the stables in Hightown, and left the Wizard's Gate to the east.

If Aerin's Crossing lies in ruins, Shara thought, *then we know there's trouble.*

They walked through the woods with as much caution as if they'd been exploring a monster-filled dungeon. Shara kept listening for any sound of the normal animal life of the forest, but the silence held, broken only by their own footsteps and Quarhaun's ragged breathing.

She smelled the smoke just a few paces before the forest fell away and gave her a clear view of the ravaged farms around Aerin's Crossing. Scattered fires still smoked on the fields nearby and the orchards on the north side of the crossroad. The houses were marked by plumes of black smoke rising to darken the sky, while no wall of the structures remained intact.

"Oh, no," she breathed.

"I can't believe it," Uldane said. "What could have done this?"

"What else? Vestapalk and the demons."

"I don't know," Quarhaun said. "We haven't seen the demons burning things before. It's easy to blame catastrophe on the evil you know. But the longer you keep yourself in that delusion, the longer the unknown evil has to plot against you."

"What is that, a drow proverb?" Shara asked.

Quarhaun shrugged. "Loosely translated."

"Well, there are plenty of evils we know of. But it's a fair point—there might be a new player on the scene, a red dragon or a fire giant."

"Or a marauding army of orcs or gnolls," Uldane added.

"A crazed cult of the Fire Lord," Quarhaun suggested with a sidelong grin at the halfling.

"So we stay alert and ready for anything," Shara said. "No delusions, no surprises."

"There's always surprises," Uldane said brightly.

CHAPTER NINETEEN

With Captain Damar's permission, Albanon led Kri out of Moorin's Glowing Tower and into the streets of Fallcrest. Though the sky was only hinting at the approach of dawn, frightened and desperate looking people were everywhere. Families huddled together for warmth against the autumn chill, taking shelter under the eaves of the larger buildings as they snatched at sleep. A few people just stumbled around, wide-eyed with shock, oblivious to the cold and dark.

"The Tower of Waiting," Kri said, for the fourth or fifth time. "It's on an island, yes?"

"Correct. We'll go to the Upper Quays and find a boat to take us over to the island."

"How far to the quays?" Kri asked.

"Across town," Albanon said. "A quarter of a mile, perhaps?"

"Quickly!"

Albanon quickened his pace, striding along the Bluff Ridge Road toward the river. Fear and anxiety welled in his chest and gripped his stomach. The town was unlike anything he'd ever experienced, the fear of its people hanging over the streets like smoke. Moorin had occasionally shared stories from his childhood, in the dark decades after the fall of Nerath and the Bloodspear War, that suggested such horrors as Fallcrest was now experiencing, but to Albanon they had been nothing more than stories, coated with the romance of memory of the distant past.

As he walked, his eyes met the despairing gaze of so many refugees—people, citizens of the town, who had lost family members, their homes, all their worldly possessions in this attack. Here and there he saw people laid low with illness, sleeping in alleys for lack of a safe sickbed. Some had great sores on their skin, and on one young man he saw a distinctive crust of red crystals growing around the sores.

For seven years, Fallcrest had been Albanon's home as he studied with Moorin, and he felt their pain. It wasn't the same town he had left behind in such a hurry, and it might never be the same even if the demons were driven off or destroyed.

"If the demons are all over Lowtown," Albanon said, "what's Nu Alin doing in the Tower of Waiting? Commanding Vestapalk's troops?"

"You saw the demons at the Temple of Yellow Skulls," Kri said. "Calling them troops implies some kind of order in the horde. Most of them are stupid brutes. I expect they have pack leaders, but I think Nu Alin has other purposes in the tower."

"But won't the tower be crawling with demons? What makes you think we can even get to it?"

"I suspect most of the demons are busy spreading chaos and destruction in Lowtown," Kri said. "A stealthy approach should serve us well, and if that fails, well, they should not underestimate our power."

"There's only the two of us," Albanon said. "And no one to keep the demons from getting too close."

"The demons that frighten the Fallcrest guard pose no such great threat to the likes of us."

"I hope you're right."

"I'm right," Kri said. "Now walk faster!"

Albanon quickened his steps again, though he was getting short of breath. "Why such a terrible hurry?"

"My divination revealed that Nu Alin was in the Tower of Waiting, but that was nearly five hours ago. He could be anywhere now, but the quicker we get to the tower, the less likely it is he'll have moved by then."

"I see." Talking was becoming too much of an effort, so Albanon concentrated on keeping up his pace and finding the quickest path to the Upper Quays.

He turned off the Bluff Ridge Road onto the Tombwood Road, which ran along the ancient forest that cloaked the southern slopes of Moonstone Hill, the site of the Lord Warden's estate. Before long, the forest crowded close to the road on their right, and the temple of Erathis stood proud on the left. The temple was brightly lit, and Albanon suspected that many of the plague-struck had found beds and care in the massive stone structure, the town's largest temple.

"There's a shrine to Ioun in the temple," he told Kri. "Do you feel the need to pause for prayer?"

"Don't be an idiot," Kri growled.

Albanon's face flushed and he hung his head, pushing himself to a still faster pace. Kri's words stung. As harsh a master as Moorin could be at times, he was never so outright insulting. *I was just trying to be helpful*, he protested in his mind.

The House of the Sun was the next major landmark along the road, an old temple of Pelor that lay abandoned for many years after the Bloodspear War. Moorin had always spoken with amusement—and a fair amount of appreciation—of the new priest who had reopened the temple, a firebrand dwarf named Grundelmar. Grundelmar's zeal for searching out the evil that lurks in the dark places of the world had appealed to Moorin's adventuresome past, and the few times that Albanon had heard the dwarf speak, he'd always come away longing for adventure.

I think maybe I've had enough adventure now, he thought. *Let me spend a few years in Sherinna's library when this is all over, and then maybe I'll be ready for another adventure.*

"We're almost there," he told Kri as they passed the House of the Sun. "See the warehouses ahead? The Upper Quays are just past them."

Kri nodded. In the predawn stillness, Albanon could hear the river rushing and the roar of the falls farther downstream. Firelight filled the sky behind the warehouses, and as he rounded a warehouse, he saw the bonfires and bright torches lining the quays. Soldiers stood by every fire, peering into the darkness and clutching their spears.

"Forget the demons," Albanon muttered. "Can we get past Fallcrest's defenders?"

"They'll let us through," Kri said. "But we need a boat first."

"Right. Follow me." Albanon turned to the right and made for the quay near the town's north wall. Fishers tended to gather there, where they could venture onto the river at a safe distance from the falls, and Albanon had heard adventurers in the Blue Moon Alehouse talk about hiring a fisher to ferry them out to explore the Tower of Waiting.

That seems like ages ago, he thought. *I wonder what happened to them at the tower.*

"No one is on the river," Kri observed.

Albanon followed the old priest's gaze out to the water. It was hard to see into the dark past the watchfires on the quay, and he couldn't make out any sign of boats on the river. He shrugged. "It's early yet."

But when they reached the place where Albanon expected to find fishers readying their gear and launching their boats, the water was just as deserted. He did spot a cluster of sun-weathered men and women, mostly humans and halflings, sitting around a table near the water and looking out at the river.

"Pardon me," he said, hurrying closer to the group. "My friend and I are looking to hire a boat."

The table erupted in laughter. "Are you mad?" a halfling woman asked. "No one is leaving Hightown."

"We just need to get to the Tower of Waiting."

"Is the guard at the Tower of Waiting?" a human man said. "Are they patrolling the river?"

"I don't understand—"

"The guard is keeping Hightown safe," the halfling woman said. "Beyond Hightown—that's where the monsters are."

Kri huffed impatiently. "Is there anyone here who will ferry us to the tower or not?" he said.

The fishers looked around at each other, then the halfling woman turned back to Kri. "Not," she said.

"Thank you. Come, Albanon, let us find someone who will."

"Good luck," someone called after them. Albanon started to look back, but Kri grabbed his arm and yanked him on.

"We have no time to waste with such impertinent oafs," the priest said.

"But, Kri, if the fishers aren't even going out on the river—"

"We'll find a way. We must."

Albanon sighed and followed Kri down the quay, scanning the wharves for anyone who might be able to help them. The sky was lightening with dawn's approach, and he started to be able to make out the shape of the island and its crumbling tower out in the middle of the river. No lights shone from inside the tower, but that didn't mean much. Local legend held that the tower had been used at the empire's height as a prison for the members of noble families who fell on the wrong side of political disputes. That would probably mean the tower had extensive dungeons underground. If Nu Alin and his allies or lackeys were there, they could burn a thousand torches and not reveal a light outside the tower walls.

"You there, soldier!" Kri called, striding toward a member of the guard who stood on the quay.

The soldier jumped, obviously tightly wound by the strain of watching for attack. "What is it?" he said.

"We seek a boat to take us to the Tower of Waiting," Kri said.

"Are you mad?" the guard answered.

Kri growled. "I tire of hearing that question," he said. "Do you know where we can hire a boat?"

The guard scratched under the edge of his helmet. "Did you check with the fishers at the north end of the quay?"

"If you mean that listless bunch of layabouts more interested in gossip and mockery than earning a day's wages, then yes, we spoke with them. They were utterly useless."

The soldier looked distinctly uncomfortable, glancing first to Albanon and then to the nearby soldiers for support, but he found none. "Well, then," he said. "I suppose you might try purchasing a boat."

"And why would I do that? I don't want to make a living fishing, I just want to get to the Tower of Waiting."

Albanon stepped between Kri and the shrinking soldier. "Where might we be able to purchase a small boat?" he asked.

The soldier visibly relaxed, and he beamed at Albanon. "There's a boatwright at the south end of the quay, near the bridge."

"Thank you for your help." Albanon took Kri's arm and led him on down the quay.

"What was that about?" the priest demanded. "We don't need a boat of our own."

"I think we might. If things are as bad as they seem here, I don't think we're going to find anyone willing to risk their lives to take us out to the island."

"Are the demons in the water?"

"I don't know, but we do know that at least one demon is in the Tower of Waiting."

"Or was, five hours ago."

"Or was. In any case, I can hardly blame them for being unwilling to venture to the island. I'm not even certain I want to go there."

"What?"

"I've seen Nu Alin before. You haven't. You didn't see what he did to Moorin, and you haven't seen the strength he gives to the bodies he inhabits. He's terrifying."

Kri drew himself up with anger. "Where is the courage you showed at the Whitethorn Spire? You choose to abandon me now?"

"No, no. I didn't say I wouldn't go with you—just that I don't want to. No one with any sense would want to, knowing what awaits us there. But I'm going anyway, because we have to. If we don't destroy him, if we don't break the siege, if we don't drive off the demons, then who will?"

"No one will."

"Exactly. We're all that remains of the Order of Vigilance. And so we must stand and fight."

Kri smiled, his anger faded. "That's right. Our oath is all that stands between the world and its annihilation."

Albanon looked quizzically at the old priest. "What oath?"

Kri stopped in his tracks and slapped his forehead with his palm. "Stones of Ioun, I can't believe I forgot," he said.

"I grew too distracted in Sherinna's tower, and neglected to teach you more about the order. I should have administered your oath while we were there."

"What is the oath? Tell me now."

"The Oath of Vigilance. To watch at all times for the appearance of the abyssal plague, the Voidharrow. To learn and pass on the traditions of the order. To fight against the creatures of the plague whenever and wherever they appear. And to guard against the construction of a new Vast Gate and its opening. We carry on Sherinna's mission, as poorly as she herself understood it."

"I swear," Albanon said earnestly. He fell to his knees and bowed his head. "I swear the Oath of Vigilance, and promise to live up to the highest demands of the order."

"You're a fool, Albanon," Kri said, but this time Albanon was sure he heard a note of pride in the old priest's voice.

CHAPTER TWENTY

Shara led the way past Aerin's Crossing, through another desolate stretch of silent woods, to the foot of the bluffs. The road wound back and forth up the bluff from there to more farms and orchards, and then to the Nentir Inn. Looking up the cliffside, she dreaded what she would find at the top. The darkening late afternoon sky had afforded her little view of the town across the river, but from what she'd seen, Lowtown seemed deserted as well. Quarhaun's description of returning home to find his city completely destroyed kept resurfacing in her thoughts, and she started trying to imagine what it would mean if Fallcrest had been obliterated. What would it mean for trade in the Nentir Vale? For the precarious balance between civilization and the monstrous races and savage tribes of the region? And what town in the region would fall next?

"How are you holding up, Quarhaun?" she asked the drow.

He sighed. "I'm tired. That bed you were talking about earlier is sounding better and better."

"Well, at the top of this bluff we'll either find beds or else discover that there's no safe place to rest left in Fallcrest. Can you make it up this road?"

Quarhaun looked up at the road. "It doesn't look all that steep," he said. "I think . . ." He frowned, staring up.

"What is it?" Shara tried to follow his gaze.

"I thought I saw something moving up there."

"Where?"

Quarhaun pointed, and Shara leaned in close to gain the same vantage on his pointing finger that he had.

"You see where the road bends the second time?" His breath was warm in her ear, and she had some trouble keeping her eyes and her mind focused. "There's a bush there, see it?"

Shara nodded, speechless.

"I thought I saw movement around the bush, the branches shaking. It might have just been a rat or lizard, I don't know."

"But we haven't seen any other living thing in more than half a mile of walking," Shara said, pulling away from Quarhaun and shaking off the distracting effect of his nearness, but keeping her eyes trained on the spot he'd identified.

"I don't see anything," Uldane said.

Shara shook her head. "Neither do I. But that doesn't mean there's nothing there. Stay on guard as we ascend. This would not be a good place to get attacked."

"Then it logically follows that this is where we will be attacked," Quarhaun said.

"Logically follows?" Shara said. "If you're suspicious to the point of madness, perhaps."

"I don't know about the point of madness, but that kind of suspicion is what lets drow live to see adulthood."

"How can you live like that? Expecting attack around every corner?"

"All I mean is that if there's something here and it's going to attack us, it makes sense that it would choose this road to launch its attack. It's a defensible position and puts us at a strong disadvantage, particularly if the attacker is better at navigating the cliff than we are."

"What's your advice, then?" Shara asked, exasperated.

"Is there another way up?"

"We could ford the stream and pass through Lowtown. Two other roads lead up the bluffs, but they're just like these."

"In the absence of a better option, then, we climb the road here. But instead of hoping we don't get attacked, we prepare for an ambush. That way, with luck, we stay alive."

Shara nodded. "All right. I'm going first. I need both of you behind me with your eyes wide open—especially you, Uldane. You'll notice any attackers long before I do. When they strike, they'll probably come from front and back, to make sure we can't flee down the road. So Quarhaun, you have to be ready to cover our rear. Uldane, stick to throwing your dagger, unless you can get around behind them on the narrow road."

"Fine," Quarhaun said. "But I think you're forgetting something."

"What's that?"

"You've planned for an attack from two directions. What if they come from three directions, or four? Or what if they come only from the top and bottom, scaling the cliffside?"

Shara blinked, trying to imagine what sort of ambush Quarhaun was used to.

Evidently Quarhaun could discern her thoughts. "My people have been known to ride giant spiders that cling to walls as easily as walking on the floor," he said. "With a large enough attacking force, we would come from all four sides in a situation like this."

"Then what defense do you recommend?"

"If there's that many of them, we're in trouble."

"You're really not helpful, you know that?" Shara started up the road. "Let's go. We're overthinking this. If we get attacked, we kill them all."

"Because that plan worked so well in the swamp," Uldane grumbled.

"We're still alive, aren't we?" Shara said.

"Sure, I'll take blind luck over careful strategy any time." The halfling couldn't hide his smile.

"Good, because I think that's all we have."

Shara found herself remembering her conversation with Uldane in the swamp ruins, discussing the day Jarren and her father died. She tried to remember the hours before the dragon attacked, the trek through the forest, the jovial banter that made up the fabric of their bond as a group, an adventuring party. They'd shared a rapport that was so hard to come by, but so easy to relax into. She still had it with Uldane, most of the time, but with Quarhaun—somebody always seemed to say something wrong, and somebody else felt hurt or took offense.

She and Jarren had shared more than a comfortable rapport, of course. Even in the moments before the dragon's attack, he'd given her one of his smoldering looks, and she'd brushed against him with a suggestive smile. By all the gods, how I miss him, she thought, wracked with the familiar ache of his absence.

Quarhaun's eyes seemed to be developing a certain smolder, too, and that left her . . . confused. Even more perplexing was the reaction his touch seemed to stir up in her, from the raw physical yearning to the damned schoolgirl blushing, which she wished she could just turn off.

She rounded the first switchback in the road, and realized she'd been ignoring her own orders, walking up the bluffs with her mind on anything but the threat of ambush. She glanced back at Uldane and Quarhaun to make sure they were paying better attention, and the drow met her gaze with a sly grin. Ignoring him, she tried to clear her mind of her other thoughts and stay alert.

Despite her best efforts, she found her mind drifting back to Quarhaun, thinking about that grin, his breath in her ear, his hand on her chin. She tried to also remind herself about his snide comments to Uldane, his outrageous attitude about the lizardfolk being expendable, and his apparent acceptance of bloodthirsty drow politics, but her mind kept coming back to the way his eyes lingered on her.

When the demons leaped out near the second switchback, she was almost relieved.

A good fight will get my blood flowing, she thought, *and not so much to my brain.*

Then her thoughts fled entirely, replaced by paralyzing fear as the nearest demon, a creature of shadow and burning blood, tore into her mind.

Roghar and Tempest rode toward Fallcrest on the King's Road from the west. The late afternoon sun cast long shadows in front of them, and the forest that lined the wood was draped in a cloak of silence and darkness.

"It's awfully quiet," Roghar said. He didn't expect an answer—Tempest had spoken little on their long journey from Nera. At times he'd almost wished he'd been traveling alone. At least then, he could sing at the top of his lungs without feeling like he was disturbing someone.

"It's not right," Tempest said.

Roghar looked around in surprise at her reply. She was peering into the woods around them, a frown creasing her brow.

"There's an unnatural presence here," she said. She met his gaze, and the anguish in her eyes drove his smile away. "It's him."

"You can feel his presence?" Roghar said.

"Not exactly. But I can feel the wrongness, all around. Can't you?"

Roghar closed his eyes and drew a deep breath through his nostrils. The smell of autumn decay and fresh earth filled his nose, but there was something more—acrid smoke, not the warm scent of hearth-fires but the sharp odor of destruction. He closed his eyes and reached for whatever sense could detect "wrongness," and felt a warm tingling at the back of his skull. Then nausea seized his stomach and cold fear gnawed at his chest.

"Oh, *that* wrongness," he said, blinking.

"We should ride," Tempest said.

From the look on her face, Roghar wasn't sure whether she meant ride ahead to discover the source of the wrongness or turn around and ride away as fast as their horses could carry them. He cocked his head at her.

"I don't know if I can do this," she said, slumping in her saddle.

After their encounter with the cult of the Chained God in Nera, Tempest had stayed in bed for three days, sleeping—or at least pretending to sleep whenever Roghar came to check on her. Finally, he had forced her to look at him and argued the case that they should return to the Nentir Vale. If the demonic influence had spread as far as Nera, then it appeared they could not flee far enough to escape it forever. It was far better, he argued, to return to the Vale and confront it at its source. In Fallcrest, he argued, they had other friends who could help them, and the mention of Albanon seemed to finally start to sway her.

It had taken all of Roghar's powers of persuasion, but he'd finally convinced Tempest that no other course of action would ever bring her peace and close out that chapter of her life. And so they had ridden for weeks from the old capital out to the frontier of the fallen empire, where the nightmare had begun.

"It's the only way," he reminded her, as gently as he could given the harsh reality of her situation.

"Remember your promise," she said, meeting his eyes.

Roghar nodded slowly. The only way he'd been able to convince her to come to Fallcrest was by swearing a solemn oath that if she ended up possessed or infected in some way by the vile red liquid, he would kill her without hesitation. He wasn't sure he could actually carry out this promise, but he had sworn it and so he supposed he must.

But he earnestly hoped he wouldn't have to.

Apparently satisfied, Tempest coaxed her horse back into motion. Roghar spurred his black stallion ahead of her, turning over in his mind the significance of the nausea and fear he had tasted.

The road wound around the base of Aranda Hill to come into Fallcrest from the north. Roghar recognized the point on the road, just ahead, where they would come out of the curve and be able to see straight down the road to the Nentir Inn. He called it the homecoming spot, the point where he always announced that he'd arrived. The thought of the inn made his body ache with longing for a soft, warm bed and a real dinner.

He kept his eyes fixed on the road ahead, and a grin of excitement spread across his face as he neared the homecoming spot, but he closed his eyes in the moment he reached it. "We're home," he said with a sigh, then opened his eyes.

The Nentir Inn was in flames, pouring smoke into the sky.

Tempest rode up beside him and stared with him at the wreckage of the inn. They exchanged a glance, then together spurred their mounts and galloped down the road. Even before they reached it, Roghar could see that they were too late to do anything. The building was an empty husk already, withered beams and posts standing above blackened fieldstone. A moment later, he realized that no one was fighting the fire—no one was even watching the inn burn down.

"Tempest, wait," he called, reining in his horse.

"What?" She slowed, but didn't stop her chestnut mare. "We have to help!"

He shook his head. "There's no help for it now. I think it's a trap."

She looked at the inn and back at Roghar, then came to a stop. He caught up with her and pointed at the burning inn.

"There's no one there," he said. "Where's Erandil?" The half-elf Erandil Zemoar had built the Nentir Inn only a few years ago. "You think he'd let his new inn burn down without even watching it? Where's the watch? Where are the spectators drawn to the disaster like moths to flame?"

"You're right," Tempest said. "That is strange. But a trap?"

"I think someone lit the fire in hopes of drawing people here to fight it."

"So what do we do?"

Roghar thought for a moment, then dismounted. "Leave the horses," he said. "Once we clear the forest, we make a wide circle around the inn and see if we can catch whoever is lying in wait."

Tempest slid out of her saddle and nodded. "Let's do it."

Roghar took her reins and led both horses off the road, where he draped the reins around a low tree branch. It would keep the horses in place for a little while, but if he and Tempest didn't come back, they'd free themselves eventually and find their own way to safety. He patted his stallion's flank and left the horses.

They hugged the forest rather than walking along the road, alert for any sound among the trees, but not even a squirrel or bird rustled in the leaves as they drew closer to the burning inn. Tempest signaled a stop just before the road left the shelter of the woods, then she drew the afternoon shadows around herself in a concealing cloak and stepped to the edge of the trees.

The inn had its own fire apple orchard, and two small farms shared the clearing on this part of the river's west bank. The road ran straight to the inn and then forked, with the left branch crossing the Five-Arch Bridge into Hightown and the right passing the farms before winding down the bluff toward Aerin's Crossing.

Tempest scanned the clearing and then waved Roghar forward. He moved as quietly as he could, but he was under no illusions about his capacity for stealth—his bulk, the weight of his armor, and the tendency of the metal plates to clank against each other despite their padding combined to make him easy to spot and especially easy to hear. He chose a path through the fields, aiming to pass close by the two farmhouses on the west side of the road.

"You don't want to keep to the shelter of the trees?" Tempest asked.

"If they're hiding in the farmhouses while they watch the road and the inn, maybe we can catch them off guard. At the edge of the woods, we'll be too far away to see them."

Roghar felt the tension in every muscle of his body. This was not his preferred way to face danger—he would rather have charged at top speed toward an obvious foe, sword in hand and divine power at the ready. Sneaking around didn't sit well with him, and waiting for enemies to reveal themselves made him anxious. Tempest seemed much more at ease, moving swiftly and all but silently through the fields, barely even making the corn sway as she passed. For all her earlier trepidation, she was facing imminent danger without a moment's hesitation.

They reached the first of the farmhouses without incident. Roghar peered in the back windows and found the home dark and apparently deserted. It seemed intact, though, so he doubted that attackers were lurking inside. After a cursory glance, he nodded to Tempest and they moved on.

As they drew near the second farmhouse, Roghar heard the sounds of fighting—the clash of steel, explosions of magic, and a great deal of shouting. It was distant, coming from somewhere off to the south, roughly where the road wound down the bluffs. He looked at Tempest, and she smiled at him.

"Sounds like your kind of fight," she said.

He returned the smile. "Let me make sure there's nothing in this farmhouse, then we'll see who's in trouble on the bluffs."

"It's the first sound of other living creatures we've heard in the last half hour," Tempest said.

Roghar nodded and broke into a run. Even before he reached the second farmhouse, he could see that it was the same as the first—dark, abandoned, empty. He signaled to Tempest and changed course, running full out toward the sounds of fighting. His body started feeling better at once, the exertion of the run soothing the tension from his muscles.

As soon as he reached the bluff and looked down, he saw the fight raging—and recognized two of the fighters.

"Shara!" he shouted. "Uldane!" His friends were locked in a struggle with dark figures of shadow laced with the same glowing red liquid that was becoming all too familiar. A white-haired, dark-skinned man in black leather fought alongside them, but it was obvious that he was using his last reserves of strength—and Shara and Uldane weren't doing too well, either.

Rather than wind his way carefully down the road, Roghar slid down the bluff with a yell, bouncing and rattling as he went but thrilling at the battle ahead.

My kind of fight, indeed, he thought, smiling.

CHAPTER TWENTY-ONE

As Kri grumbled, arms folded across his chest, Albanon paid the princely sum of sixty gold pieces to the boatwright in exchange for a simple wooden rowboat. Calling plenty of attention to his own generosity, the boatwright threw in the oars and a coil of sturdy rope for mooring at no additional charge. Kri shook his head all the way as he and Albanon wrestled the boat out the door and down to the quay.

"We should have paid a few silvers for a ride," Kri said as they lowered the boat into the water.

"But there were no rides to be had for silver or gold," Albanon said, shrugging. "The money doesn't matter."

"It should. A frugal nature is essential to the development of good moral character."

Albanon stared at Kri.

"It is!" Kri protested. "Do you want to be one of those prodigal adventurers who returns from every expedition laden with cash and proceeds to spend every copper piece in a fortnight, drinking up the town's supply of ale and enriching its thieves and con artists?"

Albanon knew exactly the kinds of adventurers the old priest meant. He'd often sat in the Blue Moon Alehouse listening to their tales and dreaming of their adventures. In fact, he would have put Roghar and Tempest into that category before he got to know them. It didn't seem like such a terrible life, as he thought about it.

Kri continued his rant. "Do you think such people spend their days in careful study before carousing through the town at night? Do you think they're prepared for the dangers they face, the dangers that threaten the world? How long do you suppose such adventurers tend to live?"

"N-not long, I suppose." A brief, glorious fire burning in the night.

Kri fixed him with a level gaze. "A true hero will light the world for ages, Albanon."

Albanon started. Did I say that out loud? he wondered. He half-expected Kri to answer his unspoken question, but the priest had returned to the work of coiling the rope.

"I don't think I ever imagined myself as a hero," he said. "I just wanted excitement."

Kri looked up from the rope. "But you've grown up since Moorin's death, haven't you?"

"I suppose I have. I've grown in so many ways."

"Nothing is holding you back now."

The thought quickened Albanon's pulse. What might I accomplish now? What heights of power might I reach?

Together they lowered the boat into the water. Albanon clambered down into it, then held the boat steady as Kri stepped in. Albanon wrangled the oars into position and pushed off from the quay, out into the dark water.

"Do you suppose there are demons in the water?" he asked Kri.

"Use your senses."

Albanon blinked in surprise. "I didn't even think of trying that outside the Feywild."

"Magic flows through the world as well. It might not be as strong or as vibrant, but it's there."

Albanon stopped rowing and closed his eyes. He felt it immediately, a current of power that ran through the river, as real as the current of rushing water. Kri was right—it wasn't as strong as what he'd felt at Sherinna's tower, but with a deep breath and an effort of will he was able to sense the weave of magic and the bright spots that marked his place and Kri's in that weave. No dark tangles of demonic power stood out in his view, but he noticed something different about Kri's brightness, a different hue or tone to it that he couldn't quite define.

He opened his eyes and found Kri staring at him.

"What did you see?" the priest asked.

"I believe the river is safe," Albanon said, looking away from Kri's penetrating eyes.

"Not if we go over the waterfall."

Albanon looked around and saw the torches lining the Five-Arch Bridge much closer than they had been. He started rowing again, fighting against the current to take their little boat away from the bridge and back on course toward the island.

"Can you see the island?" Kri asked.

Albanon nodded.

"That's good. I can't see a thing out here."

"Eladrin eyes." For some reason Albanon started thinking of the mural's depiction of Sherinna in her power and grace, the opalescent blue orbs of her eyes shining with wisdom. "Kri, who inducted you into the Order of Vigilance?"

"I had two teachers. The first was a paladin of Pelor named Channa. She was killed while trying to reclaim Gardmore Abbey from the orcs that hold it now. So a knight named Harad completed my training. The members of the order were more numerous then, so it was not difficult to find a new teacher."

"How many generations of teachers and students have passed down Sherinna's legacy?" Albanon asked.

"That's not easy to measure. Sherinna, along with Brendis and Miri, taught eight disciples, the founding members of the order. One was an eladrin who taught an eladrin student who only died a decade or so ago—so that's only two generations. Traced back through Harad, my lineage is more like six generations."

"I wonder what she was like."

"Sherinna?"

"My grandmother, yes."

"Well, I would imagine that she was something like your father and something like you."

Albanon tried to imagine what such a person might be like, searching for the qualities he most admired in his father—his magical power, his authority—and what he thought were his own best qualities, his adventuresome spirit and his loyalty to his friends. He decided that

Sherinna had led her little adventuring band with a firm but compassionate hand, that her magic had proved the decisive factor in their many battles, and that Brendis had harbored a deep but forbidden love for her.

Smiling at the image he'd constructed, he steered the rowboat into a little cove on the island. He handed the oars to Kri, picked up the coil of rope, and jumped for the shore, falling a few feet short and landing with a splash in ice-cold water up to his hips. Bracing himself against the cold, he waded to dry land and pulled the boat close, coiling the rope around a large rock. He held out a hand to help Kri to shore, then worked a simple magic cantrip to dry his clothes.

"Welcome to the Tower of Waiting," Albanon said.

"Excellent. I hope the demon is still here."

Albanon remembered the demon's strength when, in the form of a halfling even smaller than Uldane, it had grabbed and held Tempest, digging its fingers into her neck. He remembered the cracks around the halfling's eyes where the red liquid oozed and glowed, and the terrible wounds all over the body, filled with the same substance. And he remembered the demon flowing out of Tempest's nose and mouth as she lay dying. He could not echo Kri's hope, as much as he longed to be the kind of hero the priest had described.

Albanon conjured a light at the tip of his staff to illuminate their path to the tower's gaping entrance, knowing it would attract attention to them but unwilling to consign Kri to stumbling in the darkness. An overgrown gravel walkway led from the cove up to the crumbling tower.

Swallowing his fear, Albanon led the way, holding his glowing staff high. Shadows seemed to flit at the edge of his light, sinister shapes manifesting in the darkness but never venturing close enough to be clearly seen.

"They say the Tower of Waiting is haunted," Albanon said.

"Do they?"

"It was a prison once, more than a century ago, a place where the Lord Warden would put members of noble families who were too powerful or important to be killed. Supposedly some young princess was arrested on charges of demon worship and locked up here, but she hanged herself—or some say the demon she served appeared and killed her himself. Come to think of it, I've heard a lot of stories about her, most of them pretty sordid."

"And hers is the ghost they say haunts the tower?"

"Yes."

"There is often a nugget of truth to such stories, Albanon. But there is rarely more than a nugget. Vigilance demands discernment, the ability to sort the truth from the exaggerations and elaborations."

Albanon frowned, feeling puzzled. "But we are not here to deal with a ghost."

"Aren't we?"

"Well, I did wonder if perhaps the demon has used this place as a lair long enough to be the nugget of truth behind the ghost stories."

"Exactly. That kind of reasoning will get you far."

Albanon shrugged. "I'm not so sure. The demon broke into Moorin's tower looking for the vial of the Voidharrow that Moorin inherited from the order. If it had been in

Fallcrest long enough to start ghost stories, why wait until this year to attack Moorin?"

"One way or another, there are three hundred years during which the demon's activities and whereabouts are a mystery, between the time that Sherinna first encountered it and when it appeared in Moorin's tower. If it was not in Fallcrest, where was it? Wherever it was, why did it wait until this year to recover the Voidharrow from Moorin's tower?"

"What have you learned about the Voidharrow, Kri? What is it?"

"Another time, young wizard."

Albanon stopped and turned to face Kri, his feet crunching on the gravel. "No," he said. "Moorin kept information from me all the time. 'You're not ready, my apprentice,'" he said in a mocking singsong version of his old mentor's voice. "No more secrets. I'm ready for whatever knowledge you have. You have to share it—both our lives could depend on it."

Kri looked taken aback by the passion of Albanon's appeal, and Albanon almost apologized out of reflex. But he held his ground, trying to look confident and mature, ready for whatever terrible secrets the priest might decide to bestow on him.

Finally Kri nodded. "I apologize for giving you the impression that I was trying to shield you from any of the reality of what we face. In truth, I was just thinking that this was perhaps not the best spot for this particular conversation, and the urgency of our errand makes it also not the best time."

Albanon felt his face redden. "I'm sorry," he said. "I guess I'm a little sensitive about that."

"Of course you are," Kri said, clapping his shoulder. "Moorin held back your growing power in so many ways. Please know that I don't want to do that to you. You deserve all the power you can claim—and the knowledge that will help you attain it."

"Thank you, Kri. Moorin taught me a great deal—"

"Of course, of course."

"—but you're right. He was holding me back. Nothing is going to hold me back anymore."

"That's exactly right," Kri said. "Nothing can."

A shadowy form loomed up right behind Kri, great black wings rising up behind the priest like a dark angel. Crimson eyes smoldered like hot coals in its face, and veins of scarlet crystal flowed through its body, suffusing the whole creature with dim red light. Albanon yelped and loosed a bolt of arcane force that struck the monster and tore wisps of its shadowy substance away.

Kri's eyes widened in surprise, but his body froze as the shadowy demon's hands clutched at his head. At the same time, a second creature swooped out of the darkness at Albanon, stretching huge, dark claws toward him. Albanon felt irrational fear surge through him, chilling his body and setting his pulse pounding in his ears.

The demon seemed energized by his fear, and some part of his mind that clung to rational thought in the face of it could discern how the creature was drawing on his fears and shaping them into a weapon to wield against him. Understanding the process didn't help him face it, however, when his nightmares took shape before him, where a moment before the shadowy demon had stood.

He saw a towering figure, rippling with muscle and covered in skin like the thorny flesh of a rose's stem. Its face was covered with a mask made from a beast's skull, but the demon's smoldering red eyes peered out through the mask at him. Enormous antlers rose from the figure's skull, and it clutched a hunting spear with a jagged head like a whaler's harpoon. The baying of fey hounds surrounded him, and Albanon's fear sapped the strength of his legs out from under him. He scrambled on the ground, trying to get away from the nightmare huntsman.

"Albanon, my son," the huntsman said, "you are a disappointment to me."

Albanon spread his fingers and bathed the figure in fire, but it strode forward as if completely oblivious to the flames, its flesh showing no signs of scorching. It lifted the spear and aimed the terrible point at Albanon's heart.

A burst of light like the dawning sun exploded around Albanon, tearing through the huntsman in front of him. As Albanon stared, its thorny flesh came off its bones in long ribbons as it howled its agony. Then it was only the shadowy demon again, and it appeared significantly diminished by Kri's radiant assault.

The light drove Albanon's fear away as well. He found his feet and drew in a breath, sensing in an instant the location of both demons—no, all three—another one was approaching. He paused a moment, until the third demon was close enough, then engulfed them all in an inferno of arcane fire that spread out from his outstretched arms and washed harmlessly around Kri. The demon nearest him crumbled away to ash, leaving a scattering of red crystal dust in the air that blew away in the wind.

The two remaining demons scattered to the edges of Albanon's light, gathering their strength or reassessing the threat that he and Kri posed. Albanon laughed at them and sent another magic bolt streaming into the nearer demon. "You don't want to fight us," he said. "You can't handle us."

As if in response, the two demons flew near each other and seemed to flow together, combining their substance into one larger form. As Albanon watched, the form twisted and changed, taking on the likeness of the demon they'd fought at Sherinna's tower.

"They chose something we both fear," Kri said.

"Less emotional impact, but probably more physical power," Albanon said.

"Good thinking. So we don't let it get close enough to exert that power."

As one, Albanon and Kri unleashed a firestorm of devastation on the demonic figure. Lightning crackled over its limbs, fire erupted in the air around it, thunder crashed and battered it, and divine radiance tore at its substance. As spell after spell erupted around it, it took a few slow, pained steps closer to them, then toppled to the ground. Its hulking body melted into the two smaller shadows, then their shadowy forms dissolved, leaving only crimson liquid, like crystalline blood, that pooled on the ground and then seeped away.

"And *that*," Kri said, "is the power of the Order of Vigilance."

Albanon laughed, exhilarated from the sensation of all that power coursing through his body. "That is the doom that awaits all the creatures of this abyssal plague," he said.

Kri stared darkly at the blasted circle of earth where the demons had died. "All will perish," he said.

CHAPTER TWENTY-TWO

Shara stared in terror at the apparition before her. It was Jarren—not as she remembered him in life but as she dreamed of him in her worst nightmares, his insides torn out by the claws of the dragon, his neck broken and his head lolling, his eyes fixed on her. "You fled the battle," he said, his voice harsh and rasping. "You left us to die."

"I—I'm sorry, I'm so sorry." Tears streaked her face and her sword clattered from her hand onto the road by her feet.

He stepped closer, reaching a hand toward her hair. "I loved you, Shara," he said. "I put my life in your hands."

"I know. I didn't mean to flee. We—Uldane and I, we rolled away from the dragon's breath, toward the river. We didn't know—none of us knew the river was so far down!"

"I trusted you, Shara. And now you're giving your love to him?" Jarren's bloody finger pointed behind her.

For a moment, Shara didn't know what he was talking about. Then she remembered that Quarhaun was behind her, and all at once she realized where she was and what she was doing. They'd been attacked—

And the thing in front of her wasn't Jarren's ghost. It was a demon, preying on her fear, giving form to her worst nightmares and using them to weaken her.

She roared in fury as she snatched her sword up from the ground and whirled it through the apparition of her lover. The ghost's eyes widened in shock at this new betrayal, but Shara ignored its face, concentrating on the movement of her blade. She sliced and stabbed until no semblance of Jarren remained, just a gaunt creature of shadow with glowing veins of liquid crystal. Then even its shadowy substance dissipated and the red crystal turned to dust, scattered on the ground.

Only then did she see Uldane, standing behind where the creature had been, daggers in his hands and a grin on his face.

"I wondered when you were going to snap out of it," the halfling said. "But now we'd better help Quarhaun."

She whirled around and saw the drow standing transfixed, staring at two smears of shadow in the air that reached dark claws toward his head. "Quarhaun!" she shouted. Her sword cut into both demonic shades, and Quarhaun seemed to come to his senses.

Quarhaun's sword burst into purple flame as his face twisted with fury and he lunged at the nearer of the two shadows that had held him entranced. Shara found herself wondering what he had seen, what terrible fear had paralyzed him, even as she helped him destroy the creature that had pillaged his nightmares. Two more shadowy figures appeared on the road, reaching their claws toward her, and she felt them in her head, trying to sift through her mind.

A racket on the bluff above her jolted her back to full attention, and she looked up to see a dragonborn sliding down the bluff, bouncing and rattling down the steep slope with a sword in his hand and a roar in his throat.

"Roghar!" she cried, delight at seeing her friend driving away the last tendrils of fear that had worked themselves into her mind.

Quarhaun looked up as well, then gave her a quizzical glance. "A friend?"

"Yes," she said. Her joy gave strength to her sword, and the demons fell back from her assault. "A paladin of Bahamut and a strong ally. These demons are doomed."

"If he doesn't kill himself on the way down," Quarhaun muttered.

Shara laughed. Then Roghar was beside her, hewing into the demons as divine light flared around him. The demons seemed particularly perturbed by that radiance, which tore at their shadowy substance and even seemed to make Shara's sword bite more easily into them. Two demons at once reached their claws toward Roghar's head, and he paused for a terrible moment as Shara watched the fear creep into his eyes. Then he shook his head and renewed his attack, undaunted by whatever vision of terror they had presented to him.

A moment later, a bolt of eldritch fire streaked down from the road above them, and Shara glanced up to see Tempest looking down at her. The fire slammed into one of the demons and consumed it, sending the last shreds of its substance hurtling down over the bluff. Quarhaun glanced up as well and cocked an eyebrow when he saw Tempest's curling horns.

"A tiefling warlock and a paladin of Bahamut?" he said. "An unusual pair."

Roghar and Shara maneuvered into a position that kept their friends sheltered from the demons' attacks, coordinating their movements with quick, simple signals. Shara smiled to herself at how good it felt to fight alongside someone skilled and reliable.

Sorry, Uldane, she thought. It's not the same.

Shara and Roghar kept the demons at bay, their blades hacking and slicing into their shadowy forms. Uldane darted around past them to cut at the demons, then back behind the protection they offered, shouting encouragement to everyone as he went. Quarhaun and Tempest riddled the demons with blasts of fire and bolts of dark lightning. In moments, the last demon dissipated into wisps of shadow and a scattering of red crystal droplets.

Laughing with the sheer pleasure of it, Shara threw her arms around Roghar. "The paladin rushes in to save the day!" she said. "Your timing was perfect."

"Well, I was in the neighborhood," Roghar said.

"And thought you'd drop in?" Uldane said with a grin.

Roghar dropped to one knee to embrace the halfling as well. "That was pretty terrible."

"I thought it was funny," the halfling said.

Tempest made her way down from the overhanging bluff and embraced Shara. "It's good to see familiar faces," the tiefling said. "Trouble seems to be afoot in Fallcrest."

"Do you know what's going on?" Shara asked her.

"Not yet. We just arrived and found the Nentir Inn in flames. We were circling around to investigate when we heard sounds of a fight."

"*I* heard the sounds," Roghar said, thumping his mailed fist on his armored chest with a clang. "And rushed to the rescue."

"And a good thing you did," Shara said. "We were outnumbered, and Quarhaun is still recovering from our last fight against these demons."

"So you would be Quarhaun," Roghar said, extending a hand to the drow.

Quarhaun looked down at the dragonborn's extended hand for a moment too long before he clasped it. "I am," he said.

"Oh, I'm sorry," Shara said. "Quarhaun, this is Roghar, and this is Tempest. We were thrown together on a past adventure."

"And now it appears that all our various adventures are connected," Roghar said with a scowl. He squatted down and poked at a tiny pool of red crystalline liquid left behind by one of the demons.

"Don't touch it!" Shara and Tempest exclaimed together.

"It's inert," Roghar said. "I think it's... dead, I guess."

"More of Vestapalk's spawn," Shara said. "Transformed by the Voidharrow."

"Vestapalk?" Roghar said. "The dragon? I thought you killed it." Roghar had been at her side that day, in the ruins of Andok Sur, when her blade had opened the dragon's belly and sent it hurtling down into a chasm opening beneath it.

"I killed it," Shara said. "Or at least I dealt it a mortal wound. But I also provided the means for its resurrection."

"What?" Tempest said.

"When I cut the dragon, it had the death knight in its claws. I cut open the death knight's belt pouch as I swung at the dragon, and a vial full of glittering red liquid came out. It was absurd, really, a coincidence that only an evil god's tricks could have orchestrated. The liquid spilled out of the vial and flowed into the dragon's wound. The Voidharrow, Kri called it."

"Kri?" Roghar asked.

"A priest of Ioun," Uldane said. "He showed up at Moorin's tower looking for that vial of the Voidharrow, which the death knight stole from the tower."

"The demon that . . . that took me," Tempest said. "It was looking for the Voidharrow, too. And it was made of the same substance."

"That demon is serving Vestapalk now," Shara said. "And helping the dragon spread what they called an abyssal plague. We've only seen them once—and actually, that's where we met Quarhaun. The dragon's minions had captured both Quarhaun and Albanon, and the dragon tried to transform them both with the Voidharrow."

"And since then," Uldane said, "we've encountered all kinds of demon creatures that have that same crystal stuff."

"We've fought them all over the Nentir Vale," Shara said.

Roghar scratched his chin. "It appears that this threat isn't confined to the Nentir Vale," he said. "We discovered a droplet of this Voidharrow in Nera."

"Then Vestapalk's reach has grown wide indeed," Shara said.

"Not necessarily," Tempest said. "The substance was in the keeping of a little cult of the Chained God. There was no other evidence of a connection to Vestapalk. It could have come from the same source as the vial the death knight carried."

"Kri did say that the Voidharrow was separated," Shara said. "Some of it was carried east, I think he said, while the rest was passed down until it came to Moorin. So maybe what you found came from that eastern portion."

"So what is it?" Roghar asked. "Where did it come from?"

Shara looked around and saw a circle of scowling faces. "More immediate questions first," she said. "What's happened to Fallcrest? And is there any safe place in the town where we can rest, or do we need to make camp at a safe distance outside?"

"Let's try the bridge," Roghar said. "I have a feeling the Nentir Inn was set ablaze as a lure."

"Trying to draw people out from their fortifications," Shara said, nodding. "And into a trap."

"We'd better make sure we don't get drawn into the trap," Quarhaun said.

"Right," Shara said. "At the top of the bluff, we cut through the woods and around the orchards behind the inn to the bridge."

"Sounds like a plan," Roghar said.

"At least the beginning of one," Quarhaun added.

The top of the bluff offered a fine view of the land Shara, Uldane, and Quarhaun had just passed through. Shara explained what they'd seen at Aerin's Crossing and the outlying farms, and nodded as Tempest described the eerie silence of the forest along the King's Road. Shara led the group on a path through another small wood, just as quiet, around to the riverside.

As soon as they emerged from the trees, Shara breathed a heavy sigh of relief. Across the river, Fallcrest's Hightown was bright with torchlight illuminating the bridge and the opposite shore against the approaching dark.

"So Fallcrest is not yet lost," she said.

"Just under siege," Roghar said.

Their path to the bridge along the riverside brought them past the fields of one more farm, and then into the fire apple orchards belonging to the Nentir Inn. Apples hung ripe on the trees, bright red and swollen with juice.

"Pick me an apple?" Uldane asked Shara.

"I suppose thieves in the orchard are the least of Erandil's worries tonight," she said. She plucked an apple from a low branch and tossed it to Uldane, who caught it and took a hungry bite, making little grunts of delight as he chewed.

Suddenly hungry, she picked an apple for herself as well and polished it on her cloak. Fire apples were named for their brilliant red color. She lifted it to her mouth, but paused with her mouth half open. Some insect or worm had gnawed at the fruit, tearing the skin and leaving a jagged wound. The blemish in the scarlet skin conjured images in her mind of rough crystal growths and crimson liquid.

The color of the Voidharrow.

She didn't feel hungry any more. Uldane didn't seem the least bit put out by the color, though, so she handed him her apple. "Here's one for later," she said.

"They're delicious," Uldane said, sliding the apple into a pouch at his belt.

"I'm glad."

As Roghar hurried into the northern wood to retrieve the horses, the rest of the group drew steadily closer to both the Five-Arch Bridge and the burning wreckage of the Nentir Inn. Shara kept alert, looking for ambushers hidden near the inn, but no demons leaped out from the trees to attack. Once she thought she saw something moving in the blackened husk of the inn itself—something besides the leaping flames, that is—but no threat materialized.

And they reached the bridge. About halfway across its fifty-yard span, a dozen bright torches marked the position of the soldiers posted to hold the bridge against the demons.

"Safety and a warm bed," Shara said with a sigh.

"Maybe for you," Quarhaun said.

She turned to look at the drow, who was eyeing the bridge uncertainly. "What do you mean?"

"I think the chances of those soldiers welcoming me to Fallcrest are slim. Is there another way into town?"

"Why wouldn't they welcome you?" Shara said.

"Because he's a drow," Uldane said. "It wouldn't be too much of a problem in normal circumstances. We'd vouch for you, they'd give you a warning not to act up, and that would be the end of it.

Quarhaun nodded. "But with the town under attack?" he said. "Not a chance."

"That's ridiculous," Shara said.

"You think so?" Quarhaun asked. "You don't know your people very well."

"My people? I'm from Winterhaven."

"We can disguise you," Uldane said. "Or just cover you up enough that they can't really see you."

"I don't think that's necessary," Roghar said, rejoining the group with the horses in tow. "If Shara and Uldane trust you, that's good enough for me, and I'll vouch for you to the guards. They'll heed the word of a paladin of Bahamut."

Quarhaun laughed, though there was no joy in it. "You two have seen what's happening here, right? Everything Shara and Tempest were saying? You saw the demons we fought? As far as those guards are concerned, I'm part of the town's troubles. I might as well be a demon myself."

"We'll wrap you up," Uldane said. "Like a mummy!"

"He's right, Roghar," Tempest said. "Even you have encountered your fair share of mistrust, especially in more remote villages where they don't see many dragonborn."

"And that mistrust vanishes when they see my shield and witness Bahamut's presence in me."

"Well," Quarhaun said, "if people mistrust dragonborn and fear tieflings, they loathe the drow. It's not that they haven't seen many drow—it's that they've seen them and learned to hate and fear them. And I don't have a divine dragon head on a shield to make people like me. What do I have? A warlock's eldritch blade, carved with symbols of the infernal power I wield. I'm sure that will help my cause."

"Then it seems you are reaping the benefits of the life you have chosen, warlock," Roghar said.

"Roghar," Shara began.

"The benefits of a life lived without divine meddling?" Quarhaun said. "I'll take them with all their drawbacks, if it means I'm not the pawn or plaything of some supreme machinator with nothing better to do than wreck people's lives."

Roghar drew himself up to his full height, nearly seven feet of scaled fury. "I am not Bahamut's pawn or plaything," he said. "I am his champion, his agent in the world."

"I fail to see the difference. I've seen many champions sacrifice themselves in the gambits of the meddling gods."

"Champions of what god? The Spider Queen? Certainly she is a schemer with no loyalty to her agents, but Bahamut—"

"You know him well? Speak with him personally? You're so sure he's better than Lolth?"

"Of course I am!"

"That's enough, you two," Shara said, planting herself, greatsword in hand, between them. "Theological questions are beyond the scope of the matter at hand."

Quarhaun opened his mouth to say something, but bit it back with a visible effort. Roghar slowly relaxed his aggressive stance.

"Maybe not like a mummy," Uldane said.

CHAPTER TWENTY-THREE

The Tower of Waiting stood dark and silent against the slowly brightening sky. The ancient doorway stood out as a slightly darker shadow in its side, gaping open and empty, the door long since broken down or rotted away. Albanon led the way into the tower, holding his glowing staff high and scanning the shadows at the edge of its light for more demons.

The interior of the tower was as different from the Whitethorn Spire as Albanon could imagine. Instead of a spacious, graceful entry chamber that stretched the entire height of the tower, he found a small, dark antechamber that was barely high enough for him to stand. Three more doorways led out of the chamber, each one cluttered with rubble from the tower's slow collapse.

"Which way?" Albanon said, glancing back at Kri.

The old priest started and snapped his head around to look at Albanon. "What?"

"I said, which way do we go? Is something wrong?"

"No . . . no. I don't think so."

"Kri? What is it?"

"There's something . . . do you hear something?"

Albanon listened, but all he could hear was Kri's breathing, uneven, a little heavy, nervous. He closed his eyes and extended his other senses to feel the flow of magic in the tower. In contrast to the sense of a fabric or weave he'd noted in the Feywild, or the flow he felt in the river, the tower itself seemed to his senses like a storm, furious but contained, magic churning within the confined space and flashing like lightning in places it was hard for him to pinpoint. Much of the energy seemed angry, perhaps malign or even demonic, but it was much harder to identify any specific source to it, a particular demon or anything else, than it had been in the Feywild.

"Whispers in the dark," Kri said, his own voice a harsh whisper.

Albanon opened his eyes. Kri was half crouched, clutching his morningstar, looking around wildly.

"I don't hear anything," Albanon said. "Kri, what's wrong?"

"I . . . I don't know. Something's wrong. Something's definitely wrong."

Albanon's heart was pounding. He'd never seen Kri like this—his new mentor was usually so calm, in command of himself and of all around him. Even in the grip of the urgency that had propelled them from the Whitethorn Spire to the Tower of Waiting, Kri had been in charge, barking commands and making plans. Now he appeared unable to complete a sentence.

So I need to take charge, Albanon thought. And why not? I am no longer an apprentice.

"It's all right, Kri," he said. "Just follow me, and we'll get to the heart of this. We'll find out what's wrong."

To his surprise, Kri listened to him. The old priest took a deep breath and seemed to steady himself, then nodded his readiness. Albanon tried to look confident and reassuring. He swept his gaze over the three doorways and chose the one directly ahead, stepping decisively to the empty arch and ducking his head to pass through.

The room beyond had evidently been a guard post—it was equipped with a broken wooden chair, a rack that still held rusting spears, and a large, solid-looking table. No other door led out, so Albanon sighed and shepherded Kri back out the door and through a different one.

This door led to a spiral staircase stretching both up and down, which Albanon reprimanded himself for not seeing earlier.

"Up or down?" he asked, looking at Kri but not expecting an answer.

"Down down down," Kri whispered.

Cold fear ran along Albanon's spine. The priest's voice was so different, and his demeanor so completely altered, that Albanon started to wonder whether he might have been possessed. "Kri?" he said.

Kri's eyes flicked to his and then looked away, back at the staircase. "Down," he mouthed.

"Very well," Albanon said. "Down we go."

The stairs twisted down over a hundred steps before Albanon forced himself to stop counting. Without the steady count of numbers in his mind, Albanon started hearing the same sinister whispers that Kri had been hearing upstairs. He started counting again, reaching forty-seven before arriving at the bottom.

A small stone chamber was lit only by the light of Albanon's staff. A hallway stretched off into the darkness opposite the stairs, and Albanon saw archways blocked by heavy iron bars. Cells, he thought. A low table in the chamber held an unlit candle and a length of thick chain with an open cuff at one end.

"An altar," Kri said.

Albanon looked at the table again. It bore no symbol he recognized, unless the chain related to the god of imprisonment. "To what god?" he said. "Torog?"

"Not the King that Crawls," Kri said. "Not with an open cuff. The Chained God."

The Chained God. Albanon had read stories of the god who turned against the other gods, who created the Abyss in his attempt to destroy the planes and all that dwelled in them, and who the gods had bound and imprisoned someplace beyond the planes, outside of reality. The events described in these legends were so ancient that the details were forgotten—perhaps intentionally, long ago. He'd often wondered if they were some kind of allegory, describing not a real god but an impulse toward evil and destruction contained within all the gods, sort of a mythic etiology of evil. Clearly, though, to the mad cults that sprang up in devotion to the Chained God, some element of truth rang out in the myths, something that spoke to their crazed and twisted minds.

"He was here," Kri whispered.

Metal squealed from a cell door down the hallway, making Albanon's heart leap into his throat. "Who's there?" a gruff voice called. "Who dares intrude upon the Patient One's sanctuary?"

Kri stepped toward the hallway's mouth. "We seek the last true disciple of the Chained God," he said.

A bear of a man stepped into the circle of Albanon's light. He wore a flowing robe of royal purple, open in the front to reveal a coat of chainmail. His face was hidden behind a full helmet bearing a monstrous visage and topped with sharp horns. He stood a few inches taller than Albanon, and easily weighed twice as much as the slender eladrin. A jagged spiral formed of adamantine hung from a thick iron chain around his neck.

"I serve the Chained God," the man growled, "but I am not the last."

"Kri," Albanon whispered, "if that's the demon we could be in trouble." In a halfling's tiny body, the demon had been unbelievably strong. Albanon didn't want to imagine how that hideous strength might be amplified in this man's body.

Kri shook his head. "We seek the demon, Nu Alin, who was once Albric."

The man stepped a little closer. "And what business do you have with the demon?"

"We come to destroy him!" Albanon blurted.

Kri held up a hand to quiet him. "If necessary," he added.

"Then I will kill you for him," the big man said, spreading his arms.

Kri muttered something that sounded like "miserable failure," but Albanon wasn't sure who he meant—himself, the cultist, or Albanon. Albanon threw up an arcane shield around them just as a blast of black fire washed out from the cultist, spreading around the shield and dissipating harmlessly.

In answer, Albanon sent a bolt of lightning down the hallway. It sent out tendrils of blazing light to the iron bars in the cell doorways, then exploded around the cultist, knocking him off his feet. Kri followed that with a pillar of fire that roared down over the man as he struggled to regain his feet.

Kri cackled as the man roared in pain, smoke billowing from his robe and even snaking out through the eye holes in his helmet. Albanon gave him a sidelong glance, increasingly concerned that the priest was not himself. He shook the thought from his head as the cultist roared again, seeming to draw strength from the sound of his own fury, and stood up.

"You will pay for that," the cultist said.

As he strode forward, he pulled a metal-studded club from a loop on his back and rested it on his shoulder. As Kri hefted his morningstar, Albanon stepped back and sent bolts of force down the hall to slam into the big man's chest, slowing his advance. Kri could handle himself in a hand-to-hand fight if he had to, but Albanon figured that the longer he kept that huge club away from Kri, the better.

The cultist answered his arcane missiles with another roar—a monstrous bellow that shook the walls around them and the ground beneath their feet. The sound thundered into Kri and knocked him backward like a physical blow. Albanon didn't feel the force of it so much as a pressure on his mind, as if the man's howl were tearing at the edges of his sanity. He tried to call another spell to mind, but while the sound continued he couldn't focus.

The man's barrel chest seemed to have a limitless reserve of breath—his roar went on and on, and Albanon's head started to spin. He staggered back, hoping that with a little more distance he might escape the range of whatever mystic force empowered the scream, but darkness started clouding the edges of his vision and he fell to his knees.

"Enough," Kri whispered. Somehow, for all the noise buffeting his ears, Albanon heard the priest's sharp whisper clearly—and after the whisper was sheer silence.

Light and fire burst out from Kri, still utterly silent. The merest instant of the most savage heat Albanon had ever known sent him sprawling to the ground in unspeakable agony. He felt his skin char and heard it sizzle, smelled his hair burning, but saw nothing except the incomparable brightness of divine power ravaging him.

Then the moment passed. He saw the shadow-draped ceiling of the small chamber above him, heard his own ragged breathing and Kri's panting breath, felt every nerve of his body screaming its pain. He tried to lift his head, but the pain was too great.

"Albanon?" Kri said, as if noticing his presence for the first time.

Albanon flinched away as brightness washed over him again, but this time the divine light brought soothing coolness that washed away his pain.

"Did I..." Kri began, crouching over him. "Did I do that?"

"You honestly don't know?" Albanon said.

"I—I'm not sure. I . . . it shouldn't have harmed you. You should have been safe."

"I wasn't." His body still ached from the memory of the pain, and even the slightest movement sent sharp tingles through him.

"I'm sorry, Albanon. I'm so sorry."

Kri looked so stricken that Albanon couldn't sustain his anger. He sat up, wincing at the pain, and saw the smoldering remains of the cultist behind Kri. "At least I didn't end up like him," he said, trying to smile.

Kri turned and looked down at the cultist's corpse as well. He muttered something Albanon couldn't understand as he stomped over to the body, then crouched down beside it. He reached down and lifted the spiral symbol off the dead man's chest, pulling the chain over the bulky helmet and hefting the heavy amulet.

"What is it?" Albanon asked. "The symbol of the Chained God?"

Kri started, hiding the symbol behind his body. Then he drew it back out and looked back down at it—a little guiltily, Albanon thought. "This? It's the symbol of the Elder Elemental Eye. Which is the Chained God. Except most of the cultists of the Eye don't realize it."

"They think they're serving the Eye, but it's actually the Chained God giving the orders?"

"Exactly."

Albanon got slowly to his feet, his brow furrowed in thought. "Does Ioun give you orders?" he asked.

"Sometimes." Kri stared at the symbol. "Mostly I do what I think she would want me to do."

"How do you know what that is?"

"Her teachings are preserved from the Dawn War. 'Seek the perfection of your mind by bringing reason, perception, and emotion into balance with one another. Accumulate, preserve, and distribute knowledge in all forms. Pursue education, build libraries, and seek out lost and—' Lost and something. Lore— 'seek out lore.' "

"You've forgotten?"

"I'm distracted," Kri snapped, looking down at the spiral symbol in his hands again.

"So what do Ioun's teachings have to do with our mission now?"

"Ioun gives her blessing to the Order of Vigilance because its mission is the preservation and accumulation of knowledge."

"What about distributing it?"

"What do you mean?"

"It seems to me that Ioun would want you to teach the world about the threat of the Voidharrow, or whatever it is. Not hoard that knowledge. Not keep it locked up in wizard's towers."

Kri bristled. "There is some knowledge the world is not ready for."

"So you treat the whole world like your stupid apprentice, not ready for the terrible secrets that only you are qualified to learn?"

"Wait a moment," Kri said, holding up his hands. "Are we talking about the Order of Vigilance or Moorin now?"

"Moorin was a member of the order, same as you. But I'm not talking just about me. You said Ioun wants you to distribute knowledge, build libraries, educate people. Why have you and the order treated Sherinna's knowledge like a secret?"

"You're a fool, Albanon. What purpose would it have served a hundred years ago to declare the threat of the Voidharrow? To spread fear and suspicion?"

"To promote vigilance, to let all the people of the world share in the responsibility of watching for the threat, instead of appointing yourselves the guardians of the world."

"The world needs heroes. The mass of people are—yes, they're stupid apprentices. They might learn, but they'll never understand. The few who have a glimmer of understanding will try to use their knowledge to gain riches or power. And should the threat actually arise, they'll cower in fear until a hero steps forward to protect them. It might not be kind to say it, but it's the truth."

"But your order almost failed. Moorin died, leaving you the last of the order. What if you had died, too, before you could pass on Sherinna's precious knowledge? The world would have been left without knowledge of the threat it faced."

"But I didn't die," Kri said. "The gods ensured that the knowledge would be preserved."

"I thought that was your job, not the gods'."

"We are but helpers to the greater purposes of the gods."

"Just like that poor fool," Albanon said, nodding toward the corpse on the floor.

"No!" Kri screamed. "Not like that miserable, pathetic imbecile of a priest!"

Albanon backed away from Kri's furious outburst, holding up his hands in a futile attempt to placate the old priest.

"I am nothing like him!" Kri said, tears welling in his eyes. "I serve with knowledge and understanding. With purpose!" He slumped to the floor and buried his face in his hands.

Albanon looked down at the old man sobbing on the floor, his thoughts in tumult. *This is the man I hoped would be a new mentor,* he thought, *guiding me as I step into a new phase of life?*

"Kri," he said gently.

The priest only sobbed harder, shaking his head.

"I'm worried about you, Kri."

Kri nodded, rocking his whole body slightly as his head bobbed. "You must understand your enemies if you wish to defeat them," he murmured. "Albanon, I . . . might be going mad," he said slowly.

CHAPTER TWENTY-FOUR

Uldane threw himself into the task of disguising Quarhaun with all the enthusiasm of a child engaged in a game of dress-up, making Shara smile even as Roghar harrumphed. The halfling wrapped long strips of cloth around Quarhaun's head, covering his hair and most of his face until he looked like a beggar concealing some ailment or deformity. With the drow's hooded cloak in place, his face was invisible, and the cloak covered the sword hung on his back as well. An assortment of worn cloths wrapped and tied in key locations on Quarhaun's body completed the illusion, concealing his finely tooled leather armor.

"Fine, he looks like a beggar," Roghar said. "Now, what's a beggar doing in this group? Or do you plan to make us all look like beggars? Perhaps give my armor a few more dents?"

"Oh, I didn't think of that," Uldane said.

"Of course not," Roghar said.

"I could go in ahead of you," Quarhaun said. "Just a wandering hermit, nothing to be alarmed about."

"That . . . could work," Roghar admitted.

"Or you could tell the truth, Roghar," Tempest said. "As you were traveling the King's Road into town, you found this poor man under attack by demons. You hurried to his defense and agreed to escort him into the safety of the town's walls."

"The truth?" Quarhaun said. "It'll never work."

Roghar laughed and clapped Tempest on the shoulder. "It's a great plan—devious in its sheer honesty."

"I need a staff," Quarhaun said.

"Of course!" Uldane said. "That will nicely complete the disguise."

"Yes," said the drow, "and it will allow me to walk across the bridge without leaning on Shara."

"I'll cut you a branch," Shara said, starting back toward the orchard.

As she walked, she thought about the argument that had erupted between Quarhaun and Roghar and hoped they weren't starting it up again in her absence. It was interesting—a bit disturbing, actually—to introduce Quarhaun to other friends for the first time. Albanon had met the drow first, introduced him to the others. Uldane had been there when she met Quarhaun, and they'd all warmed to him quickly as he fought Raid at their sides.

Now she was seeing Quarhaun through Roghar's eyes, and it was a bit like seeing him for the first time—and not necessarily in the most positive light. The drow was certainly the product of his background, shaped by his harsh life in the Underdark and the sheer brutality of drow society. That background was so different from her own that she doubted she could ever fully understand him.

So why am I so drawn to him? she wondered.

She found a branch long and strong enough to serve as a staff and cut it from its tree, briefly considering the ruby-red fire apples she came across in the process before she decided to leave them to rot on the ground.

Fire still danced in the wreckage of the Nentir Inn, and she watched it for a moment. The flames moved almost as if they were alive, occasionally leaping where there was no fuel for them to burn.

"Elementals?" she wondered aloud. She shrugged and turned back toward the bridge.

He likes me, she thought. Despite everything, despite my grief and my failure. Uldane tells me to change—Uldane!—but Quarhaun likes who I am.

The way Quarhaun's body shifted when he saw her return affirmed that. She couldn't see his face, but she could imagine his smile from the alertness of his posture, the way she so obviously drew his attention. It made a warmth spread through her belly. And when she handed him the staff, he brushed her hand with his own. A leather glove covered his fingers, but the touch still sent a thrill through her skin.

Roghar led their procession across the bridge, while Shara brought up the rear, keeping an eye and an ear out behind them. Tempest and Uldane walked on either side of Quarhaun, as if protecting the helpless hermit from danger. Shara smiled to herself—it was a convincing illusion, at least to her mind.

"Ho there, travelers!" one of the soldiers on the bridge called. "Let me see your empty hands as you approach, please."

Shara slid her sword into its sheath on her back and held her hands out to the sides of her body. Her companions did the same—except Quarhaun, who still gripped his staff with both hands, leaning heavily on the branch as he walked.

"You in the middle, let me see your hands," the soldier called again.

Quarhaun stopped and stretched out his arms for a moment, then gripped the staff again as he hobbled forward. He was reaching the end of his strength, Shara realized, and needed to rest soon.

"Well, well," the guard said as they drew closer. "Bold adventurers come to deliver our town from the monsters and plague?"

"I am Roghar," the dragonborn announced, bowing slightly. "If my sword and Bahamut's strength can be of help to Fallcrest, I offer them gladly."

Shara counted eleven soldiers on the bridge—ten clutching longspears, arrayed behind the commander who was speaking to Roghar. That was more soldiers than she'd ever seen in one place in Fallcrest—perhaps anywhere in the Nentir Vale. She suspected that most of them were farmers or laborers drafted into the militia when the town came under attack. Fallcrest had precious few professional soldiers in its guard, and they would probably be spread around the perimeter of the walls, the bluffs, and the waterfront, commanding groups of militia recruits.

The commander returned Roghar's bow. "I apologize if I sounded flippant, paladin," he said. His apology seemed sincere, but Shara thought his voice retained a bit of its edge. "Too many would-be heroes have found their way here in our trouble and lived like leeches off the generosity of our citizens."

Was that an explanation or a warning? Shara wondered.

"When did this happen?" Roghar asked.

"We've been under attack for two weeks. The monsters swept through Aerin's Crossing and Lowtown like wildfire, driving the survivors into the relative safety of Hightown. We're crowded and getting desperate, so the last thing we need are parasites." Shara thought she saw the man's eyes rest on Tempest, then Quarhaun, during his last sentence.

"My companions and I have already slain many of the demons that infest the Nentir Vale," Roghar said. "Why, just moments ago, we rescued this poor man from a demon attack." He gestured to Quarhaun.

Shara gritted her teeth. You didn't have to draw attention to him, Roghar, she thought.

The guard stepped around Roghar to look at Quarhaun more closely. "So you're not one of these bold adventurers?" he said. "A hermit, are you?"

"That's right," Quarhaun said.

The guard frowned at Quarhaun's unfamiliar accent. "Of what order?"

"What?"

"Are you a member of a religious order? Or just one of those fanatics who think they're too good for the temples?"

"The latter, I'm afraid," Quarhaun said, drawing himself up.

Shara stretched her fingers and shifted her weight, unsure how this confrontation was going to play out.

"But now you come slinking back to the shelter of town. What's the matter, did things get too dangerous in your woodland retreat? After repudiating our ways, you come back to our walls and soldiers when things get dangerous."

"On the contrary," Quarhaun said, "I encountered no difficulties with these demons until I arrived in your fair town."

"I don't think I like your tone," the guard said.

"Commander," Roghar said, trying to interpose himself between the guard and Quarhaun. "I promised to escort this man to the safety of Fallcrest. I would not violate my sacred oath . . ."

"Don't make promises that are beyond your ability to keep," the soldier said. "What was it, then? The plague? What's hidden under those wrappings?" He peered into the shadows of the drow's hood. "Show your face."

Quarhaun stammered. "Th . . . the ways of my order—"

"You just told me you weren't part of an order. Show your face." The soldier drew his sword, though he kept the point lowered. The other soldiers shifted nervously behind their officer, making their spear points ripple threateningly.

"I will not," Quarhaun said.

"You will, or you will die where you stand."

"Commander," Roghar said.

"Stay out of this, paladin, or I might have to assume that you were complicit in this man's deception." His scowl deepened. "If it is even proper to call him a man."

Quarhaun hesitated for a long, tense moment, then lowered his hood and pulled the wrappings away from his face. The whole force of soldiers took a step back with a gasp, eyes wide with fear and mistrust.

"So our hermit is a drow spy," the commander said. "And yet, I don't see surprise or horror on any of your faces," he added, gazing around at the rest of the group. "So you all knew, and you lied to protect him." He glared at Roghar. "I've heard a lot of lies and excuses in my career, but never so bold a lie from a paladin of Bahamut."

Roghar hung his head and Quarhaun glared defiantly at the commander, so Shara stepped forward to try to alleviate the tension. "Commander," she said, "this man is a hero of the Nentir Vale. He has slain demons beyond counting and saved my life more than once. Don't judge him by his race."

"I judge him by the lies of his tongue. He hasn't acted like a hero—none of you have. Full of empty boasts and deception, the lot of you. You're not welcome in Fallcrest, not in these times."

"Officer, our deception was regrettable, but we felt it necessary. In times like these, it's natural that you would feel especially protective, more likely than usual to question the business of a drow within Fallcrest's walls. We sought only to avoid giving you alarm."

"Regrettable, indeed," the officer said, his eyes on Roghar again.

"I spoke no falsehood," Roghar said. "My companion Tempest and I happened upon these three in the midst of a demon attack on the bluffs near the Nentir Inn. Just moments ago, we did in fact rescue this poor man from demons."

"Your ability to deceive with truthful words is nothing to boast of."

Roghar turned to Shara and threw up his hands. "I told you this was a bad idea," he said.

"So we leave," Quarhaun said. "Let Fallcrest burn, if these men won't admit the champions who might save it."

"Quiet," Shara said to him. "You're not helping." She turned to the commander. "Please. Quarhaun is no spy. His reasons for coming to Fallcrest are the same as ours, and his dedication to destroying the demons that plague the town is the equal of anyone's. His sword has slain many demons, and it's prepared to slay more. If you turn him away, it will be to Fallcrest's detriment. Consider the good of your town."

"That's what I said," Quarhaun muttered under his breath, but Shara silenced him with a sharp glance.

The commander took a slow breath as his eyes ranged over the group of them, as if measuring what he could see of their character. His gaze lingered longest on Roghar and then Quarhaun. Finally he nodded. "Very well," he said. "You may enter, all of you." His upright stance relaxed slightly, and Shara realized for the first time how much the demonic attack must be wearing on the town's defenders.

"Thank you," Roghar said, bowing again to the commander. Shara and the others echoed his thanks and mimicked his bow, and Roghar led the way past the other soldiers and across the bridge.

As Roghar passed the soldiers, one put a hand on his arm. "Paladin," the man said. "Deliver us."

"I will," Roghar said. "We all will. I swear it."

Roghar scowled as he crossed the bridge, resolving never to allow this drow to force him into such an awkward position, ever again. *I'm supposed to stand for justice and honor,* he thought, *not show the world an example of deception and trickery.*

Well, he thought, *Fallcrest will see Bahamut's justice meted out at the point of my sword soon enough. And my little deception will be forgotten.*

The bridge crossed over the fastest and loudest part of the river before the falls, depositing him just south of the Upper Quays. The street was choked with people, milling around or loitering under the eaves of buildings. He saw people settling their families into makeshift camps inside wagons or in the mouths of alleys. He saw people who looked more like respectable shopkeepers than the downtrodden and destitute, standing on street corners and begging for food. He saw desperation, fear, or despair in the eyes of nearly everyone he passed.

He looked over his shoulder at Tempest, whose eyes were fixed on the cobblestones at her feet. *She and Fallcrest are the same,* he thought. *Both besieged, invaded, and violated—and reeling from the shock of it. But how do I deliver her?*

Lost in his thoughts, he led the way to the Silver Unicorn Inn—not typically his first choice of places to stay in Fallcrest, but with the Nentir Inn in flames, he had little choice. The service was better, anyway, but the group would pay handsomely for it. If there were rooms to be had at all—with Hightown so crowded with refugees from the rest of the town, it seemed unlikely.

His thoughts turned to the Blue Moon Alehouse, his favorite place in all Fallcrest to pass the time between adventures. Thanks to the labors of its brewmaster, Kemara Brownbottle, the Blue Moon offered the finest ales and beers in the whole Nentir Vale, rivaling anything he'd tasted even in Nera. He and Tempest had first met Albanon there, when the young apprentice wizard had come to hear the tales of their adventures. The Blue Moon was in Lowtown, though, which meant it was abandoned—or worse. *How long will it take Kemara to recover?* he wondered. *Assuming we do drive the demons away.*

The sound of breaking glass jolted him from his thoughts. He spun around and saw a shattered bottle on the cobblestones, and Shara glaring around at the crowds.

"Who threw that?" Shara demanded. "You want to fight him? Come out and fight!"

The drow. He'd been right after all—fear and suspicion were at terrible heights in Fallcrest, and he provided a convenient focus for those emotions. Though the crowd was silent in the face of Shara's challenge, it had all the appearance of an angry mob, and Roghar suspected they'd been shouting jeers and catcalls while he was lost in his thoughts. Shara had her arm linked through Quarhaun's and a defiant glare on her face, but Quarhaun himself looked far too weak and tired to face any challenger who emerged.

Roghar stepped to Quarhaun's other side and lifted the drow's arm over his own shoulder. "Shara," he said. "Ignore them. We've got to get him off the street and into a bed."

Shara looked at Quarhaun and blanched at the realization of how weak he was. She nodded to Roghar and hurried along toward the inn. The jeers resumed as they walked, but Roghar paid them no heed.

"They're scared, Shara," he said. "Getting angry at them isn't going to soothe their fear. They'll change their attitudes when they see what we do."

Shara nodded and gritted her teeth, and they reached the Silver Unicorn without further incident. Uldane spoke to the halfling proprietor, Wisara Osterman, and returned with the happy news that rooms were available, albeit expensive. Apparently, Wisara had addressed the high demand for rooms in Hightown by raising her already high rates beyond the amount that most of the displaced folk would be willing or able to pay. Unfortunate for the refugees, Roghar thought, but lucky for us.

He helped Shara get Quarhaun upstairs, half dragging him, and laid him into one of the down-stuffed beds for which the Silver Unicorn was justly famous. The drow's eyes opened wide in surprise at the comfort of the bed, then closed again as exhaustion claimed him.

"Platinum Dragon," Roghar whispered, "let your power flow through me to soothe Quarhaun's injuries and ease his weary body. Grant him patience to face the fears and mistrust of the good folk here. And grant him the faith to trust in your goodness and mercy."

Roghar felt strength leave him and flow into the drow, soothing Quarhaun's rest. "He'll be all right," he told Shara. "He should sleep easier now, and he'll feel better in the morning." He stood up to leave.

"Roghar," Shara said, stopping him. "Thank you."

"You're welcome, of course," Roghar said. "But I hope he truly deserves the trust you're placing in him."

Shara smiled down at Quarhaun, a little wistfully, Roghar thought. "I hope so, too," she said.

CHAPTER TWENTY-FIVE

Shara sat by Quarhaun's side for hours, watching him sleep. He seemed troubled—from time to time, he'd furrow his brow, murmur in a language she didn't understand, or even thrash his head from side to side and cry out. In the worst times, she put her hand on his hot forehead and whispered his name until he settled down again. Once, in a long string of what she guessed were Elven words, she heard her name repeated several times in what might have been an impassioned plea or perhaps an angry tirade.

If only Albanon were here to translate. Or maybe that would be too embarrassing, she thought, as Quarhaun's voice shifted to a deeper, softer tone.

She dozed in the chair beside him for a few minutes at a time, waking up each time with a painful knot in her neck or a plate of armor biting into her skin somewhere.

"Oh, this is ridiculous," she said to herself at last. With a glance to make sure Quarhaun's eyes were still closed, she started working the buckles of her armor, grimacing at the caked blood and grime that glued leather and metal to her skin in places and the painful wounds that she pulled open again as she worked.

"Do you need any help?"

Shara gasped and replaced the breastplate she'd just started pulling free from her chest, then wheeled on Quarhaun. "You're awake!" she said, holding her armor carefully in place.

"I am gifted with incredible timing," Quarhaun said, smiling weakly. He blinked hard, making an effort to keep his eyes open.

"How do you feel?"

"Stiff and sore, but that's better than I've felt in a while. How long have I been asleep?"

Shara started working the buckles that would keep her armor in place without help from her hands. "Only a few hours," she said. "I don't think Roghar and Uldane have even come up to bed yet. You can keep sleeping."

Quarhaun shook his head. "I need to get out of this armor," he said.

"Why don't I step into the hall and give you some privacy?"

"I might need help. I'm still weak."

"Well," Shara said. "Certainly I can get your boots off." She pulled her chair to the foot of the bed and sat on it. She tugged at one of his boots, but his whole body moved and he gave a yelp of pain. "Sorry!"

"Buckles," Quarhaun said.

"Of course." She loosened the buckles that held a boot tight around his calf and slipped it off easily.

"Shara?"

"Hm?" She turned her attention to the other boot, carefully avoiding his gaze.

"There are things I don't know how to say in this language," he said. "Things I've never said to anyone, expressing . . . feelings that are not really accepted among the drow. And not discussed."

"Quarhaun, I don't think—"

"Please let me finish."

"No, I don't think that's a good idea." She yanked his other boot off, harder than necessary, and he bit back another cry of pain.

"Why not?" he said.

"Gods, you're impossible!" Her face was flushed again, which only fueled her frustration. "I . . . don't want to disappoint you, Quarhaun."

"I don't think that's likely," he said, the hint of a lascivious look in his eye.

"You should get more sleep."

"I don't want to sleep. I want to know more about you."

Shara settled back in her chair. "Very well," she said. "What do you want to know?"

His eyes ranged over her body for a brief moment, then came to rest on her sword, leaned against the wall in the corner. "Tell me about Vestapalk," he said at last.

She frowned. "Do you want to know about Vestapalk or about Jarren?"

"Who's Jarren?"

"He was my lover," she said. "We . . . well, I think we would have been married, though it was something we never really talked about, except maybe once. I put him off, told him we could think about it later, perhaps when we were too old or too rich to keep adventuring."

"And the dragon killed him."

"Yes. Uldane and I were part of an adventuring band, led by my father, actually. Borojon was his name. Me, Uldane, Borojon, Jarren, and Cliffside the dwarf. We had been tracking the dragon for a while, following the carnage he left in his wake. We finally found him, or he found us."

The horror of the day came rushing back to her—the stench of the dragon's acrid breath, the sound of rending meat as it tore Cliffside apart, Jarren's horrified face looking down at her as she fell into the river.

"So you're looking for revenge."

"I suppose so." Shara ran her fingers through her hair, hit a tangle, and thought briefly about how wonderful a bath would feel. "But I already got it, in a way. I killed the dragon, or at least left it next to dead. I think the thing that irks me most is the failure of it all. I fell into the godsdamned river instead of standing with my friends and killing the dragon the first time. Then when I met the dragon again, I didn't even manage to kill it properly. Now it's back and worse than ever, and honestly, I don't know what I'll do if I find it. I think it might be more than I can handle."

"Don't count a dragon as a drake, Shara."

"What does that mean?"

"You're a dragon. You're the greatest warrior I've ever seen. The swordmasters of my house wouldn't last a minute in a duel with you. But you think you're a drake—you think you're weaker than you are. Don't underestimate yourself."

Shara looked at the floor. "You're too kind."

"And what human has ever before spoken those words to a drow? My people don't give empty compliments—well, unless there's something to be gained by it."

"So you're not hoping to gain something by flattering me?"

"Not in this case, no." He smiled. "So tell me about Jarren. Was he anything like me?"

Shara felt tears well in her eyes, and turned her head so Quarhaun wouldn't see. "Jarren was my best friend," she said. "He made it all mean something—all our adventures, all the excitement and bloodshed, all the pain we endured, all the treasures we won—he made it worthwhile. He made me feel like the greatest treasure of all. He made me laugh, and then he could be so sweet that he made me cry. He made me feel desirable when most men were afraid of me." Tears were streaming down her cheeks, but she no longer cared what Quarhaun thought. She looked at him, met his eyes, and shook her head. "He was about as different from you as I can imagine. He was a summer day, full of life and heat and passion. And you're a winter night, cold and dark."

Quarhaun looked away, disappointment plain on his face.

Shara leaned over him, cupped his cheek in her hand, and turned his face back toward her. She searched his eyes for a moment, then kissed his lips—a long, hungry kiss. When she finally drew back, her face was flushed, but not with shy embarrassment.

"And what better way to enjoy a winter night," she said, "than to huddle under a pile of furs before a raging fireplace, safe from the chill?"

JAMES WYATT

A cloaked traveler made his way into the common room of the Silver Unicorn Inn. He shouldered up to the bar, ordered a glass of the finest wine, paid in gold, and took the glass to a table in the corner.

The man was well muscled from years of farm work, and Nu Alin enjoyed the feeling of strength in the body—strength and health that he knew would slowly ebb, the longer he retained control. In these first hours after taking a new body, he always felt so alive.

He adjusted the hood of his cloak, ensuring that his face stayed in shadow. As fresh as this body was, he could already feel the skin around the eyes cracking, revealing some of his true substance. It was always the first sign that he was not the pathetic human creature he appeared to be, which meant he had to take such precautions when he wished to move around undetected. But the benefit—the terror his eyes inspired when he revealed himself in a conflict—outweighed that minor inconvenience.

He made the body as comfortable as the hard wooden chair would allow and pretended to sip the wine as he scanned the room. Only nine other people were gathered in the common room—most citizens of the doomed town were too frightened to venture from their homes at night with his demons running wild through the lower part of the settlement. Their fear pleased him, as did the serious expressions on the faces of most of the people around him. The demons had people concerned, and as Nu Alin focused his own senses—which were much more sensitive than those of his host body—he could hear their frightened whispers and conspiratorial muttering. He and his demons had nothing to fear from these people.

Then his eyes came to rest on the farthest table from his seat, where a hulking dragonborn and a diminutive halfling sat behind a dozen mugs and glasses. They were *laughing*—Nu Alin could not stomach the audacity of it—and telling stories to a tight circle of very interested listeners. And then he recognized them.

The dragonborn had pursued Nu Alin as he chased the Voidharrow and its thief from this town to the place where the trail of the Voidharrow had disappeared. He had traveled then with his wizard friend and the tiefling, who had proven a most disappointing host. After Nu Alin had taken the tiefling, the dragonborn and halfling both had been among those who confronted him in the depths of the Labyrinth, forcing him out of the tiefling's body and bringing his search for the Voidharrow to a premature end.

Nu Alin believed he was above the petty and tumultuous emotions that seemed to drive his hosts, but he could appreciate what they called hatred or loathing when he considered the two adventurers across the common room. Without question, they were the greatest threat, in the room or anywhere else in the pathetic town, to his plans—and to Vestapalk's plans. He set his glass down and focused all his attention on listening to them.

Their stories were full of improbable boasts and unlikely twists of fate, but Nu Alin recognized the danger represented by their laughter and the smiles that slowly spread out from their table through the other patrons. They represented hope for the people of Fallcrest—hope that could not be allowed to blossom into resistance.

Nu Alin was so focused on the pair of adventurers that he almost didn't notice a new figure appear in the doorway and start toward their table. He glanced in the newcomer's direction and recognized the tiefling woman he had taken—Tempest. He could still taste her delicious fear, her fury at his possession, and her determination to resist him.

"He's here!" she suddenly cried.

The dragonborn and the halfling whirled to look at her, and the room fell silent.

"Who's here, Tempest?" the dragonborn said.

"Nu Alin!" A note of hysteria tinged her voice. "I can feel him!"

The dragonborn and the halfling leaped to their feet, and it was their panic that gave Nu Alin the opportunity to escape. When the others in the room saw the two adventurers' reaction, their faint hope dissipated, replaced at once by fear. The room erupted in a clamor of confusion. Others sprang out of their chairs and milled around the room or made their way out, and it was a simple matter for Nu Alin to weave his way through the chaos to make his escape.

As he slipped out through the door, he heard the dragonborn trying to calm Tempest, assuring her that she was suffering the effects of a nightmare. Further proof, if any was needed, of the boundless capacity these mortal creatures had for self-delusion. Some part of him, perhaps tied to the emotions of his host body, wanted to laugh.

"Damn it," Tempest said, "why won't you listen to me? Yes, I had a nightmare. I woke up. I came down here to find you. And *then* I felt his presence."

Roghar nodded. "All right. Is he still here?"

Tempest closed her eyes and tried to relax, but Roghar could see that her whole body was shaking. He wanted to kick himself for not taking her seriously sooner.

"No," she said at last. "He must have slipped out in the confusion."

"Then he can't have gone far," Roghar said. "Let's look outside."

"I'll get Shara," Uldane offered, heading for the stairs.

Roghar took Tempest's arm and led her out onto the crowded street. He scanned over the crowd, looking for . . . for what? He wasn't sure. When they had faced the demon in its halfling body, the shimmering crimson of its true substance had shown through a number of gaping wounds in the halfling's flesh. By the time they caught up with the demon in Tempest's body, the only sign of its presence inside her was around her eyes. He had to assume that, if the demon had been lurking in the common room of the Silver Unicorn, it had taken pains to conceal its presence in whatever host body it was using. He decided to look for hooded figures moving quickly away from the inn.

At first glance, he counted seven people that fit that simple description. He picked the nearest, ran to catch up to him, and put a hand on his shoulder. "Excuse me," he said.

The person wheeled around and the hood fell away from his face. A middle-aged human man with a neat salt-and-pepper beard and dark brown eyes frowned at him. "What do you want?"

Roghar stared at the man's eyes, searching the shallow wrinkles at the corners for any sign of glowing red crystal liquid. He slumped. "Sorry," he mumbled. "I thought you were someone else."

Tempest caught up to him, looking around the crowd helplessly. "He could be any of these people."

"Can you feel him now? Is he still nearby?"

"I'm not a bloodhound, Roghar! It's not like I can track his scent."

"Well, I just thought . . ."

"I know. But it was just a sudden impression, overwhelming for that moment, then gone."

"Let's walk a bit," Roghar said, putting a hand on her shoulder. "Maybe it'll come again and we can do something about it, and maybe it won't."

Tempest nodded, and Roghar chose a direction and started walking.

Tempest walked beside him in silence for a while. They passed the House of the Sun and then the Temple of Erathis before she spoke again. "What do we do if we find him?" she said.

Roghar shrugged. "Kill him."

"How?"

"What do you mean?"

"Well, when he's in a body, he's so terribly strong. I'm not sure the two of us can defeat him alone. And even if we do, if we kill the body he's in, he just slips out—the way he did when Erak stabbed me. Then what?"

"Well, I've thought about that some," Roghar said. "You didn't see it, but when the demon was trying to take Falon's body, it recoiled from divine light. I figure that's the way to destroy it. Bahamut's light will consume it."

"It could be anywhere, Roghar. It could be in any of these people."

"No more overwhelming impressions?"

Tempest shook her head.

"Then let's get back. Shara and Uldane will be wondering what's going on."

"You want to just let him go?"

"I don't see any other choice. But listen—we've gained some useful information. We know he's here, moving around in the town, and we know that we have at least one way to detect his presence. He won't be able to spy on us again. And next time, we'll get him."

"But he's gained useful information, too. He knows we're here, and he knows that I sensed him. He'll keep his distance now—there might not be a next time."

"We'll get him, Tempest," Roghar said. "I promise."

CHAPTER TWENTY-SIX

Albanon knelt beside Kri and put both hands on the old priest's shoulders. "It's this place, Kri," he said. "The taint of the Chained God fills the whole tower. You can hear the maddening whispers if you listen too closely."

Kri nodded, covering his face with his hands.

"Let's get you out of here." Albanon shifted around to Kri's side and lifted him to his feet. "Come on, one foot in front of the other."

Kri's arm lashed out, striking him in the abdomen and breaking free of his grip. "I know how to walk, damn it!"

Albanon stared at him, trying to catch his breath while Kri glared wildly back. "Fine," he said at last. "Walk yourself. Follow me, or don't. I'm getting out of here." He didn't wait for a response, but turned to the stairs and started up.

Kri called after him, fury still seething in his voice. "But the demon—what about Nu Alin?"

"He's not here. And while we wander around here, other demons are overrunning the town I call home. I mean to stop them."

"Yes!" Kri hurried up the stairs behind him. "Yes! They must be stopped! But Nu Alin—we have to find the last disciple."

Albanon didn't look back. "We need to get out of here and far enough away that you can speak calmly and sensibly again."

"Wait!"

Albanon shook his head and continued up the stairs. Kri's voice seemed lined with sinister echoes, harsh whispers that conveyed what the priest wasn't saying—dire threats and fell omens. Albanon started counting stairs again so he could block out the madness.

"Albanon, I command you to stop and look at me!"

Before he could stop himself, Albanon had turned around and sat on a step facing Kri. He scowled at the priest, trying to make sense of what had just happened. "You used magic on me?"

"You weren't listening!"

"That's because you're speaking nonsense or screaming at me. I'm not your apprentice, and I'm not a slave. I won't take this from you." He stood up again, though his feet and his head felt shaky. He put a hand on the wall to steady himself.

The wall beneath his fingers was thrumming with power. The whispers became a chorus of voices in his mind, and he had to sit down again or risk toppling down the stairs. His vision was swimming, but he saw Kri staring up at him, one hand on the wall, a look of triumph on his face.

Albanon put his fingers to his temples and drew a slow breath, a simple technique for focusing his mind that he'd learned in the first weeks of his apprenticeship. He blinked several times and looked again at Kri. The priest's face was creased with concern, not gloating in triumph as he'd first thought. Not only were the voices bedeviling his mind, they'd fooled his eyes as well.

"Kri, listen," he said. "This place is full of madness. It's in the air, in the walls, probably in the stairs beneath our feet. We can't stay here, not even to look for Nu Alin. If we tried to face him here, he'd destroy us, use our own minds against us. We must leave now."

He stood up again, wavering slightly but steadying himself without touching the wall, turned carefully, and started up the stairs again.

"Albanon," Kri called behind him.

"I'm not going to stop, Kri. Come on. We have to leave."

"Don't you want to know about the Voidharrow?"

Albanon glanced over his shoulder but kept climbing the stairs. "Why are you asking me now?" he said. "It's not the best place—you said it yourself. And far from the best time."

"I want to tell you now, Albanon. I want you to understand."

Kri's voice sent a chill through his spine. The priest was not himself, and there was a threat in his tone that made Albanon want to run as fast as he could up the stairs. He quickened his pace but held himself back from an outright run.

"I don't think I want you to tell me right now, Kri," he said quietly.

"Ingrate!" Kri screamed. "First you come begging for knowledge and chide me for my reluctance to give it, then you refuse it when I offer it freely! No wonder Moorin hated you—you must have driven him mad! Just as you're driving me mad!"

"No!" Albanon shouted back, still climbing the stairs.

"Always whining about how he mistreated you—What did he say about you?"

"Kri, be still!"

"I will not! You need to hear this! You need to understand!"

"You're not yourself," Albanon said, holding back a shout.

"Oh, but I am," Kri said, his voice deep and hollow. "Never have I been so much my true self."

Albanon turned to look at Kri again, his eyes wide with terror. He half expected to see a demon where the priest stood, or some visible sign of whatever being had seized control of Kri's body. But Kri looked perfectly normal, which struck Albanon as much, much worse.

"What is happening?" Albanon whispered.

Kri advanced up the stairs, smiling. Albanon tried to back away, but found himself sitting on the stairs again as Kri drew closer.

"Listen, Albanon. Listen, and learn the truth."

Cold despair clutched at Albanon's mind, sapping his will and draining his strength. He thought of protesting, or getting back on his feet to continue up the stairs, but it all seemed futile. The stairs were endless and Kri was unrelenting—there was no escape.

"Remember the mural, Albanon? In Sherinna's tower. I told you the story of the adventurers who interrupted the ritual and destroyed the Vast Gate. What I have since learned is Albric's story."

"Albric the Accursed."

"So he is called. Albric was a dreamer who heard the voice of the Chained God and obeyed his commands. The Chained God instructed him to find the shard of the Living Gate and take it to Pandemonium. Albric used that shard to open a tiny channel into the prison of the Chained God."

"Kri, how do you know this?"

"The Chained God sent the Voidharrow through that channel. It is the distilled essence of entropy and decay, all that remains of a universe consumed by demons, and it is infused with the Chained God's will. Albric sought to do his will, but the Voidharrow spoke lies and betrayal, and Albric's acolytes were seduced. The Voidharrow defied the Chained God and transformed the acolytes into agents of its own will. Just as it transformed Vestapalk."

Albanon's mind raced, trying to absorb the information Kri was telling him and make sense of Kri's transformation at the same time.

"Then Sherinna and her friends arrived and sent the disciples into chaos. Most were slain. Some passed living through the Vast Gate into other worlds, other planes. Of all the disciples, only Albric stayed faithful to the Chained God, clinging to his purpose even as the Voidharrow transformed him."

"But he's Nu Alin," Albanon whispered.

"Yes. Nu Alin is Albric, the last true disciple of the Chained God. With the power of Tharizdun, he is the key to defeating the Voidharrow."

Albanon's desperation fueled one last attempt to break through the madness that had gripped his friend. "Kri, listen. Just moments ago you were telling me of Ioun's will, what she wishes for the Order of Vigilance. You are her priest, Kri—a priest of Ioun. She can heal your mind, restore you to right thinking—"

Kri laughed. "I did not know what right thinking was until I glimpsed the mind of the Chained God," he said. "The Chained God's will is the same as ours. Albric has been steeped in Tharizdun's thought and will. He knows what must be done."

"He serves Vestapalk!" Albanon cried. "He is a demon of the Voidharrow now!"

"You lack understanding, Albanon. The Chained God's touch has brought me a clarity of purpose and vision like I have never known." He climbed one stair closer to Albanon. "He can do the same thing for you, my apprentice."

"I'm not your apprentice, Kri." Albanon scrambled backward up two more stairs, but Kri followed. "And I think my mind is perfectly clear."

Kri stretched his bony fingers toward Albanon's head. "You cannot fight until you understand. Just let him touch your mind."

Albanon's vision swam as he felt a pressure on his thoughts, like the feeling of having forgotten something important that was struggling to be remembered. He drew in a surge of arcane power and used it to fortify the barriers of thoughts and discipline that protected his mind, but instantly recognized his very serious mistake.

Madness was everywhere around Albanon, flowing like water through the stone of the dungeon beneath the tower. It was intertwined with the flow of magic in the place, and when Albanon drew on that magic he allowed in a touch of the same madness he was trying to resist. An absurd, barking laugh escaped his mouth as he tried to correct his mistake and muster his will to drive back Kri's assault.

Kri stepped closer, and his fingers touched Albanon's forehead, sending a lance of pain searing through his head. Albanon reacted from pure instinct, recoiling from Kri's touch and lashing out with his magic. A clap of thunder exploded in the stairway, sending Kri stumbling backward. Kri lost his footing and rolled down the steps. He cried out as he fell, a sound so lost and helpless that Albanon was overcome with remorse; then he landed in a heap a half turn down from where Albanon stood.

"Kri?" Albanon asked tentatively.

The old priest groaned and stirred, starting to untangle his limbs and lift his head from where it rested against the stone wall.

"Kri, I didn't mean to hurt you."

Kri's eyes fluttered open and fixed on Albanon as the young wizard hurried down the stairs. Kri opened his mouth and Albanon slowed, expecting a moan or quiet words.

Instead, Kri shrieked, a long, tortured note too high and loud to be his natural voice, and laden with the undertones of madness Albanon had been hearing in whispers and echoes. The barrage of sound slammed him backward and tore at his mind, snatching away his senses until the scream was all that remained.

In the face of that howling storm, Albanon was a worm writhing on the stone. The whispering voices in the walls surrounding him became leering faces staring down at him, then emerged as hungry birds jabbing their beaks at him. Agony shot through him as their beaks struck him and pulled away, trailing wispy tendrils of shining silver smoke. He looked up in his torment and saw the sun burning down on him, black but ringed in angry scarlet, pulsing with life and malevolence. It was the most beautiful thing he'd ever seen.

One of the birds lifted him from the ground and impaled him on a thorn, but he kept staring up at the angry red corona, noticing the flecks of gold and veins of silver pulsing within its brilliance. He was only vaguely aware of more silver smoke pouring forth from him where the thorn pierced his body, streaming up toward the sun.

Then Albanon was no longer a worm, no longer a creature with a merely physical body. He was wisps of silver smoke and coiling tendrils of thought, a throbbing heartbeat that came from no fleshly organ, a hunger that knew nothing of food or digestion. He saw without eyes, and all he saw was the burning black sun, the Elder Elemental Eye, the unblinking gaze of the Chained God. He had no ears, but the howling scream remained, blowing over him like a gale.

Some scrap of his mind was aware of a fleeting thought. "I've gone mad."

And then he was nothing at all.

CHAPTER TWENTY-SEVEN

Shara heard the handle of the door rattle, stopped by the lock. She sat up, pulling a blanket around her shoulders.

"Shara?" Uldane's voice called through the door. "Are you in there?"

She jumped to her feet, trailing the blanket, and padded to the door, feeling her face flush. She glanced over her shoulder to where Quarhaun lay in the bed, smiling at her, his white teeth gleaming against his black lips.

"What is it?" she said at the door.

"Shara! Open up!"

The urgency in his voice overrode her embarrassment, and she flipped the lock and let the door swing open. Uldane's face was lit with excitement tinged with a hint of fear, but his smile fell as his eyes took in the scene.

"What is it?" she asked again.

"Um . . . oh! Nu Alin! Tempest thinks he was here. She and Roghar have gone to look for him." Uldane looked like he was going to say something else, but his eyes went back and forth between Shara and Quarhaun one more time and he turned away. "That's all," he added.

He started stomping back down the hall, and Shara went after him. "Uldane, what's wrong with you?"

"Nothing."

"Nothing? I'm not sure I've ever seen you so angry."

"Probably not."

"Why are you angry at me?"

Uldane wheeled on her then. "Look at you!" he said. "And him! Both of you! Back in the Blue Moon you lectured me about choosing my allies more carefully. And yeah, I've made some mistakes and I paid for them. But now you're with *him*?"

The fury of his outburst came as such a surprise that she took a step back from him. "Watch it, Uldane," she said, feeling her own anger rise. "Quarhaun saved your life in the Witchlight Fens."

"And I'm grateful, but that doesn't mean he's good for you. He's a *drow*. He comes from one of the most evil and scheming societies in the world. He has no respect for the gods, or for the lizardfolk who *actually* saved our lives. Do you really think he's what Jarren would want for you?"

"Jarren would want me to be happy."

Uldane folded his arms. "And are you?"

"I'm trying to be." She spun around, adjusting the blanket, and hurried back to Quarhaun's room to get her sword and armor.

❖

By the time Shara and Quarhaun came downstairs, Roghar and Tempest had already returned from their hunt, despairing of finding the demon. Uldane sat at a large table in uncharacteristic silence, avoiding Shara's eyes as the rest of the group settled into chairs.

"We need a plan," Roghar said. "We've got to drive the demons out of Fallcrest. And destroy Nu Alin, if we can." He gave Tempest a lingering glance.

"A couple times in the last few weeks," Shara said, "we found demons in larger groups like this. And there was always one demon in charge, a pack leader or commander or whatever. And when we killed that leader, the rest of the demons scattered. Driving the demons out should be as straightforward as finding their leader and killing it."

"Cut off the head and the body dies," Quarhaun said, nodding.

"Yes," Roghar said, "but we don't know much about this leader. It might be Nu Alin, and that presents special difficulties."

"What difficulties?" Quarhaun asked.

"We don't really know how to kill him."

"He possesses mortal bodies," Shara explained, glancing at Tempest. The tiefling's face was a mask of indifference. "If you kill the body he's in, he just tries to take another body."

"It seems possible to destroy him while he's not in a body," Roghar said, "but his natural form is like a liquid serpent, made of the Voidharrow. The last time we encountered him, that form proved very elusive."

Quarhaun leaned forward on the table, evidently interested in the topic. "So when his host body is slain, this liquid serpent, as you call it, comes out of the corpse?"

"Exactly," Roghar said, glancing sidelong at Tempest.

"Why does everyone keep looking at Tempest?" the drow asked.

"The demon possessed me," Tempest said. "And they're all worried that I'm going to fly into a hysterical rage or crying fit as we discuss how to kill the damned thing."

Quarhaun laughed out loud. Shara kicked his leg under the table, but then she saw that Tempest was smiling. Then Roghar laughed as well, and Shara allowed herself a smile. Only Uldane was still scowling.

"One of our companions at the time stabbed me," Tempest explained. "As I lay dying, the demon snaked out. I'm afraid I don't remember much after that point. But I am glad that Erak had just enough heartless bastard in him to actually do the deed, and I'm counting on you all to do the same if the demon manages to take me again."

Roghar nodded slowly, staring into his ale.

"We will," Shara said.

"I'm nothing but heartless bastard," Quarhaun added. "I'll stab you now, if you like."

"Thank you, no," Tempest said.

Roghar gave Quarhaun a nervous glance and tried to restart the conversation. "After it left Tempest, it tried to go into Falon, our cleric friend. It climbed up his body toward his face."

"But it didn't get there?" Quarhaun asked.

"It started flowing into his mouth and nose," Roghar said, making Tempest shudder slightly. "But I had noticed that it seemed particularly averse to divine radiance, so I blasted it and it withdrew long enough for Falon to hit it harder. That's when it fled."

The drow stroked his chin. "Divine radiance, you say? Well, we have you. I can muster some radiance, though it's not exactly divine. Tempest, have you mastered the third invocation of Hadar?"

Tempest blinked at him. "I don't know what you mean," she said slowly.

"Perhaps you learned different terminology. Do you know the invocations of Hadar? The spells that draw on the light of the dying star?"

Tempest's face showed no sign of recognition, and Roghar shifted uncomfortably.

"Gibbeth's shadow, woman, did your teacher tell you nothing of the baleful stars?"

"I had no teacher," Tempest said.

Quarhaun arched an eyebrow. "You made an infernal pact with no one to guide you?"

"Not everyone has the luxury of a life of study," Roghar said, the hint of a growl in his voice warning the drow to back off.

"Certainly, but those without learning shouldn't dabble with powers beyond their understanding."

Tempest's eyes smoldered with anger, and Roghar drew himself up in his seat. "She is no mere dabbler," Roghar said. "I've fought alongside her for years, and I dare say her power surpasses yours."

"I don't doubt it," Quarhaun said. "If I recklessly seized all the power I could without regard for the consequences, out of ignorance or desperation, I suspect I'd be more powerful than you can even imagine. But I choose a more moderate path. I'd like to survive long enough to enjoy my power."

Shara looked between Quarhaun and Tempest, realizing for the first time how her experience of Tempest had colored her impressions of the drow warlock. They were different in many ways, starting with the eldritch blade Quarhaun wielded to channel his power. Tempest preferred standing back from her enemies, sending her spells coursing through her rod to blast them from afar. But some part of her, Shara realized, had figured that Quarhaun's power was more or less accidental, the way Tempest's was. To think that he had sought out the infernal power he wielded was a bit disturbing.

Tempest's anger burst its banks and she stood up, leaning over the table to glare at the drow. "We are both thieves, Quarhaun, wielding power that isn't ours. You can pretend you're a wizard if you like, couching it all in the language of academic study, but it doesn't change that fact. Sooner or later, our crimes will catch up with us."

Quarhaun laughed in her face. "You're right, of course. But I am a master thief, always staying one step ahead of the law, hiding myself behind layers of intermediaries and deception. And you? You're a master of the smash and grab, utterly lacking in subtlety and technique. Which of us do you think will be caught first?"

Tempest fumed at him for a long moment, then turned and stormed out of the room. With a parting glare at the drow, Roghar followed her out. Left alone with Shara and Quarhaun, Uldane got up and left without a backward glance.

"So much for a plan," Quarhaun said. He grinned at Shara. "Perhaps we should return to what we were doing before we were interrupted."

Shara frowned, looking after her friends. What's keeping me from storming out with them? she wondered. Shouldn't I be outraged at the things Quarhaun said?

She smiled back at Quarhaun, weighing his suggestion. Not if he's right, she thought. She stood up and held out her hand to him.

Glass crashed somewhere in the inn, and a scream pierced the quiet night. Shara hurried to the door of the common room and looked around. People were shouting both upstairs and outside on the street, but she couldn't figure out the source of the commotion.

Then a living flame smashed open the door beside her, and a monstrous face formed of glittering red liquid leered at her from the midst of the fire.

Kri stood and looked down at Albanon's limp body on the stairs. "Now you understand," he said. The eladrin didn't stir. Blank eyes stared upward, seeing nothing at all.

Kri bent his head and lifted Ioun's holy symbol off his neck. "You taught me to pursue knowledge and understanding," he said to the symbol. "And so I have."

He twisted the bottom of the symbol, the crook that extended from the bottom of the stylized eye, and it opened. He slid out the tiny crystal vial that held his miniscule fragment of the Voidharrow. He closed his fist around the vial and felt the two wills at war within it—its own and the Chained God's.

"I renounce you now," he said quietly. He let the symbol fall, clattering to the stairs and tumbling down into the darkness below. "Your knowledge is vain and empty. Your understanding is futile. The will of the Chained God is my will."

He reached into his robes and pulled out the jagged iron symbol he'd taken from the dead priest and put it around his neck.

"I will destroy the Voidharrow and finish what the Chained God commands."

At last the eladrin moved.

He opened his eyes and tried to figure out who he was. The Doomdreamer stood looking down at him, grinning madly, surrounded by a wreath of leering spirits. The floor beneath him was hard, uneven—stairs, stone stairs.

"Rise, Albanon," said the Doomdreamer.

He obeyed without thought, then decided that his name must be Albanon. He focused all his attention on the Doomdreamer, eager to learn more of his identity, eager to fulfill his next command.

"Follow me," the Doomdreamer said, and started down the stairs.

Albanon followed, adding his quiet voice to the babble of spirits surrounding them, flowing in the walls and floor as well as hovering around the Doomdreamer. Seventy-two stairs they descended, eight nines, six dozens, two squares of six. Formulas flitted through his mind and fire danced across his fingers in response, and he emerged into a chamber at the bottom of the stairs.

"Ah, you have remembered your magic." The Doomdreamer was pleased, and Albanon rejoiced. "Let me see you destroy that corpse."

Albanon followed the Doomdreamer's pointing finger with his eyes, and saw the body lying on the floor. Two cubed times three squared. With a flick of his fingers he filled seventy-two cubic feet of the room with roaring flames. A little pressure of his will kept the fires burning until the corpse was a smear of ash on the stone floor.

"Now you know the extent of your power," the Doomdreamer said. "At last you understand."

"Yes," Albanon said. "I think I do."

"He was a false servant," the Doomdreamer said, nodding toward the ashes. "He failed, and his death was well deserved. His obliteration was required, so no memory of his failure remains. Together, you and I will succeed where he failed."

Albanon nodded, but he was no longer sure he understood. He wanted to use his magic again, to turn the numbers and formulas over and over in his mind, to explore every permutation and calculation. Seventy-two was a mystic number to him now, a perfect inversion of exponents and primes, a source of power and an expression of a far greater power. What would it take to pierce the Doomdreamer with seventy-two arrows of pure magical force? He started toying with that calculation.

"We have one more task to complete in this place," the Doomdreamer continued. "And then we must find Nu Alin."

"What one task?" Albanon asked.

The Doomdreamer scowled at him. "Such impertinence," he said. "Expected from the old Albanon, but not from the new."

What old Albanon? he wondered. He couldn't remember anything before opening his eyes on the stone stairs a few moments ago.

"Which makes our one task all the more important," the Doomdreamer said. "We must see the one we serve."

Albanon stepped closer to the Doomdreamer, curious and anxious. The Doomdreamer moved to stand beside a makeshift altar, decorated with a single candle and an opened manacle. With a word from the Doomdreamer, the candle burst into flame, and a chorus of mad whispers filled the room. Albanon murmured something senseless, adding his voice to the chorus, and shuffled still closer to the table.

The Doomdreamer snapped the manacle into place on his own wrist and wrapped the attached length of chain around his forearm. "Chained God," he intoned, "Patient One, He Who Waits, my fate is bound to yours. While you are chained, I am chained. When you are free, only then will I be free."

The whispering chorus grew louder, and here and there a keening wail rose above the other voices. Albanon chanted numbers, factors and multiples of seventy-two, the seeds of arcane formulas that could create or destroy.

"Dark God, Black Sun, God of Eternal Darkness, I bring this candle to your darkness, seeking a glimpse of your majesty."

The chorus was more wails than whispers. Thirty thousand, three hundred and seventy five was the product of the next two primes with their exponents inverted. That number would produce a much larger burst of flame.

"Anathema!" the Doomdreamer screamed over the unearthly chorus. "Undoer! Ender! Eater of Worlds! Reveal yourself and end our clinging to the false reality of this world."

The next product was so large that Albanon could barely calculate it, but he was confident that he could scorch the earth across an entire farm by manipulating those numbers. Could he create more than a billion magic missiles to tear the Doomdreamer's body to ribbons?

The Doomdreamer's eyes rolled back in his head and he convulsed, dropping to his knees behind the makeshift altar. Albanon dropped to his knees at well, unsure what he was supposed to be doing.

The wailing chorus ceased and the Doomdreamer collapsed on the floor. "One billion, three hundred and thirteen million, forty-six thousand, eight hundred and seventy-five," Albanon said, and then he, too, fell silent.

Panting with exertion, the Doomdreamer lifted himself off the floor. "Did you see, Albanon?" he asked. "Now do you understand?"

"I understand," Albanon said. You are Kri, he realized suddenly. I understand perfectly.

CHAPTER TWENTY-EIGHT

Shara yanked her sword from its sheath as the fiery demon surged forward. "Quarhaun!" she shouted.

Dozens of tiny flames caught in curtains and on posts and floorboards as the demon entered the inn and lunged at her. Its entire substance was fire, except the crystalline head in its core, and Shara couldn't see any difference between the flames left in its wake and the demon itself. It extended a tendril toward her and she slashed at it with her sword, but as the blade passed through the fire she didn't feel any resistance and it didn't seem to slow or hinder the attack at all. She followed her blade's arc, twisting her body out of the tendril's direct path, but it still seared across her back, igniting her cloak.

With a muttered curse, Shara loosened the cloak's clasp and let it fall smoking to the floor. Sweat trickled down her face as the demon's heat washed over her, and she smiled. "Into the fire," she muttered, and inched closer to the inferno.

A bolt of blue-white light whistled over her shoulder and struck near the demon's leering face, blossoming into a sheet of ice that spread across the surface of the fire, stilling the dancing tongues of flame for a moment. Shara took advantage of that moment and followed the bolt's path with her sword, striking hard where the demon's substance had grown solid and—she hoped—brittle. Her blade struck something hard, making a loud crack, and the demon recoiled with a monstrous roar. Its fury seemed to intensify its heat, melting away the coating of frost that Quarhaun's spell had created, and it curled in around Shara, extending more tendrils of flame to enfold her.

She ignored the coiling tendrils and drove her sword into the demon's face. She expected to hit solid crystal, hard as rock, but instead found liquid that flowed around her blade. The demon's light and heat faltered with the blow, and the tendrils that struck her stung but didn't burn her. Pressing her momentary advantage, she sliced her sword clean through the demonic face, drawing a trail of crystalline liquid out with her blade. The face dissolved into floating globules of red liquid as the demon's fiery form contracted. A moment later, the liquid globs fell to the floor, burning like lantern oil, and the demon was no more.

She bent to pick up her cloak, then used it to swat out the little fires left behind from the demon's passing. Quarhaun added his own cloak to her effort, then put his hand on her shoulder.

"You fight like you have nothing to live for," he said.

Shouts from the street outside suggested that the threat had not passed, but she clasped Quarhaun's hand anyway.

"If I had killed Vestapalk when I thought I did," she said, "would these demons be here now?"

"We are the same, you and I."

She arched an eyebrow at him, and he responded with a wink and nodded at the door. "There's more killing to do," he said.

Smiling, she stepped to the wreckage of the door left behind from the demon's entrance and peered into the street.

Roghar looked up and down the hall, trying to find the source of the scream that had stopped him in his tracks as he came upstairs. Wisps of smoke snaked out around a door midway down the hall, and another cry for help came from the same direction. He glanced at Tempest, who nodded, and then sprinted to the door. Drawing a deep breath, he kicked the door open, releasing billowing clouds of smoke into the hallway.

Flames roared in the room beyond, lighting the room in lurid reds. The thick smoke made it hard to see what was happening, but Roghar plunged in without a moment of hesitation, following the sound of a man coughing. He stumbled over something on the floor, looked down, and found a woman's body.

"Tempest!" he shouted. "Get her out of here!" He crouched beside the woman at his feet, and a word of prayer sent Bahamut's power into her, simultaneously strengthening her against the fire and smoke and lighting her like a beacon so Tempest could find her in the smoke.

As he stood again, a column of fire roared up right in front of him. A demonic face, mouth open in a shriek of fury, floated in the midst of the flames, evidently formed of a glittering liquid similar to Nu Alin's true substance. Roghar drew his sword.

"Vile spawn of chaos and destruction," he said, "you are not welcome in this world. Get back where you came from."

He didn't expect any kind of response, but the demon answered him, in a voice like the crackling of flame. "The Plaguedeep grows, mortal. Soon this world shall be consumed."

As long as the demon was willing to talk, Roghar used the opportunity to get his shield off his back and into position on his arm. "I don't know what the Plaguedeep is, but I'm here to make sure that this world stays as the gods intended it to be."

"The Plaguedeep is the place whence I came, and it is in this world. Until it grows to consume the world. As I shall consume you!"

I guess it's done talking, Roghar thought, interposing his shield between himself and the demon's fiery tendrils. His sword erupted with brilliant light as he swung at the demon's liquid crystal face. It recoiled from the divine light, and his blows seemed to burn the liquid crystal in a way that the roaring flames could not.

Roghar fought with righteous fury, confident in the knowledge that he was doing Bahamut's work, helping to defend and protect the defenseless citizens of Fallcrest. His confidence gave strength to his arms as Bahamut empowered his weapon, and in just a moment the demon was gone, its fires extinguished and its crystalline substance shriveling to black residue on the floor.

Snarling with satisfaction, Roghar turned to check on Tempest. Smoke still clouded the air, but he didn't see any sign of her. White light still shone near the floor, marking the location of the woman he'd tripped over. Tempest hadn't retrieved her.

Another cough, weaker than before, came from the floor near the window, where fire still roared in the curtains. Roghar plunged deeper into the smoke, yanked the curtains to the floor and smothered the flames, then found the suffocating man slumped in a chair. He invoked Bahamut's healing power as he lifted the man to his shoulder.

"A more moderate lifestyle would serve you well, friend," he muttered to the heavy man. "The blessings of food and drink were meant to be enjoyed within sensible limits."

He staggered to the woman's side and dropped to one knee. Groaning with effort, he lifted her under his arm—grateful for a much lighter load—and carried both unconscious people out the door.

The hallway was in chaos. Smoke billowed along the length of the hall, mostly clinging to the ceiling. Near Roghar, Uldane stood facing one of the nightmare demons they'd encountered on the bluff, standing firm against it though his face was contorted with fear. Behind Uldane, a clump of terrified looking people, mostly clad in bedclothes, huddled together, recoiling from the shadowy tendrils the demon lashed toward them. At the far end of the hall, Tempest stood facing another demon near a broken window.

Tempest seemed paralyzed with fear, and Roghar could imagine why. These demons used fear as their weapon, taking on the appearance of whatever their foe feared most. And they came from the same source as Nu Alin, apparently, so it was likely a trivial matter for them to draw on Tempest's terror of Nu Alin and her fear of being possessed again.

I have to help her, he thought.

He lowered the two people he was carrying to the floor, as gently as he could, and scanned the clump of terrified bystanders for someone who looked at least vaguely competent. A teenaged girl caught his eye, wearing a look of defiance as she held a younger boy.

"You," he called, pointing to her. "I need you to get these people into the middle with the rest of you. I'll keep the demon busy. Can you do that?"

Her eyes went wide and flicked to the demon, but when she looked back at him she nodded. He smiled as he drew his sword again. He roared and charged the demon.

"Fiend of the Plaguedeep!" he shouted. "Your doom is here, in Bahamut's name!"

The demon whirled to face him, and it changed. The snaky tendrils of shadow and liquid crystal that served the creature in place of legs lifted up off the ground and became five draconic heads in five different colors. The burning inn fell away until he stood alone on a desolate plain before Tiamat, god of greed and vengeance, queen of evil dragons.

"Worship me, dragonborn," all five heads said in unison. "I am also of the blood of Io."

Bahamut and Tiamat were two sides of the same coin, in dragonborn thinking. Both gods had arisen from the corpse of the first dragon god, Io, when he was slain by the Lord of Chaos in the Dawn War. But they embodied opposite extremes of Io's philosophy, and dragonborn believed that they all had a choice to make in life between the path of Io and the path of Tiamat.

Doubt gnawed at Roghar's heart, a doubt he'd never previously admitted or acknowledged. *Did I choose the right path?* he wondered, putting the doubt into words for the first time.

The dragon-god roared, five earth-shaking bellows of pain and fury, and Roghar saw Uldane's dagger stuck into the back of the demon as it turned. Tiamat was gone, and Uldane had taken advantage of the demon's distraction to deal what might have been a mortal blow, but the demon was reaching out to retaliate. Light flashed around Roghar and he lashed out with his blade. The demon's horned head toppled from its shoulders and its body began to dissolve into shadow and red liquid.

Roghar glanced around. The girl had accomplished her mission perfectly, and the two people he'd retrieved from the room were awake, looking around with terror as they huddled with the others. At the end of the hall, Tempest was wrapped in the coils of the other demon's tendrils, her body limp in its grasp.

"No!" he roared, pushing his way past the bystanders to reach her.

Just as he came to her side, an explosive blast of lightning engulfed the demon, and Tempest's body with it, roaring with thunder that knocked him back into the knot of people behind him. The demon released its grip on her as it staggered backward, too, and Tempest fell on her face onto the floor.

Roghar pulled himself up and free of the bystanders, and Tempest managed to lift herself to her hands and knees. The demon surged toward her again, but she lifted one hand and spat what sounded like an infernal curse at it. Flames spilled out from her outstretched fingers and over the demon. Roghar stepped up as it reeled back and plunged his sword into its chest.

As the demon's form dissolved, he bent beside Tempest and lifted her to her feet. "Are you all right?" he asked.

She shook her head and didn't meet his eyes.

"They use our fear as a weapon," he said.

Tempest looked at him, fear still haunting her eyes. "Roghar, what if the drow is right?"

"About what?"

"About me and my power," she said. "It's true that I'm dealing with forces I don't really understand."

"But you're using your power for good."

"Are you sure?" Tempest looked away before he could answer. "It doesn't always feel that way."

"Destroying demons? Of course that's a good purpose."

"Ultimately, yes. But in the moment, it just felt like destruction. Self-preservation, perhaps, but there's nothing noble about that."

"Tempest, you can't—"

"Roghar!" Uldane shouted. "The inn is burning!"

CHAPTER TWENTY-NINE

Albanon rowed the boat back toward the quays as Kri manned the rudder, keeping his eyes fixed on a plume of smoke rising up from a building just beyond the north end of the quays. Glancing over his shoulder as they drew nearer, Albanon guessed it was the Silver Unicorn Inn in flames.

"We'll find Nu Alin where the demons are attacking," Kri said.

Ninety-seven full strokes of the oars brought the little boat to the quays. Albanon frowned at the prime number. He started toying with multiples of it, poked at its square and cube, and found his mind filling with formulas again.

"Albanon!" Kri barked. "Pay attention!"

Fire shot out from Albanon's fingers and caught in the rope he'd been using to tie up the boat. He swatted out the flames and counted thirteen hemp fibers reduced to glowing embers. Another prime.

He finished tying up the boat and clambered onto the dock after Kri. Together they hurried toward the column of smoke. Thirty-eight steps—twice nineteen—brought him into the thick of the terror around the Silver Unicorn. Demons like the ones they had fought at the Tower of Waiting haunted the streets outside the inn, catching lone bystanders and feasting on their fear. Animate forms of living fire stalked around the burning inn as well, setting fires in buildings and townsfolk alike.

Thirteen, thirty-eight, ninety-seven . . . calculations danced through Albanon's mind. Settling on the formula he wanted, he reached a hand toward one of the burning demons and snuffed out its fire. He saw a suggestion of a shape remaining when the fire was gone, then something like a red crystal skull fell to the floor. Eight seconds after he extinguished the flame, the demon was gone without a trace.

"Impressive," Kri said. "But we are looking for Nu Alin."

Eight words, Albanon thought. Eight seconds for the demon to die. An unlikely coincidence.

"There he is!" Kri said, pointing to a broad, strong-looking man who walked without fear among the demons. "Don't kill him! Not yet."

Eight words again, Albanon thought.

Kri hurried toward the man, whose face was hidden beneath the hood of his cloak. "Albric!" he called.

Nu Alin stopped and lowered his hood.

Albanon stared. The body was completely different, but the eyes were the same—the eyes of the halfling creature that had clung to Tempest's back, digging its fingers into her throat while demanding that Albanon activate the teleportation circle in Kalton Manor. The same creature that had killed Moorin.

"Albric has been dead for a long time," Nu Alin said slowly.

Eight words.

"Not completely," Kri said. "His will yet survives in you."

"He is gone and long forgotten, old fool."

"The Chained God commands you! Finish your task!"

"I have come with a different purpose now."

Eight eights, Albanon thought.

As Kri was about to speak again, someone barreled out of the inn, a red-haired woman with a greatsword. Her name bubbled slowly to the surface of Albanon's thoughts, and he mouthed it to himself. *Shara.*

She launched herself at the nearest demon, one of the shadowy nightmare creatures, and hacked into it with her massive sword. The drow who had come with them from the Temple of Yellow Skulls came out of the inn after her, his eldritch blade burning in his hand. He leaped at the same demon, and together they made quick work of it, apparently undaunted by the nightmares it induced.

"Albanon?" Shara cried.

"Albanon," Nu Alin said, looking at him as if seeing him for the first time. "I remember you. You sent me and your tiefling friend into the Labyrinth after I killed the old wizard."

Anger welled in Albanon's chest, but he tried to keep his face a mask. As long as Kri believed that his mind and will were shattered, he would not have to fight the priest. He wasn't ready.

"His mind has been broken by the Chained God's touch," Kri said. "He will not remember."

But I do remember, he thought. I remember everything, Kri.

"Too bad," Nu Alin said. "Do you suppose he remembers finding the wizard in his tower? It was a work of art, what I did to him. A masterpiece."

He's trying to provoke me, Albanon thought.

"Albanon, what are you doing?" Shara called. "We could use your help here! Roghar, Tempest, and Uldane are still inside!"

Tempest is here?

"He remembers more than you think," Nu Alin said.

Kri looked at him sharply, but Albanon made his face blank again. As Kri peered into his vacant eyes, Shara leaped over the corpse of another demon and ran toward them. As she drew close, Nu Alin spun around and slammed his fist into her gut, hurling her back the way she'd come. She crashed to the ground and lay still.

"Servant of the Chained God," Nu Alin said to Kri, "I serve another master now."

"Betrayer!" Kri spat. "You fought the Voidharrow's will even as it transformed you. It is not too late. You can still help me free the Chained God."

"Impossible."

"No. I have the shard of the Living Gate. I have a fragment of the Voidharrow. We can finish what you began. I need only your knowledge."

"Then look upon my masterpiece," Nu Alin said, grinning at Albanon.

Quarhaun was helping Shara to her feet, and they both gaped at Nu Alin with fear and confusion on their faces.

One of the flaming demons swept toward them from behind. Albanon extended his hand and snuffed its flame as he had done to the other one a moment before.

Nu Alin turned and started walking toward the quay. Shara shouted, and Quarhaun leveled his sword, sending a bolt of frost hurtling after the demon. The bolt crashed into Nu Alin's back and stopped him in his tracks as Shara ran after him.

"Come, Albanon," Kri said. "We have all we need."

Without a word or a backward glance, Albanon turned away from Shara and Nu Alin and followed Kri into a shadow-cloaked alley.

Frozen flesh cracked and splintered as Nu Alin turned to face Shara and meet her charge. Where his body tore, red fluid appeared in the gaps—not blood, but the all too familiar liquid crystal of the Voidharrow. Shara drew back her sword, but Nu Alin lunged at her with blinding speed, ducking under her sword and slamming his fist into her again. She managed to twist away from the full force of the blow so that he only sent her sprawling on the ground rather than hurling her through the air again. His strength was unbelievable. *If he keeps hitting me like that,* she thought, *I'm going to stop getting back up.*

"So I take it you're Nu Alin," Quarhaun said, standing beside Shara as she got to her feet again.

"Indeed."

"And are you familiar with the third invocation of Hadar?"

"I am not." Nu Alin curled his clawlike fingers into fists and stepped toward Quarhaun.

"Observe!" Quarhaun shouted. He held out his hand alongside his eldrich blade, contorting his fingers into a bizarre shape, and light erupted in front of him.

It was as different from the clear, pure radiance of Roghar's divine magic as that holy light was from the illumination of a lantern—a difference not of brightness or color but of *quality*, somehow. There was a wrongness, an alienness to it, as if it came from some distant star, pale and faint in the midnight sky.

The light's effect on Nu Alin, however, was every bit as dramatic as what Roghar's light had done. The demon sprang backward, throwing his arms up to shield his face from the unearthly glow. Where the red liquid showed in his joints, it smoldered and shrank back. The light congealed into an orb the size of Quarhaun's fist that sprang at the demon and took up an orbit around him, sending little jolts like lightning to stab at him.

Shara got to her feet and cautiously circled around the demon. He snarled and coiled as if to spring at her, but the orb flared brighter and its light held him in place. He swatted at the orb of light instead, and it shattered into a million tiny fragments of light, dispersing into the darkness.

"Parlor tricks," Nu Alin said. "Even if you dress them up with fancy names, they remain but tricks."

"Then let's see what you think of the seventh—"

Before Quarhaun could finish his sentence or even begin his invocation, Nu Alin was on him, bony fingers clenched around his throat. Blood welled where the clawlike tips of his fingers dug into the drow's skin, seeking the great arteries that carried blood to Quarhaun's brain.

Shara sprang at him and swung her sword down with all her might, but with impossible speed and strength, Nu Alin twisted around and lifted Quarhaun into the path of her assault. In horror, she tried to stop her swing and pull the blade back, but it still bit deep into the drow's arm, sending his eldritch blade clattering to the ground.

Nu Alin started to laugh, then his voice became the dragon's voice. Vestapalk was laughing at her failure, even as his minion drove sharp claws into Quarhaun's throat.

"You care for this man?" Vestapalk's voice asked. "Once already this one has nearly killed him. The feel of claws sinking into his chest is vivid in the memory."

"I will kill you, Vestapalk," Shara said. She lunged again, and once more Nu Alin lifted Quarhaun to intercept her blow. The drow's eyes were wide as he gasped for air.

"Listen, mortal fool," the dragon's voice said. "Your interference is not welcome. The Plaguedeep grows and the plague spreads, with or without your meddling."

"I'll stop you and your plague. I swear it." Shara rushed at Nu Alin again, feinting a swing from her left shoulder until the moment Nu Alin brought Quarhaun into the path of her sword, then twisting the blade around so it came up under Nu Alin's unprotected left arm, cutting deep enough to draw a gush of blood as well as a welling of the liquid crystal.

Nu Alin roared in pain, in his own voice once more, though Shara thought she heard the distant laughter of the dragon still echoing around her. He hoisted Quarhaun by the neck and hurled him at Shara, knocking them both to the ground in a tangle of limbs.

Shara sat up and saw Nu Alin running away, into the darkness. "Get off me," she shouted at Quarhaun, pushing him away and scrambling to her feet.

Too late. The demon was too fast. She saw Roghar emerge from the burning inn, leading Tempest and a train of townsfolk, but Nu Alin was gone, lost in the shadows in the direction of the quays.

Before Shara could get Roghar's attention, two more of the nightmare demons swept toward her. At the same time, she saw five fiery demons closing in around Roghar and his little ragtag band. A handful of soldiers approached from the other side, clutching swords and spears as they drew near the demons.

"He's getting away!" she shouted to no one in particular. "Don't let him get away!"

Suddenly the dragon stood before her, roaring and spreading its jaws to bite or breathe its toxic gas. "Damn you," she muttered, pushing back her fear and stepping forward to meet the dragon, slicing into its throat. It batted at her with a claw, but she sidestepped its clumsy attack and cut it again. Then it was once more just a shadowy demon with a trail of red liquid dripping from its deep wounds.

She saw Uldane slip out from the group around Roghar and look around the street. He looked at her and shrugged.

He's trying to stop Nu Alin, bless him, Shara thought. She pointed her sword in the direction Nu Alin had gone, then brought the blade around to cut through the demon's torso, destroying it.

Quarhaun stood facing the other demon, fear and anger warring on his face. With a roar, he swung his eldritch blade at the demon, but it knocked him aside before his blade could connect. Shara leaped into the opening it left and sliced into its head. It spasmed, raking sharp claws down her arm before it, too, dissolved into nothing.

The wound stung, but she ignored it and raced after Uldane. *He probably won't catch up to Nu Alin,* she thought, *but what if he does? He can't take on the demon by himself.*

She ran along the town's outer wall toward the quays, past looming warehouses and smaller businesses catering to the river trade. As she reached the quays, she saw Uldane walking along the riverside. He had a dagger in each hand, and his posture was alert, searching for a sign of Nu Alin.

"Uldane!" she called.

He looked up, saw her, and turned away. A sudden fear gripped Shara. *What if Nu Alin took him? Would I be able to tell?*

She hurried to catch up with him, keeping her sword ready. As she went, she watched the way the halfling moved, trying to spot any telltale sign that the demon was in control of his body. He seemed a little stiff, but that could be explained by the tension of searching for the demon—or by his anger at her.

What does he have to be so angry about, anyway? she thought. *It's my life.*

She replayed her conversation with Uldane in the inn. *Is this what Jarren would want for me? It's a ridiculous question,* she decided. *If he were alive, he'd want me to be* with him, of course. But he's not, so it no longer matters what he wants.

A voice just like Jarren's whispered in her mind, and she imagined she could feel his breath in her ear. *What do you want?*

I want to be happy again, she told the memory of him. Like we were.

And are you? Jarren's memory or Uldane or the mocking voice of Vestapalk asked her again.

She remembered falling into the river with Uldane, looking up at Jarren a moment before the dragon killed him. She saw the dragon falling into the chasm at her feet, the red crystal flowing into its wounds. She felt her shame and fury as the dragon spoke to her through the demons she'd fought, mocking her, taunting her with her failure.

"I don't deserve to be happy," she muttered aloud.

CHAPTER THIRTY

Albanon's thoughts and feelings were a jumble as he followed Kri through the tumult caused by the demons' attack on the Silver Unicorn. He found a rhythm in counting his footsteps, a stability in the steady beat of his boots against the cobblestones and packed dirt of the streets and alleys. Slowly, as Kri led him through Hightown, Albanon found a focus, a burning point of fury and hatred at the center of his mind's storm. Kri had done something to him, something that shattered his mind and sapped his will. All the rest—thoughts of Nu Alin, memories of Shara and Quarhaun, the sudden recollection of Tempest—was fragmentary and uncertain, but he found comfort and stability in staring at Kri's back and calculating the various ways his spells could tear the old man into tiny pieces.

Their winding path meant nothing to him until suddenly a tall tower came into view, limned with eldritch light in the night. The Glowing Tower, he thought. Moorin's tower.

Blood. Blood everywhere, sprayed on walls and floor and ceiling in patterns of intricate geometry—angles and curvature danced through his mind, undergirded with formulas he had not noticed before. "It was a work of art, what I did to him," the demon had said. "A masterpiece."

Not art, Albanon realized. Mathematics. Magic.

His head spun as he contemplated the mystery that Nu Alin had woven from Moorin's blood. The fabric of space and time was rent apart and woven back together, differently, subtly, intricately. He stumbled, overcome by a wave of nausea.

"Albanon!" Kri snapped.

Albanon made sure his face was blank before he looked up at the old priest. Kri stopped and searched his eyes as Albanon stared straight ahead.

"Perhaps Albric was right," Kri said at last. "Your mind was stronger than I gave you credit for. It seems that Moorin was not a total idiot after all."

A spark of anger flared in some shattered corner of Albanon's mind, enough to make him realize that Kri was trying to provoke him, testing him.

"Did you see Shara back there, Albanon?" Kri asked. "Did you hear her call out to you?"

Another test. Albanon kept his face a mask and didn't answer, didn't even allow his mind to pursue the questions that surfaced in his mind. *Who is Shara to me? Should I care about her?*

"Come along, Albanon," the Doomdreamer said, apparently satisfied. "We have work to do."

Two hundred thirteen, Albanon thought as he started walking again. He had stopped counting steps as he contemplated Nu Alin's mathematics of blood, and counting again was the only way he could keep his mind away from the madness contained in those formulas.

Two hundred and fifty-six steps—sixteen sixteens, the square of a square of a square—brought him to the threshold of Moorin's tower. Crossing the threshold brought another wave of memory, the trepidation he felt entering the tower the night of Moorin's death, seeing that the tower's wards had been disabled. He pushed the memories away and counted the seventy-seven remaining steps up to the top of the tower.

"Be gone!" Kri shouted when he reached the top of the stairs.

Albanon looked past him and saw a squad of soldiers, staring wide-eyed at Kri.

"The defense of this tower is no longer your concern," Kri said.

"But Captain Damar—" one of the soldiers began. Albanon recognized only that he should know the name— no further memory would come to mind.

"Tell your captain that the guard is no longer welcome in the Glowing Tower. We will deal harshly with trespassers."

"Our orders—"

"Sergeant, if you utter another word you will become trespassers." Albanon felt power gathering around the Doomdreamer, dark and dangerous.

The sergeant must have felt it, too. He nodded to the other soldiers, who immediately filed to the stairs, casting nervous glances at Kri and Albanon as they passed. The sergeant was the last to leave, and he dared a parting word of defiance as he started down the seventy-seven steps. "You'll hear from the Lord Warden about this."

"Be gone!" Kri roared, and the force of his voice seemed to drive the sergeant forward, making him stumble on the stairs. Only the quick reaction of the men in front of him kept him from tumbling down to his death.

"Now to work," Kri said. "First, disable the ward on the teleportation circle."

Albanon followed an arcing path across the room where, months ago, Moorin's blood had traced a line of very precise curvature. He closed his eyes as he walked, seeing in his mind the spray of blood and feeling the flow of power that still followed that line. He sidestepped the table he knew lay in his path, but kept his hand in the flow of magic. *What did Nu Alin create here?* he wondered. *And does Kri know it's here?*

He reached the teleportation circle and suddenly remembered arriving there with Kri just hours before. *How did I forget that?* he thought. The shimmering dome of the ward that kept them in until . . .

Disabling the ward was trivially simple, barely an effort of calculation. A guard had let it down before, so whoever established it—the High Septarch, he realized—must have created a control even a fool could use from outside the circle.

"Excellent," Kri said, appearing behind him. "Your power has grown, quite dramatically, now that you're free of Moorin's fetters."

You have not yet seen how my power has grown, Albanon thought. *But you will.*

Kri reached into the folds of his robes and withdrew a chunk of reddish crystal followed by a glass vial holding a tiny sample of the Voidharrow. He strode into the center of the circle and closed his eyes, reaching out to sense the magical energy that flowed through the patterns and sigils. Albanon did the same, his mind flooding with formulas and arcane syllables as he did. He bit his tongue to stop himself from giving voice to the magic he felt, not even consciously aware of what the spells would have done if he'd unleashed them.

Kri was right, he realized—his power had grown. In the Feywild, he'd been struck by how easy it was to access the magic that flowed through everything there. Now, the same power—no, even more power—was at his fingertips in the world, practically leaping from his fingers and spilling from his tongue without his conscious effort.

But can I control it? he wondered.

He opened his eyes again and saw Kri's brow furrowed in concentration. Now he sees Nu Alin's magic, too, Albanon thought. Will he fathom its purpose?

Kri opened his eyes and looked down at the items in his hands. "Just as Albric did, so we now do. Together, the Voidharrow and the fragment of the Living Gate will open a portal like none ever seen before in this world."

"The Vast Gate," Albanon said. Words echoed dimly in his mind—a new Vast Gate, construction and opening. To guard against it, he remembered suddenly. The Oath of Vigilance.

Kri frowned. "You remember," he said.

"I remember," Albanon blurted. "*Alak tashar—*"

"That's enough," Kri said. "I can't decide if your mind is too whole to be safe or too broken to be useful." His eyes dropped to the fire still dancing across Albanon's fingertips. "Or perhaps too broken to be safe."

Kri had asked no question so Albanon gave him no answer, but he let the fire that had sprung up unbidden fade from his hands.

"But I need you," Kri continued. "I can't kill you, and I can't risk shattering your mind completely. So as long as you remain . . . pliable, I suppose we will carry on as planned."

With a last searching look at Albanon, Kri lowered himself to his knees in the center of the circle. He laid the chunk of crystal on the floor. "Chained God, guide me," he breathed. He lifted the tiny vial and strained at the stopper with a visible effort. He thrust the vial at Albanon and growled, "Open this. Carefully!"

The stopper was stuck fast. Peering into the vial, Albanon noted that the glass had fused together somehow, as if the substance within had heated like a furnace and shaped a new orb around itself. Albanon formed his finger and thumb into a ring around the neck of the vial and concentrated for a moment, creating a thin plane of magical force within the ring that made a clean cut through the glass.

The substance within surged up the sides of the vial and out the mouth, defying gravity as if thrilled to be free, and splashed onto his hand. It was cool and slick, and it spread quickly into a thin film covering his whole hand.

"No, you fool!" Kri shouted. "Get it onto the shard!"

Albanon stared, transfixed, at his red hand and wrist. A distant memory surfaced in his mind—a serpent of red crystal snaking out of Tempest's dying body, surging onto Falon's flesh, reaching for the young cleric's face and forcing itself into his mouth. Like the demons he'd fought, the red liquid was a dark snarl in the fabric of magic, out of place even in the more tangled weave of magic in the world.

Kri was on his feet now, clutching the crystal and holding it up near Albanon's hand as if its mere proximity would draw the substance away from Albanon's flesh. Sure enough, a drop of the Voidharrow fell onto the shard. A flash of brilliant light cast stark shadows all around the chamber, and Albanon imagined that he saw the trails of Moorin's blood in the darkness.

A more recent memory fought its way into his awareness. The thing that had been Vestapalk, the dragon that was now a demon, looming over him and drooling the Voidharrow onto his forehead, infusing him with the substance of its corruption. Then Kri tending to him before the red substance took him completely, purging his body clean with divine light.

A formula took shape in his mind and rolled off his tongue, and his hand began to glow. First red light shone in an orb around his hand, but then the liquid began to burn away and the pure white light shone through, growing steadily brighter.

Kri snatched the crystal away before the light could sear it, shouting, "No! You're destroying it!"

Albanon allowed the light to die and examined his hands. None of the substance remained, either on his skin or in the vial.

Then Kri's fist slammed into his jaw, knocking him backward and jumbling his thoughts. He felt like he'd been on the cusp of an important realization or insight, but it was gone, like a word that vanished from the tip of his tongue.

"I would kill you where you stand," the Doomdreamer said, "but now is the moment I need you."

The Voidharrow had fused with the shard and expanded around it. Albanon closed his eyes and extended his other senses, and he felt and understood the crystalline structure forming around the shard, matching its internal structure, channeling magical energy in a precise pattern. He also noted that the liquid was replicating itself, like a living creature, forming more of its substance from nothing.

Kri thrust the shard toward him again, holding it in both hands as it slowly expanded. "Place your hands on the Vast Gate with me and help it grow, shape it with me."

The liquid slithered over the surface of the crystal, expanding it and fusing with it so Albanon couldn't tell where the original shard ended and the new substance began. He was hesitant to touch it, for fear the liquid would try to fuse with him again, but he didn't want to—no, he *couldn't* disobey the Doomdreamer. He placed both hands on the crystal and felt the magic surging through it.

Kri stared at him and spoke in a tone of firm command. "We are shaping the Vast Gate, forming an archway, creating a pathway between worlds. Keep those thoughts in mind and no others."

As they guided its growth, the crystal expanded into a slender column that they soon had to rest on the floor.

They shaped it up and over into a curving arch, then—with agonizing slowness as the amount of liquid flowing over the surface diminished almost to nothing—back down to touch the floor again.

Albanon heard the soft pop of air as an unknown landscape, a dark and forbidding castle on a high promontory, appeared in the archway. The scene then disappeared as quickly as it had appeared, replaced by a foam-washed seashore.

The Vast Gate was open.

CHAPTER THIRTY-ONE

Roghar led his new ragtag army—the handful of soldiers who had helped him and Tempest defeat the fire demons—on a triumphant march through the shattered doors of the Silver Unicorn. Smoke still wafted around near the ceiling—more smoke than usual, anyway. Besides the front doors, a few other windows and doors were crashed in, curtains and bedsheets scorched or incinerated, and timbers here and there were blackened with fire, but the inn had escaped a far worse fate thanks to their efforts. To her credit, Wisara Osterman acknowledged that fact, promising that the "heroes of Fallcrest" could drink at the Silver Unicorn for the rest of their lives, on the house.

"She obviously doesn't know you very well," Tempest whispered to Roghar.

"I'm not sure I want to do my drinking here, anyway," Roghar said. "It's sort of a dump."

Uldane stalked in a few minutes after they got settled and silently took a seat at the table.

"No luck?" Roghar asked.

Uldane shook his head with a glance at Tempest.

"Where are Shara and the drow?"

Uldane shrugged.

"What's the matter with you, Uldane?" Roghar said, clapping the halfling on the shoulder. "We won, didn't we?"

"I don't want to talk about it." The halfling crossed his arms and seemed to fold in on himself, turning away from Roghar.

Shara burst in then, scanning the room, and the drow loomed at her shoulder. "Where in the three worlds is Albanon?" Shara said.

"Albanon?" Roghar said. "I haven't seen him since . . ."

"He was there," Shara said, storming to the table. "I saw him, and Kri as well, *talking* to him."

"Kri was talking to Albanon? Who's Kri?" Roghar asked.

"They were both talking to Nu Alin!" Shara said. "They let him get away!"

"You found Nu Alin?" Tempest asked, leaning forward.

"He got away," Uldane said. "I'm sorry, Tempest, I tried to catch him."

"He would have killed you," Roghar said. "None of us is strong enough to handle him alone."

Quarhaun rubbed his throat, where several lighter spots in his dark skin marked recent wounds only partially healed by magic. "True enough," he said, his voice hoarse.

"But he got away," Uldane said.

"I can't believe Albanon would let him go like that," Tempest said. "He hates the demon almost as much as I do."

Roghar scratched his chin. "Is it possible he didn't recognize Nu Alin?"

JAMES WYATT

"Maybe at first," Shara said. "But he watched the demon hit me and he didn't lift a finger. Then he just walked away."

"I'm sorry to say it," Roghar said, "but I think we need to treat the elf as an enemy until we know what's going on."

"Eladrin," Tempest said automatically.

"Whatever. But perhaps Nu Alin has powers of mind control we're not aware of."

"Or else Kri does," Shara said.

"Tell me again who this Kri is?" Roghar said. "A priest of Ioun, you said?"

"Yes. Kri helped us deal with another demon, another servant of Vestapalk. He knows more about the threat we face than anyone, and he said he was the last member of an order that Albanon's mentor also belonged to. After we destroyed that other demon, he took Albanon into the Feywild, looking for a weapon we could use against Vestapalk."

Roghar rumbled as he absorbed this information. "You think he was lying?"

"I don't know," Shara said. "I trusted him—I think we all did. But he seemed to be doing most of the talking with Nu Alin just now."

"Imagine," Quarhaun said, his voice dripping with sarcasm. "A trusted servant of the gods turns out to be not so trustworthy after all."

"What in the Nine Hells is that supposed to mean?" Roghar said.

"You think only priests of the Spider Queen are capable of treachery? I am not so naive."

"If you expect treachery from every quarter, you're certain to find it."

"And if you don't expect it," Quarhaun said with a wry smile, "it will find you."

"So you won't be surprised to hear that I don't trust you outside the reach of my sword arm," Roghar growled.

"But a dagger in the ribs comes from inside that reach." The drow was still smiling, but there was a look in his eyes that Roghar found even more threatening than his words.

"You're right," Roghar said, rising to his feet. "I don't trust you at all, and I wouldn't miss you if I never saw you again."

"Roghar, sit down," Shara whispered, glancing around at the soldiers and citizens who had paused from their celebrations to listen to him. "Quarhaun's just toying with you."

"Like a cat toys with a mouse before it pounces," Roghar said as he lowered himself back down to his chair. "But I warn you, drow, I'm no mouse."

Quarhaun shrugged. "And I'm no cat."

"Stop it," Shara said to the drow, squeezing his hand. "And you, too," she added with a sharp glance at Roghar. "This whole thing started with Albanon and Kri. They're the ones who let Nu Alin escape, not Quarhaun."

"Well." Roghar took a deep breath, biting back another angry retort for Shara's sake. "The important thing is that we've scored a first victory. We killed a lot of those demons, and showed the citizens of Fallcrest a ray of hope. Now we take the fight to them and retake Lowtown!"

The nearby soldiers cheered, and the inn patrons who'd been dragged from their beds in the middle of the night joined in, and Roghar felt, however briefly, like a proper hero. But a glance at Shara, Tempest, and Uldane showed him that he'd failed to inspire them in the slightest.

"Fine," Shara said. "You can be the hero of Fallcrest. But I have a dragon to kill. I'm tired of facing his exarchs and letting him mock me through them. I need to find him and take him out, once and for all."

"What, and leave Fallcrest defenseless?" Roghar said.

"Cut off the head and the body dies, too," Shara said, with a glance at Quarhaun. "Nu Alin isn't the head. It's Vestapalk. He's out there, somewhere to the west, and I mean to find him."

"Is Vestapalk the head of Kri and Albanon as well?" Tempest asked.

"I assume so," Shara said. "Why?"

"What if he's not? What if there's another head behind them both? When does it stop?"

"Sooner or later, we'll find whoever's in charge of all of this. I think it's Vestapalk. Do you have a better idea?"

"I'm just trying to say that it's not necessarily a good idea to ignore these evils just because they're not 'the head,' you see? If we discovered tomorrow that Vestapalk and Nu Alin and Kri were all servants of Tiamat, for example, would you abandon your quest for vengeance against Vestapalk and go hunt down the dragon queen?"

Shara frowned. "No," she admitted. "But this is different. Vestapalk—not Tiamat, not any other evil mastermind, Vestapalk has taunted me through the mouths of two of his demon pawns. I'm through fighting pawns."

Roghar glanced around the room. Soldiers and citizens alike were talking quietly among themselves, their initial fervor after his pronouncement fading quickly. "Listen," he said. "A moment ago, half the people in this room were ready to charge out the door with me and drive the demons out of this town. With every second we spend bickering, that number drops. If we want to use their excitement, we have to act now."

"You have to keep your pawns in play as well," Shara said. "I see."

"They're not my pawns," Roghar protested.

"Of course they are," Quarhaun said. "At least the priests of Lolth have the honesty to admit it."

"This is their town!" Roghar said. "I'm just encouraging them to retake it for themselves."

"Fine," Shara said. "Then let them retake it while we go hunt down Vestapalk."

"They need leadership," Roghar said.

Quarhaun arched an eyebrow. "The silken words of every tyrant."

"Tyrant?" Roghar got to his feet again, drawing the eyes of every soldier in the room—and a few cheers. Emboldened by the cheers, he gave up on arguing with the drow and turned to address the room. "People of Fallcrest," he said, "the time to liberate our town from the demons is *now*!" He drew his sword and held it over his head, inspiring more cheers.

"Now it's *our* town," he heard Quarhaun mutter behind him.

Roghar ignored him. "Soldiers, take up your arms! Gather your comrades! We gather in the square to free Lowtown and drive the demons back to the pits that spawned them! For Fallcrest, for Bahamut, and for glory!"

A roar of cheers nearly deafened him. The soldiers and many of the citizens were on their feet and crowding out the door to the square, ready to begin their counterassault. Roghar's heart was pounding in his chest in anticipation of the coming battle.

"Well, I guess that settles it," Shara said.

Roghar turned back to the table. Uldane and Tempest were on their feet as well, both looking ready to follow him out the door. Shara and Quarhaun still sat at the table, their arms folded and their faces dour.

"You're not coming?" he said.

"What have I been saying all this time?" Shara said. "Have you even been listening?"

"But I thought—"

"You thought your stirring speech would change our minds, or that we'd be too embarrassed not to accompany you when the rest of the town was on your side. Or you just got caught up in the excitement and didn't think at all. It doesn't matter."

"Shara, listen to reason."

"Good luck with the demons, Roghar," Shara said. She looked at Tempest. "I hope you find Nu Alin, and kill him for what he did to you."

Roghar scowled. "Well," he said, "I hope you get your revenge on Vestapalk as well."

Shara extended a hand, and he shook it. He nodded to the drow, who returned the gesture, and turned to the door.

"Uldane?" Shara said.

"Good-bye, Shara," the halfling said, his words clipped.

"I still don't—"

"Maybe this never occurred to you, caught up in the mad whirlwind of your love for Jarren, but I loved him, too. He was my friend—maybe my best friend. And he wouldn't have wanted this for you."

As he went out the door, Roghar looked over his shoulder and saw Shara stiffen. She stared at Uldane for a long moment, then nodded. "Good-bye, Uldane."

CHAPTER THIRTY-TWO

Albanon's head spun and his stomach sank as a kaleidoscope of worlds appeared and disappeared within the frame of the Vast Gate. He felt magic flaring in the channels created by Moorin's blood, drawn to the opening of the gate, tugging at the forces within the gate as if to channel them in a particular direction. Kri finally seemed to become aware of the additional magic at work in the tower, casting nervous glances around at the rest of the room even as he tried to concentrate on focusing the gate on a single destination—the prison of the Chained God.

"Chained God!" Kri called. "Ender and Anathema, Eater of Worlds, Undoer: Come and wreak destruction!"

Albanon's stomach churned and he remembered finding Moorin dead in his tower, the blood and gore everywhere, the reek of the wizard's spilled guts and acrid blood. This is all wrong, some part of his mind declared. We're supposed to prevent this, to work against the killer of Moorin, not according to his purpose.

The chaos in his mind sent the image in the Vast Gate spinning dizzily from world to world. Albanon lurched out of the magic circle and emptied his stomach onto the floor, falling to his hands and knees as his gut contracted again and again until nothing remained to heave up.

When he looked up, the archway of the Vast Gate was filled with utter darkness. Kri stood transfixed before it, gazing into the void, a look of bliss on his weathered face.

"Tharizdun," he whispered.

"No," Albanon gasped. "Kri, wait!"

"Patient One. He Who Waits. Chained God." Kri's voice grew slowly louder as he intoned the appellations of Tharizdun.

Albanon's throat burned and his head was pounding, but he staggered to his feet. "Kri, remember your oath! The Oath of Vigilance!"

"Your waiting is over and your freedom is at hand!"

The darkness in the Vast Gate changed subtly. It remained an inky black that repelled all light, but red liquid flowed behind and beneath it, too, gleaming here and there like tiny, dim stars in an awful night sky. Albanon had the fleeting sense of something poised and waiting in the darkness, ready to spring.

And then it erupted through the gate and emerged into the world.

First was a wave of sheer power, like a blast from a furnace but without light or heat, just raw energy that washed past him, overwhelmed him, battered him to the floor, and left him for dead. He was nothing to it, utterly insignificant, like an ant beneath the foot of a titan. It filled the tower and extended farther, probing into the world beyond.

Albanon's mind reeled from trying to take it in, unable to comprehend the vastness of what he perceived and what was perceiving him. Somehow whatever was left of his mind understood that it was the eye of Tharizdun—the mere attention of the Chained God, extended from his prison in the void into the world on the other side of the Vast Gate. None of the god's power or substance had yet passed through, but the simple fact of his glance passing over Albanon had left him wrecked and teetering at the brink of madness.

Kri had already plunged over that brink, and he babbled and wailed long strings of nonsense syllables as Tharizdun's gaze seemed to focus upon him. He stood with his arms spread open to the gate, eyes open but rolled back in his head, his body arched in ecstatic torment in the sight of his god.

Next through the gate came a slow seepage of liquid red crystal, more of the Voidharrow probing through the gate. Albanon gasped as the first snaky tendrils surged out toward him, but they passed him by, coursing out along the pathways that Nu Alin had laid with Moorin's blood.

Once more Albanon perceived the pattern of the whorls and arcs of blood, the channels that directed both the flow of magic and the movement of the Voidharrow. Arcane formulas gave structure to his thoughts again, and he understood what had escaped him until that moment, what Kri still had not grasped. The Voidharrow was forming a lattice, a net that would catch and bind whatever emerged through the Vast Gate.

Even the Chained God.

A moment before, Albanon would have found it impossible to conceive of anything worse than the Chained God emerging through the gate that he and Kri had opened. Then he tried to imagine a demon like Nu Alin, or like the monster at Sherinna's tower, but infused with the power of the Eater of Worlds.

"No no no," he murmured.

He staggered across the room to the place where Moorin's body had lain, slumped on the floor against the far wall. Tears stung his eyes as he fell to the floor, just as he had done on the night of Moorin's death. It had never before occurred to him to wonder who had cleaned the tower and what had become of the body, and he was stung with guilt as he realized that he should have ensured that Moorin was properly laid to rest. But he shook the feeling from his thoughts, putting himself in the position Moorin had occupied, the focus of all the lines and whorls of energy in the room.

He felt the Voidharrow coursing toward him along dozens of different pathways. Hundreds of wordless, whispering voices pressed against his mind, overwhelming him with a sense of eager hunger. Terror set his whole body quivering. The red liquid of the Voidharrow gleamed like blood on the walls, floor, and ceiling.

Is this what Moorin saw as he died? Albanon wondered.

He fought back his terror and focused on the magic. Numbers and formulas danced in his mind. He felt power welling up in his heart like a sun, then his body started to glow. He spread his arms wide and felt the magic course out from him, sending light flowing like pure water back along the channels that laced the room to meet the approaching Voidharrow. Where the flow of light met the red liquid it flared into white fire, and in a moment the room was lit with a hundred stars where his light burned the Voidharrow.

The Voidharrow's fury was a palpable pulse in the air of the room, but it was an impotent rage. The light burning out from Albanon filled the channels, and the Voidharrow seemed unable to flow outside the lines that had been prepared for it. All it could do was inch slowly back the way it had come, back to the Vast Gate, until the room was filled with an intricate lacework of Albanon's light.

Then the Voidharrow was gone entirely, but the attention of Tharizdun, which had diminished to a mere brooding presence in the room, surged outward again, as if it had been waiting for the Voidharrow to get out of its way. Albanon rehearsed the formulas in his mind, focused his power to keep his own lattice in place, thinking perhaps he could hold the Chained God back.

He quickly realized how foolish a hope that had been. With eagerness born of untold ages of imprisonment, a flow of shadowy slime began to pour out from the Vast Gate. A dark mist rose up from the slime, and Kri stood in a billowing cloud of it, breathing deeply as if to draw the Chained God's power into himself. The dark slime flowed out into the channels of Albanon's light, and all his exertion couldn't stop its flow or even slow it down. It ran like a surging river along every channel at once, converging around him before he could move from his position on the floor.

Soul-numbing cold gripped him as the liquid shadow surrounded him on every side. His body convulsed with what would have been agony if the cold hadn't deadened his every nerve. His mind reeled once again, driving away all sense of purpose, shattering his memory and robbing him of his power.

He watched dumbly as Kri drew in more and more of the shadowy mist, gathering it in a dark nimbus around himself. The old man seemed to grow younger, stronger, and even taller as the power flowed into him. He strode through the eddying mist to stand beside Albanon's inert body, and Albanon stared up at him without managing to form a coherent thought.

Kri crouched down and seized Albanon's shoulders, lifted him effortlessly from the floor, and stood him on his feet. Albanon's head swam but his feet stayed under him somehow. Kri stared into his eyes and smiled, but there was no hint of humor or kindness on his face.

"The Chained God is chained no more, Albanon," he said. "He emerges from his prison. And you are a witness. You will be my right hand in the new temple of Tharizdun."

The words washed over Albanon without registering any meaning, but they left a foul taste behind. Billowing shadow loomed up around him, threatening, but Albanon could feel the promise of power beneath the threat—power that could destroy him or exalt him. Kri wielded that power already, and slowly Albanon understood that Kri was offering to share it with him.

Not offering, he realized—Kri presented him no option to refuse.

His mind grasped at the last word he'd heard, Tharizdun. Three syllables, nine letters, three threes. Each third was a microcosm of the whole, and the whole could be expanded into an ever-growing geometric formula . . .

Albanon's body shook with building power and he let it out in a flash of lightning and roar of thunder that hurled Kri away from him and across the room, shook the Vast Gate, and even seemed to push back the billowing mist for a moment. In that moment, he threw himself at the gate.

A snaky tendril caught his ankle and sent him sprawling. Black slime crept toward him on every side, and he felt the full brunt of the Chained God's awareness focused on him. That more than any physical restraint kept him pinned to the ground, straining to keep a hold on his fragile mind. The physical manifestation of the god, he realized, was just the tiniest extrusion of Tharizdun's power, like a fingertip poked through the little hole between worlds created by the Vast Gate.

Then Kri was beside him again, looking down and shaking his head. "Albanon, you fool," he said. "You could have become one of the mightiest beings in all the worlds. Instead, you will be the first thing destroyed when the Eater of Worlds makes his return. The first of many."

Albanon felt himself lifted up, like an insect pinched between the fingertips of a mighty giant, and drawn toward the Vast Gate. Tendrils of black slime held him aloft, dangling upside-down, as wafting shadow swirled around him. With a jolt of fear, he realized that the tendrils holding him were part of Kri now—the old priest's legs were gone, replaced or fused with the sickening mass of sludge that extended out to cover the room.

Albanon hung before the Vast Gate and stared into the void beyond. The vastness of nothingness threatened to unhinge his mind again, but he forced himself to consider the curvature of the gate's archway and the crystalline structure of its substance, which he had helped Kri to form and to focus.

Focus. With the power of the Chained God still flowing through the gate, its focus was fixed in place, the connection between the world and the god's prison firmly established. That didn't mean it couldn't be changed, though.

He had no time for thought, not with the Chained God's eye fixed on him. Swinging in the grasp of Kri's snaky tendrils, he planted a hand on the crystal of the Vast Gate and exerted his will to change its destination.

Kri yanked him away from the gate and the smooth crystal fell away from his hand, but too late. The blackness within the arch blinked and vanished, and the power and will that had filled the room was gone. Slimy tentacles still writhed everywhere, and a cloak of misty shadow still surrounded Kri like a manifestation of the power that churned within him, but the Chained God was cut off. Where there had been inky blackness and roiling malice on the other side of the portal, now there was only a dry plain.

"Damned fool," Kri said. "You are wasting my time. I will kill you, then, and refocus the Vast Gate myself."

Another inky tendril wrapped around Albanon's neck, and Kri began to pull from both ends of his body, as if to tear him apart.

CHAPTER THIRTY-THREE

Roghar stepped out of the Silver Unicorn and was greeted by a cheer—a handful of ragged voices raised in his honor after too much to drink in the local public house. Their acclamation had seemed much louder in the confined space of the inn's common room, and their numbers had looked greater as well. He looked around the cluster of soldiers and counted about a dozen, all clutching torches and weapons, stamping their feet and clanging steel against their shields.

"What in the Nine Hells was I thinking?" he muttered to Tempest.

"Hush," she said. "These people need leadership, and they know a hero when they see one."

"That certainly explains the welcome we received on the bridge."

"You promised them what they need. Now give it to them."

He glanced down at Uldane and saw the halfling beaming up at him, the anger of the last hour and the bitterness of his final exchange with Shara apparently forgotten in the excitement of the moment. "You raised an army, Roghar!" Uldane said. "Well, it's more people than we had when we fought the demons on the bluffs, anyway."

Somebody set a wooden crate on the cobblestones in front of him and he stepped onto it, looking out over his little army. A line of vermilion across the eastern horizon marked the approach of dawn, though a few stars still burned brightly overhead, shining through chinks in the cloud and smoke that draped the sky. He drew his sword to more cheers, and lifted it high over his head.

"People of Fallcrest!" he said.

Slowly the cheering diminished as the soldiers quieted to listen to him. He let his eyes range over the crowd—he counted fourteen this time—and tried to size them up. A couple were professional soldiers, judging by the quality of their arms and armor, but most were militia, ordinary folks who had risen to the defense of their homes. That was perhaps the only advantage he could claim in the battle ahead. His soldiers would be dedicated to protecting their town. That would have to suffice.

"We face a foe unlike any you have faced before," he said when the cheers had quieted. "These are not orcs from the Stonemarch, come to sack and burn the way they did ninety years ago. These are not bandits united under some warlord, come to plunder and pillage. You've seen them. These are demons, spawned in the dark pit of the Abyss with just one purpose—to destroy everything we know and love. The farms of our neighbors are burning, the Nentir Inn is aflame. Lowtown has become their haunt, and the forests across the river are silent."

Roghar looked at each soldier gathered there—now he had eighteen—and saw fear in every eye. Good, he thought. They should be afraid.

"But they can be fought," he went on. "You saw that tonight. Some of them are creatures of living fire, others are nightmare made manifest. But they're all still flesh and bone that sword and spear can pierce and break. Their greatest weapon is fear. Ours is hope—hope that casts out fear, hope that strengthens our arms to protect our homes, hope that shines light into the darkness!" He lifted his sword again and it began to glow, growing stronger until it was a blazing sun, a beacon of divine light shining across the square.

The little army erupted in cheers again, and at that moment the sun broke over the horizon, sending beams of light into the clouds.

"For Fallcrest!" Roghar shouted over the cheers. "For Bahamut, and for glory!"

Twenty-four soldiers stood before him now, cheering and rattling their weapons. His army had doubled in strength in the time he had taken to speak to them. He wondered how much larger it might grow if he spoke longer, but he shook off the thought. His soldiers were ready to fight, and there would be no better time to strike.

"To the bluffs!" he called. "First we take the Market Green!"

Roghar stepped down off the crate. All around him, soldiers clapped him on the shoulder or slapped their swords against his shield. Tempest and Uldane found their way through the soldiers to his side, and together the three of them led the way down Market Street toward the bluffs.

"Well done," Tempest whispered to him as they walked.

"Thank you."

"Your timing was amazing," Uldane said. "Did you know that the sun was going to rise at that exact moment?"

Roghar laughed. "I had my eye on it, but I basically got lucky. Or else Bahamut put in a good word for me with Pelor."

"I'm not sure it works that way," Tempest said.

"Lucky, then."

"Let's hope our luck holds," Uldane said.

Roghar glanced over his shoulder at the soldiers following them—following him, really. He was almost certain their numbers had swelled still further.

"More of them keep coming," he said to Tempest.

"Of course they do."

"I hope the Lord Warden doesn't take offense at me for presuming to lead his troops."

Tempest smiled. "Well, I can think of two likely outcomes. Either you lead them to victory, in which case he can't really complain. Or you lead them to annihilation and he gets furious, but you're not around to get punished."

"I like the first option," Uldane said.

Roghar nodded. "I agree. Let's aim for that."

"Do you have a plan?" Tempest asked.

"When have I ever had a plan?"

"You sound like Shara," Uldane said with a grin that quickly dissolved into a scowl.

JAMES WYATT

Roghar walked a few paces in silence, confident that if the halfling wanted to talk about whatever was bothering him, he would. Uldane could generally be counted on to speak up in any circumstance, even on the way to a battle that might be his last.

"It's like she just doesn't care any more," Uldane said at last. "I mean, she always enjoyed fighting, but after Jarren died she just got reckless. And you know nothing scares me, but I don't like the feeling that my friend doesn't care if I live or die—doesn't even care if she dies. Jarren cared. Jarren cared for us both."

Roghar put a hand on Uldane's shoulder as the halfling rubbed at his eye. "And the drow?"

"He doesn't give a damn. He doesn't care about anything but himself. It's like being with him is just another way for Shara to put herself in danger."

"You think she's in real danger?"

"Yes! I don't think he'd pause a minute before turning on her if he thought he could save himself."

Roghar scratched his chin. "Shara told the soldiers on the bridge that he had saved her life, more than once."

"He helped us fight the demons, it's true. But he's just looking out for himself."

"Hm. I think that's a little different than saying he himself is a danger to her."

Uldane shrugged. "I don't see how."

"Well, Uldane, Shara's heart was broken. And I think she blames herself for Vestapalk's return when we all thought he was dead."

"So she's punishing herself?"

"I think so, yes."

"That's stupid. It's like . . . like making a wound larger because it doesn't hurt enough."

"People who are hurting sometimes do things that don't make much sense."

"All you tall folk do things that don't make sense, all the time. I guess it's nothing new."

Roghar stopped walking. The straight and level road had come to an end, and ahead was the winding track leading down the bluffs to Lowtown and the Market Green. "Like leading a ragtag gang of militia into battle against a horde of demons?" he said.

Uldane stepped to the very edge of the bluff and leaned over so far that Roghar felt a rush of vertigo on his behalf. "Exactly like that," the halfling said. "Look, you can see some of the burning ones moving around down there."

"Do you see any on the trail down the bluff?" Roghar asked.

"No sign of fire. But it was the nightmare ones that attacked us over on the west side. They're not so easy to spot in this light."

"Right. They're hard enough to spot right before they attack. Eyes and ears wide open as we head down, then. We've got to spot them before they attack the soldiers behind us."

Uldane and Tempest both nodded, their attention focused over the edge of the cliff.

Roghar turned to face his little army again. The numbers had swelled further, to more than he could quickly count, and he felt a surge of gratitude that made his chest ache.

"Warriors of Fallcrest!" he called. A chorus of cheers, louder than anything he'd heard back at the inn, answered him. "We march into enemy territory," he said. "But we're not going to find massed lines of demon soldiers waiting for us—they don't fight that way. They'll send little squads to harry us, to bite at our flanks and nip at our heels. That means we need to be as nimble as they are. If there's too many of them and too few of you, fall back and find help. There's no disgrace in it."

He let his eyes range over his troops. He saw nods of understanding, faces set in determination as soldiers steeled themselves for battle, and a few of them taking nips from little flasks of liquid courage. The early rays of sunlight gleamed on their steel caps and spearheads, resting like the favor of the gods on each of them.

"On to victory!" he shouted.

"Victory!" came a cheer in response.

Roghar lifted his glowing sword over his head and started down the trail, Uldane and Tempest close behind him and a surge of desperately eager soldiers pressing him on.

The cliff that divided Fallcrest in two offered a sheer drop of more than two hundred feet in the center of town. The track made use of natural ledges and dwarf-cut switchbacks to provide a path a wagon could follow, albeit slowly and very carefully—especially on the turns. It was only barely wide enough for a wagon, and every time a wagon started the descent a runner would hurry to the bottom to make sure a different wagon didn't start up at the same time. But even that arrangement was better than what the other two roads that traversed the bluffs offered—riders and small carts could navigate them, but wagons were out of the question. That made Market Street the best option for his soldiers, but still not a great option.

Roghar tried to listen for any sign of an ambush, but the soldiers behind him made an unbelievable amount of noise. Wayward footsteps sent trickles of gravel down the cliffside around him, and even the whispers of more than two dozen men added up to a constant low murmur that made him despair of hearing anything else.

"Up ahead!" Uldane said suddenly. He pointed to a narrow stretch of the trail, where the cliff edge was marked with red warning banners. Roghar knew that at least one wagon had slipped over the edge there and plummeted down, killing several people and as many horses. It was a logical place for an ambush.

He followed Uldane's pointing finger and tried to make out what the halfling had seen, but his eyes showed him no sign of danger.

"I see it," Tempest said. "One of the nightmare demons."

"More than one," Uldane said. "Look up the bluff from the road."

Roghar looked up and spotted at least some of the demons Uldane saw—three or four of the shadowy demons, lurking among the scrub trees that clung to the bluffs. "Well done, Uldane. Let's get them!"

His sword blazing like the sun, Roghar charged forward. As he neared the point where he'd spotted the demons, he called on Bahamut's power, and a gust of wind like a swooping angel lifted him off the ground and set him down in the midst of the demons on the bluff. One foot slipped as he landed, and for a moment he feared he was about to tumble down the cliff, but he got his feet under him again and stood his ground as three shadowy figures surged toward him.

"You killed us," one of the figures said, no longer a demon of shadow and Voidharrow but a soldier just like the ones behind him, clad in leather and clutching a spear. The man's eyes were dead and his flesh gone gray, but he moved with all the speed of the living. The other two figures took on similar shapes, and they reached for him with their dead hands, whispering words of condemnation.

"You led us to our doom," one said.

"Foolhardy," said another.

The ground beneath Roghar's feet began to rumble, matching the pounding of his heart. His mind knew that these demons could prey on his fears and turn them against him, but when faced with his deepest terrors given flesh, he found it nearly impossible to listen to that part of his mind. He glanced around and saw gravel tumbling down the bluffs, and he realized what the rumbling meant.

A landslide would obliterate his entire, pathetic army in one blow.

"You did this to us," a dead soldier said, clawing at his eyes.

Roghar whirled his sword around him in a wide circle, trailing light like a comet. Steel and radiance bit into the walking corpses that threatened him and they recoiled, allowing their true demonic faces to show through for a moment.

"Hurry!" he yelled to the soldiers behind him. "Landslide!"

The demons in their dead-soldier guises closed around him again, and the rumbling of the earth grew louder. His sword exploded in light as he slammed the blade into the middle demon's shoulder, cutting through red crystal and shadowy flesh until nothing remained but dust. He spun to face the two remaining demons and roared his triumph, punctuating his roar with a blast of dragonfire from his mouth. As he conquered his fear their faces with their haunting eyes melted away—and he realized with a start that the rumbling of the earth stopped as well.

There was no landslide—it was just another weapon of the demons, playing on his fears.

But it might have been their most effective weapon yet. In his fear, he had shouted an order to his soldiers that had instilled the same fear in them. Fear could turn an army of soldiers into a panicked mob in an instant, and a glance behind him confirmed that his warning had done exactly that.

"Halt!" he shouted, but he had no confidence that his voice would be heard over the tumult of the panicking soldiers. And before he could do anything more, the other two demons redoubled their assault.

"I've heard a lot of lies and excuses in my career," one demon said, taking on the appearance of the commander on the bridge and glaring at Roghar, "but never so bold a lie from a paladin of Bahamut."

The other stood back and seemed to grow. Its face was a mirror of Roghar's own, and great leathery wings spread from its shoulders.

"Kuyutha," he murmured, awe and fear seizing control of his thoughts. Kuyutha was an exarch of Bahamut, a dragonborn who had been a paladin like him in life, but ascended to his god's right hand. Dragonborn revered Kuyutha as Bahamut's particular emissary to them, who had shepherded the scattered clans after the fall of the empire of Arkhosia centuries ago. He was said to train the bravest and purest dragonborn paladins personally, in his halls in the celestial mountains.

"You have failed Bahamut," the exarch said. "I share our god's disappointment."

Roghar glanced between the two figures expressing their condemnation, and he knew the exarch's words were true. He was a failure as a paladin, a disappointment to Bahamut and a mockery of all his god's ideals. He fell to his knees and bowed his head, feeling unworthy even to look at Kuyutha. The commander stepped closer and drew a sword, as if to carry out a sentence of execution.

"For Fallcrest!" came a shout from somewhere behind him.

"For Bahamut, and for glory!" more voices cried.

Roghar looked up just as the commander swung his sword at Roghar's neck. A reflex brought his shield up to block the blow, and he sprang to his feet.

A wave of soldiers was about to break around him. As he stared, trying to remember what was happening, the first soldiers reached the commander, hacking him with swords and prodding him with spears. He made a sound somewhere between a hiss and a roar and changed, his human face transforming into a blank, alien visage of leathery black skin and red crystal.

Roghar spun to face Kuyutha—or rather, the demon that had adopted Kuyutha's visage and presumed to speak with his voice. "Blasphemy!" he spat. "You dare to speak with the voice of my god!"

"You are the one putting words in your god's mouth," the demon whispered.

Roghar's sword flared with divine light as he drove its point through the demon's gut. Kuyutha's face faded as the demon crumbled into dust and ash. "For Bahamut," he muttered, looking down at the scarlet residue left in its wake.

A cheer erupted from the soldiers as the other demon fell under their blows. Roghar turned to survey the scene. Tempest and Uldane had led an assault on the demons on the other side of the road, and they stood in the midst of another clump of cheering soldiers.

"Our first victory is won!" Roghar shouted, and another round of cheers erupted from the soldiers. Four demons, he thought. How many more do we have to face?

CHAPTER THIRTY-FOUR

Albanon stared at the Vast Gate as Kri pulled at him, peering through the billowing blackness at the dry landscape that had appeared in the archway. He thought he saw a tiny speck in the crystal blue sky beyond the gate, but it was too far to be of help.

I have to face Kri on my own, he thought.

An effortless gesture sent a bolt of arcane force hurtling at Kri—a weak attack, but it was all he could manage as his spine creaked and popped, sending waves of agony through his body. The bolt glanced off Kri's shoulder, but it was enough to make the grip of the slimy black tentacles weaken just slightly. Albanon used that moment to slash with his dagger at the tendril that held his neck. It relinquished its hold and he dangled from his ankles again, gasping for air.

"Why do you struggle?" Kri mused. His voice had grown larger—deeper and stronger, and with a resonance that defied the acoustics of the stone chamber, as if he were speaking in some other space. "Do you not see the power I wield? I am the exarch of Tharizdun, the extension of his reach into this pathetic world. You cannot resist me."

"And yet I do," Albanon said, slashing at the tentacles that held his feet. Other tendrils batted at his arms, deflecting his blows.

"Because all mortals are born to futility. Mortal life itself is a futile exercise, a vain struggle against an inevitable doom."

Albanon stretched out the fingers of one hand and engulfed Kri in a roaring blast of fire even as more tendrils coiled around his legs and arms. Kri roared in pain, but this time his grip didn't falter. A thick tentacle wrapped around Albanon's waist and squeezed, forcing the breath from his lungs.

A distant sound like the baying of many hounds wafted through the Vast Gate. Albanon roared with the last breath in his chest, and a clap of thunder erupted between him and Kri, drowning out the sound from the gate. The force of the blast pushed Kri backward and knocked away the tendrils that held Albanon, sending him sprawling onto the floor near the gate.

Please hurry, Albanon thought, willing his thoughts to travel through the gate.

"What are you doing?" Kri said. "You're waiting for something, trying to buy time. What feeble hope are you clinging to?"

"I can beat you," Albanon said through gritted teeth, climbing slowly to his feet.

Kri laughed. "I admit that your power has grown since you left that fool Moorin's tutelage," he said. "And the shattering of your mind seems to have expanded your power even more. But you have no idea what you're facing."

"Moorin was no fool," Albanon said.

"He held you back, kept you from the full extent of your power."

"He trained me in the responsible use of my power. He gave me all the tools I needed to make use of it, even if I didn't realize it at the time."

"Oh, you've found it in your heart to forgive the old man, have you? How touching, in the last moments before your own death. And in the same room where he met his grisly end, no less."

That gave Albanon an idea. He glanced around the room again, his eyes darting over the arcane pattern formed by Moorin's blood.

"What are you doing?" Kri demanded. A thick tendril of inky blackness darted at his head, but Albanon ducked it and slid a few steps to his right.

Formulas danced through his mind and lightning shot from his fingertips. He saw Kri recoil, but the lightning coursed all around him, tracing the eldritch lines in the chamber, forming a net of deadly power that surrounded him.

"No!" Kri screamed. His flesh seared and some of the inky substance that formed his lower body burned away to greasy smoke as the lightning net closed around him. But he raised his arm and swept it in a wide arc, trailing darkness behind it. As the darkness spread it stifled Albanon's lightning and extinguished the fire.

"I will not suffer any further indignity at your hands, whelp," Kri growled, surging closer to Albanon on his liquid mass of tentacles. He raised his arms over his head—and paused.

The baying of hounds had grown much louder, and Kri hesitated as he looked around to find its source. His eyes settled on the Vast Gate and he frowned.

"Your father's demesne," Kri said. He made a dismissive gesture that hurled Albanon out of his path, and he slid over to the gate. "Thought to call for help, did you? So that's what you were waiting for."

As Kri lifted his hands to the Vast Gate, Albanon sent another bolt of force hurtling into him, delaying him just an instant—and just enough. As Kri reeled back from the arcane attack, the first hound leaped through the gate and sank its teeth into Kri's arm.

The hounds of the fey hunts were no ordinary dogs. Their pelts naturally manifested patterns of arcane power, whorls and lines of lighter or darker hue than the surrounding fur. Their eyes glowed like emeralds lit by fire from within, and bright green flames licked from their mouths as they barked and yelped, launching themselves at their quarry. These hounds had held their own against the demons at the Whitethorn Spire, and they showed no fear as they navigated the writhing mass of tentacles that had taken the place of Kri's legs.

Immeral was the first eladrin to follow the hounds through the gate, his slender sword shining with eldritch light that sliced through the darkness even as his blade bit into Kri's flesh. Another half dozen fey knights appeared through the portal and took up positions surrounding their foe.

"This changes nothing," Kri said. A slimy tentacle yanked one of the fey hounds off him and hurled it against the wall as another tendril batted Immeral away. "You have summoned this hunt to its doom." His tentacles were everywhere, batting at hounds and coiling around the ankles of knights, weaving in the air and emitting their constant stream of dark vapors.

Albanon felt his head spinning again, his grip on his thoughts slipping and madness threatening to claim him again. Kri was no longer human, and what he had become was . . . it seemed impossible, like something from a nightmare or a lunatic's visions. Albanon caught himself counting tentacles instead of casting spells, marveling at the fractal division of what seemed like coherent liquid strands, and tried to force his mind back to the threat Kri posed—both to him and to the allies he had summoned to help him.

"You still hear the call of the Chained God, Albanon," Kri said, staring into his eyes. Even from across the room, his gaze was intense, and it amplified Albanon's sense of vertigo. "Heed it. Release yourself to it."

Albanon felt himself falling, and the room dissolved around him. Instead of stone and mortar, he saw the tower as endless expanses of crystalline structures. The Vast Gate was a hole in space, and the Feywild beyond disappeared from view. The eladrin and their hounds were blobs of amorphous flesh and glowing spheres of magic and soul, coexistent but not united. He himself was much the same, except that his magic swirled around him in great glowing arcs, like comets hurtling through the void of space.

Only Kri seemed unchanged from his new perspective. He remained a thing of madness and nightmare, an intrusion into this reality from somewhere else. He reached a slimy tendril out past an eladrin globule and dipped it into one of the circles of Albanon's power and siphoned off some of his magic, turning it into a blast of fire that leaped at him and washed over hounds and eladrin in its path.

Albanon had no hand to raise in warding, no mouth to give voice to a spell that might counter Kri's attack, no mind to channel his magic at all—but he had will, somehow, some ability to desire and to effect that desire. And the slightest exertion of that will caused a whirling circle of magic to flare into life as the fire crossed it. The fire dissolved back into the magic that made it, reabsorbed it into Albanon's own power.

"That's not possible," Kri said. "Your mind should be broken by now, your power shattered."

Shaping his will into pure defiance, Albanon reined in his mad perceptions and reshaped his sense of reality, forcing his mind to see stone and eladrin and hound and Albanon again in place of the abstractions he had created. One more figure emerged from the Vast Gate, a tiny dragon—Splendid! The dragonet swooped in and perched atop the gate, surveying the scene.

With a jolt like an arrested fall, Albanon began to think again, and suddenly he realized what Kri's weaving tentacles were accomplishing—more than fending off attacks and tangling footsteps, they were *feeding*, sipping from each glowing orb of life and magic, the soul and power of each eladrin and hound arrayed against him. The more opponents he faced, the stronger Kri became.

So Kri had been right. Albanon had summoned Immeral and his hunt to their doom, because their presence only made Kri stronger. Unless . . .

Albanon loosed his grip on his thoughts just slightly, let them wander where they had begun to stray earlier, and let his mind fill with seemingly random patterns—the branching and weaving of Kri's shadowy tendrils. He sank back against the wall as dizziness overcame him, but he saw the patterns, like looking down onto a network of streams and rivulets flowing into a river and feeding the sea. Seeing, he understood, and his understanding gave him power.

An eldritch word, an effort of will, and the focus to keep the patterns and equations fixed in his mind cut off the flow of energy. A second word reversed it, and the backlash was so enormous that every other creature in the room—eladrin and hound and dragonet alike—was hurled away from Kri and sent sprawling to the floor. Albanon screamed a third word to moderate the flow, but it was too late. His allies were reeling from the sudden influx of energy, energy that carried some taint of Kri's madness with it.

Albanon's own mind was nearly overwhelmed by the power flowing into him from Kri, and his perceptions fluctuated back and forth between normal vision and the mad abstractions of crystal, flesh, and magic. His thoughts were a flow of formulas and patterns that sometimes seemed like a stream circling the quivering orb of his flesh. In a way, the mad view of things was helpful, because he could separate himself from that flow of thoughts—it became a resource he could draw upon, instead of a torrent that overwhelmed him.

What his eyes showed him only served to create a current of fear that churned the stream of his thoughts. Kri had erupted in fury at the loss of so much power, and he retained enough might to wreak havoc among the hounds and hunters surrounding him. Three hounds and a huntsman lay dead or dying on the floor, blood pooling around them. Kri was pulling the slimy tentacles back to himself, trying to contain the leakage of his power, and lashing out all around him with bolts and blasts of dark energy and thundering booms.

Power spun around Albanon in ever-widening circles of blinding light, fueled by the energy he'd stolen from Kri, the touch of his dark god. He drew a deep breath and watched the eddies of air and magic around him as he stilled his thoughts, he dipped his mind into the current of patterns and numbers, and he spoke a string of arcane syllables. All the fury of a summer thunderstorm erupted around Kri—lightning crackled over his skin, thunder buffeted him from every side, and wind whipped around him with a furious howl.

To Albanon's mad-sight, Kri seemed to diminish, to get smaller without changing in any other regard. His eyes saw flesh scorched and torn, inky tendrils dissolved into smears of residue on the stone.

Kri's hand fell on the archway of the Vast Gate, and Albanon's heart pounded a warning. The image within the archway flickered and changed—the texture of the hole changed in his mad-sight, in a way that defied description—and then Kri slid through the portal.

No no no, Albanon thought, a beat of denial in the river of his consciousness. He stretched out a hand and extended his will, trying to pull Kri back through the gate, but his magic couldn't reach through to whatever world Kri had entered.

But Kri was not all the way through. Tentacles coiled around the crystalline archway as his body hung suspended on the other side of the gate. His face was contorted with hideous effort, as if his physical exertion was keeping him from passing fully through the portal. A loud crack signaled the fracture of the arch, and the Vast Gate went blank.

Kri was gone, carried off to some other place, and the Vast Gate was just a dead archway, a door to nowhere standing in the midst of Moorin's tower. Albanon stood before the arch, staring through it to the blank stone floor and walls beyond.

"Where did he go?" Immeral said, appearing at Albanon's side, the Elven words flowing like a clear stream from his tongue.

Albanon shrugged. "I don't know," he said.

"To the Feywild?"

"I don't think so. He changed the focus of the gate before he passed through it, and it was still changing as he hung there."

Albanon turned around and surveyed the wreckage of the room. It seemed strangely normal, after the madness of the past hours—quiet and stable and sane, just a room in a tower in a perfectly normal town.

The other eladrin were tending to the dead, and even the hounds stood solemnly in a vigil for their lost pack mates.

"It appears another journey to Moonstair is in my future," Immeral said. "And with a rather larger entourage this time."

"Not as large as the one you brought with you, I'm afraid. I'm sorry."

"The riders of the hunt know the danger they face. Eshravar died bravely."

"I'm grateful for your aid, Immeral."

The huntmaster bowed. "I am at your service, my prince."

Albanon smiled. "In that case," he said, "I have one more request before you ride for Moonstair."

CHAPTER THIRTY-FIVE

Roghar's army reached the bottom of the bluffs without further incident. Once they were off the narrow trail, they could spread out more, sweeping like a wave through the streets of Lowtown. Almost immediately, a group of three fiery demons appeared, and just as quickly scattered before the combined fury of Roghar and his soldiers. One demon was badly wounded, perhaps mortally, but mostly it seemed they lacked the will to make a stand and hold their territory.

"They're pulling back," he said to Tempest and Uldane. "Or circling around to attack where we're weaker."

"They'll pick off stragglers," Tempest said. "You should tell them to stay close together."

A rumble of thunder drew Roghar's attention to the sky, but the dawn was driving the clouds back. The noise, he realized, came from Hightown. A flash of fire or lightning caught his eye, and he found himself staring at a familiar tower perched near the edge of the bluff. Moorin's tower.

"Roghar?" Tempest said, putting her hand on his arm.

"Sorry. What?"

"The soldiers. They should stick together."

"Right. I was thinking about Albanon."

"Albanon?" she asked.

Roghar nodded toward the bluffs. "That was his master's tower. Something's going on there."

"There's no time to worry about that now."

"No." He gave orders to the soldiers nearby who had become his lieutenants more or less by default, trusting them to get the word around. "Stick together, don't let demons lure you away from your fellows, and don't hesitate to run from a fight you can't handle—as long as you run toward help, not away from it."

He led them slowly through the streets of Lowtown. The Market Green was deserted, but resistance seemed to grow stronger as they drew closer and closer to the Lower Quays, along the river west of the market. He formed his troops into a wide wedge, with him in the center, and drove onward to the river.

"Nu Alin is near," Tempest said suddenly, clutching Roghar's arm.

A figure stepped out of the shadows near a warehouse, not ten yards away. "You can still taste me," he said in a deep voice, his words stilted and strangely slurred. "As I can still taste your fear—your delicious fear."

Demons began emerging from inside or behind the warehouses—dozens of them, both the fiery kind and the nightmare fiends. Here and there stood four-legged beasts and four-armed brutes, and beyond them a cluster of what looked like hundreds of swarming spiders made from the Voidharrow crystal. The demons ranged the length of the quays, stretching as long as Roghar's line of soldiers, if not as deep.

Nu Alin stepped into the sunlight that spilled over the bluff and brought dawn to Lowtown at last. He yanked the cowl off his head and Roghar felt a sudden jolt of horror and fear. The face had once been human, but now it was bone and blood and liquid crystal, the flesh mostly dissolved away by the demon inside.

"I need a new body, Tempest," Nu Alin said. "This one is starting to fall apart."

Tempest shuddered and leveled her rod at Nu Alin. Flames streaked out from the rod to burst around the demon, setting his clothes and even his flesh on fire. He didn't seem to notice, but strode toward her undeterred by the flames and smoke billowing around him.

As if Tempest's attack had been a signal, the demons arrayed around Nu Alin and the soldiers lined up behind Roghar surged forward to meet in the middle. Roghar shook his head as he realized that this was exactly the kind of fight he had told his soldiers not to expect—an orderly line of demons facing their assault head-on.

Perhaps I'll stick to adventuring after all, he thought.

Several of the fiery demons surged ahead in front of Nu Alin, so Roghar moved to intercept them and keep them from hindering Tempest as she kept hurling spells at their leader. He saw Uldane circling around them, so he made sure the demons' attention was firmly fixed on him, roaring a challenge and whirling his blade in a glowing arc that bit deep into two of the creatures. A chill touch of fear at the base of his skull told him that a nightmare demon was closing in behind him, so he turned his head and exhaled a cloud of dragonfire without even looking.

Then he saw what he'd done—Tempest was engulfed in a cloud of fire, reeling back as the flames consumed her.

The fiery demons clutched at him as he pulled away to help her, searing his scaly skin, but he ignored them, shut out Uldane's shouts, focused on nothing but helping Tempest. "Platinum Dragon," he muttered in prayer, "please undo the harm I've done." He willed divine power into his hands, ready to send healing through Tempest's body.

"You've killed us all," Tempest spat as he reached her side. She swung her flaming arms at him, trying to batter him back.

"Let me help you!" he cried, filled with the terror that he might be too late.

A bolt of coruscating black energy, exactly like one of Tempest's eldritch blasts, hurtled through the air and struck Tempest in the spine. Her eyes opened wide and her mouth stretched into a scream.

"Tempest!" Roghar shouted.

As she writhed in agony, her face peeled away to reveal the monstrous visage of a nightmare demon, and Roghar felt all his terror ebb away, replaced with the profound realization of what an idiot he'd been.

He followed the path of the eldritch blast back to Tempest—the real Tempest—and gave her a sheepish grin. She just laughed, shaking her head, and sent another blast of fire into the fray.

Somewhere, not too far off, Roghar thought he heard a trumpet. He glanced to the skies, wondering if Bahamut had sent a flight of angels, but then he heard the baying of hounds, and he'd never heard of angels traveling in the company of hounds.

"Roghar!"

He spun around and searched the chaos for Uldane, finding the halfling more or less where he'd left him. However, the three fire demons, rather than chase Roghar, had moved to surround Uldane, who was clearly having trouble dodging the flaming fists of all three creatures.

"Sorry," Roghar called as he hurried to rejoin that fight. His sword quickly drew the attention of one of the fiery demons. It roared as it wheeled on him, lashing out with long tendrils of flame that licked at his armor but didn't get through to his flesh.

The demon's angry roar was cut short suddenly as Uldane's dagger sank into what must have served as its spine. The flames of its body blew outward and extinguished, and the liquid red substance in its center spilled to the ground, first hardening and then crumbling to dust.

"Where is he?" Tempest shouted behind him, a note of panic in her voice. "Where's Nu Alin?"

Roghar scanned the area as the two remaining fire demons circled cautiously around him and Uldane. He caught a demon's fiery fist on his shield, batted it aside, and spotted a corpse on the ground near where a clump of soldiers were fighting one of the nightmare demons. The cloak draped over the body matched what Nu Alin had been wearing.

"There!" he shouted, pointing at the body. "He's down!"

"I see the corpse," Tempest called back, "but where's the demon?"

Oh, no, he thought. He could be anywhere—sliding like a serpent unseen in the chaos, or inhabiting any of these bodies, friend or foe.

He was sure the same thought was haunting Tempest, as her wide eyes darted around to every soldier and demon nearby. She tried to keep a wide circle around her free of any potential threat, even pushing a soldier who stumbled too close, sending him dangerously close to a demon's fiery claws.

Roghar roared and launched a fierce assault on the fire demons that kept him pinned down. His sword erupted in light and sliced into the crystal heart of one demon as his shield forced the other one back, knocking it off balance. Uldane took advantage of the demon's moment of imbalance and drove his dagger into its skull, and both demons died at once, their flames extinguished.

"He's going to come after Tempest," Roghar said. "We have to keep him away from her."

"He might try taking one of us," Uldane said. "Even if it's just to get closer to her."

Roghar fixed Uldane with a steady stare. "He hasn't taken you already, has he?" He searched the halfling's face and eyes for any sign of the red crystal, but Uldane's face broke into a broad grin that was unmistakably his.

"It's creepy, isn't it?" the halfling said. "He could be anywhere, anyone."

"Yes. Now keep her safe." Roghar started toward Tempest. "We're coming to help you," he called to her, keeping his sword low.

"Stay back!" she shouted.

"Tempest, it's us. We're safe."

"I don't know that. You can't prove it."

A soldier, a woman who had fallen into the role of one of Roghar's lieutenants, approached Tempest from behind, her eyes fixed warily on Roghar. Roghar tried to remember her name—Beven? Beren?

Belen, he decided.

"The demon has him," Belen said to Tempest. "Strike him down, quickly!"

Tempest spun to face her, backing away without getting too close to Roghar. "Stay back, all of you!"

Belen's eyes widened and she pointed at Roghar. "Behind you!" she screamed.

Tempest wasn't fooled. She glanced at Roghar without turning away from Belen, but even that momentary distraction was all the opening Nu Alin needed. In Belen's body, he leaped into the air and came down on top of Tempest, smashing her to the ground. Belen's fingers scrabbled at Tempest's neck.

Together, Roghar and Uldane rushed to Tempest's side. Roghar planted a kick in Belen's gut that sent her sprawling, though her fingers left a long gash in Tempest's neck. Blood spurted from the wound as Tempest cried out in pain and fear.

Nu Alin was unfazed by the blow, making a rasping sound that might have been laughter as he lifted Belen's body to its feet. "It's fascinating," he said in an approximation of Belen's voice. "She's so furious with you, Roghar. She followed you, trusted you, believed that you would keep her safe. You failed, and now you're ready to kill her in order to get to me. She feels so betrayed."

Uldane stood near Nu Alin, a dagger in each hand, looking for an opening. Keeping his eyes on the demon, Roghar fell to one knee beside Tempest and muttered a prayer, closing the wound in her neck.

"Does it matter to you what body I wear?" Nu Alin said. "It appears that it does. None of you knew the farmer whose body I just abandoned, and you thought nothing of lighting it aflame to drive me out. But when I took Tempest"—he looked at her with something that might have been hunger in his eyes—"you couldn't bring yourself to attack. Are you torn, now? Was this Belen someone you cared enough about that you'll hesitate again? She certainly hopes so."

"She would rather die than live as a prisoner in her own body," Tempest said, getting to her feet.

"True," Nu Alin said, "but she's desperately clinging to the hope that you can free her without killing her. She has such *faith* in you, Roghar. But she's so afraid that her faith has been misplaced."

Roghar and Tempest spread out so that they and Uldane more or less surrounded Nu Alin. Roghar knew they were fooling themselves—if the demon wanted to, it could escape with ease through one of the gaps between them, or even jump right over the halfling's head to get out of their grasp. It certainly didn't seem to feel threatened as they closed in around it.

But he had to admit that the demon's words were giving him pause. What right did he have to hurt or kill Belen, just because she'd fallen prey to the demon? He had a responsibility to her, to free her if he could.

"Look at you," Nu Alin said, turning in a slow circle. "You didn't hesitate for a moment when I wore the flesh of that farmer. You set me aflame, burned the flesh from my bones. Did he offend you? Or was it something I said? Will you kill poor Belen if I start describing how eager I am to taste Tempest again? It's strange, actually—I've never felt this way about a host before. Usually I wear them out and discard them. But I feel as though I've been deprived of a particular pleasure because I didn't have the opportunity to really use you up." Belen's face leered at Tempest with an almost lascivious grin.

That was more provocation than Tempest could stand. "You never will," she snarled. "And you'll never do that to another host. *Rekhtha murkuhl Hadar rash!*"

Wind sprang up around Nu Alin, engulfing him in a whirlwind that lifted Belen's body from the ground. Dust and debris rose up in a cone, and eerie lights shone all around him, weaving into a prison of light and wind that held him fast.

"What is that?" Roghar said.

Tempest shot him a wolfish grin. "I believe Quarhaun would refer to it as the seventh invocation of Hadar," she said. "It's worse than it looks."

Belen's body writhed helplessly in the whirlwind for a moment, then her back arched in what seemed like horrible agony.

"But Belen—" Roghar said.

"Don't worry about her," Tempest spat.

"I have to worry about her. I led her into this."

"Tempest!" a voice called from somewhere nearby. It was familiar, but Roghar couldn't quite place it.

Tempest didn't turn toward the voice. Her eyes were fixed on Belen's body, one hand outstretched to keep the whirlwind in motion.

A man broke from the mass of warring demons and soldiers and ran toward them. Roghar shifted so he stood between Tempest and the onrushing man, then he recognized Albanon and the pseudodragon perched on his shoulder.

"Stay back, elf," he growled.

Albanon stopped in his tracks, and the smile fell from his face. "What's wrong?"

"Shara said you were talking to the demon, that you let it escape."

Albanon's brow furrowed and he looked down. "I . . . I don't remember," he said, meeting Roghar's gaze again. "Listen, Roghar, a lot has happened. But I'm the one who brought a fey hunt to kill all these demons."

Roghar looked behind Albanon and noticed for the first time that the battle was clearly going against the demons. Hounds were barking and yowling, and he saw several green-eyed, flame-tongued beasts in canine form biting and tearing at demons. Eladrin warriors cloaked in starlight fought alongside the Fallcrest militia who had followed him, and Roghar could clearly see the hope written on the faces of his soldiers. Against all odds, this battle was looking like a victory.

Perhaps I haven't failed them after all, he thought.

Albanon was staring slack-jawed at something to his left, and Roghar followed his gaze to where Belen's body still hung suspended in the whirlwind. Her mouth was stretched open in a silent scream, and a long, snaky tendril of shimmering red liquid was emerging slowly from her throat. The eldritch lights of the windstorm shone brightest around that tendril—around Nu Alin as Tempest's magic extracted him from Belen's body. Roghar could see the lights searing Nu Alin's substance. A black crust of ash constantly formed and reformed across the liquid surface, each layer blowing away in the wind before being replaced by the next.

"Is that the demon?" Albanon asked. "Nu Alin?"

Roghar nodded.

Albanon stepped closer and looked up at the writhing serpent whose substance was slowly eroding under the alien lights of Tempest's spell. "Worm," he said. "You killed my master, possessed my friend, and sacked the town I called home. Now you and your plans are dust."

He stepped to stand beside Tempest and put one hand gently on her shoulder. With his other hand, he lifted his staff and pointed it at Nu Alin. The wind intensified and the lights grew brighter, dancing with lightning and fire in the heart of the windstorm. Nu Alin burned faster, and in a moment the serpent was reduced to a cinder, the cinder to ash, and then there was nothing.

Albanon and Tempest lowered their hands and the whirlwind died, lowering Belen slowly to the ground. Roghar fell to the ground beside her, relieved to find her breathing in ragged gasps, though she was unconscious.

"She'll be fine," Tempest said, coming to stand behind him.

"Is he really gone?" Roghar asked.

"He is."

Roghar stood and put a hand on her arm. "How do you feel?"

Tempest blinked, and a tear streaked down her cheek. "Pretty good," she said. She pulled him into an embrace, one of her curling horns clattering against his breastplate. "Pretty good indeed."

EPILOGUE

Roghar led the triumphal procession back to the Silver Unicorn as the clouds melted away into a glorious blue autumn sky. His soldiers had suffered serious losses, but Albanon's unexpected arrival with a half dozen fey knights and their hunting hounds had kept the demons from taking a much heavier toll. After Nu Alin's death, the handful of demons that remained had scattered, offering no more resistance, and a circuit through Lowtown had turned up no further pockets of demon infestation.

Fallcrest would have a long journey to recovery, from rebuilding burned buildings to treating the citizens and soldiers who showed signs of the demonic contagion. That harsh reality was in the forefront of Roghar's mind as he approached the flame-scorched inn.

But then the cheering started. People spilled out of the inn and gathered from the square to welcome back the victorious soldiers, throwing hats in the air and flowers at their feet. Roghar scanned the crowd, looking for Shara's red hair or the drow's black-skinned face, but he saw neither of them.

As he drew near the doorway, a portly man he recognized as the Lord Warden, Faren Markelhay, stepped out. The Lord Warden's arms were crossed over his chest, and he cut an intimidating figure.

Roghar leaned close to Tempest and whispered, "He can't complain, right?"

"Right. You're a hero."

The Lord Warden stepped out of the doorway and spread his arms wide, smiling just as broadly, as if the crowd were cheering for him.

"Heroes of Fallcrest!" he shouted over the crowd, prompting them to cheer even louder.

Roghar braced himself for a long speech and perhaps some attempt to claim credit for the victory. Instead, he was pleasantly surprised to see the Lord Warden step out of the doorway and gesture for Roghar to enter.

"There will be time for speeches and acclamation later," the Lord Warden said as Roghar ducked through the doorway. "But the last thing Fallcrest needs right now is for me to stand between it and a good party."

Roghar clasped his hand and clapped the Lord Warden on the shoulder. "Well said, my lord."

Shara shifted her pack and stepped out of the inn. She looked down Market Street and saw the last straggling soldiers of Roghar's little army disappear out of sight behind the temple of Erathis. Shaking her head, she set her back to Roghar and his army and made for the Knight's Gate out of town, Quarhaun at her side.

At least half the garrison of the gate had abandoned their posts, probably running off to join Roghar. Nobody challenged them or gave them more than a glance as they passed through the gate. The road took them a quarter mile out of town and then hit the King's Road, stretching off to the east and the west. Westward lay the Cloak Wood; Gardbury Downs and its ancient, ruined abbey; and eventually her home town of Winterhaven, nestled in the foothills of the Cairngorm Peaks. To the east was the lush vale of Harkenwold and then the forbidding Dawnforge Mountains, or they could take the Trade Road northeast through the Old Hills to Hammerfast. She stood at the crossroads for a long time, considering the road in both directions.

"Where are we going?" Quarhaun asked at last, rather stupidly, she thought.

She stared straight ahead, and her eyes rested on the gleam of the Nentir River under the morning sun.

"Forget the road," she said. "We're going north. Sooner or later, we'll figure out where Vestapalk is hiding."

"And in the meantime?"

"In the meantime, there's a whole world out there to explore. I've never been north, up to the Winterbole Forest, so we're going there."

In the meantime, she thought, we're together.

◆——◆

Belen stumbled into the common room, looking wild-eyed and frantic, as if she'd just awoken from a nightmare.

Roghar was reminded of the way Tempest had barged into the same room the night before, and half expected the soldier to proclaim that Nu Alin was in the room.

Instead, she forced her way through the crowds of revelers to the table where Roghar sat with Tempest, Uldane, and Albanon, celebrating their victory.

"Roghar," she said, "I need to tell you something."

Tempest stood and put an arm around Belen's shoulder, then gently lowered her into the chair she'd vacated, at Roghar's left hand.

"How are you feeling?" Roghar asked gently.

"Never mind that," Belen said. "Listen. The thing—Nu Alin, when it was inside me." She shuddered. "It tried to shield its thoughts from me, but I saw something. Something it didn't want me to see."

Roghar leaned forward on the table. "What did you see?"

"A . . . a memory, I suppose. Nu Alin stood before an enormous creature of green scales and red crystal, a hideous monster something like a dragon, but not any of the dragons I've ever seen in a book."

"Vestapalk," Albanon said.

"The dragon-thing was lying in a pool full of red liquid, almost like blood, but also like the red crystal on the demons we fought. The pool bubbled and churned, and at the edges where it met stone, it flashed with fire and lightning. The pool was at the bottom of an enormous shaft, and the shaft was full of the same sort of—of chaos, like the earth unformed and reduced to its component elements."

"Has Vestapalk made his lair in another plane?" Tempest asked.

"No," Belen said emphatically. "Nu Alin had a name for it—the Plaguedeep. But it's in the world, Nu Alin knew this. It's in a volcano to the west of here, past the Ogrefist Hills, not more than a hundred miles from Fallcrest."

"Are you sure?" Roghar asked her, meeting her eyes.

"I'm positive."

Roghar sat back in his chair and looked around the room, his thoughts a jumble.

"That's not all, though," Belen said, seizing his hand. "Roghar, we fought perhaps two dozen demons this morning. But in the demon's memory, I saw hundreds of them. They gathered all around the pool, like it was some sort of spawning place for them."

"Hundreds of demons," Roghar said. "And so close." He sighed and took a deep drink of his mead. "Tomorrow, Fallcrest begins its work of rebuilding. And we head west."

ABOUT THE AUTHOR

James Wyatt is the Creative Manager for Dungeons & Dragons R&D at Wizards of the Coast. He was one of the lead designers for 4th Edition D&D and the primary author of the 4th Edition *Dungeon Master's Guide*®. He also contributed to the Eberron Campaign Setting, and is the author of several Dungeons & Dragons novels set in the world of Eberron.

THE ABYSSAL PLAGUE

From the molten core of a dead universe

Hunger
Spills a seed of evil

Fury
So pure, so concentrated, so infectious

Hate
Its corruption will span worlds

The Temple of Yellow Skulls
Don Bassingthwaite

Sword of the Gods
Bruce R. Cordell

Under the Crimson Sun
Keith R.A. DeCandido

Oath of Vigilance
James Wyatt

Shadowbane
Erik Scott de Bie
September 2011

Find these novels at your favorite bookseller.
Also available as ebooks.

DungeonsandDragons.com

DUNGEONS & DRAGONS, D&D, WIZARDS OF THE COAST, and their respective logos are trademarks of Wizards of the Coast LLC in the U.S.A. and other countries. ©2011 Wizards.

DUNGEONS & DRAGONS

An ancient time, an ancient place . . .
When magic fills the world and terrible monsters roam the wilderness . . .
It is a time of heroes, of legends, of dungeons and dragons . . .

THE MARK OF
NERATH

Bill Slavicsek

THE SEAL OF
KARGA KUL

Alex Irvine

UNTOLD
ADVENTURES

Short stories by Alan Dean Foster, Kevin J. Anderson,
Jay Lake, Mike Resnick, and more

THE LAST
GARRISON

Matthew Beard
December 2011

Bringing the world of Dungeons & Dragons alive,
find these great novels at your favorite bookseller.
Also available as ebooks.

DungeonsandDragons.com

DUNGEONS & DRAGONS, D&D, WIZARDS OF THE COAST, and their
respective logos are trademarks of Wizards of the Coast
LLC in the U.S.A. and other countries. ©2011 Wizards.

In the fall of 2012, scientists at the Large Hadron Collider in Geneva, Switzerland, embarked on a series of high-energy experiments. No one knows exactly what went wrong, but in the blink of an eye, thousands of possible universes all condensed into a single reality...

Sooner Dead
Mel Odom

Red Sails in the Fallout
Paul Kidd

Earth. After the apocalypse. Never mind the radiation—you're gonna like it here.

GAMMA WORLD™

Find these great novels at your favorite bookseller.
Also available as ebooks.

DungeonsandDragons.com

DUNGEONS & DRAGONS, D&D, WIZARDS OF THE COAST, GAMMA WORLD and their respective logos are trademarks of Wizards of the Coast LLC in the U.S.A. and other countries. ©2011 Wizards.

MANY ROADS LEAD TO NEVERWINTER

RETURN WITH
GAUNTLGRYM

Neverwinter Saga, Book I
R.A. Salvatore

NEVERWINTER

Neverwinter Saga, Book II
R.A. Salvatore

CONTINUE THE ADVENTURE WITH
BRIMSTONE ANGELS

Legends of Neverwinter
Erin M. Evans
November 2011

LOOK FOR THESE OTHER EXCITING NEW RELEASES IN 2011

Neverwinter for PC
The Legend of Drizzt™ cooperative board game
Neverwinter Campaign Setting

HOW WILL YOU RETURN?

Find these great products at your favorite bookseller or game shop.

DungeonsandDragons.com

NEVERWINTER, DUNGEONS & DRAGONS, D&D, WIZARDS OF THE COAST, their respective logos and THE LEGEND OF DRIZZT are trademarks of Wizards of the Coast LLC in the U.S.A. and other countries.
©2011 Wizards.

WELCOME TO THE DESERT WORLD OF ATHAS, A LAND RULED BY A HARSH AND UNFORGIVING CLIMATE, A LAND GOVERNED BY THE ANCIENT AND TYRANNICAL SORCERER KINGS. THIS IS THE LAND OF

DARK·SUN WORLD

CITY UNDER THE SAND
Jeff Mariotte

UNDER THE CRIMSON SUN
Keith R.A. DeCandido

DEATH MARK
Robert Schwalb
NOVEMBER 2011

ALSO AVAILABLE AS EBOOKS!

THE PRISM PENTAD
Troy Denning's classic DARK SUN series revisited! Check out the great new editions of *The Verdant Passage*, *The Crimson Legion*, *The Amber Enchantress*, *The Obsidian Oracle*, and *The Cerulean Storm*.

Dungeons & Dragons, D&D, Dark Sun, Wizards of the Coast, and their respective logos are trademarks of Wizards of the Coast LLC in the U.S.A. and other countries. ©2011 Wizards.

Enjoy these fantasy adventures inspired by
The New York Times **best-selling**
Practical Guide series!

MONSTER SLAYERS

A Companion Novel to *A Practical Guide to Monsters*
Lukas Ritter
978-0-7869-5484-1
Battle one menacing monster after another!

NOCTURNE

A Companion Novel to *A Practical Guide to Vampires*
L.D. Harkrader
978-0-7869-5502-2
Join a vampire hunter on a heart-stopping quest!

Aldwyns Academy

A Companion Novel to *A Practical Guide to Wizardry*
Nathan Meyer
978-0-7869-5504-6
Enter a school for magic where even the first day can be (un)deadly!

The Faerie Locket

A Companion Novel to *A Practical Guide to Faeries*
Susan Morris
978-0-7869-5562-6
The locket will whisk you into the world of faeries— and the adventure of a lifetime.

DUNGEONS & DRAGONS, D&D, WIZARDS OF THE COAST, and their respective logos are trademarks of Wizards of the Coast LLC in the U.S.A. and other countries. Other trademarks are property of their respective owners. ©2011 Wizards.

BOOKS FOR YOUNG READERS